THE WINTHROP AGREEMENT

A Novel

ALICE SHERMAN SIMPSON

HARPER

NEW YORK · LONDON · TORONTO · SYDNEY

HARPER

HarperCollins books may be purchased for educational, business, or sales promotional use. For information, please email the Special Markets Department at SPsales@harpercollins.com.

FIRST EDITION

Designed by Jamie Lynn Kerner
Ornament throughout © soosh/Shutterstock

Library of Congress Cataloging-in-Publication Data

Names: Simpson, Alice, author.
Title: The Winthrop Agreement : a novel / Alice Simpson.
Description: First edition. | New York, NY : Harper Paperbacks, [2023]
Identifiers: LCCN 2023013160 | ISBN 9780063304086 (pbk.) | ISBN 9780063304093 (ebook)
Subjects: LCGFT: Novels.
Classification: LCC PS3619.I56326 W56 2023 | DDC 813/.6--dc23/eng/20230324
LC record available at https://lccn.loc.gov/2023013160

23 24 25 26 27 LBC 5 4 3 2 1

"I came to America because I heard the streets were paved with gold.

When I got here, I found out three things:

First, the streets were not paved with gold.

Second, they weren't paved at all.

Third, I was expected to pave them."

—UNKNOWN IMMIGRANT

1

"I CAME TO AMERICA . . ."

1893

After what seemed an endless fourteen-day journey across the wave-tossed Atlantic in the belly of a filthy, overcrowded steamship, the first thing sixteen-year-old Rivkah Milmanovitch saw as she entered New York's harbor was the Statue of Liberty. She wept for having survived the voyage and the idea of a new life awaiting her in America.

Jacob would be waiting for her onshore. She could hardly wait to see his smile, which made her breathless, and to tell him the news: she was pregnant.

They had hardly begun their life together in Marijampolė when he began talking about going to America. Not only was the eighteen-year-old Jacob the handsomest boy in her village, but also he could fix things. Anyone who needed anything repaired came to Jacob— even the Gentiles hired him—to mend their wagons, plows, pumps, and farm machinery. He had described to Rivkah that in New York *the streets were paved with gold* and it was there he would make his fortune. They would have a home of their own in America—perhaps even a farm, which was not permitted to Jews in their Lithuanian shtetl.

One week after the rabbi married them, Jacob admitted to her that he had borrowed money from his brother to buy two steerage tickets for New York. Rivkah was taken completely by surprise and excitement until he told her his plan, which was that he would leave at the end of the week and that she would come a month later. Despite her tears and protests, and notwithstanding the furor of Rivkah's family when they found out, Jacob kissed her goodbye, promising that when she arrived, he would be waiting for her at the port with a job and a place for them to live.

When a month passed and she was ready to leave for the ship, she still had not received any news from Jacob.

"You're a fool," Papa said, gesturing wildly with his hands.

Mama, hands clenched, rocked back and forth, weeping. "Oy, what kind of husband leaves his wife after one week? Did you make him happy, Rivkah?" Her mama looked her in the eyes with suspicion. "You know what I mean . . . in the bed?"

"Mama." Rivkah looked away, humiliated at her mama's accusation in front of her papa.

"What if he's not there, Rivkah? Maybe he got drowned at sea. If he's not there . . ." Her mama shook her finger in Rivkah's face. "What will become of you? Listen, if that *meshuggener* isn't waiting for you in America, you go to New York, and then go to Lottie Aarons'," Mama insisted. "Right away. Before it gets dark, Rivkah. You hear me? She, at least, has a good head on her shoulders. Yitzak and Lottie will take care of you. That Jacob, I never liked him. With that smile of his." Mama spit three times to keep away the evil eye. "Do you have Lottie's letter?"

"Yes, Mama." Rivkah pulled out the last letter she had received from her friend Lottie, with her address on the envelope.

"Put it somewhere safe. . . . You shouldn't lose it. You lose everything. Oy, will I ever see you again, Rivkah?"

Rivkah had to remain on the ship till morning before taking a ferry to Ellis Island that hot August day. She never left her carpetbag, made from a worn rug, unguarded. It held what she thought she would need in America: one white cotton shirt, one blue wool skirt, a babushka of yellow wool with blue flowers, a pair of black boots, one black hat, two pairs of woolen hose, underwear, the nightgown her grandmother had made for her wedding night, a hairbrush and comb, their wedding picture, a photo of her family taken in Marijampolė when a traveling carnival came to town, and, wrapped in brown paper, a few bites of hard bread with prunes from the ship's breakfast. She wore everything else in layers. On her feet she wore her white wedding boots. Holding her brunette braided hair in a crown were the two tortoiseshell combs her mama had given her.

With difficulty differentiating between her anxiety and excitement as she stepped off the ship, Rivkah could not possibly have known what was waiting for her unborn child in this promised land of milk and honey. Destined to wreak havoc, it waited on Millionaire's Row in the Fifth Avenue mansion of a family named Winthrop.

2

NEW BEGINNING

When the large gray rat brushed between her legs and the foot treadle of her Singer, Rivkah held her breath. Her body stiffened as she made two fists, pressed her elbows against her ribs, closed her eyes, and then bit her lower lip until she tasted blood.

"Rat?" whispered her friend Lottie.

Rivkah put her finger to her pursed lips.

Rivkah had arrived at Ellis Island, waited on endless lines, answered the twenty-nine questions, and passed a medical examination that took about two minutes. She lied when the doctor asked her if she was pregnant, fearful they might send her back to Lithuania. The inspector couldn't pronounce her name and therefore wrote *Milman* instead on her papers.

Jacob was not waiting. She searched the crowds of passengers and people waiting along the pier. Walking this way and that. It seemed hopeless. There was an ocean of foreign-looking people. Light- and dark-skinned, dressed in strange garments and headwear, they carried their belongings in suitcases, baskets, and bundled blankets and sheets. But nowhere did she see his smile.

She had no idea where he lived. No way to find him. She hadn't expected New York to be so big—larger than Marijampolė—with so many buildings. There were taller buildings in the distance than she could have ever imagined. Hours passed. Gathering her thoughts, she decided to find Lottie Aarons' house, and then tomorrow together they would look for Jacob. What if, she worried, Lottie lived on the top of one of those buildings and she had to climb all the way to the top? She showed Lottie's address to several people. Everyone knew the street called Delancey.

Once she learned how to pronounce it, she asked people to point the way. Most spoke languages she did not understand, but they knew Delancey Street, so she followed their pantomimed directions—first one way, then another—through the crowded streets. She learned that Delancey Street was in "New York," not "America."

Rivkah was pushed and shoved on the busy, narrow sidewalks, and while at first she was bombarded by the voices speaking in foreign tongues, soon she discovered that most people spoke Yiddish. They were bargaining with pushcart peddlers, selling fruit and vegetables, fish, clothing, and even prayer books and Shabbos candles.

Fortunately, it was still light but her mouth was so dry, she longed for something to drink, and wished she had not put on her wedding boots, which were too small and pinched her toes so that it pained her to walk. Her carpetbag seemed as heavy as a trunk. She walked and walked, pushed and jostled by the hordes of people who were rushing past her. Sometimes it seemed as if she were walking in circles. Remembering the dry bread in her bag, she considered stopping on the steps of a building, but there were rats and stinking garbage everywhere.

At long last, a plump, stooped elderly woman who looked exactly like her Nana with her basket filled with cabbages, onions, and bread pointed to a five-story redbrick building.

"Across the street, *meydeleh*," she said in Yiddish, and smiled sweetly at Rivkah.

The converted row house was no different than any other on the street. Steel stairs led to its open, arched front door. The building sat atop two shops. One sold ladies' undergarments, the other looked to be crammed from floor to ceiling with stacks and rolls of fabric. Both shops seemed to lean weightily against the steps to support its five floors. The balding shopkeeper, in a collarless shirt, worn pants, and suspenders, leaned forward and craned his neck to look down the block. He cupped his hands to his mouth and shouted a boy's name, "Eitan!" repeatedly.

There were hordes of people attempting to either make their way along the bustling street or push closer to peddlers and their push-carts.

Rivkah maneuvered herself and her carpetbag between two wooden pickle barrels and a woman, shaped similarly, who had set up between two chairs an old door covered with at least fifty pairs of men's shoes, worn but polished. On her other side, another woman sold cheap, damaged eggs.

In Marijampolė, Jews were not allowed to rent or own land, and like on Delancey Street, peddling had become a way to earn a living as they dreamed of their own shops.

Rivkah excused herself in an attempt to get past the children shouting and laughing on the steps and, finally, making it to the top, found the doorway blocked by a huge bald man with a bulbous red nose, practically bursting out of his tight clothes. He sat precariously, tilted back on the two legs of a spindly wood chair, while reading a Jewish newspaper—and refused to move.

Finally making her way into the shadowy hallway, and thoroughly exhausted from her journey through this foreign city, she began to weep. She sat on the stairs, uncertain if she could climb four more flights, when—like an angel—Lottie appeared.

"Rivkah, is that you?"

Her dearest friend had gained weight since she left Marijampolė with her handsome husband, Yitzak, to find a new life in America. But the warmth of her mahogany eyes hadn't changed. Lottie had been overjoyed to see her and welcomed her with a warm embrace. Rivkah breathed in the familiar scent of vanilla that Lottie wore. She told Rivkah that Yitzak had disappeared without a trace.

"How do you manage alone?" she asked.

Lottie shrugged. "I manage."

When Lottie took off Rivkah's wedding boots, now covered in mud, ruined beyond repair, and bathed her raw and bleeding feet with cold water, Rivkah wept with relief and disappointment.

That had been three months ago. Lottie had generously shared her one room and small bed, taught Rivkah about life on the Lower East Side of New York, and helped her get this job at Hein & Fox Company on West Third Street and Wooster, where they sewed linings for golf and yachting caps.

"No talking!" shouted the foreman in Russian. "Work!"

Rivkah stepped on the foot treadle and the machine hummed back into action. She continued the endless work of pushing cap lining after cap lining through the Singer sewing machine, which Hein & Fox made her buy and for which they deducted fees from her paycheck each week—for the machine, thread, and her pressing iron. She worked twelve hours a day and earned four dollars and fifty cents for six days. They expected a certain number of pieces at the end of the day. Always fearful that the foreman might tell her not to come to work, Rivkah reminded herself that every cap liner she sewed allowed her to pay her share of the six-dollar-a-month rent, food, and other necessities. In order to pay a midwife, she also needed to save what little was left and put those extra pennies, nickels, and dimes in a coffee can on the shelf.

At Hein & Fox, she and Lottie shared a small sewing table next to the windows. In front of them sat the three little Zalensky girls, sleepily bent over, running their machines with knee treadles. The Feingold twins bookended the little ones.

"Those three Zalenskys are from Minsk," Lottie had once mentioned with disapproval.

"If they're twelve, I'm twenty-five!" Rivkah had complained. Children under twelve were not allowed to work in the factories.

"More like seven, if you ask me," Lottie had said. "Their legs . . . they don't even reach the floor pedals!"

"Mr. Zalensky pays a penny a day to Mrs. Feingold. Her twins make certain they stay awake," Rivkah said. "And work."

My child, Rivkah thought, *will never work in a factory. He'll go to school. Get an education.*

Rivkah wasn't sure if the remaining ten women in the twenty-by-eight-foot room were eighteen or eighty; they looked so forlorn and worn-out.

As the sun rose at midmorning, cloudy beams of sunlight broke through the holes in the two filthy windows and streaked across the width of the intolerably dark and crowded workroom, lit only by two small kerosene lamps. For a brief moment they lifted their gaze off their Singers' feed dogs, the place where the needle punched in and out of every liner, to squint at the golden shafts that filled the room.

"Jesus sent the light to let us know he is watching over us," a Polish Gentile shouted one morning, breaking the company's rules of silence. They all watched in horror as she was dragged out of the room, begging to be given another chance. Rivkah could hear her pleading that she had nine children to feed.

Rivkah didn't believe in Jesus or that he was watching over them. The beams made it possible to see the fabric fibers and dust that filled her eyes and nose and made her cough from her sore throat.

If only they would open a door or window so she might be able to escape from the sour, pungent stench of human sweat. Her eyes burned, her shoulders ached, and she felt sharp, intermittent pinpricks in her shoulder from bending over the machine for hours on end. And she was always thirsty.

The day after the woman with nine children was fired, at midmorning when the light beams appeared again, Rivkah felt the first flutter of life: small bubbles, like gas, that rose in her belly. She took her foot off the pedal for those few moments and closed her eyes.

Time passed slowly. The Seth Thomas alarm clock rang each morning at six. Rivkah was certain she couldn't go on much longer. But every day, in all seasons, along with hundreds of others, she climbed the nine flights of rickety wooden factory stairs on West Third Street. There was an echo of sighs and groans as the workers ascended to get to their Singers on time. Lottie, a step or two ahead, counted in a whispered breath each of the hundred and twenty steps on the way up each morning and then again at night when their workday finally ended.

The small bed she shared with Lottie grew more and more uncomfortable as her pregnancy progressed. Night after night, Rivkah lay with her swollen legs raised on a rolled-up blanket. She tried to be as still as possible so as not to disturb Lottie, who slept with her hands folded across her chest like the dead, snoring noisily and never moving throughout the night. While Lottie fell right to sleep, Rivkah lay in bed staring at the ceiling and worried about everything. Was Jacob alive or dead? Had he abandoned her? Was he somewhere in the city searching for her? She wondered if they had passed on the street. Or if he was on the trolley she missed. How would she work and be a mother? She hid her pregnancy under layers of clothing and worried whether the baby would be healthy. Would it be deaf? Dumb? Would it have all its arms, and legs, and fingers, and toes? She missed the old country, her mother, her father, her two brothers and four sisters, her grandparents, and the mad uncle they kept locked in the small room—all together in one noisy house. Why, she asked herself, had she come to America?

Rivkah's water broke late one Sunday in April while she was on the street, buying a baked sweet potato from Mrs. Abramowitz, who sold them from a baby carriage. Two neighbors gossiping at their open windows saw what happened and came to help her up the four long flights. She lay on the bed, moaning with pain, waiting for the midwife and hoping Lottie would return in time from the bookkeeping classes she was taking at Henry Street Settlement.

She gave birth to a beautiful baby girl—with two arms and legs and ten fingers and toes—and named her Miriam after Jacob's grandmother. When she and Jacob were finally united, she was certain he would be pleased. There were moments that she marveled at the infant's movements, the thrusting motions of her tiny arms and legs, which only weeks before she had felt in her belly. But when Miriam was swaddled and still, she worried about whether she was capable of this huge responsibility for another's life—and one so fragile and vulnerable. She knew only a few words of English; she could barely read or write. What did she have to give?

Two weeks after giving birth, she returned to Hein & Fox. Six days a week she got up at four to bathe, feed, and care for Miriam; washed the diapers in the sink and hung them out the window to dry; and prepared something to eat at work—usually a slice of stale bread smeared with *schmaltz* (chicken fat), or something left from dinner. Lottie's friends Lena and Max Schenkein, in their seventies, who owned a bakery on the street floor of a building on Eldridge Street, offered to care for Miriam while Rivkah worked.

"What are you eating for lunch?" Max would ask each morning and then, holding his finger to his lips, slip her a warm roll wrapped in brown paper. "You shouldn't waste away!"

"There are rooms in our building," Max told Rivkah one evening after work. "You could be closer with Miriam. You would have your own bed. There's one room, not so nice, in the basement. Another is on the sixth floor—a small one but with a window. I took a look. It faces a brick wall but the rent is cheap. Four dollars—plus fifty cents for the baby. Let me see if I can talk to him about the fifty cents."

"Not the basement." Rivkah waved her finger back and forth. "It would be like being dead and buried." She liked the idea of her own place and worried that she was becoming a burden to Lottie, eating her food, taking up half the small bed, tossing and turning, and now Miriam crying and fussing.

"Take a look, Rivkah." Max shrugged. "What do you have to lose?"

"You should hurry," Lena whispered, as though someone might be listening. "Someone else shouldn't grab it."

That Sunday, Rivkah rented the top-floor room. It had a polished pine floor and the walls were freshly painted in rose varnish. The potbellied stove was next to a small iron bed and there was a deep, four-foot-long soapstone sink divided into two basins, which could be used as a wash or bathing tub. With the cover on, it could be a table. There were two wooden chairs. Unlike Lottie's place, this building had no electricity or toilets. Lottie brought her a kerosene lamp and a chamber pot to keep under her bed. Tenants, she soon learned, emptied the pots out their back windows. Easier than going up and down four flights to outhouses in the alley.

"Be happy you're on the fifth floor," Lottie joked.

The one window in the room, as Max had described, was inches away from a brick wall. It was dark, day and night. A family of six lived in the room next door. Rivkah could hear everything that went on. The wife had a terrible temper and was always clamoring, until one day the husband vanished and her fury turned to bewailing.

There had to be a hundred people crammed into that small tenement from the basement to the top floor, speaking and shouting in Russian, Polish, and Yiddish. As soon as Rivkah entered the front door and began her trek up to the top floor, the pungent stench of cabbage and onions, the stink of sweat and piss and garbage that filled the stairways and halls overwhelmed her.

Those first few nights, lying in bed with her newborn, Rivkah missed Lottie's heavy body and breathing beside her. She tried not to toss and turn, worried she might roll over and suffocate Miriam during the night.

When Lena and Max came to visit a week later, he was carrying a dresser drawer, which he had painted pink and to which he had added wheels. It was the perfect bed for Miriam. Lena had made tiny sheets and knitted a wool blanket as a surprise. It was made up of small pink and yellow squares. Each pink square had a rose in the center.

Every creak of the building, every sound of footsteps on the stairway, terrified Rivkah. She wedged a chair under the doorknob to keep out the intruders she imagined roamed the halls at night. She wished Jacob would come.

It seemed Miriam never stopped needing something—to nurse, to be changed, and to be held. Rivkah worried every time the baby cried that something was terribly wrong: that she hadn't enough milk to nurse her; that the child was ill; that she wasn't a good mother. Every part of her body ached. All she wanted was to sleep.

The monotony and repetition of piecework left too much time for Rivkah to worry. Lottie reminded her again and again that Miriam was safe in the warm, fragrant kitchen while Lena and Max baked bread, challah, strudel, and *rugelah*.

Lottie had successfully completed her secretarial and book-keeping courses. Her first interview was uptown and they wanted her to begin immediately. She gave notice at the cap factory and she and Rivkah made a navy blue business suit just in time for her first day at the Winthrop Company. She missed Lottie but never said a word.

When a fire leveled the Hein & Fox cap factory in 1898, Rivkah found work at another factory—that was paying fifteen dollars a week if she worked twelve-hour days. Conditions were no better than at Hein & Fox. But they kept all the doors locked—all the time. When Rivkah thought about being locked in, her belly ached and she felt trapped and couldn't catch her breath.

But it was the same for so many of those she knew—determined, fiercely ambitious—with dreams of buying land, farms, and homes, and educating their children.

Rivkah sewed shirtsleeves and pockets from 7:00 a.m. to 8:00 p.m., six days a week. Climbing four flights, carrying Miriam to her one tiny room and trying to find enough energy to care for her child, when all she wanted was to get into bed and close her burning eyes.

Rivkah Milman had never been beyond Fourteenth Street. She had no knowledge that uptown, far from Eldridge Street, the city was becoming the center of world commerce. She had no interest in the fact that titans of industry like the Winthrop family were pouring extraordinary sums into building mansions bordering Central Park to publicly display their wealth and importance.

Instead, Rivkah worried about the persistent cough she had developed. Her fingers were raw from the fabric, her feet were swollen from sitting so many hours, and her shoulders ached from bending over her sewing machine. Of what possible interest was it to her that, uptown, the dirt roads, empty lots, and what had once been Seneca Village with its population of African Americans, Irish immigrants, and Germans were being replaced with copies of the Fontainebleau château, Florentine palazzos, and Beaux Arts mansions being built by architects Stanford White, Richard Morris Hunt, and Thomas Winthrop?

3

FRIENDSHIP

1898

S uch borscht!" Lottie sighed. "And pumpernickel with butter! From
Lena and Max?"

"Tss! You think I have time to bake bread!" Rivkah said.

"I help Lena make bread," said Miriam, now four, sitting on the floor, practicing writing numbers on pieces of paper. "When Mama's at work."

"You're a good helper, Miriam," Lottie said as she cleared the table and set up their portable Singers in order to work. "The only four-year-old on Eldridge Street that knows how to make bread! But more important, the only four-year-old who can write her numbers."

"Sit on the rug, Miriam," Rivkah demanded. It had been a long day, sitting at the machine and caring for Miriam.

"Can I help, Mama?"

"Do what I say: sit on the rug," Rivkah insisted.

"Rivkah, be nice. What has happened to your heart? You'll make the child cry."

It was this life she led—in cramped, small spaces—no time alone, no room for air or sunlight. Little time for laughter or joy. Old before her time. Scrimping and saving to pay bills—hoping for a better life one day—and always the doggedness of hunger.

It seemed to her, though she never said it, that everyone in New York was like her—poor, hungry, and exhausted—yet there was still a small fire in her belly, an eagerness to find that America that Jacob had promised her. Could she find it herself, without him?

She missed Marijampolė. Dark, airless tenements like this one had become her grim, hopeless world. Miriam couldn't even play in the sun. Lottie had told her that uptown, far from Eldridge Street, the streets were clean, buildings were rising, and the city was an exciting place. Lottie said that rich people lived in grand houses near a great park. None of that mattered to Rivkah. All that mattered was getting up every morning and climbing the factory stairs, sewing sleeves or caps, whatever the bosses wanted sewn, and then dragging herself home at the end of the day to scrub, clean, and care for Miriam.

Lottie kept asking her if she had any dreams for the future. Pfff! She had left all her dreams in Marijampolė. She had no pleasure. All she wanted in life was a red rocking chair like the one Papa had made for her.

Lottie had dreams; she had had them since they were children. To be a bookkeeper. She was good with numbers; was ambitious; had taken free classes, studied, and practiced; and now was making good money working for that rich Winthrop family. Lottie saved so she could go to concerts, the Jewish theater—even bought a new hat every now and then. She had even left Delancey Street and found a nice apartment in Brooklyn on a tree-lined street. Rivkah was making Lottie a pincushion for Hanukkah from a scrap of forest-green velvet, with a tassel made from silk threads—a surprise for Lottie's collection of hatpins.

"Damn it. The thread broke," Lottie muttered.

"You want I should make you a glass of tea?"

"Sure. How many sewing machines do you suppose are running tonight on Eldridge Street?" Lottie sighed, rethreading the bobbin on her machine.

"A hundred?" Rivkah said, rubbing her aching shoulders. Lottie asked the oddest questions.

"More like thousands. Except uptown where the Winthrops are

sleeping in their comfortable beds." Lottie laughed. "No wonder they are millionaires. I bet he owns half of Singer's patents."

"He makes patterns?"

"Not patterns: patents," Lottie said.

"What's a patent?" Rivkah got up from the table without waiting for an answer and put the kettle on. "Now that you're a bookkeeper, working uptown, I don't know why you do this."

"I get to spend time with you—and you, Mimi."

Hearing the name Lottie called her, Miriam looked up from the floor where she was still writing.

"And"—Lottie shrugged—"I make a few extra dollars."

"Which you spend on Miriam and me." She was so grateful. Sometimes she would think about what she would have done if she hadn't found Lottie when she arrived and Jacob, that louse, wasn't at the pier.

Lottie paused her machine. "Rivkah, you're my family. What more do I need? I don't mind sewing as long as I'm not locked in those factories. When they locked those doors and the windows were all closed." Her face flushed. "I thought I'd choke to death."

"'He who can't endure the bad will not live to see the good,'" Rivkah said as they sipped their tea.

"Oh, pish with your sayings from the old country, Rivkah. You sound like my mother . . . always *kvetch*ing."

"What choice do I have?" Rivkah asked. "You have your book-keeping."

"The factories need *you*. More than you need them. Don't forget. Are you listening, Rivkah? Demand more. They pay the men twice as much," Lottie said.

"Yes, yes. I hear you, already. I'm taking home fifteen dollars a week now. That's something."

"Pish," Lottie said. "Do they treat you any better?"

Rivkah hated when Lottie got started.

"If you had your own business, you could make a lot more than fifteen dollars. I'm telling you. After the fire, Hein & Fox collected thousands of dollars from the insurance company," Lottie continued, angrily. "Did you get one damn cent for your Singer? That *you* paid for?" Lottie blew the wisps of her unruly hair that fell around her face as she furiously pushed cap pieces through the feed dog. "They're all the same. Miserable *gonifs*!"

"Stop, Lottie. Please. I need the work. I can't be making trouble at the factory. It's all I can do to get through the day and then care for Miriam. I have no time for unions. Besides, they fire agitators." That was all she needed—to lose her job. Lottie was braver than she was.

She stopped the machine to wipe her burning eyes with an edge of her apron.

"You gotta think about doing something else with your life, Rivkah."

"Like what?"

"We're still young. You have to have dreams."

Rivkah waved her off and went back to stitching her pile of sleeves.

Soon their machines were whirring nonstop.

Lottie stood and stretched. "Oy! My back. Funny: my back doesn't hurt when I'm doing bookkeeping or typing."

"You've always been so good with numbers. Even when we were girls."

"They're like music to me, numbers," Lottie said. "I count everything. I count my footsteps, windows, stairs, and even the carriages that pass on the cobblestone. I like writing them in columns. Right, Mimi?"

Miriam stood up and ran to her side. "Aunt Lottie, show me your book," she begged.

Lottie took her purse off the back of the chair and, after searching, proudly showed Miriam her little notebook with the brown cover. Turning the pages, she explained which numbers went into each of the columns. "One day very soon, little one."

Rivkah watched as Lottie took Miriam's chin in her hand and brushed her hair off her face with a gentle hand.

"I will teach you," Lottie said. "Are you learning your numbers?"

As Miriam carefully counted to ten, Lottie acted spellbound. When Miriam handed her the paper with numbers written on it, Rivkah put it on the table without a glance.

"Rivkah, pay attention. Your little Miriam can count to ten. That's extraordinary. You must give her a kiss for this."

"I'll give her a kiss when she goes to sleep. Come, Miriam, time to get in bed," Rivkah said harshly. "Oy, soon I got to climb all them stairs again."

"And that's exactly why, my dear friend, you need a dream."

"Tss. That again? I've got no time for dreaming, Lottie," said Rivkah. "I've got laundry to wash and hang."

"Come, Mimi, Mama's tired." Lottie took the child from her arms. "I'll put this little one to bed and kiss her. Once for me and twice for Mama."

Rivkah watched as Lottie put Miriam to bed and kissed her tenderly. "Sweet *big* dreams," she whispered in the child's ear. Rivkah felt a surge of jealousy, thinking that Miriam must love Lottie more than her. Lottie was so gentle. When, she asked herself, had she become so hardened? Then, as if to shake away her bad thoughts toward the friend who loved her like a sister, she stood, lifted her apron, and began shaking it in the air, and soon she was spinning around and around. She and Lottie were in the meadow, filling their aprons with wildflowers to weave together—yellow, orange, and red poppies for crowns—the Marijampolė wind blowing the field of wildflowers in a jubilant dance. She imagined flower petals and leaves flying into the air from the apron's skirt. She remembered that Lottie had loved two boys and couldn't choose. She remembered, too, how Jacob had whispered in her ear when he walked her home that he might marry her—for a kiss. Everything had been possible then.

"What *are* you doing, Rivkah Milmanovitch?" Lottie asked.

"Milman. Our name is Milman now!" Rivkah corrected. "We are Americans."

Miriam sat up and pointed. "Mama's dancing, Lottie! Mama's dancing!"

And she was *laughing*. Dreams were for fools, Rivkah thought but let her mind wander, searching for the happiness there had been in Jacob's kiss. And the dreams: to dance with Jacob on Saturday nights, to marry him—to make pretty dresses.

When she stopped spinning, she put her hands to her heart. "Oh, please don't laugh at me," she said breathlessly.

Lottie took hold of her hands. "I'd never laugh at you. You are my dearest friend."

In that moment, there in the center of the room, she allowed her hard edges to dissolve.

"You know, Lottie . . . I remembered a dream." Lottie was standing at the open door, about to go home. Rivkah felt the heat rise to her cheeks. She felt like the wide-eyed, softhearted girl who had arrived at Lottie's door almost five years ago, optimistic about a promising future and certain of the husband who would provide. "I've . . . I've been thinking I'd like to have a little dress shop."

1902

1

SZYMON MOSKOWITZ

Miriam Milman did not believe that Szymon Moskowitz was an idiot, despite what his father said, how he looked, or how everyone in the building treated him. She could hear Mr. Moskowitz calling his oldest son names—*yutz*, *shmo*, and *shmendrik*—through the thin wall that separated their rooms on the fifth floor at 245 Eldridge Street.

For one thing, Szymon never got a proper haircut. One side was longer than the other, and the bangs, which hung over his eyes, were cut zigzag. His clothes were those of a ragamuffin—like the boys with no homes who slept in stairwells and stole bread and pickles. His shirtsleeves and jacket were too short, his frayed pants were too big, and he wore a rope for a belt to hold them up. He made strange faces and constantly blinked. None of the other five Moskowitz children—Nadia, Little Boris, Alina, or the twins, Igor and Anton, whom Miriam could not tell apart—looked so foolish.

In all four years that they lived next door to one another, Miriam never saw Szymon doing anything or playing with anyone. Instead, he sat alone on the front steps or up on the roof. Mr. Moskowitz would send one of the younger children to get him for dinner and then shout at him as he slammed their apartment door. No one in his family, in the building, or on the street was nice to Szymon. Miriam believed everyone should have someone who cared about them and she worried that no one cared about Szymon.

"Mama, why does Mr. Moskowitz call Szymon bad names?" she began asking when she was six.

Mama looked up from the Singer. "Don't ask so many questions."

"Why doesn't Mr. Moskowitz like Szymon?" she asked when he beat his son.

"Mind your business. I got to sew these cap linings for Monday."

"What's wrong with Szymon's leg, Mama?" she asked when the boys in the building playing marbles in the hall called him "Cripple."

"Leave me alone with your 'Why this? Why that?'"

Always the hum of the Singer night and day when Mama wasn't washing things: the sheet, the towels, rags, dishes, the floor, and the rag rug. Always the impatient huff and puff of her breath and never any answers to Miriam's questions.

Without an answer, Miriam decided that Mr. Moskowitz didn't like Szymon because his right leg was shorter than the left and caused him to limp. His leg, the faces he made, and the way he blinked his eyes all the time—those were the reasons.

She didn't believe he was an idiot.

It was always the same. Mama would be washing the floors and muttering under her breath, and Miriam knew Mama would soon explode with anger—that Miriam was lazy . . . made a mess . . . would never amount to anything other than someone who picked up coal on the streets. Washing the floors made Mama cranky. She said she wanted her to help, but nothing Miriam did pleased her. She was used to Mama's harsh words; Lottie always said that Mama worked hard, was tired, and to "go about your business."

Now that she was eight, Miriam was realizing Lottie was right. If she went outside, got out of Mama's view and her thoughts, Mama forgot all about her, did her work, and then cooked a good dinner.

"Where do you think you're going?" Mama would demand. "Don't talk to nobody and don't go nowhere with anyone," Mama warned every time she went outside. "And stay off the roof."

That's why Miriam preferred to sit on the top step, where she could forget about Mama's outbursts while watching everyone and everything: neighbors shopping from the pushcarts, haggling, pushing one another to get closer to the peddlers or get past one another on the crowded streets. Horse-drawn carts clopped by, kicking up the stench of dust, manure, and rotting garbage.

This spring afternoon, looking up at her from two steps below, sat Szymon Moskowitz, who nodded his head, twisted his mouth, blinked again and again, and then turned away to look out onto the street. Szymon, like Miriam and all the children in the building, preferred to be outside. Every room in their building on Eldridge Street was filled with people shouting and babies crying, sounds that echoed through the walls and halls and up and down the stairways. Mama would complain, "There's no peace. Not a moment." She and Mama were quiet but that didn't keep out the neighbor's noise. Mama never hit her the way other mothers hit their children. Mama didn't have to because all Miriam wanted was to please her, but nothing ever did.

Mama worried about everything.

"Hi, Szymon. What are you doing?" she said, smoothing her skirt.

He shrugged. "Nothing, miss."

Szymon was polite, calling her "miss." That was one reason she didn't think he was stupid.

Mrs. Epstein, from the third floor, carrying baskets of food, her wiry brown hair flying in every direction, the baby on her back and two other children in tow, stood at the bottom of the stairs. "Move over, *yutz*." Szymon's face turned dark as he stood up to let her by. Miriam cringed when Mrs. Epstein spit on him as she passed.

Szymon wiped the spit off the front of his jacket with his sleeve. Miriam watched his eyes blink rapidly and repeatedly. His face was twisted as if he were in pain—inside of him.

Mama didn't like Mrs. Epstein.

Mrs. Epstein dragged three-year-old Rachel by the arm. Sometimes, she left four-year-old Lev in the hallway, howling and wailing, begging to be let into the apartment. That's when Mama would say, "That Mrs. Epstein, she's the devil."

Sometimes Miriam could hear Mrs. Epstein shouting at her husband that he was good for nothing and lazy, that he should leave and never come back. Mrs. Epstein hated that he read books and she threw things at him as he ran down the stairs—glass that shattered, pots and pans that clattered against each step as they fell from the third to second floor—only seconds after Mr. Epstein himself attempting to escape her terrifying temper.

He always had a book with him—when he left for work in the morning, when he came home, and even when his wife chased him out of the apartment. In the summertime he would sit on the steps to read until there was no light. In the winter Mrs. Epstein would shout out the window to him up on the roof, accusing him of reading when she needed his help.

Mama didn't want Miriam to go to the roof, even in the summer to cool off, but every now and then she just had to. She had to because she felt like she could see the whole world from the sixth floor. She could see both down- and uptown: the buildings, the river, the ever-changing cloudscape in the sky, and the waves of laundry on lines stretching from building to building, dancing in winter, motionless in summer.

Mama said it was because of Isaac Tannenbaum that she didn't want her on the roof. Isaac was twelve and always in trouble. Everyone in the building talked about the Tannenbaums. They said that Isaac and his brothers and sisters stole from the pushcarts and that Officer Thomas Reilly had arrested Isaac—more than once. Miriam once watched as he pulled Isaac down off the front steps by his ear.

Miriam heard that Isaac and his family lived in the basement—twelve people, and that they slept on rags, under pipes and beams, with no furniture, in the dark. Szymon's twin brothers said that the ceiling was so low in the basement, the Tannenbaums couldn't stand up and that a hundred rats crawled over Isaac's family while they slept—every night—and that they ate potato skins and onion peels—and cats.

Mama said they were vermin, *drek*, and that Miriam should stay away from them or she would bring bugs into the apartment.

Isaac kept pigeons on the roof. He built them houses from wood he found on the street when buildings were torn down, and Mr. Epstein brought scraps of food for them. Isaac would hold the pigeons tenderly to his chest. Miriam wondered what secrets he whispered into their feathers. When he stood at the edge of the roof, waving the stick with the rag attached, Isaac's face was full of joy when suddenly the sky was filled with his birds returning home.

A peddler's voice broke through her thoughts. "Hot potatoes, hot potatoes. Five cents."

Szymon put his hands over his ears.

"Why are you doing that?" Miriam asked.

He shrugged.

"What do you like to do, Szymon?"

He shrugged again.

"You must like to do something. Everyone likes to do something. Read books. Play ball."

The minute she said "play ball," she was sorry, having forgotten about his leg. She had never seen him join in when the other boys played in the street. They called him "Cripple" as though that were his name. Once, when Mama was sitting on the bed, drinking a glass of tea, Miriam asked her why Szymon's leg was shorter, and she said she didn't know, that he was born that way and there was nothing you could do.

"I can't read and I can't play ball," he whispered, making that face he made, looking away, and then rubbing one finger back and forth across the steel step.

"Where do you go to school?" she asked.

"I don't, miss."

"Why not?" She couldn't believe that.

"I don't know."

"Don't you want to?"

"I guess not, miss. What about you? What do you like to do? I see you go to school every morning." He was banging the heel of his normal leg on the step below him. Miriam wondered why his mother didn't put a hem on his pants so they weren't so raggedy.

"You know my name is Miriam—Miriam Milman?"

"Yes, miss."

"Please call me Miriam." She waited for his response, which didn't come. "So you can't read?"

He shrugged.

"Why not?"

"I just can't"

"How old are you?"

"Seven."

"You're one year younger than me. I'm eight. You should know how to read."

"Because of my leg, I can't go to school."

"That's ridiculous, " she said. "What does your leg have to do with your brain?"

"Papa says cripples can't go to school."

"What do *you* think?"

"I don't know." He began blinking furiously and twisting his mouth.

"Well, you must think about things," Miriam said. "Everyone thinks about something."

"I like to look at the stars."

He sat up, his expression relaxed, and he almost smiled.

"At night. I go up on the roof when the sky is clear. Sometimes Mr. Epstein is on the roof, too. He reads there or helps Isaac feed the birds. He knows all about the stars, shows me pictures of them in his library books. I know their names."

"The stars have names?" Miriam asked.

"They do." Szymon moved up two steps to sit across from her. "There's Orion, Ursa Major, and Centaurus." He counted on his fingers. It was as though he were singing: he was so proud, knowing those names, and his voice was filled with wonder. The words flowed; he wasn't twisting his mouth or blinking. His eyes were lively and blue. "You can recognize them in the sky, too. The stars make pictures." He paused and punched his finger in the air. "You can learn to connect each star in your mind. Some night I could show you from the roof."

He was looking at her as though waiting for her to say something. But she was trying to imagine how stars could make pictures.

"Did you ever notice that the moon looks like a man's face?"

Mama didn't want her to go up on the roof, especially at night. "No, I never noticed that."

"I could show you that, too. The next time there's a full moon."

"Okay." She didn't mention that she wasn't supposed to go up there.

"Mr. Epstein told me that he saw a moving picture once, *The Man in the Moon*."

"What's a moving picture?"

"You sit in the dark and there's this story that moves on the wall. Mr. Epstein says that in this moving picture there was a giant cannon that shoots this big bullet into the sky. There were men on it called astronomers."

"Astronomers," Miriam whispered.

"They study the stars and moon and the planets."

She wished she understood because he was so excited and sure of himself. He knew every word he wanted to say and his cheeks blushed with pleasure.

"You mean the men, the astronomers, get shot into the sky?" She tried to imagine how that would feel, leaving Eldridge Street, passing through the clouds and stars, and watching everything she knew disappear.

"Yes, the astronomers. They are inside this . . . Mr. Epstein calls it a spaceship."

"Would you be brave enough to do that?"

"Yes, I would. Right now, even." He opened his eyes wide and grinned.

She had never seen Szymon happy before.

"And then the spaceship hits the man in the moon in the eye!" He burst out laughing.

"And then what?" Szymon was so much braver than she was.

"Mr. Epstein said the astronomers got out of the spaceship to look around, and from where they were standing on the moon they could see the earth. The earth looks like a ball when you see it from far away," he explained.

"But how do they get home?" Miriam asked, worried about being so far away from home, Mama, and Lottie. Suddenly she felt the late afternoon chill, buttoned her sweater, and then put her cold hands under her armpits. She would never look at the moon the same way.

"The astronomers, they fall off the moon and fall down—through the stars and clouds—and finally"—he paused for drama—"they land in the ocean."

She had never heard anything so interesting. "Like Brighton Beach ocean?"

He shrugged and twisted his mouth. "Maybe. They were saved by a passing ship, brought home. Everyone gave them a parade."

"Gee, I wish I could see a moving picture like that. I'd like to see the stars, too."

"I'll come and knock on your door next time there's a full moon."

Miriam thought about how exciting it would be to understand what the sky was about.

"I bet I could teach you how to read, Szymon. I could."

"You think I could learn? Do you really think I could read about astronomy?"

"I do. If you know all those star names, I'm sure you could."

They were both startled when Igor and Anton, Szymon's twin brothers, shouted, "Szymon!" in unison from the building's doorway. "Mama says come in for dinner. *Now.*"

2

LIBRARY

Aguilar Free Library

Lottie, would you take me to a library? I need to find a book for Szymon Moskowitz."

"What? You're a teacher now?"

They were walking to Iceland Brothers' for lunch. Miriam had thought all morning about what she would order and decided on a pastrami sandwich on rye bread with mustard.

"Szymon can't read and he's seven and his papa and mama won't let him go to school because of his leg and he knows all about the stars and astronomers and spaceships and I'm sure he can learn to read. I'm absolutely sure. They just don't take good care of him. That's why he looks the way he does. His father makes fun of him and everyone laughs at him and calls him names and I promised I would teach him. Please, please."

"All right already, *meydeleh*. Stop." Lottie waved her hands up and down. "Take a breath."

"And you know, I was thinking about Szymon's leg and thinking that if the shoemaker made something to put on the bottom of his shoe, maybe he wouldn't limp so much, and then his Papa would say he could go to school. What do you think, Lottie?" She had so many ideas that she couldn't stop talking. "Maybe we could find him a shirt and jacket that fits. Secondhand. Do you think Mama would fix his pants so they're not so raggedy?"

"You've got a smart head on those shoulders. That's what I think, Mimi Milman. But you talk too much!"

Lottie hugged her close and Miriam felt her soft belly and breasts. She had a comforting body, Miriam thought. Mama got stiff and you could tell she was uncomfortable.

"I don't think your mama has time to fix Szymon's pants."

She had to do something for Szymon. She didn't know what, but she just had to.

On one of Lottie's days off, they went to the Children's Room at the Aguilar Free Library on East Fifth Street and patiently waited on line to get two seats at the reference table.

"The librarian looks like a princess in a storybook, doesn't she?" she whispered. "She's very pretty."

"Miss Spencer's also well educated and knows a great deal about books. And look at her good posture," Lottie said quietly. "I wouldn't be surprised if she practices walking with a book on her head."

Miriam decided right then and there that she would do that every day so she would have good posture, too.

When they were finally seated, Miss Spencer asked how she might help them.

"Would you have a book about the stars and moon for my friend Szymon?" she asked. "He's seven, and his father won't let him go to school because he limps." Lottie patted her arm to indicate not to talk too much.

"Oh, my." The librarian looked sad. "Let me see what we have."

When she returned a few minutes later, she handed her a book. "If your friend Szymon is interested in astronomy, this is the perfect book for him. *Smith's Illustrated Astronomy.*" She opened the large book to show Miriam a splendid black-and-white picture that filled the entire page. "Do you think your friend will take good care of it?"

Miriam began turning the pages.

"Look, Lottie, it's a teacher and his students. He's showing them the night sky and the stars. I like the checkerboard floor, don't you?"

Lottie liked the book as much as she did.

"Oh, Miss Spencer. This is . . ." She was embarrassed, as she didn't know how to describe her happiness.

"And *you* might like this book, *Marigold Garden* by Kate Greenaway."

Miriam opened the book and gasped with pleasure at the picture of five young ladies sitting at a table in a garden. "The Tea Party!" she exclaimed. "Just look at the beautiful dresses. Look, Lottie. I want dresses just like these someday. I love the library! Thank you, Miss Spencer. I can't wait to show Szymon his book. I just know he can read. Especially when he sees these pictures."

"May I suggest that you keep the book for your friend at your home, since it is your responsibility?"

Miriam understood that, even though no one said it, both Lottie and Miss Spencer were afraid that Szymon's father might not like him to have the library book.

She could hardly wait to give Szymon his book, to help him with the words—and to read the Kate Greenaway book. Miriam was never without a book after that. Wherever she went, she carried a book with her and particularly enjoyed reading on trolleys and trains.

1908

1

245 ELDRIDGE STREET

At fourteen Miriam was embarrassed when people noticed her hands, with their long, slender fingers. "It's why her sewing stitches are so small," Mama would say. Work mattered to her mother.

She and Mama were sewing for people in the neighborhood—mostly alterations, but now and then someone would ask for a blouse, dress, or suit for special occasions. Miriam was eager to help, but Mama insisted that school came before work for her daughter. She even worked on Saturday, the Sabbath, so Miriam could go to school, and reminded her of her sacrifice at every opportunity.

Recently, Lottie had been referring them uptown customers: friends, acquaintances, and business associates of the Winthrops and their wives for clothing alterations. "You have a natural sense, Mimi," Lottie said. "Of style, fabric, and color."

Miriam convinced Mama to buy fabrics on sale that caught her eye—to offer to their customers. She saved her money to buy fashion magazines—*Ladies' Home Journal*, *Harper's Bazaar*, and *Vogue*—and noticed every detail of what women of higher position wore.

"Look at this vicuna wool, Mama. Imagine how warm that would keep you."

"Don't look at what you can't have."

"Close your eyes and feel this silk, Mama. It's as smooth as a river."

"Mrs. Klein can't afford silk. Mind your business, Miriam."

"Look at that velvet. It's as blue as Lottie's eyes. Imagine Lottie in a gown made from blue velvet instead of brown."

"Stop all that business. Your head is in the clouds," Mama would say. "Remember where you come from."

"But what about our uptown customers? Mrs. Winthrop's clothes are made from the finest fabrics."

"I guess," Mama agreed, with hesitation.

Nothing pleased Miriam more than to close her eyes and run her hand over textiles. Then, at odd moments, images would come to her head of garments she might make. She daydreamed of a wardrobe of garments made from fine wools, mulberry silks, satins, and velvets but kept it a secret from Mama. Occasionally, when she economically made use of a fabric, Mama would tell her to make herself something. She even made clothing for the neighbors' children from remnants.

Mama sat at the window with the shawl with blue flowers on yellow wool that she brought from the old country around her shoulders, sipping her glass of hot tea so she could watch what was happening on the busy street below.

"What time is it? I hope Lottie didn't miss the trolley."

"She'll be here soon."

"She's usually here by now. I hope she didn't get run over by one of those new electric cars."

"You say that every Sunday. Stop worrying so much."

"How would we get paid without her?" Mama fretted.

Mama had not gone beyond fourth grade in school, so, under Lottie's careful watch, Miriam learned how to write each month's income and expenses in pencil—neatly and in the proper column in the account book Lottie bought for her. Unlike Lottie, she depended on an eraser. Each customer had their own page, and there was a page for expenses. When Lottie came by on Sundays, she checked the numbers, rarely finding errors. Despite Mama's concerns, their little business was thriving.

Mama's hacking cough erupted.

"I'm worried about you. That cough's getting worse, and you have dark circles under your eyes." She coughed all night and agonized all day—about everything: finishing work on time, pleasing customers, collecting payment, delivering garments, and always about paying bills. Her hands were never still. That was how Miriam knew she was worrying. No matter how much Miriam reassured her, Mama fretted and wrung her hands.

"I only hope it's not the tailor's disease." Mama spat to keep evil away.

Tailor's disease was what workers in the crowded clothing factories called tuberculosis.

"Everything's got to be clean." Mama agonized as she looked out the window. "Take up the rugs and wash them, Miriam. Germs shouldn't settle in the fibers."

"I did already. This morning I scrubbed the floors with soap and boiling water the way you showed me—and the dishes and clothes, too. Everything's clean."

"It's important, Miriam. Oh, no." Mama stood, raised the sash, and leaned out. "Read the sign, *shmendrik*!" she shouted down as the curtains danced wildly in the onrushing wind. Then, cupping her hands together, she bellowed, "It's against the law!"

"Mama, you're letting in the cold!" Miriam pulled down the window and the curtains lay still again, the street noise subsiding into a dull hum.

"Those imbeciles are spitting on the sidewalk, spreading disease." She began coughing, her face turned red, and she sat back in the chair, rocking back and forth, lost in her woes.

"Come in! Come in!" Miriam greeted Lottie as she came up the stairs covered with snow.

"And where's my hug?" She reached out and folded Miriam into her warm embrace.

"Ooh, your cheeks are like ice," she exclaimed with glee. "Come, take off your coat, sit by the stove, and get warm. Look at our new place!"

"What a *shturem*. So snowy and muddy. Oy, my hem. Filthy."

"Wouldn't it be wonderful if hems were shorter?" Miriam asked.

"Miriam!" Mama looked aghast. "Such foolishness."

"Tea's ready. It will warm you up." Miriam took Lottie's wool hat, scarf, gloves, and coat, shook them to get the snow off, and then led her to a chair near the stove.

"Take your boots off, Lottie," Mama commanded, handing a rag to Miriam. "Quick, wipe the water off the floor. Use this rag before it should leave a mark."

"Wait. I want to take a look at this beautiful child of yours with her dreamy eyes." Lottie held Miriam and stepped back as Miriam blushed.

"Don't flatter the child; she'll get a swelled head."

"I like the way you are wearing your hair, Mimi. Like a crown of braids." She lifted Miriam's chin. "Look at people when they speak to you. Be proud."

"She's always late for school, fussing over that hair every morning," Mama said. "And never stops chattering. A wonder she gets any work done. Hang Lottie's things."

"Just like you were when you were young, Rivkah! You've forgotten. Like an old lady."

"Yes, Mama." She hung everything on a peg and then wiped up the melted snow from the floor. Mama watched critically.

"Put newspaper inside Lottie's boots. Over there." Mama pointed. "You missed a spot."

"Rivkah, stop worrying about everything already. Bring me some hot tea," Lottie demanded, holding her hands near the pot-bellied stove to warm them. "They painted the place nice. It looks fresh. A new beginning. So tell me, Rivkah, where did the Lefkowitzes move?"

"They needed more room. Would you believe twins? They found a place in Brooklyn. Not by you. Two rooms," Mama said, handing Lottie a glass of tea. "*Oy gevalt!* Imagine? Eight children and two boarders. How did they all live in this room?" She shrugged and then suddenly chuckled. "Their loss is our gain! No more looking at a brick wall. We have the parlor, four hundred square feet, with two front windows, a view, and close to the outhouse. Look. The high ceiling." Mama was so proud!

They stood at the parlor windows and looked out onto Eldridge Street, which was a white haze. Despite the blizzard, the street was lined from end to end with pushcarts. Throngs of shoppers, bent against the gusty winds, were bundled against the storm. The fire escapes were a tracery of lace and icicles hanging like chandelier crystals against the brick buildings. There were mucky horse and wagon tracks in the streets.

"Look!" Lottie pointed to the street. "Mrs. Epstein and Mrs. Moskowitz are trying to get across the street. They're holding their coats so they don't step in horse shit"—she laughed—"but they've forgotten they're walking in the mud."

"They look like two big Russian bears," Miriam said.

"Well, I would never describe Mrs. Moskowitz as a big bear." Mama chuckled. "Look at their dirty petticoats. That Mrs. Epstein. I'm telling you, she's the devil."

"You made these curtains?" Lottie asked. "So quick?"

"Miriam found the lace on sale. She's got a good eye. Twenty-five cents," Mama said with pride, holding one up. "She made them last night. They cheer me up. And there was a little left over, so she made a bow and cuffs on her blouse."

"So smart, your daughter."

"Mama loves looking out the window. Now she can see a sliver of sunrise that peeks between buildings."

"And only the front steps instead of four flights to carry the Singer," Mama said.

"Mama, you don't have to carry the Singer anymore." She pointed to the corner of the room. "It's right there." Miriam closed her eyes to take a deep breath. "Can you smell the bread baking? I tell Mama that the smell of Max and Lena's baking brings us customers." She tried to put her arms around her mother, but Mama struggled free.

"I smell pickles," Mama complained.

"I bought one sour, and one soaked in horseradish. Also, fresh herrings with sour cream and onions. For your breakfast. And, since I passed by a knishery, sweet potato knishes."

"Lottie, you come every Sunday; you don't need to bring."

Miriam and Lottie stifled their mutual smiles as Mama grabbed the bag from Lottie.

"You like our new table?" Miriam rubbed her hands across the polished oak.

"Why do we need such a table?" Mama shrugged. "Fancy-schmancy. And *four* chairs, even. It was expensive but I *hondl*ed a little and got a good price: ten dollars. Sit! I made borscht, and we have some fresh rye bread from downstairs."

"Would I say no?" Lottie asked. "Your mama makes the best borscht on the Lower East Side. Such a beautiful table and chairs . . . A set?"

"I do know how to cook," Mama said with pride. "And *hondl*!"

"And she has her rocking chair." Miriam was always trying to make Mama see things in a more positive way but could never do so. "I'm going to buy some red paint."

"My papa made me a rocking chair and painted it red." Mama smiled one of her rare smiles. "I loved that chair. This one's not so good."

"But now you have one again. And didn't I tell you that you could afford the table and chairs?" Lottie coaxed. "You planned. You saved. You've even raised your prices."

"I suppose," Mama admitted against her will.

Putting her glass in the sink, Lottie took the Coca-Cola calendar off the wall and handed it to Mama with a pencil. "Now, when will you give notice at the factory? Pick a Friday. You've worked there long enough."

"I worry, Lottie," she sighed as she put the calendar on the table.

"Pick a date already," Lottie insisted, poking the calendar. "Your mama's such a *kvetch*."

"Mama, most factories pay fifteen dollars a week. We make double that now," Miriam said. She hated factory work.

"Thanks to you, Lottie, and the customers you send from uptown, we're making two ladies' suits and a gentleman's suit—with a vest," Miriam said. "Also, we have three party gowns to alter."

"And I took your advice," Mama said. "I put money every week in the bank."

"Jarmulowsky's?" Lottie laughed. "They call him the 'East Side J. P. Morgan.'"

"I hope he don't steal it."

"He won't steal your money, Rivkah. He's a Talmud scholar. And rich. He buys steamship tickets cheap and then sells them for a profit to the Jews leaving Europe. Such a businessman." Palms up, she waved her hands.

"I don't trust banks." Mama shrugged.

"Speaking of business, the customers I sent thank me every time they see me. Last week a woman saw me in the suit you made and she noticed Miriam's fine buttonholes."

"The minute I saw that pin-striped wool, I knew it would be perfect for you with your beautiful auburn hair—and it was on sale," Miriam said.

"She's a fine lady—from Madison Avenue. I told her to come next Sunday at two o'clock. So I brought you some fabric. You should make a curtain, Miriam. Get a rope to go across the room, and when the bell rings, by the time she climbs the flight of stairs, you'll pull the curtain across to hide your bed. More businesslike. More professional."

"Oy, she thinks of everything." Mama clapped her hands.

The burlap that Lottie took out of the package reminded Miriam of sacks of potatoes. She wished they could have a velvet curtain instead, especially with uptown customers.

Lottie slapped her hand on the table. "And give your notice at Triangle, Rivkah. You, too, Mimi."

"I only work two days. Mama wants me to finish school."

"Two weeks!" Lottie insisted.

"All right already." Mama heaved a long sigh as Lottie circled the date on the calendar.

True to her word, Mama gave notice two weeks later at work and placed a hand-painted sign in the window: MILMAN'S ALTERATIONS—1ST FLOOR.

UPTOWN: 1890–1899

1

SMALL CATCH

1890

Hoping to escape his new tutor's eagle eye, Frederick Winthrop climbed up the rocky outcroppings above Bethesda Fountain in Central Park. He could hear his name being called, and the distant crunch of Patrick's shoes in the brush. Patrick was never supposed to let him out of his sight, and he had to admit that Patrick was the fastest and fiercest yet. The first day he arrived, he had told Frederick, by way of warning, that he had been a bare-knuckle heavyweight champion in Ireland. Until Patrick, Frederick had been able to elude all his tutors—or *captors*, as he imagined those hired to care for him and who kept him from his adventures in the park.

Today was his tenth birthday. Father was traveling, and Mother hadn't come out of her bedroom to wish him a happy birthday before he left for school that morning. There was no party planned. None of the children ever came to his parties. That was fine with him. He didn't care.

He had no interest in playing ball, the carousel, goat rides, or tennis on the lawn. He only wanted to bring home one small bird for his collection—preferably a cedar waxwing.

Believing he had dodged Patrick, he no longer felt the need to stay hidden. Reaching the top of the hill overlooking the lake where he ice-skated in winter, Frederick found one of his classmates sitting on a large boulder.

"Hello, Edgar." Before the boy could escape, Frederick reached him and stepped on his hand. They were both the same age, equally small for their age, yet Frederick recognized the fear in the startled boy's expression—how he struggled not to cry. Like a frightened rabbit, he thought.

"You're hurting me." In terror, Edgar looked for a way out. Frederick knew his only option would be to jump off the boulder onto the rocks below.

He pushed Edgar flat, sat on him, and grabbed hold of his wrists. "Empty your pockets."

"Leave me alone."

"Give me your money." He twisted the fellow's arm until he cried out in pain. While Edgar rubbed his arms, Frederick emptied the pockets of Edgar's clothing one by one—found three pennies, a ball, and a small ornate sterling silver pen on a white velvet ribbon.

"How come you have a pen with flowers on it? Are you a sissy?" Frederick put everything in his pocket.

Edgar cried feebly. He looked terrified as he struggled to throw Frederick off his chest. "Come on," he pleaded. "I need to bring that pen home or I'll get a beating. It's silver."

"Shut your bone box." He laughed, picking up leaves, bark, and dirt from the ground and pushing them into Edgar's mouth. "Bring me twenty-five cents tomorrow."

"Frederick." It was Patrick calling his name.

He took hold of Edgar's jacket, pulled him up, put his face very close to Edgar's, and squinted as he spoke. "Keep your mouth shut."

Edgar was spitting and coughing. "I have no money."

"You'll find some, crybaby," Frederick said in a whisper. He'd been taking things from classmates for so long that it was second nature. "Or how would you like to fall off the school's roof?" he threatened. He might be small, but the other boys were afraid of him. He'd started a rumor that he had thrown a boy off a rooftop.

Pushing Edgar to the ground again and pleased that he had frightened him, Frederick quickly left to find a bird.

The walk home with Patrick was delicious. Secreted in Frederick's jacket pocket was the small cedar waxwing, quiet but still alive. At first it had fluttered, desperate to be free.

It was precious game. Waxwings subsisted on a diet of bugs and berries. When they ingested overripe berries that had begun to spoil, they became intoxicated. It had been easy for Frederick to capture with his bare hands.

Behind the locked bathroom door, he filled the basin, closed his eyes, and tried to calm his breath and ever-quickening heartbeat, as he held the small bird underwater until it was dead. He loved the exquisite feeling of its final flutter. What had it felt in those last moments? Distress? Surrender?

Each bird was placed in a jar stolen from Cook's canning supplies in the kitchen. In his school's science room, when no one was about, he filled the empty jars with formaldehyde. Over the past year, at the library, he learned how much liquid each bird required. His collection included a blue jay—known for intelligence and family bonds—and a hermit thrush—shy by nature, it stayed hidden except when it sang. They mainly ate insects but were known to eat small amphibians and reptiles as well. Recently, he had added a pair each of finches, sparrows, and doves.

He neatly printed their Latin names on canning labels taken from the kitchen. One of the housemaids actually found his specimen jars in his closet—told Mother, and then Father called him into his study for one of his "talks." He was even angrier to find his older brothers, Jonathan and Thomas, seated around Father's desk, witnesses to his humiliation. They joined Father in treating him like their naughty child.

Having promised to get rid of the collection in order to avoid his father's beating, he waited until the house was dark and quiet, and then, tiptoeing through the mansion's dark wood-paneled halls, carried the jars two at a time to the third floor.

One of the unused dusty storage rooms beneath the mansard roof, filled with broken furniture and cobwebs and clearly never visited, was the perfect hiding place.

He found everything he needed among the room's shabby contents. He placed a wooden board between two chairs, evenly lined up eight jars, placed another board atop the lids, and then added another row of specimens.

With a fierce adherence to an invented procedure, Frederick planned the capture—secreting them in a pocket with his hand upon their soft feathers—and the means of death: drowning. At that one final moment when he placed his finger over their hearts and felt life end, he felt a strange and pleasurable stirring in his loins. When executed correctly, there was an exquisite symmetry to each death as well as in their placement on his shelves—a measured inch between. A few more birds and he would have the perfect number of specimens: two dozen. Locking the door as he left, he hung the key on a string around his neck. When he finally crawled into bed, the grandfather clock in the hallway chimed three o'clock. His heart beat so heavily in his chest, he had difficulty falling asleep.

The tiny, helpless specimens were elegant and grew even more beautiful as they aged, he thought, particularly when the window's light filtered through the amber liquid. The small American goldfinches (*Spinus tristis*) were the most beautiful, he thought. But he was tiring of small birds and began imagining larger, more complicated specimens.

Occasionally, he came across hawks drowning small rabbits in the Ramble of Central Park. To gain power over an accipiter would certainly be a grand prize, like overwhelming one of his classmates.

2

CARNEGIE HALL

December 16, 1893

The Brahms was extraordinary. Thank you, my dear." Jonathan Winthrop bent down to kiss his wife's forehead. They were celebrating his forty-third birthday at one of the season's most exciting social events. It was the premier of the New York Philharmonic performance of Dvořák's *New World Symphony* at the newly renamed Carnegie Hall.

Alice French-Winthrop, Jonathan, and his younger brother Thomas, all in their finest evening clothes, made their way to the first-tier lounge for the intermission. There was a murmur of voices and occasional polite laughter as women fanned themselves. Couples strolled the area as though at a ball; a sway of gemstone-colored gowns partnered with starchy tuxedos. It was, Alice understood, where one should be this evening if you were important in New York Society.

"It was as though Marteau were playing the violin in our music room again." Alice gazed up at Jonathan. She stood on tiptoe in order to rearrange his long, unruly hair, which, along with his mustache, was beginning to turn salt-and-pepper. After a whirlwind romance, they had been married for more than ten years, and at thirty-one, she still adored his patrician looks, attentions, and intellect. She was pleased that they shared a love for music and painting, and that he was both observant and curious. Not to mention how divine he looked in formal attire.

"That was a hell of a lineup on Fifty-Seventh Street." Thomas chuckled. "Did you ever see so many horse-drawn carriages? I'd say a line a mile long. Damn!" He chuckled. "Just wait until this crowd tries to find their own carriages at the end of the night. They'll need the coppers to break up the brawls!"

He was an exuberant man and having traveled the world by land, sea, and rail, life never failed to amuse him. Both brothers had such adventurous stories to tell. It was one of the reasons they were invited absolutely everywhere.

"Brawls?" Jonathan scowled. "Not likely with this crowd—not at two dollars a ticket."

"Even at that price, there isn't a single empty seat," she said.

"Andrew has built a concert hall as pleasing to the ear as it is to the eye," Thomas said, waving at someone he recognized.

"Speaking of which, Tom"—she laughed—"you *did* read the invitation, which called for white tie, didn't you? How naughty to choose blue to match your eyes, you rascal." His hair, brows, and short beard were prematurely snow-white. He was as tall as her Jonny but much more flamboyant. She appreciated how petite they made her look at five feet three.

"I like breaking with convention." He grinned and straightened his bow tie.

She urged, "Come, let's promenade," eager to walk about, to be seen in her new pearl-embroidered, periwinkle satin and velvet gown, which she'd ordered from Paris—and in the company of the dashing Winthrop brothers.

Jonathan, whom she'd met at the Art Students League, was one of the city's most renowned portrait painters, and Thomas was much in demand, designing many of the new Beaux Arts mansions surrounding Central Park and on Long Island. With the keen understanding that the possession of patents was the key to triumph in commerce, her father-in-law, Winston W. Winthrop, attorney-at-law, had made the family's fortune in partnership with Isaac Merritt Singer, the sewing machine developer. She had married well—and for love. The Winthrops were a fine family, Alice believed—with the exception of their horrid younger brother, Frederick.

"Everyone who is anyone is here this evening." She looked about the crowded red-carpeted lounge, considering which way they should saunter—in order to see the most important people—and be seen.

"Wish Sarah had been up to joining us," Thomas said despondently.

"I worry about dear Cousin Sarah. There's melancholy in the Collingwood family, Tom."

When Jonathan put his arm around her waist to draw her close, she worried his hand might stain her silk gown. "Let's see who's here."

The crowded, overheated space was filled with the mixed scents of varied perfumes, gentlemen's hair pomades, and winter tuxedos, which had been stored for months with mothballs in trunks or rented for the occasion for three dollars. It was overbearing if one stood still for too long, and made her feel faint.

"Seriously, Jon and I worry that she suffers from the same illness as your mother."

"Remember? After Frederick was born," Jonathan agreed.

Thomas stopped, scowled, and whispered angrily, "Sarah's young. Mother was in her fifties and Father was seventy when Frederick was born."

"I just think you could meet someone . . . livelier, that's all," she said. It was more than that. Sarah was fussy and prim. At the end of an evening together, Jonathan would complain about Sarah's constant whining about her ailments and his brother's fawning. They both hoped Thomas would tire of her. "I have a friend I would like to introduce you to. She's pretty, well traveled, and quite energetic and intelligent." Passing acquaintances, she nodded and waved ever so slightly.

"Thank you, but I care for Sarah," Thomas said. "Damn, my shoes are too tight. I'd just like to sit."

"Walk!" She pushed him forward. People were circling the floor in a counterclockwise movement as in a waltz. "Well, it wouldn't hurt to just meet her."

"Will you both stop? I don't want to discuss this. I love Sarah."

"Is that the future you want? A wife, like your mother, who never came out of her bedroom?"

"That was *all* because of Frederick," Thomas argued, looked about to be certain they wouldn't be overheard, and then whispered, "Mother *disliked* Frederick from the moment he was born. Sarah has *health* issues."

"Stop bickering, you two." Alice detested Frederick. He was only thirteen but had a strange way of looking at her, which made her quite uncomfortable. He was always creeping about, popping out from behind doors and columns, and suddenly appearing in the garden when she least expected him. "We can all agree he's a *dreadful* boy," she said.

They strolled, smiling and nodding at those they knew. She could tell her gown was being discussed—approvingly. But then, she understood style.

"It was because of Frederick that Mother neglected her duties," Thomas said, affecting a smile as though discussing pleasantries.

"No parties. No salons. She even refused to give our annual masked balls," Jonathan said.

"I absolutely adore entertaining." Alice lived for the menu planning, flower selection, decorating, and dressing for parties and musical salons. It was what she was born to do. "Without parties and balls, I would absolutely die of boredom," she added.

Looking about, she was certain her gown was the most startling, especially with her pale skin and dark hair, which she wore rolled in an upsweep topped with a bun, and wisps in the style of a Gibson girl. Jonathan said she was "fragile and voluptuous" and appreciated her full bosom, narrow waist, and wide hips. She wore a swan-bill corset, all the rage in Paris, to create an S-curve torso shape despite how uncomfortable it made her.

She whispered, "Frederick can't return to Groton—bad behavior."

"Last week, he set fire to the bed of one young nanny. She fled." Jonathan chuckled.

"Oh, God. No. Look who's coming," Thomas said under his breath as Cornelius Vanderbilt II and Alice Vanderbilt approached. "Shh. No more about Frederick."

"What an absolutely gaudy dress she is wearing," she whispered. "Can you believe? Pale pink—in December?"

"Ah." Jonathan squeezed Alice's arm as he bowed gallantly. "I'm surrounded by the two most beautiful Alices in the city."

"Jonathan Winthrop. Always saying *just* the right thing, you handsome devil." The matriarch of the Vanderbilt family blushed. Alice couldn't help but notice the sparkle of pink diamonds at Mrs. Vanderbilt's neck—and the sparkle in her eyes. All the women flirted with Jonathan. "What a beautiful purple gown. Madame Buzenet of Paris, I'd guess?"

"Oh, my dear, I would never wear purple. It makes me look sallow. It's periwinkle. Your gown is divine. You are *always* the best dressed in any room. Isn't she, Jonny?"

"Cornelius," Thomas interrupted. "How's construction going on the Breakers?"

She knew that Thomas had little patience with fawning women and their mockeries, but what could she do? In society one was expected to flatter—especially Alice Vanderbilt.

"Hunt was a breeze to work with. Great spirit," Vanderbilt answered with a chuckle. "No pretense. No drama. We'll be done before the season, I'm certain." He bowed, indicating their conversation was over. "Enjoy the concert." The couple moved on.

"One hardly notices her scoliosis," Alice whispered.

"Bores. Was he saying that I am pretentious?" Thomas asked. "Difficult to work with?"

"Tom. Don't be ridiculous," Jonathan whispered. "The other night at dinner I remember distinctly you said, 'The Breakers will represent the boorish taste of an American upper class—socially ambitious but lacking a noble pedigree.'"

"Your words . . . exactly." Alice laughed.

"You know quite well, Tom, that Cornelius is determined to imitate—and surpass—the European aristocracy," Jonathan added.

"But it will be the most talked about in Newport," Thomas said.

"Pretentious, you mean?" Jonathan added.

Thomas' expression quickly melted into a grin. They all laughed. Alice raised her finger to her mouth to remind them that they were among society.

Thomas sighed. "I wanted my name on the Breakers." He'd been devastated to lose that commission to old Richard Morris Hunt.

"Don't be greedy, Tom." She poked her finger at his outrageous blue plaid dress vest.

They sauntered about the floor again, smiling and nodding.

"God, if only I could take off these goddamn shoes," Thomas complained.

"We'll be back in our seats soon."

"I've had this idea, Jon," Thomas said. "How about, after Sunday dinner with Mother and Father, we look around to see if Frederick still has his dead birds in jars?" he suggested mischievously. "We can say we are going for some air."

"Whyever would you want to do that, Tom?" Alice asked. "You think he's still at it?"

"My dear little Alice, I actually think his specimens are getting larger," Thomas teased, and then, lowering his voice, added, "Last month, Cook said her red tabby was gone."

"Are you serious?" Jonathan asked. "I have no interest in this idea of yours."

"What if he *has* put Cook's cat in a jar?" She fanned furiously, attempting to maintain a pleasant expression as they circled the lounge again. "Why *does* he kill birds?"

"Would you both stop discussing dead animals?" Jonathan whispered angrily.

"I asked him once, and he just looked me straight in the eye and laughed in that devilish way he does." Thomas shook his head and rolled his eyes. "Grotesque, our little brother."

"Your brother gives me the willies," she said. "I think he'd like to put *me* in a jar."

"Stop," Jonathan said so loudly that the couple walking in front of them turned about to see who had spoken so loudly. Fortunately, at that very moment the usher's handbell announced the end of the intermission. They began walking toward their box.

Alice, keeping her voice modulated, said, "Tom, before we go back into the hall, I want to beg of you to just *meet* my friend. She's an excellent dancer, and you do love to dance."

Pausing to nod to Dvořák, they entered their box, which was next to the composer's.

"You know, Tom, Frederick seems smitten with Sarah," Alice continued. She was seated between the two men. "He just might steal her from you," she warned with a smile and a shake of her finger.

He shook with laughter. "He's the only one who can convince her to take her Fowler's."

"Fowler's?" she said with alarm. "But there's arsenic in Fowler's solution."

"Where*ever* did you hear *that*?" Thomas asked with scorn.

She placed her finger on her lips as the ushers turned down the gaslights and pretended not to notice that Thomas had used the opportunity to unbutton his shoes.

Leaning forward to look into the orchestra below, Jonathan turned to whisper to her, "Look. So many variations of silk and taffeta—like a sea of gems. It would make a stunning painting . . . with you in the foreground."

Everyone applauded as Seidl entered the stage, walked to the podium, and then tapped his baton in readiness. Sitting upright, her head high, Alice smiled at Jonathan as she lay her hand on his, wondering if she would be able to sit through the rest of the concert in the corset that was crushing her ribs. He leaned close to her, brushing her cheek with a kiss, and she whispered, "Don't let up with Tom."

3

STOLEN THINGS

Small and gaunt, his mother sat like royalty in her ochre silk wing chair, waiting, in her room where the amber velvet drapes were always drawn. The only light in the darkened bedroom was from the fireplace. Anna, her maid, had come at four to fetch him. She stirred the fire, discharging a firework of sparks, before leaving the room.

"I have something I want to say to you, young man," Eleanor Winthrop said. "Look at me when I speak to you. You're thirteen now," she said. "You distress me."

Another lecture. If there was anything he hated, it was the incessant reprimands—from his parents; older brothers, Jonathan and Thomas; his teachers; and his latest tutor, Timothy.

You distress me. He perfectly mimicked her voice in his head. Instead of looking at her, he watched the ornate timepiece on her mantel: French porcelain and gilded bronze under a glass dome. Louis XVI, he was certain. He knew the value of things.

It was halfway between 4:16 and 4:17.

"Give me your hand," she demanded, sitting forward in her chair. He never liked the disdain in her voice when she spoke to him. Her frosty hair was pulled back, revealing the remains of her aristocratic expression. She wore an antique lace shawl over a black velvet dress. She was always in mourning.

"I have schoolwork." How he hated the touch of her dry, thin-skinned hands, which lace cuffs could not hide.

"There are often things missing after you visit my rooms. I imagine you think I don't notice. I've given you the benefit of the doubt. Considered it childish behavior." She paused. "I want to speak to you about the netsuke. You know the piece."

"You mean the seventeenth-century, Japanese netsuke from the Edo period? Yes, I remember it."

"It's gone," she said. "Missing."

"Oh, too bad. Have you asked the servants?"

She had first told him the story when he was seven, and even then, he thought it was a preposterous story. An old, childless woman who was washing clothes found a giant peach floating down the river. She brought it home as a gift to her husband, and when they tried to divide the peach to share, the couple discovered a child. He told them that he'd been sent from heaven to be their son. They named him Peach Boy, and Momotarō grew up to bring them much joy and become a Japanese national hero.

"That netsuke has been in our family for generations. It was special to me," she said. "It was to be given to Jonathan when I die. It's missing from the bookshelf."

"And?" he asked with the empty expression he used when confronted about mischief. He stared directly into her red-rimmed, rheumy blue eyes. "Why would you think I have it?" It gave him pleasure to take small objects, the precious tokens of appreciation and things that mattered to other people. "Have you asked Anna?"

"Anna has been with me since before you were born, my dear boy."

The netsuke was skillfully carved, he had to admit. The craftsman had been skillful in capturing the velvety texture of the fruit despite the cold surface of the ivory. The ivory even had the faint blush of a peach. But such a silly story. What mattered was that his mother treasured it. He'd thought about it since he had first held it, seen how worried she was that he might damage it, imagined what it would be like to take it, considered when would be the best time, and then pondered where he might hide it and how distressed she would be.

On the infrequent occasion that he visited her rooms, he could think of nothing else. But she kept it on the end table by her chair, where she kept whatever book she was reading.

And then one day, for some reason, she moved it to the shelf below where she kept her precious collection of Meissen porcelain birds.

Her voice interrupted his thoughts. "How dare you. How dare you accuse my maid. Anna does not steal. You do—and I want you to stop. Are you listening?"

He tried to pull his hand from her grasp but she held him in her steely grip.

"I can't imagine of what use or interest the netsuke or the French perfume bottles, for that matter—things missing from my room— might be to you, yet they mean a great deal to me." She paused and then asked, "Is that why you take them?" He was astounded by her question.

She knew. About the things he'd taken.

She let go of his hand and stood. "Do you think I'm a fool? Look at me, Frederick," she demanded. "I would not like to mention any of this to your father. It would upset him terribly."

He could stare anyone down. And when she blinked, he turned and walked out of her bedroom, past Anna, who was standing guard, and into the foyer. He stopped momentarily in front of her ornate hallway mirror, glimpsed his own fierce expression, and held his head higher.

She had followed him. When she reached out to put her hand on his shoulder, he expected one of her dry kisses. Instead, she pushed him out the door, saying, "For the life of me, I don't know what is wrong with you."

As he walked down the corridor past all the family portraits and climbed the stairs to his room, he put his hand into his pant pocket and felt the sharp edges of his mother's earrings with their cascade of glittering emeralds.

4

THE WINTHROPS ON LONG ISLAND

1896

The East Coast was experiencing day after day of hot humid temperatures above ninety degrees, which didn't even subside at night. Frederick; his father, Winston; his mother, Eleanor; and his brothers, Jonathan and Thomas, had escaped the sweltering city for their forty-room Long Island cottage, where cool breezes blew off the North Atlantic. In preparation for a board meeting in September, his father had invited their new bookkeeper, Lottie Aarons.

Much to Frederick's chagrin, the buxom Miss Aarons, in a brown wool suit, was seated across the table from him at lunch, unavoidable in his line of sight. She was to spend the week—and, to his disbelief, dine with them—when she belonged in the kitchen with the rest of the help. He decided it would be amusing if he took every opportunity to provoke her.

"Frederick, stop slurping your consommé and sit up straight." His mother gestured with an upward movement with her hand, lifted her chin, and feigned a smile. He hated being reprimanded as though he were a child. He was sixteen, after all. Turning his back, he spoke to the bookkeeper, who was delicately tasting the foie gras—with her salad fork, of all things.

"Do you sail, Miss Aarons?"

Her eyes flashed a distress that he recognized from frightened animals as she shook her head, her mouth full of the unctuous foie gras.

"Swim?"

"No, I do not swim, sir."

"A shame. It's a beautiful day for a sail. But . . . if . . . something should happen, you *would* need to know how to swim."

"Frederick!" barked his brothers in unison.

"Grayson!" Mother called out.

"Yes, Madame."

Grayson, the dining room butler—Frederick never did learn his last name—moved with exquisite grace, unnoticed, around the large dining table with the silver platter. With his silver hair, patrician profile, and pale gray uniform, he blended perfectly with the sterling.

"More foie gras, Grayson." Frederick pointed to his plate. He ate the slice in one quick bite and moaned with pleasure. "Perhaps Miss Aarons would like more." He saw the defiance in her stare, the discomfort in her refusal.

No one spoke.

"Motor carriages are the future," Alice said, breaking the silence. "I'm simply dying to drive."

"Excuse me, Grayson," Thomas asked. "Have you brought my wife her consommé?"

"Mr. Frederick brought it to her earlier, sir."

"How thoughtful of you, dear," Mother cooed. "Did Sarah take any?"

"Yes, Mother."

"Dear, dainty Sarah." She sighed.

Thomas had convinced Sarah to go to Paris for their honeymoon. Upon their return, her color was rosy and she even seemed carefree. She confided in Frederick that she no longer felt the need for her Fowler's solution, which she had been taking for assorted ailments. This had frustrated his plan to increase her dosage, so he found opportunities to surreptitiously put it into her food—a little here, a little there. Consommé was the perfect occasion.

His brother designed and built one of his most elegant, light-filled Beaux Arts mansions for his new bride, adjacent to the family's mansion and that of Jonathan and Alice's on upper Fifth Avenue, the rooms decorated with the crystal chandeliers, Persian rugs, and furnishings he had collected during his youthful travels throughout Europe. The rooms were filled with roses. Within a month of their return, the color faded from Sarah's cheeks, light hurt her eyes, music her ears, and she couldn't bear the fragrance of fresh flowers. There were no parties, balls, or visitors. She rarely came out of her darkened rooms.

"Was she any better today?" Mother asked, her pained expression painted with phony pathos.

He almost laughed aloud. She had no interest in attending to her daughter-in-law—just as she had never tended to him. He enjoyed the theater of her lackluster imitation of empathy.

"I'm certain she will join us for dinner," Thomas said cheerfully, unwilling to accept that his bride was growing weaker. Sarah would not be joining them—ever. This afternoon, rather than one teaspoon of Fowler's, Frederick had stirred two into the clear broth, having grown impatient. He was eager to observe the signs of her organs beginning to fail, the weakening of all her systems.

Just as he had observed in the birds, the small rabbits, and the occasional stolen pet, the effects of his exquisite design of her death proceeded in a satisfying and dependable order. He kept a small leather-bound diary in his inside breast pocket in which he wrote observations of her symptoms and complaints. He noted she was having increasingly incapacitating episodes of stomach pain and her pale skin was erupting with boils.

He wanted to be alone with Sarah, his finger over her heart at the exact and voluptuous moment when her heart stopped. Over the years, beginning with those small finches and waxwings, final moments like these had become ecstatic—and now that it was happening with Sarah it was . . . erotic.

"You are the only person who seems to be able to get the poor dear to eat. What *is* your secret?" Mother cut off small bites of the filet of beef macédoine.

"She says I'm a comfort."

"You?" She laughed. "The poor, poor child." She forced an expression of concern and paused, her sorrowful expression quickly turning into a smile. "We *are* fortunate to have Newport, aren't we?" Mother rarely discussed anything disagreeable, and Sarah's condition was definitely that. "With the doors open, we get such a delightful breeze off the Atlantic."

"It's quite lovely, Mrs. Winthrop. I am so grateful to be here," the bookkeeper said. "I read it's a hundred twenty degrees in the city."

He hated Miss Aarons' obsequious smile. He stood, wiped the edges of his mouth with his napkin, brushed crumbs from his lap onto the red Persian carpet, and then walked to the open French doors to look out to sea. He overheard his mother whisper, "He has no manners at all."

It would be a delightful afternoon for a sail. But he hated giving up taunting the bookkeeper. It was like Cook's cat teasing a half-dead mouse with its paw.

"Why don't we take our coffee and dessert on the loggia?" Mother said, calling forth a flurry of servers and carts, the clatter of porcelain and silver, as the family settled themselves at a table among the potted palms. While they daintily picked at Cook's charlotte à la parisienne, a crown of ladyfingers filled with cream and dotted with fresh raspberries from the garden, he noticed how the bookkeeper licked her lips, relishing her dessert. Turning toward her just as she was about to put a spoonful to her mouth, he said, "Tell me, Miss Aarons, is it true that the folks *downtown* piss out the window?"

Everyone, including the bookkeeper, gasped. His mother began ringing the silver bell quite furiously without realizing that Grayson was standing behind her chair.

"Madam."

"Clear, Grayson."

The bookkeeper put the spoon down noisily on the plate. Her distress excited him.

"Well, is it?" he repeated as he inhaled the fresh sea air. She made nervous attempts to fix wisps of her hair that had come undone.

Jonathan said, "Such a rude question."

"Especially while we are eating," Thomas added.

Father pounded on the table. The dishes and silver bounced and rattled. "Young man, you are incorrigible! Keep your conversation pleasant!"

"Boys, boys," Mother interjected. "Can't we just enjoy dessert?"

Father rose and poured himself a Scotch from the crystal decanter on the side table.

"Those people down there," Frederick said, "just want free hand-outs."

"You try living on the wages those poor folk earn!" Miss Aarons' outburst of indignation startled him, and apparently everyone else. She turned crimson and was pulling at the collar of her blouse as though she were choking.

"Miss Aarons, are you all right?" Alice asked. "Grayson, quick! Pour Miss Aarons some water."

"Deep breaths," Thomas said. "Deep breaths, Miss Aarons."

Frederick stood and waved his hand in a grand gesture he imagined his hero Henry Clay Frick would use. "Mark Twain says we are living in the Gilded Age. Like the Golden Age of Greece."

"Oh, sit down, you imbecile," Father admonished him. "You have absolutely no understanding of Twain. He meant that these times glitter on the surface but underneath it is corrupt, you fool. Bring me a cigar, will you, Grayson."

"Certainly, Mr. Winthrop."

BLACKMAIL

September 13, 1899

Lottie pursed her lips and smoothed the fingers of her new kid gloves, checking for the third time to make certain she hadn't lost any of the tiny pearl buttons. She felt like a frightened child riding in the building's newfangled elevator—even though she was accompanied by Jonathan and Thomas Winthrop.

"I detest these monthly meetings with Frederick," Mr. Jonathan whispered. " Nineteen, and that arrogant twit thinks he knows it all."

Mr. Thomas was adjusting his bright yellow bow tie. "Too bright, Miss Aarons?"

"Oh, no, sir. If it gets too gloomy, I will be cheered just by looking at your tie."

"Then you will like my yellow plaid vest as well."

"One day you will have a yellow suit made." Mr. Jonathan poked his brother in the belly. Mr. Thomas attempted to tame his white mane and then pulled the ends of his white moustache, which Lottie noted he always did after he laughed. Both over six feet tall, the two brothers towered over her by almost a foot.

She took pride in waiting with her handsome employers for the elevator in the lobby of the World Building on Park Row and Frankfort Street.

"I can't breathe in that office."

"Sorry to say, Mr. Thomas, your brother has nailed the windows shut." She turned to Mr. Jonathan in an attempt to change the subject. "How is your father, sir?"

"Thank you for asking." He checked his pocket watch for the time. "It doesn't look good. His pneumonia seems worse, and he's quite incoherent. The doctors don't hold much hope. He's almost ninety."

"I'm so sorry. And what about your plans for the school?"

"Yes, yes." Mr. Jonathan's face brightened, his voice animated. "Since William H. Maxwell has become superintendent, there are changes in the public system. An eight-year standard curriculum— for all elementary schools. Imagine! Kindergarten for children under six—on every city block. Even in the poorest neighborhoods. We plan to open the Winthrop School in the New Year."

She listened nervously for the sound of the elevator starting its descent from an upper floor.

"Here it comes! Would you like to hold my arm, Miss Aarons?"

"I'll be fine, sir. Thank you. Counting helps."

When Jimmy Riley, the elevator operator, in his beige cap and uniform with a triple row of brass buttons, opened the door, he nodded to them and said, "Twentieth floor?"

The door clanged shut and she felt like a trapped animal. Usually she walked up the twenty flights. The elevator lurched into action and she grabbed Mr. Jonathan's arm.

"Sorry, miss." Jimmy nodded.

"Quite all right, Jimmy." She forced a smile.

"With the influx of immigrants," Mr. Jonathan continued, "there must be vocational and technical programs—sewing and manual training—to prepare these young people for the city's industries." He continued with enthusiasm, "And for those who can't speak English: special classes."

"I read in the *Journal* that these poor children eat only one meal a day." She was counting each floor. They had just passed the eighth.

"Maxwell believes in school-sponsored breakfasts and lunches for poor students."

"We thought you'd appreciate that, Miss Aarons. The timing is right for our school. The city schools are overcrowded, with morning and evening shifts."

"Ninth floor," she chirped.

"We're searching for exceptional students. Keep your eyes open for us, Miss Aarons."

"Eleven."

"No need to count the floors."

"Sorry, sir. I cannot get used to riding these newfangled elevators."

"You're perfectly safe," Jimmy Riley said.

"That's what *you* say."

"Furthermore," Mr. Thomas continued, "children will benefit from small classrooms and more attention."

"Yes. Keep children from temptations like boxing matches, dance clubs, and pool halls." She felt extremely uneasy at the sound of the metal elevator slowly moving up the interior of its confined space. *Fifteen.* She expected the chains to give way, imagined them plummeting to the ground. Crushed. She took a huge breath. The next few floors passed more smoothly. "I hope your father will live to see the school's first day. It would make him proud."

"I doubt that will be possible. But thank you for your thoughts," he said, and Mr. Jonathan added his thanks as well.

"Twentieth floor, Winthrop Company," Jimmy finally announced. It took him some adjusting up and down and with some bouncing to get the door and the floor lined up properly, during which Lottie's stomach did somersaults and she was unable to stifle a moan.

"Sorry, miss."

"Thank you, Riley," they said in unison.

Lottie stepped out of the elevator and took a deep breath. "Safe and sound." Taking a lace hanky from her purse, she patted her face.

"Take your last breath of fresh air." Mr. Jonathan ran fingers through his salt-and-pepper hair, opened the office door, and stepped across the marble threshold. "Frederick awaits."

The air was fetid, a mix of cigar, sweat, heat, and cuspidor. Several hours had passed when Mr. Frederick finally slammed the book closed. "Well, that should do it!"

Lottie looked at her watch. No wonder she was hungry. It was almost eight o'clock and everyone was testy. She began to tidy Mr. Frederick's desk while his brothers gathered their paperwork. While all three brothers were officers of the corporation, Mr. Jonathan and Mr. Thomas, with their father's approval, were investing corporate funds in the development of the Winthrop School. As bookkeeper to the corporation, the school, and the three brothers, her work was complicated. Winston Winthrop had long ago asked her to keep particular watch over Mr. Frederick, his finances and real estate deals, the buying and selling of tenements on the Lower East Side, and to make certain they were not part of the corporation's business.

Mr. Thomas stood up, stretched, and then grumbled, "You've taken Father's office, with the best views of the city, locked the windows, and closed the drapes. Why don't you allow us some of the fresh air blowing off the Hudson River, for God's sake?" He pulled the drape aside to reveal a dark sky. "There's not one bit of air in here."

"I like it this way."

"It's not your office. Father isn't dead *yet*, Frederick," Mr. Thomas said.

"He might as well be."

She was certain she had gasped aloud. She couldn't believe that Mr. Frederick actually laughed when he said that.

Mr. Jonathan leaned forward and, pointing an accusing finger, said, "Behave yourself! We are quite aware of how you feel about Father, but be civil."

Taking a seat, she looked through the notes she'd taken during the meeting using Gregg shorthand. Based on bisecting elliptical figures and lines, it allowed her to take notes faster than longhand. In the morning she would transcribe them on her typewriter.

"Next time, open the windows. Do you want to suffocate us?"

"Not a bad idea, Tom."

"Frederick!" said both brothers.

Mr. Frederick stood, taking his pocket watch from his vest; announced, "I'm going to be late for my Delmonico's reservation"; and started toward the door.

"Just a moment." Both brothers blocked him from moving.

"Delmonico's will just have to wait. Sit down," Mr. Thomas said, forcing him back to his seat with a prodding finger to his shoulder. "There is one more thing. You are to stop this business with young girls," he demanded. "You're jeopardizing our family's reputation."

"Hearsay. Pure gossip." He seemed caught off guard.

"I was told she just turned fifteen," said Mr. Jonathan.

Mr. Frederick burst into laughter. "She's young and eager for adventure. And with only an investment of small flattery and a few sparkles!"

"Father would be upset if he knew you are carrying on with the daughter of our family friends," Mr. Jonathan threatened.

"Most likely he'll be dead in a matter of days."

Lottie gasped again.

"Meeting adjourned, gentlemen." Mr. Jonathan stood.

There was an awkward silence as Mr. Jonathan and Mr. Thomas stood to get ready to leave the office. They gathered their coats, hats, and umbrellas. Lottie, already in her coat and gloves, had quietly moved closer to the door. In the tense, overheated room, she could feel the drops of perspiration rolling down her back.

"Oh. Uh. Just . . . one . . . moment." Mr. Frederick drew out each word. "I . . . intended to tell you earlier." He paused and then took a cigar from the humidor, not bothering to offer one to his brothers. He looked like the cat that swallowed the canary. Leaning back in his leather wing chair, he said after a lengthy pause. "You know . . . that property—the one on Sixty-Ninth off Fifth? That you've had your eyes on for that school? Well, it's mine." He grinned as he lit the cigar, seemingly filled with pleasure that he'd taken them completely by surprise. They sat, each with his mouth agape. Lottie couldn't believe what she had heard. "It's too valuable for such nonsense as a school."

"That's quite impossible, Frederick. Jon and I signed the papers weeks ago."

"Bliss changed his mind."

"Henry H. Bliss?" Mr. Thomas jumped up from his chair, crossing toward Frederick's desk, and raised a fist as if to strike his brother. "Why, that's part of Millionaire's Row," he said.

Mr. Frederick laughed. "I know!"

Mr. Jonathan quickly leapt forward to hold Mr. Thomas back.

But Mr. Thomas' temper, once raised, was always difficult to contain. He slammed his fist on the desk. "We're ready to begin construction. We showed you the plans. Trusted you. It's our family's legacy to the city. To honor Father and Mother."

"Of no interest to me, Tom. I thought I made that perfectly clear."

Lottie believed in this school as much as Mr. Jonathan and Mr. Thomas. Public schools in the city were as overcrowded as the tenements. *Mind your business,* she told herself, and folded her hands in her lap.

Mr. Frederick laughed as he looked up at his two brothers, who were leaning on their fists in front of his desk. "I think you will discover that Bliss may have, uh, forgotten to register your paperwork!"

"Forgotten? We signed papers last month. I should never have shown you our drawings. You underhanded son of a—" Mr. Thomas broke off when Mr. Jonathan placed a hand on his shoulder, reminding him there was a lady present. Mr. Thomas' cheeks and nose were flushed with fury.

Mr. Frederick stood up to face his brothers. "Bliss registered the property in *my* name," he said in his cockiest tone. "It's done!"

Mr. Jonathan was outraged. Leaning forward, he gripped the side of the desk for control. "So that's why Bliss came to speak to me last week, rambling about difficulties filing the papers—and letters—begging for their return. I had no idea what he was talking about."

"Have you blackmailed Bliss to bury our paperwork?" demanded Mr. Thomas.

His two brothers suddenly seemed to loom over Mr. Frederick. But he only gave them one of his wickedest smiles.

Mr. Jonathan took a hard grasp of his brother's wrist and twisted it.

"Have you returned the letters?" Mr. Jonathan demanded, as he let go of his grasp.

Mr. Frederick shrugged, rubbing his wrist. "I can't remember, actually. I have so much to attend to."

"Our school would ensure rich and poor have the finest education."

"Do you think I give a fig about the poor?" Mr. Frederick spit into his cuspidor. "Jews, most of them! Can't even speak English."

Lottie thought about Eldridge Street: families with handicapped children; families with twelve children living in the basement; her downstairs neighbor's beautiful daughter, deaf and dumb; and the Moskowitz family, next door to Rivkah, with the boy with a clubfoot. These children didn't go to school. Their clothes were worn hand-me-downs. They couldn't speak English. But they could learn.

While she kept her gaze on her shoes, she listened, wondering if there was any way she could have known. Tomorrow she must check the books to be certain that not one cent had been paid to Henry Bliss from the corporation.

"Bugger off. Build your damn school somewhere else." Mr. Frederick stood, buttoned his vest, put on his coat, and walked to the door, where he stopped to put on his hat. "Lock up, Miss Aarons," he ordered. And without tipping his hat, he walked out the door.

6

SUSPICION

SEPTEMBER 30

On his deathbed, Winston Winthrop had confided to his eldest that he had grave concerns about the welfare of the company, the workers, and their families under Frederick's ideas of management, and both Jonathan and Thomas promised him that they and Lottie Aarons would oversee Frederick's every move.

"Ah, here we are." Lottie, seated in the back of the Winthrops' car, gathered her purse and gloves. "Such a beautiful funeral, sirs; sad, but your father would have been pleased." She wanted to offer some caring gesture but decided it wasn't right for someone in her position.

"You are a great comfort to us, Miss Aarons," Mr. Jonathan said, his usually unruly hair combed and pomaded in place for the occasion.

"Father *and* Mother were very fond of you," added Mr. Thomas, in his mourning clothes with neither colorful tie nor vest.

"Thank you for bringing me home. The trolley would have taken me more than an hour—and *so* crowded. I might have had to stand the entire way."

"Certainly, a gentleman would have given you a seat."

They were at the front of the West Seventy-Sixth Street brick row house where she had recently moved, thanks to the generosity of Winston Winthrop. A gas streetlamp and smooth pavement marked the block of new homes. The chauffeur had opened the car door and both Winthrop brothers stepped out as well.

"It's been a long day." She lifted her skirt so as not to soil the hem. "I'm glad I no longer have to make that trip to Brooklyn."

"It was Father's wish that you have this apartment, and we agree. We're pleased to see you settled in the city, Miss Aarons."

"I'm so appreciative and proud to have worked for your father. And to be working for you both."

"He was, as are we, very grateful for your work," Mr. Jonathan said.

"And keeping an eye on Frederick for us," added Mr. Thomas, as if in the same breath.

"It's awful about Henry Bliss," she mentioned, casually. "Getting run over." She couldn't help herself; she found it highly suspicious.

"He seemed almost pleased about Bliss, didn't he, Tom?" Mr. Jonathan said.

"Almost? I'd say he was *damned* pleased! Excuse me, Miss Aarons."

"He's a devious one. Wouldn't put it past him," Mr. Jonathan said. "Let's just keep it between us, though."

"But of course, sirs."

"We wouldn't want unnecessary attention brought to our family. You understand?"

"Absolutely, sir."

Mr. Thomas sighed and tipped his hat. "Good evening, my dear. See you Monday morning. Thank you for your assistance. Thank you for watching over and protecting our—"

"Finances," Mr. Jonathan said, finishing his sentence. "Please wave to us from your parlor window, Miss Aarons, so we know you're safe inside."

"Why don't we see you to your door?"

"That's not necessary. Good night to both of you. He was a great man."

By December, there were complaints of unpaid wages and deteriorating working conditions at the Winthrop Corporation. In February, Frederick fought ferociously with workers against unionization. He didn't want to pay sick workers' medical care or lost wages. He watched as families were evicted from their homes and refused any family assistance.

1909

1

SEWARD PARK

It rained the entire first week of March. Every day the streets were
flooded and muddy. Finally, on Sunday the sun came out.

"Miriam, get some fresh air. Go to the park. Take a sandwich."

"Come with me, Mama. The sun will be good for your cough."

"I have work," she said. "Mrs. Kovitz is coming today."

Miriam couldn't stand Mrs. Kovitz and was glad to leave.

She found an empty bench in Seward Park, at the corner of Essex and
East Broadway, where she ate her pot roast sandwich on Friday's challah. She saved some crusts for the birds. Robins came and danced
around her feet and made her laugh.

"May I sit here?"

The first thing she noticed was his highly polished brown oxford boots. Few men in the neighborhood had shined shoes. As her
gaze rose, she was aware of his well-made brown, pin-striped Kup-
penheimer sack suit with matching vest and starched high-collar
shirt.

When she looked at people she met, Miriam quickly gathered
an impression of what their mannequin would be like. This young
man's proportions were perfect from his shoulders to his feet.
He had a confident and balanced stance, grounded in those shiny
brown shoes. He was young, about eighteen, she decided. Although
he approached her in a friendly manner, there was something about

him that struck her as ever so slightly insincere. She noticed small things like this about people she met, and they made her uneasy. She often considered that she would be a happier person if she didn't notice everything.

"I'm Frederick," he said, and removed his bowler. She was somewhat taken aback by the intensity of his gaze. Unsettled. Bowing slightly, he went to seat himself on the bench. "And you?" As he sat down on the bench, the cluster of birds at her feet flew up noisily, all at once, and disappeared into the trees.

"Mimi," she answered. That was what her friends at school called her. And Lottie. Only Mama called her Miriam. Suddenly feeling quite shy, she looked down. She could feel that the color had risen to her cheeks, revealing her lack of self-assurance.

He slid closer. "Do the boys tell you that you look like a Gibson Girl?"

She was embarrassed. The boys she knew wouldn't say such things. She moved away.

He reached over and took her hand in his. "Such delicate fingers. No wedding ring?"

She laughed. He certainly had a sense of humor. "I'm not married."

"Do you live nearby?" he asked. His hand was soft.

She pulled her hand out of his. "I live with my mother."

"And your father? Where is he?"

She was uncomfortable with his questions. But perhaps he only wanted to know her.

"He will arrive any day," she lied. "And you?" she asked boldly. "Do you live nearby?"

He watched her feed a brave bird that had returned. "The birds like you, too, I see."

She wasn't used to talking with boys other than Szymon next door and Isaac, who lived in the basement, and the boy on the second floor who helped his father sell fish from a pushcart. Mama said to keep away from boys in the building; they were low-class.

Frederick took out a gold pocket watch from his vest. "I must be on my way." He stood, took a few steps, and then returned. "I would like to see you again. If you will meet me here at seven p.m. tomorrow, I will take you to dinner. Would you like that?"

Standing next to him, she found that she had to look up to see his eyes. He was quite a bit taller than she had first realized.

Dinner? She didn't know what to say. She had never been out for dinner in her life. What should she do? Say? He checked his watch, lifted his eyebrows, shifted his weight from one hip to the other. "Well?" he asked impatiently, interrupting her thoughts. "Where shall I pick you up?"

Oh, no, he mustn't see where she lived! Or Mama with her apron and cough. She didn't know what to say. She wanted to say yes more than anything.

"I'll wait at the entrance to the park at seven," he said boldly. "If you're here at seven, we shall have dinner." He walked off before she could say anything more, without even asking her last name.

Her heart was racing with excitement as she started home. He seemed a gentleman. She had, on occasion, seen people through windows eating in restaurants, and now she would be on the inside. But Mama would certainly say no, and so she decided that she would tell her that she had been invited for dinner at her friend Sina's. Just a small lie. He was very handsome.

It was still light when Frederick beckoned to her from his black automobile the next evening at the entrance to the park—just as he had said—at seven. She wore a simple black skirt and the blouse to which she had added a ruffle from the leftover lace from the window curtains. A liveried driver opened the door of the Pierce-Arrow—she recognized it from the pages of *Vogue*—and Frederick offered his hand to her from the darkness of the back. She stepped onto the running board and slid onto the soft, leather-cushioned back seat. She had never ridden in an automobile. Her heart was racing.

At the Old Homestead Steakhouse on Ninth Avenue, the waiter showed them to a small table along the wall. As they passed a window, she brushed her fingers over the plush pine-green velvet drapes. Frederick ordered with grace, clearly accustomed to having everything as he desired, cooked in a specific way: the sirloin rare, the potatoes hashed, the spinach creamed. There were starched white linens and more utensils than she had ever seen before. Everything sparkled. There was a hum of voices interspersed with occasional laughter, the sound of silverware on china, and the scent of herbs and spices and women's perfumes. Violins played softly. It seemed a million miles from the commotion of Eldridge Street.

She savored every bite of her dinner, especially the delicate slices of rare, pink beef. At home, they cooked meats for hours: pot roast, brisket, and stew. The potatoes, crisp and brown, and the creamy spinach, with a hint of nutmeg, were nothing like the boiled potatoes Mama made almost every night.

Frederick talked about the expansion of the city, buildings that he admired. He described how his office was on the twentieth floor and attempted to explain to her that his company worked with the man who made Singer sewing machines. It never occurred to her that Singer was a person. She delighted in hearing about his travels, especially Paris. She watched how he ate, following his example. How he held his fork, cut his steak, held the knife and used it to move food around the plate, and wiped his mouth before each sip of water or wine.

At every opportunity she took in the details of all the elegant women in the room—how poised they looked in their beautiful feathered hats, the fit of their silk blouses with embroidery on shoulders and sleeves.

When the waiter brought the cheesecake Frederick had ordered, he abruptly turned all his attention to her. She felt warm and special in his presence. He took a small tissue-wrapped parcel from his pocket and handed it to her. He told her it was a perfume bottle from Paris—very old, having belonged to his grandmother—and that he wanted her to have it. She pulled the stopper, and the fragrance of oranges filled the air. He asked permission to place a drop on her neck.

He wanted her to see his mansion on Long Island, he said. Overlooking the ocean. As he described its gardens and ponds, listed its gilded rooms, Mimi began to imagine herself as Aschenputtel, a young woman who lived in awful circumstances that suddenly changed when she went to the ball of a prince. Dressed in a gold-and-silver gown and shoes, she and the prince danced until midnight, when she had to return home. The prince searched for her after finding one of her lost golden slippers. Mimi had borrowed the book of fairy tales many times from the library. It was still her favorite story.

After dinner, Frederick's driver was waiting and drove them across town and, at her request, dropped her at Seward Park. Frederick kissed her hand and thanked her for her delightful company. She felt giddy when he suggested they meet the following week—same time, same place.

She was relieved that Mama was asleep and snoring loudly. She undressed and slipped into bed beside her and then went over the details of the evening, remembering his fragrance of citrus and spice.

Work slowed the following week, so she was able to meet him again. Mama was happy that she was seeing a friend, and Frederick was waiting at the entrance to the park promptly at seven.

They ate dinner at a dimly lit café. Frederick ordered in French: for himself, squab wrapped in bacon with juniper berries and grapes. He suggested that Miriam might enjoy a beautiful piece of sole with lemon butter and capers.

"Too beautiful to eat," she cried in delight.

He sat quite close to her and fed her small forkfuls of food. Chills ran through her.

"In Paris there's a small music hall—originally it was an opera house—near the *rue* Bergère. There are acrobats, sometimes a snake charmer, a boxing kangaroo, trained elephants, the world's tallest man, and a Greek prince covered in tattoos as punishment for trying to seduce the Shah of Persia's daughter." He fed her a taste of his squab and then a small roasted grape.

"How exciting your life is," she said. "So full of adventure."

She had a million questions to ask. How did one charm a snake? What was a kangaroo? What was a Shah of Persia, and how do you train an elephant? She didn't ask.

"All the dancers at this music hall are the same size," he said. "One can hardly tell them apart. Petite, like you, and almost as beautiful. They glitter and sparkle like little birds, all aflutter onstage. They wear nothing but feathers and pearls," he whispered in her ear.

"Nothing else?" she asked. As the waiter removed their dishes, she thought she felt Frederick's hand against her thigh.

"Nothing else." He laughed. "I can just imagine you, my *petite*, dressed in yellow feathers, like a little goldfinch."

"I think I once saw a Follies girl in *Modes de Paris* magazine. My mother's friend called the photo *risqué*, which she explained was French for 'naughty.' Her skirt was very short."

"Some might say so, I suppose," Frederick said. "It's all in the observer's point of view. Did you know that in nature it is the male birds with the most beautiful costume? A male hovers above a female, flapping its wings." Frederick paused to raise and dramatically move his arms like wings. "He sings to her." Placing one arm around her shoulder, Frederick hummed a song in her ear, which made her shiver.

"Ostrich feathers are all the style," she said. "For neckpieces, hats, and on hems. Why, I've counted a dozen in this room. They're quite pricey, you know."

When he said, "I'll buy them for you. A dozen, if you like," the idea of coming home with a dozen ostrich feathers made her burst into laughter. While she laughed, he brushed her hair aside and kissed her neck. Fortunately, no one seemed to notice in the candlelight.

"Close your eyes. This is for you." He took her hand in his and dropped something in it. "What do you think it is? Keep your eyes closed." He took his hand away.

She felt the cool, slender cylindrical object and its connection to a long and delicate velvet ribbon. She held it to her nose, smelled cinnamon, oranges, and flowers. When Frederick took it from her hand, she opened her eyes.

"It was my mother's. My father brought it to her from Paris. I want you to have it. I've filled it with fragrant ink so you can write me love letters. Do you recognize the flower?"

She shook her head.

"Jasmine."

"I've never smelled jasmine," she admitted shyly. Such a beautiful thing, pierced silver and engraved with flowers, hanging on a white velvet ribbon. She had never received gifts before meeting Frederick.

The driver had stopped at the park entrance.

"Meet me at six on Saturday. It will be a special evening I've planned for you."

"Tell me, please," she begged, stepping out of his car. "I can't bear surprises."

"Tell your mother that you will be staying the night with a friend, and wear that pretty white blouse with the waterfall of lace and all the tiny buttons again."

Before she could tell him she couldn't possibly do that, his car drove off into the night.

"Where's my birthday kiss?" Frederick asked on Saturday as they rode uptown.

"You never said it was your birthday!" She had never asked Mama if she might spend the night with Sina. There was too much work, and Mama would need her help.

"Here, let me hold your purse for you." He placed it inside his coat and then held both her hands.

"And how old are you?" she asked.

"Guess."

"Eighteen?"

He threw his head back and laughed. "Eighteen? No . . . try again."

"Twenty?"

He shook his head.

"Tell me, tell me. I give up."

"I'm an old man!" he whispered. "Twenty-nine! Too old for you, do you think?"

She let out a gasp and pulled her hands out of his. He was almost the same age as Mama. Mama would be very angry.

"Give me back your hands," he demanded, interrupting her thoughts. She was shocked when he held her hands up to his mouth and felt his tongue against her palms. He took each of her fingers into his soft, wet mouth. When she attempted to pull her hands away, he took hold of them. His laughter echoed against the walls of the automobile.

He reached into his pocket and took out a small velvet box. Opening it, he removed a little gold ring and slipped it onto her finger. When she held up her hand, a small stone sparkled in the street's lamplight. She had never seen anything so beautiful.

"Oh, how can I resist those pretty green eyes, that mouth like an angel's?" His hands held her face still. He leaned close enough that she could feel his breath. "I would love to see you with your hair down. Kiss me boldly."

She leaned forward and kissed him with daring.

His kisses grew more ardent than she expected, and she was surprised at the strange sensation of his tongue as it circled her lips and then entered her mouth. He pressed her close to his chest, and she had an awareness of a fluttering, a curiously sensual sensation. But it also filled her with apprehension.

"We'll be at Raptor in no time. Have you ever seen the sun rise over the ocean? Listened to the mourning doves and finches at dawn? I can't wait to share it with you."

"I can't." She pushed him away. "I can't. I've never stayed a night away. I wouldn't dare ask. My mother's not well. It's not possible. I'm sorry if you thought I could. I can't. She would worry."

"Stop." There was a flicker of anger, a momentary spark, she noticed, and then it passed.

"I'm so sorry." She felt wretched to have disappointed him, especially on his birthday. "Please don't be angry with me." She kissed him again.

"I liked that." He laughed. "Don't look so sad. No apologies." He paused and looked out the window. "I know. We'll have dinner at my hotel. It's exquisite: French—Beaux Arts. It has its own laundry, power plant, ice-making machines, and telephone system," he rattled on. She had no idea what he was talking about.

Then he seemed to catch himself. "I'm going on and on, aren't I? I'm just disappointed that you won't go with me to Raptor. Another time, perhaps. I had so many plans. Kiss me again," he murmured. "With your tongue, my sweet little bird."

Her emotions were in upheaval. She felt exhausted and helpless. She had never lied to Mama.

When they entered the Wolcott Hotel on Fifth Avenue, she was startled by the brilliance of its lobby, the elaborately carved decorations, gold and crystal, and the plush feel of carpeting beneath her feet.

"It's quite grand," she exclaimed, but—seeing her reflection in the multitude of lobby mirrors, wearing a skirt and blouse—she felt like a country bumpkin in a royal palace.

"It's Louis XVI," Frederick said. Taking her arm, he led her quickly to a private elevator. People were staring at them—at her.

"Where are we going?" She didn't belong here. There was tightness in her chest as the elevator rose, and she struggled to breathe.

In the privacy of the elevator, taking her in his arms, he whispered, "Don't be afraid."

A servant welcomed them, and then seemed to magically disappear through one of the hallway's mirrored doors.

"You live here?" she asked, taking a deep breath and looking about. Everything was gilded, its décor as ornate as the hotel lobby. She had thought they would dine in a restaurant.

With his arm around her waist, Frederick guided her through the living room and into an intimate study lit only by candelabras. She had never imagined he would bring her to his rooms.

"I'll see what we can put together in the way of dinner," he said, and then excused himself.

Walking about the room, Mimi paused to look at a series of miniature framed paintings of small birds and ran her hand over the leather-bound books that filled the bookcases. On a small table sat a bell jar filled with nine enchanting birds with brightly colored feathers, perched upon branches. She had always wanted a canary, certain its beautiful songs would bring cheer to Mama and fill their little apartment with springtime. Mimi watched the birds for several minutes before realizing in horror that they were dead.

She picked up a small, pale pink stone carved in the shape of a peach and, when it came apart, feared she had broken it. To her surprise, fitted inside was the figure of an infant boy.

There was a group of photographs in silver frames, at which she looked more closely. They were not photographs of his family, as she had expected, but rather photos of girls her own age doing unspeakable things with men. They were shameful. Naughty. Some were naked; others raised their skirts to reveal private parts. Curious, she picked one up to have a closer look. A young girl with blond curls was lying across a bearded man's lap and he was spanking her. Why would anyone want such an awful picture? she wondered.

"Naughty little girl! You shouldn't be looking at that."

She dropped the photo and the glass shattered.

"I'm so sorry," she said, kneeling to pick up the pieces of glass.

"Stop," he said angrily, pulling her up from the floor. Then just as suddenly he laughed. "Just leave it." He led her away.

He was no longer wearing the tuxedo coat, vest, or tie. Instead, he wore a claret-colored paisley silk jacket with velvet lapels that tied like a robe. His shirt was opened at the collar, and on his bare feet were burgundy velvet slippers. He poured her a glass of champagne and, when she resisted, assured her that it would be fine for her to drink because she was with him.

After some time, the servant served them dinner: tender pink chops—lamb, Frederick explained—and potatoes carved into ovals, as well as the tiniest green beans she had ever seen. And he kept refilling her glass. Amused by her pleasure, he moved his chair beside

hers and fed her bites of dessert, chocolate cake with fresh berries
and whipped cream. When they had finished, the servant appeared
as if by magic, then quickly and silently removed all signs of their
dinner.

"I'm feeling just a bit dizzy," she told him as he helped her from
her chair.

"Don't worry. You'll be safe with me," he assured her as he led her
to a divan. When she lay back, luxuriating against the velvet and silk
pillows, he sat at her feet and took off her shoes. "One of these days I
will take you to Raptor." He gently caressed her feet.

"Can you really see the ocean from your windows?"

"Yes. You can hear the waves breaking on the shore, see the moon
and stars. We could walk along the beach as the sun sets; in the morning, see the sunrise."

How could she not tell Mama she had met such a fine gentleman,
kind and smart, and who could change their lives? She would want to
tell Mama everything he had told her about Raptor's elegance. Frederick called it a cottage, but it had forty rooms, ten ponds, gardens,
wild birds, and a maze, which he had explained was a maze of hedges
in which you played hide-and-seek. Mama would be excited for her.
She would need a gown. But where would they get the money for the
fabric or find the time to make one?

"I'm afraid I don't have a ball gown," she said.

His resonant laughter seemed to fill the room as he took off his
velvet jacket, unbuttoned his shirt, and lay down beside her. "I only
want to be alone with you." He took her hand and placed it inside his
shirt. "Besides, you don't need beautiful clothes." She felt him shiver
as she touched the smooth skin on his chest. "Do you feel my heart
desiring you?"

When he untied and removed the lace bow at her neck, she held
her breath, didn't know what she was supposed to do. As one by one he
slowly opened the pearl buttons of the high-collared blouse she had
copied from *Ladies' Home Journal*, he counted and kissed her tenderly
for each one. She laughed when he forgot seven, corrected him, and

soon was counting with him. She could feel his breathing intensify with each number whispered against her ear as he began kissing her neck, and then, as he undid her braids and spread her hair around her face and shoulders, the sensation of his fingers running through it. When he pushed the blouse off her shoulders and took each arm out of its sleeve, she felt the tickle of his lips on her bare arms, his tongue on her underarms.

She lay still as he lifted her skirt, luxuriating in the confidence with which he removed her stockings. But when she felt his warm hand on her thighs, she experienced something quite different: a feverish stirring somewhere in her belly. He removed her under-garments with surprising ease. When his mouth moved down to her breasts, she began to feel a yearning for something unspeak-able. The heat of his bare chest against hers. The susurration of his breath. The sounds of her own.

"Tell me you want me," he whispered. "Say it."

"I want you," she whispered. There wasn't enough air to breathe for her longing.

"Again," he insisted, and she said the words again and again.

Mimi felt the urgent stirrings of desire, more intense than those she sometimes had in the dark: longings to touch down below, which she fought against because of the fierce pleasure that followed. It was a pleasure, she had been certain, that must be shameful. Suddenly she was jolted out of the inexplicably invasive feelings to her body by a loud and angry moan, like the sound of a wild animal dying.

She was awakened by the sound of knocking and startled to find herself alone in what must be Frederick's bedroom.

The butler entered the room to tell her he would see her to the cab that was waiting. She freshened herself as quickly as she could. He took her down what seemed endless flights of stairs and then led her out by way of the servants' entrance, into the darkness, where the cab was waiting.

After telling the driver her address, as the cab headed downtown, she said, "Oh, no, I seem to have lost my purse."

"Does you want me to take you back to the Wolcott, miss?"

"I have no money to pay you, sir," she said with embarrassment.

"The gentleman, he paid yer fare."

Arriving on Eldridge Street, she slipped quietly into the apartment, got undressed and into bed next to Mama, and breathed a sigh of relief that she didn't stir.

2

BETH ISRAEL HOSPITAL

Mama's cough worsened. For weeks, even after being diagnosed with pneumonia, she refused to take the doctor's advice that she be hospitalized. She was in a constant fear that Miriam couldn't manage without her.

They tried cupping. Miriam heated the insides of the cups and then attached them to the skin on her mother's back.

"Cupping doesn't do anything," Lottie declared. "It's an old wives' tale! Listen to me, Rivkah. If the doctors tell you it's pneumonia, then it's pneumonia! You can't play around with that."

"Once the heated cups draw the phlegm from my chest the illness will be sucked to the surface," Mama insisted.

"Listen to the doctors," Lottie urged.

"She's as stubborn as a mule!" Miriam laughed.

When Lottie rolled her eyes and shook her head, Rivkah said with annoyance, "Don't think I didn't see that."

"As helpful as cupping a corpse." Lottie threw up her hands in dismay. "Oy, I suppose it can't hurt. And you, Mimi, see that your mama gets sunlight. *That's* what kills germs."

Miriam was able to get her mother to take her medicine, and for a while she seemed to improve. Her energy returned; she was able to get out of bed and work for part of the day.

On Saturday morning they walked to Seward Park and fed the
birds and squirrels.

"What are you looking for?" Rivkah asked.

"Nothing."

"You look like you're looking for something."

"Well, I'm not," Mimi lied. She searched the passersby and automobiles, hoping to catch a glimpse of Frederick. She had to take care
of Mama, the apartment, groceries, and the business. There was no
time to go to the park, and she realized her chance to go to Long
Island with Frederick was slipping away.

Mama coughed throughout the night, she had no energy during the
day, and within days her breathing became labored. There were dark
circles under her eyes. She made Miriam sleep on the floor on rags so
she wouldn't get sick.

Miriam woke during the night and placed a hand on her mother's
forehead. It felt hot to the touch. Mama was agitated, tried to sit up.
"What time is it? Are we late for work? Hurry, hurry, or Mr. Blanck
won't pay us. The rent is due."

"We don't work for Mr. Blanck anymore. *Gey shluffen*, Mama. Go
back to sleep. It's nighttime."

Rivkah sighed, fell back onto the bed, and began snoring. Miriam
tossed and turned. Could they afford for the doctor to come again? It
was her decision to make. Mama kept saying, "No, I'm almost better."

In the morning she was wheezing, feverish, and once she fell
asleep again, Miriam went to fetch the doctor. He came to the house
and insisted she go to Beth Israel, the hospital for the city's Jewish
immigrants. Mimi's fifteenth birthday went unnoticed.

Visiting the hospital the first night, she fought her exhaustion. White
walls, curtains, rows of white iron beds that lined the length of both
sides of the room, each with a small white enamel nightstand and a
white enamel water pitcher and cup. A curtain could be drawn for
privacy. Like a white ghost ship.

The quiet broken only by imperceptible moans and coughs. The powdery smell of borax and the exhalations of the sick and dying. Was this what death was, a vast endless place of white? Even the staff, doctors, and nurses were dressed in white from shoes to caps, drifting like ghosts through the room, stopping here and there for a task, a few whispered words. It was quiet except when the sounds of patients' cries filled the empty spaces. She searched for Mama in every bed.

"Miriam, Miriam. Hire Mrs. Kovitz. Pay her what she asks, Miriam." Mama spoke with a force as though she had been holding the words in her mouth, ruminating over them, all day and night, waiting for her arrival.

Miriam pulled a white metal chair close to Mama's side, held her hand. "How are you? Did you sleep?"

"Sleep? With all these strangers? They snore. They moan. How can I get well here among the sick and dying? Did you hire Mrs. Kovitz?"

"She stinks of cabbage."

"So hold your nose. Do what I tell you, Miriam."

But Mrs. Kovitz was slow. "Oy. Oy. My back and my neck. Right over here, oy, oy," she moaned, pushing up her tangle of greasy brown hair and rubbing the back of her dirty neck. Miriam had to remind her to wash her hands when she arrived. Mrs. Kovitz didn't like that. "I hurt all the time from this work. Like someone is pushing a dagger in my neck. And here, too." She rubbed the lower side of her back. "It's hard to work. Like someone set a fire to my spine . . . and my neck. And once it starts, the pain, I see stars." She would wave her hand at Miriam and say, "What would you know, with your ladylike ways?" Always about her pain, her debt, her family of lazy invalids, and then calling Miriam "Princess" in Polish.

Hannah Kovitz's work was careless, and often Miriam had to do the tedious work of pulling out her stitches and resewing. It took all Miriam's strength to get through each day.

It was strange to be without Mama: alone in bed, alone at breakfast. The silence of one, except for the voices that came down the stairs, through the floors and walls, and through the windows—like the cawing of angry birds.

"It has no taste. It needs salt, and put in some onion and garlic," Rivkah complained when Miriam arrived at the hospital the next night. "Didn't I teach you to make soup?" Miriam couldn't stand the smell.

"Close the curtain. I don't want anyone should know my business."

She pulled the curtains around them, enclosing them in an otherworldly space—a spaceship. Like the one Szymon described that flew astronomers to the moon.

"Come closer, Miriam. Strangers shouldn't listen. You don't look so good. Are you eating?"

"I'm just tired, Mama. I have no time to eat." The truth was she had no appetite.

"Sit down." She patted the space next to her. "Here. On the bed. Beside me." She took hold of Miriam's hand. "Your hand is cold. Did you finish Mrs. Callahan's party dress?

"What about Mr. Zeitz's coat?

"Don't forget, Miriam, Jacob Cohen's bar mitzvah is in three weeks.

"How will we ever pay the rent?

"Remember, Miriam, make little stitches.

"Don't forget Mr. Zeitz's coat. I promised.

"Wrap everything nice. With string."

All Mama thought about was business. Miriam pulled her hand away. Her mind was spinning.

"I do everything you say, Mama. But I can't work with Mrs. Kovitz."

"Don't shout, Miriam. There are strangers here." She waved her hand as though shooing flies. "What will they think?" Her voice was low and phlegmy, her eyes wild with fever.

"Rest, Mama. You need to rest so you can come home. Don't worry about the others."

Lottie insisted that she let Mrs. Kovitz go and hire two young girls instead. One was thirteen, the other fourteen. That was a good decision. They listened to her.

The hum of machines, the harmony of their voices, filled the small room. Sometimes they even sang songs. By midweek, business finally began to go smoothly.

But then, long after the two seamstresses left—alone in bed with only the voices of the Moskowitz family next door, the grown-ups arguing, the children screaming and crying—anxiety crept in beside her like a presence where Mama used to lie. Sleepless, she held the little gold ring she kept on a ribbon around her neck, thinking about Frederick and what she had done. Ashamed that his kisses and touches had aroused feelings, unfamiliar and wonderful. Yet she missed them and wanted more.

She had been weak, allowing him to take advantage of her. She could find no answer other than she had felt powerless. His kisses were sweet. She wondered whether, if she had gone with him to Long Island for that weekend, he might have asked her to marry him. She was so glad Mama didn't know. Mama was so sick. It would surely kill her.

What had happened? She didn't understand all the confusion of feelings she had each time she had been with Frederick and he touched her certain ways. Kissed her the way he did. The thing that had happened that night. She knew it was wrong but not why. She didn't know where to turn to get answers. What she knew about women things was from her friends at school, who had whispered about where babies came from. Sina said she often woke in the night to see her father and mother actually having sex. She described how her father lay on top of her mother and moved back and forth while touching her breasts. They all laughed.

She didn't menstruate on time, and began throwing up in the morning, and was certain that God had punished her.

3

TRUTH

Sitting in the hard white metal chair by the side of Mama's hospital cot, the curtain drawn around them to satisfy Mama's need for privacy, Miriam told Mama in a whisper how it all began, how she had lied, ridden in a car with a stranger, gone to his rooms at the Wolcott Hotel, and drunk champagne until she forgot everything. She had to tell her; what else could she do? Poor Mama, weak and frail, held her breath, listened, her hand tightly fisted at her mouth as though to stifle the anger, like shrill, wrathful crows waiting to fly out.

When it seemed that Mama could no longer hold her breath, her hand moved from her opened mouth and the words flew out, dark and ugly. *"Gevalt. Gey avek.* I can't look at you." She sobbed. "You want to kill me . . . How could you do this? How?" She broke into convulsive coughing. Miriam gave her water to sip. "You're pregnant, aren't you?"

She didn't understand. So she sat quietly as Mama condemned her.

"What will become of you? *Vey is mir!*" The expression in her strained eyes, a look sorrowful and full of anguish, Miriam knew she would never forget. "Did you bleed this month? Tell me. Did you?"

Miriam looked down in shame as she whispered no. "Please forgive me." She apologized over and over for the shame she had brought to her. She begged, but Mama turned her head to the wall. Miriam wanted to die.

When Miriam returned to the hospital the next night after work, the doctor told her that Mama was not improving.

"*Kindeleh*," Mama said, her voice raspy and low, "I know I'm dying." Her eyes were swollen with fever and crying. "Promise me you won't tell anyone about him." She pushed herself to sit up in bed. "He's not going to help you. Do you hear me, Miriam? Do you understand? *Farshtaist?*" Mama gripped her hands. "He's from another world—a *gonif*. He's stolen your life. You're only a child, your head always in the clouds with fancy ideas. *Oy-oyoy.*" She let go and fell back onto her pillow. "Don't get any notions he will marry you," Mama said angrily, then was overcome by a paroxysm of coughing. Miriam offered her a sip of water.

"*Got in himmel*, Miriam," she said, gasping for breath. "You don't even know his last name. And I won't be able to help you. What will you do?"

The weight felt enormous. "I'm a terrible daughter and have brought such disgrace to you. I'm so sorry." They wept together.

On Friday night, propped up in bed, Mama's hair was like a wild woman's. Sitting by her side, Miriam brushed out the tangles. Neither said a word. The unbearable stench of disinfectant, death, and the air of sorrow in the ward made Miriam feel weak.

Finally, Mama spoke. "Come closer to me. No one should hear." When she was certain no one was listening, her voice barely above a whisper, she said, "One of the nurses, she wrote me the name of someone on Hester Street. Go tomorrow. At five o'clock." Mama handed her a piece of paper with a name and address, then looked around again to be sure no one had heard. "She's not a doctor. She's a midwife from Poland. The nurse says you will be safe. She charges twenty-five dollars. Take the money from the coffee can."

"Is it dangerous?" Miriam asked.

"If anything should happen—after. If you shouldn't feel so good. Promise me: if you're bleeding or you have a fever, you'll go to the hospital—right away. Promise me." She was gasping for air.

"I promise. Rest. I'm so sorry, Mama." She apologized again and again.

"Tell Lottie. I don't want you should go alone."

"I can't. I can't tell her."

"She's like family. She'll understand. God forbid something should happen."

But Miriam couldn't bring herself to tell Lottie. On Saturday afternoon she sent the girls home early. As she got ready to go to her appointment, she sat with the coffee can in her lap, counting out twenty-four one-dollar bills and four quarters. That would leave only six dollars. Mama had saved this money. It had taken years. She couldn't do this. She was frightened. It was taking a life. She would find a way, somehow, to manage.

When she went to Beth Israel that night, she told Mama. Miriam was surprised that her mother looked relieved.

"Then go to the Foundling Asylum on East Twelfth Street in Greenwich Village. You could go live there until you have the baby. Afterward"—she paused and took a deep breath. "Afterward, they will find a good home for the . . . the . . . baby. No one will know. You'll say you . . . you've been away."

"But what about the apartment? The rent? The business? Mr. Zeitz's coat and the Cohens' bar mitzvah? We'll lose everything." She wept.

Mama sighed, shook her head, and lay back. She rubbed her frail hands the way she did when she was troubled. "How would you live with such shame?" she asked after some time. "By yourself it's too much. Too much." She began coughing.

"Shh, don't talk, Mama. You'll get better. I'll bring you home. Take care of you."

"You're only a child. Oy. The neighbors, they'll gossip, say bad things about you." Mama was having difficulty breathing.

"I don't care about the neighbors. You were alone, waiting for my father, and he never came. I was just a baby. You managed. I'll manage."

Mama reached out, held and rocked her, and then, with her feverish hand, smoothed her face, wiping the tears away with the sleeve of her hospital gown. "I wanted more for you."

"Don't talk, Mama."

When the nurse came and said that visiting hours were over, Miriam kissed Mama goodbye, hoping she would make it through another night.

4

SITTING SHIVA

Mama had told her that she wanted a proper Jewish burial. In Jewish tradition, the next day, Lena and Max Schenkein from downstairs helped her with funeral arrangements.

In addition to her grief, she was torn between the tradition of sitting shiva for a week and the necessity of getting the work done so she could pay the bills. Although her mother had followed the religious traditions of her own parents in Marijampolė and carried on their work ethic, Miriam wanted to be as American as she could. Mama was content, steering sleeves and collars through the Singer's feed dog, but Miriam saw beyond that. She observed lifestyles from the magazines, cutting images of dresses, suits, and gowns from the pages and pasting them into a notebook along with images of hats, shoes, bags, and even hairdos, which changed from season to season. She collected magazine photos of beautiful homes and furnishings, read about life uptown and the members of high society. One day she hoped to move out of the chaotic, crowded tenement life of Eldridge Street—leave this all behind—and be part of a better life in America. In the meantime, she had neither time nor interest in prayers.

It was a sunny April afternoon and Lottie had come by to offer comfort. She reached forward, held Miriam's face gently in her hands, and looked into her eyes. They were seated on low boxes rather than chairs, which suggested being brought low by the sorrow of the loss.

"I don't like how you look, *meydeleh*. You look drawn. This is too much responsibility for you. You're just a child."

Since taking Mama to the hospital, everything had become a blur other than getting the work done. Always the work.

Miriam stood to close the window. The noisy shoppers bargaining for foods and wares, as well as the smells from the street, made her feel woozy.

"I'm not a child. I'm fifteen!" she argued as she turned back toward Lottie, walked to the stove, put the kettle on for tea, and then returned to sit.

"Pfff," Lottie responded, searching her eyes again. Miriam looked away. "Tell me, Mimi, are you eating? Sleeping?" Miriam liked that Lottie called her Mimi rather than Miriam.

"Yes, yes," she lied. She was sick every morning. "I'm a strong girl!" She held her arms out like a strongman. "I hired three seamstresses to help me. It's crowded, but I must finish the work."

"Do they listen to you?"

"They better!" Mimi laughed.

"It's good for you. Speak with authority."

"I ask people to pay their respects in the evening."

"Listen," Lottie said. "Customers only want their clothes finished on time. You think they care about grieving? So, Mrs. Kovitz?"

"Gone and good riddance." Mimi handed Lottie a glass of tea. "And I've decided from now on, I want to be called Mimi."

"Easy for me. I've always called you that. So be it!"

She wanted to confide in Lottie but it was her burden. Mama said her eyes gave away everything she thought and felt. Lottie had brought a feast from the delicatessen. It was more than she could possibly eat, even if she had an appetite. All she'd eaten that week was chicken soup and slices of apple.

"The *rugelah* is delicious." Mimi forced herself to take a small bite. "Better than Lena's," she whispered, as though the Schenkeins might hear.

"They're from Willie Entenmann's in Brooklyn. He bought a

horse and carriage, delivers bread and baked goods door-to-door. Such an idea!"

"Please, Lottie, eat."

"Well, maybe just one more. The rest should be for you and your visitors. I miss your mama. Sometimes when she would take in or let out my clothes, we'd talk."

"What about?"

"Our husbands. Such *fershtinkiners*!—excuse me for saying. My Yitzak disappeared. Pffft. The first year. Went out for a paper and never came back. It's a good thing I didn't want children right away. And anyway, you're like a daughter to me."

Mimi felt a swell of emotions. These two important women in her life, both abandoned by their husbands, built lives for themselves. So different from one another. Whereas Mama had neither patience nor kindness, never showed affection or offered a kind word, Lottie believed in her and herself, and had love to share. What, Mimi wondered, would her future be like?

"Did you ever look for him?"

"Of course I looked. Everywhere. I even placed an advertisement in the *Forverts*. That newspaper prints pictures of Jewish husbands who disappear. I put it in the 'Gallery of Missing Husbands': 'Yitzak Aarons, eighteen years old, from Marijampolė, Russia-Poland, umbrella peddler, five foot eleven inches, with brown hair, and missing the end of his left thumb.' Then I wrote my name and address in case anyone saw him."

"And?"

"Not a word. Not a letter. Vanished. But your mama and I, we waited. Can you believe? Your mama was certain she would run into your papa on the trolley." Lottie laughed. "And my Yitzak?" She sighed, "I waited for him to return—with the *Tribune*! But after a while I didn't miss him at all. I come and go as I like. Your poor mama, she waited for your father her entire life."

"She *never* said a word. I don't know anything about him. She refused to tell me when I asked."

Lottie looked astonished. "She never told you that he didn't meet her at the port? That she got off the boat—practically a bride—waited and waited in her wedding boots?" Lottie muttered Yiddish curses under her breath. "She showed up at my door, that poor girl: sixteen, pregnant, her feet raw and bleeding. That *gonif* was nowhere to be found."

Mimi swallowed her anger. "Did you know him? My father."

"Of course." She clapped her hands together and rolled her eyes toward the ceiling. "*Oy gevalt!* What a charmer! Him and that smile. I bet you didn't know your mama was the prettiest girl in the village."

When Mimi thought of her mother, she saw her at the stove, stirring the soup, bent over the wash bucket scrubbing clothes in her old brown skirt and the blouse she wore day after day with its worn collar. Even though she sewed for others, she seemed to have no interest in making herself a new skirt or blouse. Mimi had made Mama a simple blue wool skirt for Hanukkah. She promised to wear it, but no occasion was "special" enough, and it hung on the peg on the wall. "I don't need fancy clothes to live in this *shmutsik tsimer*," Mama said.

"It's not a filthy room," Mimi had argued.

Mama was either bad-tempered, argumentative, or lost in her thoughts. Reminding Mimi constantly to *know her place—sit still—be quiet.* Tired, always tired. Mimi had made herself a promise. No matter what, she would never admit she was tired. Never.

Mama had never spoken of Mimi's father other than in passing, calling him names in Yiddish: *shmuck* or *shmendrick*.

"He was a scoundrel, with a smile to break a girl's heart. All the girls were after him. But he chose Rivkah." Lottie paused and then shook her head.

"What was she like in Marijampolė?"

"Oh, your Mama. How she loved to dance. All the boys wanted to dance with her. She would make herself pretty costumes with embroidered flowers on the sleeves and colorful skirts—the colors of the flowers: yellow, red, white with embroidery around the hem. Her stitches were beautiful and fine. Like yours. She and Jacob danced like . . ." Lottie closed her eyes. "I can see them like it was yesterday.

Round and round, her lace petticoats flying, her brunette curls with the crown of flowers and colored ribbons in her hair. Everyone watching and clapping for the two of them.

"I knew this field where there were wildflowers. We kept it a secret. When there was a dance on a Sunday night, we would sit under a tree all afternoon, weaving colored ribbons and fresh flowers. And," she whispered, "we would talk about how the boys kissed." Lottie was smiling; her cheeks blushed with the pleasure of her memory. "You look like her, you know. When she was your age."

"Did you dance, too?"

"I wasn't such a good dancer. But I liked to sing."

"I've never heard you. Ever."

"What's there to sing about in these times? In this place?"

She could not imagine that Mama or Lottie had ever been young. The idea of Mama dancing and Lottie singing was impossible. Mama's wedding photo had faded long ago.

"She would never answer my questions. None." She began to cry. "She never wanted to talk about anything."

Putting her glass down, Lottie took hold of Mimi's hands. "Because this life disappointed her. She expected more."

Mimi bit her lower lip, trying not to cry. She had disappointed Mama, too. She stood and began clearing the table, wrapping the food.

"You'll take this food home. I couldn't eat it in my lifetime."

"Maybe just a little," Lottie said.

Eager to change the subject, Mimi asked, "How's work? Tell me about the Winthrops." Mimi loved hearing about life uptown.

"It's good," Lottie said, easily distracted.

"I love when you describe the dinners and parties. I can almost picture them. Be sure to find out what costumes everyone wears for the Winthrops' masked ball in March. Take notes."

Suddenly, Lottie banged both hands on the table, enough to make the glasses bounce. "Now, *that* would be a good piece of business for you. Why didn't I think of it before?" She took her little book and pencil from her pocket to write a note. "You just wait and see, I'm going to send you such business. When you're ready, that is. For next year's Winthrop ball!" She closed the book and put it and the pencil back in her pocket before continuing. "For now, what I worry about is how you will manage on your own."

Yes, on my own, Mimi thought. And soon there would be no hiding the fact that she was pregnant. No husband and no father for her unborn child. Did he ever return to the park? Or wonder what had become of her? If she saw him, would she find the courage to tell him she was expecting? Would he marry her?

Lottie interrupted her straying thoughts. "Don't forget to pay the rent on time, Mimi."

"I'm hearing that people are buying up buildings in the neighborhood and tearing them down. I can't sleep, worrying that they might come for this one."

"Oy!" Lottie said. "Don't tell me you are becoming a worrier like your Mama. Let me put my arms around you. Come, *meydeleh*."

Accepting Lottie's comforting embrace, she feared she would burst into tears and admit to her condition. "Everything will be all right. I'm going to make something of myself, like you. You wait and see. For Mama!" She forced a smile and then jumped up from her box, taking Lottie's glass. "I'll make you more tea."

"Sit." Lottie took hold of her. "If I have another, I wouldn't sleep." She reached for Mimi's hands. "I want you should take good care of yourself."

"Of course, I will." She was holding back tears.

"She asked me to watch over you. She loved you, even if she didn't say so. Even if she didn't show you. There were things she just couldn't say. She had a hard life. Look at me, Mimi." She held Mimi's chin, forced her to meet her gaze. "You can tell me anything. I'm here for you. You're like a daughter to me. My family." Her gaze was unyielding. Mimi lowered her eyes. Would Lottie stand by her? She was filled with so much shame. Another day she would tell her, but not today.

5

THE MOSKOWITZ FAMILY

June

Most nights when the Moskowitz family who lived next door sat down to dinner, it was a noisy, boisterous event. They, too, had moved downstairs and were now ten, living in a room the size of hers and Mama's but without the window that looked out onto Eldridge Street.

Since Mimi borrowed *Smith's Astronomy* from the library and began teaching Szymon to read and write, his appetite for learning had flourished. He found his way to libraries, old bookstores, and peddlers' carts in search of books about astronomy, the sciences, and history. He left his growing collection—more than forty books—at Mimi's apartment for safekeeping, and now fourteen-year-old Szymon had come to the realization that he wasn't stupid.

Mimi found secondhand clothes for her young friend and neighbor, mending and hemming them properly. Szymon allowed her to cut his hair—on the roof when no was around to see them. Over time he had stopped blinking and grimacing.

At Mimi's suggestion, he had asked the shoemaker to put a thick sole on his right shoe, and so he limped less, had fewer back pains, and even stood up straight.

It had always upset Mimi to see the hatred in Szymon's father's eyes, to hear it in his voice when standing around the front steps with his friends, imitating how his son walked and blinked—to make the men laugh.

Szymon confided in Mimi that he'd registered for school and his teachers were helping him to catch up, and it was Mimi to whom he proudly showed his report cards.

On this steamy night in June, with the humid breath of inevitable rain—even inside the apartment, even on her skin—she could hardly imagine how there was air enough in that one windowless room next door for their family of ten to breathe. Ever since Mama had gone to the hospital and then died, Mimi wished they were her family. Hearing their voices through the wall reminded her that she was alone when she sat at the table or just stood at the stove to eat out of the pot, too exhausted to sit down after her long days at the Singer, keeping the business going, visiting Mama, and doing schoolwork.

There were the voices of the children—Nadia; Little Boris; Alina; and the twins, Igor and Anton, whom Mimi could not tell apart. She never heard Szymon's voice. "Big Boris" Moskowitz's bearded younger brother and his red-cheeked bride had arrived the previous year, moved in, and grown quite fat, and every step they took shook the floorboards under Mimi's bed. Usually the children laughed and fought, and the adults spoke Russian. While Miriam didn't understand what they said, over time she had a sense of what they were saying—a word here and there. Most nights she lay in the iron bed she had shared with Mama and tried to differentiate their voices until she fell asleep. She wondered if the Moskowitz family ever slept.

Tonight, it began with Boris—his deep, raspy, monotonous voice that seemed to come from the depth of his belly, insisting on something in what sounded like a repetition of the same sentence. His wife, Anya, shouted, "Stop!" There were several moments of silence and then he began again—a thunder of intensifying rage.

Big Boris Moskowitz was a dirty man, brawny and foul, who stank of horse dung. Miriam was sure that he never went to the baths. His broken-down boots were caked with muck, his pants were baggy at the knees and crusted with dirt or horse feed, and his shirtsleeves, rolled up above the elbows, revealed the burly arms that cleaned the city streets of manure.

Their newborn began to cry louder and Boris, impatient, hammered his fist on the table, shouting Russian curses. Anya pleaded. Chairs were knocked over. Boris' voice grew louder. Dishes and glasses shattered on the floor as he bellowed, and a bottle crashed against the wall next to where Mimi huddled in her bed, her heart a jackhammer.

She was certain from Anya's tone that she was pleading with her husband in an attempt to protect her children. Mimi imagined her kneeling on the floor, hair caught up in that frowsy bun, all skin and bones and in the same brown wool dress she wore every single day, its opening held together with safety pins.

She wondered if Anya had been a beautiful bride in Russia when she married Boris, like the faded photo of Mama and Jacob with his radiant smile on their wedding day. A smile, which meant nothing.

Whatever Anya Moskowitz had been like as a bride, now she walked with her shoulders pulled up to her ears, slightly stooped. Dark circles surrounded her weary eyes. Each year there was another baby on her hip, if it survived, and there was even more strain in her expression—as though she awaited the next blow. Women in the building gossiped that the reason Anya lost so many babies was because Boris kicked her when he was drunk.

Soon everyone would begin to talk about *her*: Mimi Milman, fifteen and pregnant, and another missing husband.

Lying alone in Mama's bed, she recognized each voice through the wall. The uncle, who Mama had said drank as much as his brother, was shouting at Boris to stop, and soon these two came to blows and Igor's wife, who Mama had said was *meshugga*, was shrieking.

And then Boris began beating the children. Nadia, four years old, blond-haired with a face pretty enough to be on a Coca-Cola calendar, shrieked like a seagull in distress. Mischievous Little Boris, seven, always hiding somewhere, was pleading, "*Nyet, nyet*, Papa." Alina, ten, with only four fingers on her right hand, bleated like a sheep in static outbursts. The twelve-year-old twins, Igor and Anton, howled in unison like wolves. Above it all was the constant sound of leather hitting flesh, each blow followed by Anya's shrill pleading.

It was Szymon's voice that surprised Mimi. It rose from somewhere inside him like the roar of a lion and with an intensity she could not have imagined possible from the gentle boy who had taught her about the constellations. And for a moment everyone in the next room was quiet. Szymon was almost as big as his father now, and Mimi had wondered if one day he would strike back.

"Why do you stay?" she had once asked.

"My brothers and sisters need me . . . and where would I go?"

Mimi, frightened, slipped out of the iron bed she used to share with Mama, moved it away from the wall, and then slid a chair under the doorknob. She feared that Boris' voice, his rage, the tables and chairs, the cast-iron pots in which Anya fried sausages and cooked cabbage stews, might burst through the wall that separated their apartments.

People on every floor began pounding on the walls with their fists, stamping with their feet, and banging on the floors with brooms. Some must have poked their heads into the hallways to shout.

Mimi covered her ears with her hands to muffle the sounds, folded her arms across her swelling belly, and then prayed to a God she didn't know to protect the baby growing inside her as well as the family next door from their father's temper.

She despised and feared Boris Moskowitz. How he looked at her, passing in the dim, narrow hallway; how his hand would brush against her; the stench of beer on his breath when he'd been drinking, and the stink of horse dung that followed him like a shadow; the murmured vibration of hunger he made whenever he saw her, his chin jutting forward, his tongue circling his lips. That smutty grin.

Mimi looked at the Big Ben clock. It was almost midnight, yet the air was no cooler. She heard Officers Thomas Doyle and Michael Callahan banging on the door with their nightsticks and shouting, "Open the door, Boris, or we'll be havin' to break it down. You wouldn't want that, now, would you?" There was a scuffle and shouts of "Hold him down" and "Get the cuffs on him." She heard them dragging Mr. Moskowitz down the hall to the street, kicking and bellowing and putting up a great fuss. She got out of bed to watch from behind the lace curtain as, shirtless, he tumbled down the front steps, landed with his legs straight up in the air, and how the two policemen, laughing, kicked him, and then beat him with their nightsticks.

When things were quiet in the Moskowitz apartment again, Mimi went back to bed, waiting for their voices to lull her to sleep.

She felt a gentle motion in her belly as the baby moved inside her for the first time.

The next evening after dinner, the intense heat brought everyone out of their sweltering apartments: into the hallways, onto the front stoop, and onto the fire escapes. Szymon Moskowitz was gone. Mimi heard it from Isaac Tannenbaum on the roof. Her heart felt broken. She decided that he must have left sometime during the early hours when everyone in 1B was finally sleeping, snoring, and dreaming of streets paved with gold, without a word or note of goodbye—without his books.

1910

1

EVICTION NOTICE

Thursday, January 13, 1910

Haber & Troy, Attorneys-at-Law
149 Broadway, 47th Floor
New York, NY

> *Dear Mr. Troy,*
> *I got your letter telling me to be out of my apartment by the*
> *end of this January. I've looked, but can't find a place to live.*
> *Please give me one month.*
>
> > *Sincerely,*
> > *Miriam Milman*

"Get her out," Frederick Winthrop demanded as he looked out the window of his new office in the Singer Tower, with its breathtaking forty-seventh-floor views. "Any way you have to."

"Impossible," said Timothy Troy. "She's a child—same age as my daughter, for God's sake. She has no place to go."

"And she's got a newborn baby, Frederick," argued Lawrence Haber. "Give her a break."

"What do I care? Don't give me any sob sister story. She's the only one who hasn't left. You gave her fair warning. Two weeks, the property's coming down, and for all I care anyone in it." Picking up his briefcase and bowler hat, he strode to the door.

"Out! I want her out!" he shouted as it closed. Demolition was scheduled. That was that.

When the elevator reached the lobby and he stepped out, he noticed the grandeur of the Singer Tower's lobby. Its celestial ceiling was made up of multiple small domes with delicate plasterwork met by a forest of marble columns trimmed with bronze beading. At the top of each column was the monogram of the Singer Company, a huge needle, thread, and bobbin rendered on large bronze medallions. Three years earlier, when it had been built, it had been the tallest building in the world. His father, his family—he, for that matter—had worked and prospered with Singer, and one day soon he would build an opulent skyscraper taller than the Singer: the Winthrop Tower, his name embedded in its concrete and steel. The world and history would recognize his contribution to the city, and he would do it without his brothers, even Thomas. He would be damned if he'd ever ask for his advice. He chuckled at how angry Thomas would be to learn he had hired McKim, Mead & White.

Two weeks later he shouted over the telephone, "Well?"

"Well what?" asked Tim Troy.

"Is that girl out?"

"We won't do it, Frederick."

"Then I'll get it done myself, and get a new law firm as well."

2

EVICTED

Matthew's birth before the New Year had been surprisingly easy. He was the dearest baby, as though his personality were already defined and all he wanted in his life was to please. In return, Mimi loved nothing more than to kiss his fingers, toes, and cheeks and breathe in his sweet fragrance. The songs and lullabies she had learned as a child came back to her. Everyone celebrated his birth. Perhaps everyone gossiped, but no one asked her any questions.

She hadn't wanted to trouble Lottie with her *mishigas*, so she had kept the eviction notice a secret, certain she would somehow manage.

The week before the building would be demolished, Lena and Max Schenkein had wept just before the wagon took them and their belongings to a small building they bought in Brooklyn, where they would live above their new bakery on Atlantic Avenue.

But between the bitter cold weather, customers' work to complete, recuperating from giving birth, and caring for Matthew, Mimi had had no time to search for a new place to live. She had believed that the goodness in her landlord's heart would have given her till the end of February.

On the first of February, Officer Michael Callahan, in a gray shirt and pants and leather suspenders, pounded the door with his fists and, when Mimi opened it, practically pulled her from the front room on Eldridge Street.

"I can't believe you're still here, Mrs. Milman. You and the baby, you're the only ones. The buildin's comin' down. You ain't got much time. Let me help you." He picked up her Singer and Mama's carpet-bag. "Hurry!"

As she and Officer Callahan made their way down the front steps, she saw that a crowd had gathered across the street to watch the demolition. Ashamed, she pulled the collar of her coat up, covered her face with scarves, and lowered her head. Matthew was protected, close to her chest. She stumbled with the weight of all she carried.

The building fell quickly, the space it had held on Eldridge Street empty, replaced with mounds of shattered brick, the air heavy with concrete dust—and memories.

It was then that she noticed a black Pierce-Arrow and one well-dressed gentleman, heads taller than the throng. She was absolutely certain it was Frederick.

"Well, that's done," she heard him say to his driver, who held the automobile door open for him. Taking off his top hat, he stepped into the car. "The opera house," he directed.

"Yes, Mr. Winthrop."

Mimi was aghast. Winthrop! Of Lottie's Winthrop Corporation?

With Matthew, suitcases, bundles, and her sewing machine at her feet, Mimi turned to watch him pull away. As the car vanished, she realized she had nowhere to go.

3

A HOME FOR MIMI

Two days later, Lottie followed close behind Thomas Winthrop as he burst into his brother's oak-paneled office at the Winthrop School.

"Frederick's done it again, Jon!" he exclaimed. Lottie caught his coat and hat, which he practically threw into her arms. He probably would have dropped them on the floor if she hadn't been there to catch them.

"How often must I remind you? First, a greeting." Mr. Jonathan sat at his desk, where she could see he was working on student applications. He was fastidious about his person, his painting studio on Union Square, his school director's office, as well as his grand Chippendale mahogany desk. Mr. Jonathan stood and nodded. "Good morning, Miss Aarons. Good morning, Tom. Dashing vest!"

Mr. Thomas laughed sheepishly, patting the red plaid vest over his broad chest. "Good morning, my dear brother." He went around the desk and gave his brother a bear hug and then, as always, made certain his paper-white mustache was twisted properly.

Lottie hung their coats in the closet, then sat down in the chair next to Mr. Jonathan's desk with her hands folded in her lap and her legs crossed at the ankles. She had her stenographer's notebook and pencil on the desk, ready for dictation, should that be necessary.

"Now, sit down, Tom, and tell me what that rascal's done. More evictions?" He pushed the school applications on his desk off to the side into a neat pile and then made certain his pen was where he preferred it to be. "Or is it women again? Sit, sit."

Tom sat across from his brother, picked up the pen, and began tapping it nervously on the desk.

"Tom, he's a goddamn womanizer, and foolishly feckless, too. Oh, excuse my profanity, Miss Aarons. And stop tapping my pen!" Mr. Jonathan grabbed it from his brother's hand and placed it back where he liked it to be. "Remember when Frederick was caught climbing out of a window without his pants?"

"Barely!" Mr. Thomas picked up the pen again, trying his hardest not to laugh, yet clearly enjoying his own pun.

The two brothers broke into shared laughter. Lottie bit her lip so as not to smile.

"More than once," Mr. Thomas continued, winking at her mischievously.

With her hand over her mouth to stifle her laughter, she stared down at her steno pad.

"It seems, sir, that your brother has evicted my dearest and oldest friend's daughter," Lottie said. "From the parlor room at 245 Eldridge Street. There's a bakery a few steps below the street. Excellent bread."

"Our little slum-landlord brother owns that building."

"How do you remember so many details, Tom?"

"I just do." He puffed up with pride.

"After my friend Rivkah Milman died last year—pneumonia—I've watched over her daughter, Mimi, as best I could. The poor child is only fifteen, Mr. Jonathan.

"Fifteen? On her own?" Mr. Jonathan shook his head.

"And, uh, excuse me, sir." She felt the color rise in her cheeks. "She has a baby."

"Oh, my." Mr. Jonathan's eyes were wide in disbelief. One by one, he rearranged the papers and his blotter and pens on his desk into neat arrangements. She knew when he did that, he was organizing his thoughts.

"Your attorney Mr. Troy evicted them two days ago. With two

weeks' notice, sir. I'd no idea Mr. Frederick owned that building until Mimi told me for the very first time yesterday!"

"He tore that goddamned building down, Jon. Excuse my language, Miss Aarons."

She wished they would stop asking her forgiveness for their salty language. She was used to it by now and heard worse on the streets downtown.

"The first night, she and the baby—Matthew is only two months old—were sleeping on a bench in Seward Park, Mr. Jonathan," she continued.

"Sleeping in the park? We can't have that."

"Last night they showed up at my door at midnight. I don't know what she will do. She's a seamstress. A hard worker. She will lose her little business without a place to live."

Mr. Thomas took a deep breath, pulled an envelope from his breast pocket, and then handed it to his brother. "Miriam Milman, Jon. Is that name familiar?"

"Mimi," Lottie corrected as Mr. Jonathan opened the envelope and read the letter. It was Mimi's order of eviction.

Dropping the letter on his desk, his expression changed to utter astonishment. "Mimi! How could we forget?" He let out a loud sigh. "Yes. In March, Frederick took a young girl to the Wolcott. Walked the child through the front doors like she was the Queen of Sheba— through the lobby and up to his suite for all of New York to see. Called her Mimi. Gossip travels quickly amongst servants."

Lottie was stunned. Mimi at the Wolcott Hotel.

"We had done all we could do to keep *that* scandal quiet," Mr. Jonathan explained. "When I asked how old she was and her name, he laughed. 'Mimi, like in the opera.' Said he never asked her surname. Imagine? Walked her through the hotel. One of his showgirls, for God's sake." He was pensive for several minutes. "Sorry, Miss Aarons."

Lottie was taken quite by surprise. "She's not a showgirl. She's a seamstress, my friend's child."

"Only fifteen?" He shook his head from side to side.

"What a predicament, Jon. Could she have had a child?"

"It would seem so." He silently counted on his fingers. "The timing is right."

Rivkah had confided that Mimi was pregnant and asked her to watch over her. She had marveled at how Mimi handled the awkwardness of her pregnancy while caring for her mother until her death, gave birth with quiet dignity, then immediately went back to work and sewed by commission to make ends meet, without complaint. Lottie respected Mimi's need for privacy, and was relieved when she finally revealed her circumstances. It was a lot for Mimi to carry alone, and she was able to offer advice and loving support. But learning that Frederick Winthrop was Matthew's father took her breath away. She was enraged.

"It has to be Frederick's child," said Mr. Jonathan.

"Oh my God, Jon, can you imagine the scandal?"

Lottie grabbed the pen, which Mr. Thomas had once again picked up, and put it back on the desk.

"We must help her. Discreetly, of course!"

"Absolutely, Jon!" Mr. Thomas stood, adjusted his vest, and when he fussed with his mustache while he thought about what to do, it was all Lottie could do not to shout at him to leave it alone.

"Didn't he recognize the name?"

"Obviously not, sir," Lottie replied.

"From what I understand, Haber & Troy wrote the letters but wouldn't help with the eviction. So our little brother hired his buddies at the precinct to handle it. After hours."

Mr. Thomas rubbed his fingers together, indicating a bribe.

"How has the poor child managed?"

"She's quite diligent," Lottie said.

"What is wrong with that man, Tom?"

"We'll handle this between the two of us. Once again, as far as Frederick, of course, we *must* avoid a scandal."

"Absolutely," Mr. Jonathan insisted. "No rumormongering—at any cost."

"We must find her a place to live." Mr. Thomas paced the room

and, of course, pulled on his mustache. "What about that little building on Madison and Ninety-Third Street?"

"Hmm. I suppose. She could work downstairs and live upstairs
rather comfortably," Mr. Jonathan agreed.

"Has she told you who the father is, Miss Aarons?"

"No, sir. She kept her . . . condition a secret for the longest time.
She absolutely refused to reveal the father's name. I assumed it was
some *shlemiel* in the neighborhood." Immediately, she wished she had
not used the Yiddish expression for someone stupid or, even worse,
insinuated that their brother was stupid. She was usually careful in
the office. The Winthrops were fairly liberal minded—except for Mr.
Frederick, who despised Jews.

"Let's set the wheels in motion, Tom." Mr. Jonathan slapped his
hand on his desk with a resounding bang, which startled his brother,
causing his papers to fall into disarray, pens to fly out of the ink-
stand, and the ink blotter to roll back and forth like a rowboat in a
storm. He stood up and walked around his desk to stand beside his
brother. "Now, Tom!" Then, leaning back to observe Mr. Thomas, he
added, "One of these days perhaps you will let me paint your portrait,
Thomas, you handsome devil! In that wingback chair." Then, pulling
his brother up and placing his arm around his shoulder, he steered
him out the door. "Come, Miss Aarons, we'll drive you home."

She quickly put Mr. Jonathan's desk in order, gathered the gentlemen's outer garments from the closet, and then, loaded down
with three coats, hats, scarves, and gloves, ran down the school's
hallway after them. She was comforted that Mimi and Matthew
would be taken care of by the Winthrops and pleased that she had
spoken up.

"How could he put a young girl and an infant out onto the street
like that? And just when we are in the midst of school interviews.
Damn him," said Mr. Jonathan as he locked the front door of the
school.

"We have applications from so many bright, promising children,
Miss Aarons. Even from the tenements. It's going to be a superb year."

As they headed across town, Mr. Jonathan spoke quietly. "Listen, Tom, we must make sure that Frederick never hears about this business."

"Yes, we'll set things up with the attorneys. With the utmost discretion."

"We wouldn't want him to get tangled up with this girl again." Mr. Jonathan paused to consider.

"Or for him—or anyone else—to know about the boy," Lottie added. "What would people say?"

"By all means, Miss Aarons," both brothers said in unison.

4

1313 MADISON AVENUE

They had been staying in Lottie's parlor on Seventy-Sixth Street and Lexington Avenue when the Winthrops' attorney Mr. Troy came by.

"Hope you're not superstitious, Mrs. Milman," said Mr. Troy when he handed her two door keys tied with string and a tag marked *1313 Madison*.

"Not in the least, sir."

If she didn't look at Mr. Troy's face, she would have been certain, by his boyish build, that he was a lad of twelve or thirteen. But his gaunt face with its deep-set, sorrowful blue eyes revealed that he was closer to fifty. She also noticed his well-tailored three-piece suit in its unusual size and fine Irish wool. She was used to the way men dressed downtown: in clothing that was secondhand, patched and repaired, made from heavy wool or corduroy, with suspenders or belts to hold up pants that were usually a size too large.

"Take a look at the place and I shall come back next week with papers for you to sign, if it meets your satisfaction. We prefer you don't come to the offices," he said somewhat sheepishly. "For reasons I believe you understand."

"Yes, Mrs. Milman understands," Lottie said.

"Be sure to give Miss Aarons a list of the furnishings you'll need, Mrs. Milman, and we will do our best to provide them for you as soon as possible. The Winthrop family sincerely hope you and Matthew will be comfortable at 1313."

Restless on Lottie's front room sofa, Mimi got up and began to put together a list of what she would need: a bed, blankets, and a pillow; a table and two chairs, in case she had a visitor; a soup pot and a fry pan; two plates, cups, and glasses; two forks, knives, and spoons; a teakettle; and a coffeepot. She had hated having to leave Mama's soup pot and well-seasoned cast-iron skillet, which she had taught Mimi to clean with kosher salt. Never soap. She missed Mama's coffeepot. Mama insisted that her good coffee had to do with the pot—and measuring properly. There was only so much Mimi was able to take from the apartment with so little time. Sadly, she had left so much behind when the building was torn down.

Would it be too much, she wondered, to ask for a small rag rug for Matthew to play on when the floors were cold? Overwhelming sadness was followed by rage at Frederick—Mr. Frederick Winthrop—and brought her to tears.

It was past three, Matthew's final feeding, before she was able to fall asleep.

At breakfast the next morning, Lottie seemed very thoughtful. She hardly spoke as she sat at the kitchen table eating her cornflakes.

"Are you upset with me?" Mimi asked.

"What makes you ask that?"

"You're so quiet."

"Am I?" Then Lottie put her spoon down, took a deep breath, and began speaking so fast, Mimi could barely keep up.

"I need to tell you," Lottie began. "The Winthrop brothers—Mr. Jonathan and Mr. Thomas—they were discussing how to help you, and the story came out. About you and Mr. Frederick. People saw you, Mimi. Friends of the Winthrops saw you. At the Wolcott Hotel. At a hotel. What were you doing there? Society people saw you." She paused. "Oy. Those people love gossip. I didn't say a word. The Winthrops are very smart people. They are part of society—the Four Hundred. People saw you—people who have nothing better to do than gossip—and with . . . with Mr. Frederick. Those people, they know Mr. Frederick. They know he likes young girls. And you, fourteen years old. They didn't know *you*, of course, because you're not an Astor or a Frick . . ." The color had risen in her cheeks, and her hands rose to cover her face and emotion. Her head shook in an unspoken "no."

Mimi was speechless, caught off guard, found out.

"You told them, didn't you?" She reached across the table to put her hand on Lottie's arm, feeling forsaken. Her throat filled with a stew of anger and sadness. After Mama died, she believed that no one would ever know. She had had no intention of telling anyone—ever. And now Lottie had betrayed her. "How did you know?"

Lottie cried out. "Your mama told me. She loved you and asked me to watch over you. I would never tell the Winthrops. My word of honor, child."

"Then how did they know it was me?" Her breath hung somewhere midway in her throat. "There's nothing you love more than gossip."

Lottie's expression turned dark and fierce. "Don't you go thinking I told them anything, because I didn't. It was your name, Miriam—Mimi—and the building on Eldridge Street. Frederick Winthrop owned that building."

"But he didn't know where I lived."

"Are you certain?"

"We always met in Seward Park. He never asked my last name or where I lived. He was a gentleman, and . . ." The words stuck in her throat.

Lottie reached across the table for her hand. Her touch was comforting. "Then Mr. Thomas and Mr. Jonathan—they must have simply put two and two together."

"I was ashamed." Mimi began to cry.

"You're not the one to be feeling any shame. Frederick Winthrop is a grown man. He should know better. Oy! And you? A child, for God's sake. His brothers *do* understand. Believe me when I say, absolutely not one person in that . . . that *upstanding family*," she said with scorn, "wants a scandal. That's why they're giving you and the baby a

place to live. And I will make very sure you get all that you deserve."
Lottie's fury rose up the sides of her neck, flushing her cheeks the
color of Mama's rocker. She let go of Mimi's hand to fan her face with
the *Herald* and, with the other hand, sweep tousled hair off her face.

"I couldn't sleep. How will I pay the rent?" she asked. "My business is gone. Nothing's left."

"You don't need to pay rent. The Winthrops represent the Singer
Corporation, and they will provide for you."

"Will they, Lottie? But how will I ever repay them?"

"You won't have to. How many times must I tell you? Shh, now.
Drink your coffee." Lottie paused. "I hear crying."

Mimi wiped her tears, cleared the table, and started out of the
kitchen to care for Matthew when she remembered her list and, taking a folded paper from her pocket, handed it to Lottie. "This is what
I think I'll be needing."

Lottie looked at her list. "Oh, Mimi. They will give you everything you need—and then some." She stood, came around the table,
and held Mimi while she wept. There was endless comfort in Lottie's
abundant embrace.

"A table and two chairs?"

"A table and *four* chairs. You mustn't worry," Lottie said, holding
her at arm's length. "Better than you could ever hope to provide for
the boy. You'll see."

"I want a good life for him. I don't want him to work in the factories."

"The Winthrops will keep their promises. But they'll expect in
return that you never tell anyone—about Mr. Frederick. You will sign
papers to that effect. You can have nothing to do with him, whatever
silly ideas you have in that head of yours. Nothing."

"I would never tell," she whispered. Matthew's cries pulled at her
and the milk in her breasts.

"You're young. You'll meet a feller one day and he'll ask about
the father." Lottie paused. "And what will you tell Matthew when *he*
asks about his father? And he will. It's human nature. You must think
about that."

She pulled her shoulders back and said with pride, "Just the same thing I always say: that his father died at sea."

"Then that's that. *Ge'endikt.*"

"Yes," Mimi agreed. "Finished."

"Go, go." Lottie waved her out of the room. "Don't forget to take the keys."

Matthew rested on her hip as she walked along Madison Avenue past rows of brownstones, searching for 1313. The walk in the brisk, clear air had put him to sleep. She couldn't believe how charming and quiet the neighborhood was.

She was wearing a new outfit of her own design: a long, shawl-collared cable-stitched sweater jacket Lottie had knitted from her sketch and that kept her warm against the cold and windy February gusts. It was the color of pale mustard, and she wore it over an ankle-length, darker mustard wool skirt. The new straight-line style did not go unnoticed by passersby.

She had knitted herself a striped scarf from the same yarn with the addition of pale yellow and coral stripes. Lottie had been startled at the combination; she was so used to navy and brown, which made up most of her own somber wardrobe. The jacket had a double row of beautiful carved wooden buttons that Mimi had found at the button store when she was fourteen and had saved, knowing one day they would be perfectly suited for one of her designs.

Matthew slept snugly within the sling she made of the scarf.

The two cold brass house keys were in a pocket. Every now and then she reached for them to be certain they were still there. They reminded Mimi that they were her new beginning.

LAWRENCE LOFT

1313 Madison Avenue was a four-story redbrick and brownstone similar to four other row houses on the east side and three on the west of the avenue. It seemed quite a grand house to her, one intended for people of modest fortune. She wondered if she would find a garden in the back, even a small one.

Looking up, she noticed that the upper two stories each included three-sided bay windows and that the facade of the building was decorated with stylized leaves and flowers. She was happy that it was a cheerful building. She stood, hesitant to open the door. Matthew stirred.

"We are home, little one," she whispered, taking the keys from her pocket.

Taking a deep breath, she put the larger of the keys into the lock and struggled to open the door. She tried the second key and then the first one again but the lock would not turn.

"Need some help with that door, young lady?"

A tall, slender sandy-haired man, well dressed in taupe tweed, stood on the sidewalk.

"I think I've been given the wrong keys."

"May I try?" He took the keys and, with a bit of force and the noisy creaking of rusty hinges, opened the door. "There you go." He offered his hand. "I'm Lawrence Loft. I live three blocks down. Is this your shop?" He spoke with an English accent.

"Yes, my . . . our new home. I'm Mimi Milman and this is Matthew."

"Your brother?"

"My son."

"Excuse me, Mrs. Milman. Such a beautiful child. How old is he?"

"Almost three months."

"He seems a peaceful baby. Will you live here as well?"

"I have a business. I'm a seamstress . . . I mean, I do clothing alteration and custom designs . . . and suits for gentlemen—like yourself, sir," she said with the confidence she had been practicing lately. "That is a very fine suit you are wearing, Mr. Loft. I recognize its good quality."

"You have a discerning eye." He smiled. "It was custom made for me in London. I travel there for business frequently." When he took out a gold watch on a chain from his vest, she noticed the sparkle of his cuff links. He was the most elegant young man she had ever seen. As though he might have modeled for one of J. C. Leyendecker's Arrow Collar Man illustrations in the *Saturday Evening Post*. "Well, I must open my shop by ten sharp. When you get settled, Mrs. Milman, stop by and say hello." He handed her a card from his vest pocket. His name and address were printed on cream-colored paper in raised gold letters: *Lawrence Loft, Objets d'arte*.

"What a beautiful card."

"I sell art objects," he explained. "You will need a business card for your new enterprise, and it would be my pleasure to create one for you as a welcome gift. When you are more settled, we will discuss the elements you would like included."

"How kind of you, sir."

"I'll leave you to get settled." He tipped his bowler and turned to leave. "By the way, Mrs. Milman, may I say that your ensemble is quite chic—and most becoming?"

His approval and compliment almost made her forget how terrified she was to step over the threshold into the building.

Her mouth was as dry as burlap; she was barely able to swallow. Her stomach was queasy. She placed her hand where the fear rested.

Breathing in the stale smell of dust and mildew was like opening a trunk that had been in a basement for a long time. What surprises awaited? she wondered.

She entered what would be the shop, turning round and round in the enormous space.

"Matthew, this must be the size of the entire first floor on Eldridge Street. Don't you think?" She danced over to the two windows facing the avenue. "We can put actual clothing in the windows. On mannequins. A man's suit in one, a lady's in the other."

She moved to the middle of the room. "May I help you, madam?" she said to an imaginary customer, a debutante from Fifth Avenue. "A ball gown? In silk? Velvet? Both? Oh, yes, madam. Certainly, madam. For the Astor ball? Of course, madam." She pretended to write the order in a book. "You know, madam? Cobalt blue would become you."

She waltzed around the outer edges with Matthew, his eyes open wide, laughing gleefully. "How many seamstresses should I hire for the season, Matthew? Eight, you say? Then I shall need eight Singers, eight chairs, pegs for my threads, shelves for fabric rolls, a large worktable in the center of the room, and a tall mirror and stand. And I've always wanted canaries in a brass cage. Where do you suppose that door leads? Come, let's explore.

"Oh, look, Matthew, there's another room," she exclaimed as she opened the door, "where we can sleep—and eat. And look: there's a real kitchen." She turned on the water. "Hot *and* cold. I can give you a bath in the sink. I won't have to boil water. Imagine that!

"Curtains would be so charming on this window." She leaned forward over the sink. "Oh, look, Matthew, there's a garden. Shall we take a quick peek?"

When she unlocked the door, Matthew's mouth and eyes opened wide with surprise when the draft of cold hit his face. She held him close. "But it's been neglected," she said sadly. "It will need some serious tending. I'll have to learn how to do that. Will you help me?" She kissed him on his nose. "I'll give you a spoon and you can dig in the dirt. When you're a *big* boy. Then we'll plant flowers. And one day, shall we have a peach tree?

"I can do this," she murmured. "I can. Our new life begins today. I will fill our new home with my dreams. Give you, my sweet, a good life. The Winthrops have given their promise to help us. Oh, if only Mama could be here to see this."

Closing the door to the garden, she noticed a narrow stairway in the shadow. She climbed to the second floor, where she discovered a sunny front parlor facing Madison Avenue. In the rear, overlooking the garden, was a spacious room with what appeared to be two closets, one for clothes and the other a white, tiled toilet with hexagonal black and white tiles on the floor. There was a sink and a bathtub with enamel faucets; one marked *hot*, the other *cold*. Over the tub the daylight shone through a leaded glass window in shades of blue. A yellow-breasted bird perched in a tree had been hand painted at the center.

"We can live upstairs and work downstairs," she explained to Matthew. "Oh, my," she gasped. She ran about the room, looking at every detail, every window's view. Finding another staircase, she whispered, "I wonder who lives upstairs." The third floor was the same as the second. Empty. It, too, had its own bathroom.

There was one more staircase, which led to the fourth floor. Halfway up the stairs, the air turned musty. She knocked on the closed door, then listened. No one answered. She gently opened the door and could see that the low-ceilinged room was something of a storeroom filled with odds and ends of furniture under sheets; plumbing parts, bricks, sheets of tin ceiling, floorboards, rakes and shovels, garden furniture with peeling paint and in serious need of repair—all sorts of broken things.

She was suddenly overwhelmed with exhaustion. There was a pair of matching upholstered chairs under a sheet. They were shabby but could be salvaged and reupholstered. She sat down to think and to nurse Matthew, who had begun to fuss.

"No one lives here, Matthew. No one at all. It's completely empty. Do you suppose the entire house is intended for you and me? Did the Winthrops give us this whole house?

"I'm going to make the most beautiful clothes from the most

luxurious fabrics I can find, in the most beautiful colors. I see them. I dream them." Matthew just looked up at her with wistful eyes, lost in the contentment of suckling. She held his hand, kissed each tiny finger, filled with tenderness for him and the sudden awareness that her entire life was about to change.

She felt herself slipping into sleep in the comfort of the chair.

6

THE WINTHROP MANSION

MARCH

Dressed in her freshly washed and ironed white shirtwaist and navy wool skirt, her black boots cleaned and polished with wax, Mimi stood in front of the full-length mirror to put on the straw boater. She chose a wide, bright blue grosgrain ribbon for a hatband and pinned onto the ribbon a small bouquet of velvet roses in varied shades of blue and lilac, with pale olive leaves.

When she had found the flowers in the peddler's cart, they were tired and wilted.

"Ten cents," the gnomish old man had demanded.

Mimi took five pennies from her pocket, held them in her outspread palm. "This is all I have," she said. She waited a moment, silently counted to five, and then turned to walk away.

"Wait," he shouted. "What's your hurry? Okay. Seven cents," he suggested.

"Five is all I have, and besides, they are almost ready for the dust bin."

"All right. Take them." He reached out greedily for the pennies.

Mimi stepped back, clenched her hand shut. She put out her other hand for the flowers, waiting for him to offer them before giving him the pennies.

"They're velvet, you know. Uptown they would ask twenty-five cents. You got a bargain."

"Those things? They're old and tired. I bet you've had them for years."

She was still pleased with her purchase. Just as she'd suspected, with steam from the teakettle, the velvet roses had bounced back to life.

She turned her head this way and that, tipped the hat at a slightly jaunty angle over her upswept hair, and then smiled at her reflection. With the velvet flowers, it would look a great deal like the pricey one she had seen on the cover of *Vogue* magazine. She pinned the flowers with the pearl hatpin Lottie had given her for her sixteenth birthday. Lottie had told her stories about women who defended themselves with hatpins. One prevented a train robbery. Lottie had read in the *Herald* that a woman in Chicago stabbed a masher who had tried to put a chloroform rag over her nose, and that President Theodore Roosevelt said, "No man, however courageous he may be, likes to face a resolute woman with a hatpin in her hand."

She sparingly dabbed L'Origan, the French perfume Frederick had given her, onto the underside of one rose petal, even though it smelled like orange blossoms. She'd read that it was the favorite fragrance of fashionable society.

It was a lovely day, and into a cloth satchel she had made, she put her library book, *The House of Mirth*, and an apple in case she decided to read for a bit in the park. It had been almost a year since she had seen Frederick.

"When do you think you'll be back?" Lottie asked, holding Matthew on her lap, feeding him oatmeal.

"I should be back by three. I'm going to the Metropolitan Museum."

"Enjoy yourself, Mimi. Matthew and I won't miss you a bit, will we?"

"Thank you. This will be an adventure."

The Winthrop family's mansion sat splendidly across from the Metropolitan Museum of Art on Fifth Avenue. While the same height and width as Mimi's old building on Eldridge Street, that was clearly where any similarity ended. The vertical white stone surface, elabo-

rate details and decorations, garlands, vines, and medallions sparkled in the sunlight. The elegant arched front door was carved wood
above which perched a lacy iron railing and two floor-to-ceiling
French double doors topped with seashell designs. Above were two
more floors of ornate double windows that rose to the mansard roof
and another lacy iron balustrade. Topped with more windows, a
rounded wooden roof was edged with what looked like a necklace of
pearls. Lovely enough for royalty, she was certain.

Nowhere was there the stink of garbage, no barrels of pickles
brining in a swill of garlic, dill, and vinegar. Not one peddler shouting the prices of onions, cabbages, turnips, or Shabbat candles would
dare line these curbs. There were no filthy dogs, feral cats, or rats to
be seen scouring for bits.

Nowhere in sight was there a fire escape or laundry flapping like
sails from the multitude of windows. And there were no shrill sounds
of mothers hollering out the windows for their youngsters to come
home, or ragamuffin boys playing barefoot in the street. No vulgari-
ties. No sounds at all, other than the wheels of passing carriages, the
clopping of hooves, and the occasional motorcar engine.

The Winthrop mansion rose from its plot like a monument.

Along the park side, under open blue skies filled with billowing
clouds and flocks of birds, genteel couples strolled: handsome men
in dark suits and hats, corseted women with hourglass figures and
refined appearances, wearing hats that looked like capsized ships
adorned with birds, flowers, netting, and bows.

Young wives held their husbands' arms while pushing babies in
proper prams. It was the world she knew about from Edith Wharton's
books—one of quiet refinement. Not illustrated figures from *Vogue* or
words in a library book that fed her imagination but one in which she
could turn round and round and see in its entirety. Each building on
Upper Fifth Avenue had been distinctively designed to show off and
vie for the title of Belle of the Ball. Like its surrounding neighbors,
the Winthrop Mansion was stunning with its ornate borders and
trim, but rather than cut from fabric, it was carved from stone. It an-
ticipated the arrival of guests dressed for tea or parties.

She stood at the edge of the curb in her polished boots. Time was at a standstill, and she was filled with apprehension. With a deep exhale, she took one step off the curb onto the immaculate street and crossed to the other side, where she suddenly felt dwarfed by the mansion's grandeur and heritage. Looking up at the façade, the multitude of floors and windows, she wondered what it would be like to awaken each morning, stand at those third-floor French doors in a silk robe, move that red velvet drape aside, and gaze out upon Fifth Avenue's grand views of the museum and the park. A row of gray pigeons standing at attention like soldiers, guarding their perch between the second and third floor windows, inspected her with disdain.

The world belonged to people like the Winthrops. All of it. Could they see as far as Eldridge Street from their roofs? Did the rich ever look downtown?

And then, as though a cruel storm had driven out her joy, she was overcome suddenly with questions. Why had she come? What did she expect to happen? What if a servant came out the door and asked her what she wanted? What was her business on Fifth Avenue? What if one of the Winthrops should appear? What if it were Frederick? And he recognized her this time? There was danger in that possibility. It had been childish to come. She did not belong here.

Married to a Winthrop, she might have a different life. Matthew would have a future of opportunity and privilege. As always, when she thought of what might have been and what was, she reached for the gold ring, which since Matthew was born she wore on her wedding ring finger, and turned it around and around mindlessly.

It was all so futile. She turned away from the Winthrop mansion and started for home.

THE CORSINO BROTHERS

Mimi and Matthew stayed with Lottie, waiting for word when the furnishings on her list might be delivered. She still had not received papers to sign. Lottie assured her they would arrive in due time. During the day, Mimi went to clean and scrub the wood floors, walls, and windows while Matthew lay on blankets on the floor. By the end of the week, she had no energy to go back to Lottie's and instead bought bread, cheese, and fruit and simply slept on the floor.

On Monday, a knocking at the side door woke her. When she looked out the window, there sat a truck. She quickly slipped into her old dress, picked up Matthew, went to the door, and then opened it a sliver.

"We got yer furniture."

There stood a giant of a man with wide cheekbones and a strong jaw, a heavy stubble and a thick mustache. When he removed his flat cap, his thick, dark hair fell over his eye.

"The Wint'rops sent us." He mispronounced their name as he nodded over his shoulder. "Me and Anthony—my brother." He seemed very rough.

"Please wait a moment," she said, closing the door.

Putting her boots on, gathering up Matthew, and then wrapping a blanket around him and herself, she walked out to the street, where an open truck was filled to overflowing with more furniture than she had ever seen, all wrapped in cloth and tied with rope.

"For me?" she asked.

"If you's Mrs. Milman, then it's for you," he answered snappishly.

The morning was chilly, and she made certain that Matthew's head was covered.

"I'm Frank Corsino and this is my brother, Anthony Corsino." His voice was coarse, his manner rude.

Anthony, younger, shorter, slimmer, and more clean-shaven than Frank, had a waxed handlebar mustache. Despite the bone-chilling cold, he was dressed in overalls over a wrinkled white collarless shirt, a misshapen suit jacket, and fedora, all of which had seen better days. He politely removed his hat as he nodded. She couldn't help but notice how blue his eyes were against his tanned, leathery skin.

Mimi noticed the fluttering of drapes as neighbors peeked out of their windows. Just like Eldridge Street, she thought.

"Is all of that for me?" She gasped.

"Yes, ma'am." Frank shifted his suspenders to pull up his thread-bare pants, tucking in a turtleneck sweater, unraveling at the shoulder. "We ain't got a lot a time, so where do you wants everything?"

"I don't know."

"Well, you better make up your mind, lady. You wan' us to leave it on the sidewalk?"

"Oh, no!" She gasped. "You mustn't do that. Please, I'll do my best." Tears welled up in her eyes.

"This ain't all there is, neither." When he wiped his forehead with his sleeve, she noticed his dirty fingernails.

"You mean there's more?" A tear ran down her cheek. She didn't know what to do.

Frank turned to his brother. "She wants to know if there's more, Tony." Anthony grinned a big toothy smile of agreement.

"My brother, Anthony—Tony—he don't say nothin'."

"You mean he can't speak?" she whispered.

"Nah, he could if he wanted. He just don't wanna." He spoke loud enough for Anthony to hear. "Hey, are you cryin'? There ain't nothin' to cry about. I'm sorry." He bent down to look in her eyes. "I didn' mean to upset you." He smiled and she noticed a gap between his front teeth that made her laugh. Taking out a huge handkerchief, he handed it to her. "Don'a you worry. Me an' Tony, we'll take care of everything. Eh, Tony?" He patted her shoulder. "Okay, we figure this out. Your business is in the front. Right? And what's in the back?" As he strode across the wood floor and through the doorway into the kitchen, in his workman's boots, she could feel the vibration. "The kitchen's back here," he shouted.

He climbed up the stairs, taking two at a time, and then yelled, "Where da ya want your bedroom? In the front or back?"

She made a quick decision. "The back, please."

When he returned, he assured her that they knew where everything needed to be.

"Your gonna like looking out on that garden in spring. Good choice."

Anthony never said a word as they moved the contents of their truck into and through the house. Frank spoke to his brother as though they were having a conversation, but Anthony just shook his head in agreement or disagreement. As each piece was carried inside, Mimi attempted to see what it was they were carrying. They made it look easy.

Gathering her wits and growing more confident, she began directing them as they took each piece off the truck and soon noticed that they worked together like dance partners. As they carried things into the building, they would stop inside the door and wait for her instructions.

"Upstairs, front parlor, please," she ordered as they carried a velvet sofa through the front door. With Matthew in her arms, she ran up and down the stairs making on-the-spot decisions as to where they should place each piece: the sofa, a pair of brocade armchairs, and several end tables. She had only seen beautiful furniture like this in magazines.

"Upstairs, back room, please," she directed for the large iron four-poster bed.

When they had assembled it, she exclaimed that it was large enough to hold an entire family.

They assured her the mattress would be arriving soon. There was a dresser and a matching mirror, an armoire with mirrored doors. Looking inside, she laughed. She had few clothes to hang on all the wooden hangers.

"Over there, please." The brothers placed a highly polished bentwood mahogany crib and dresser and a child's play table and four chairs in the corner of the room. She let out a cry of excitement when Anthony walked through the bedroom door carrying a wooden rocking horse and placed it on the floor, where he set it rocking back and forth. She had never seen anything so delightful.

"Tony made it," Frank said proudly as his brother nodded in agreement. "He made one for my boys, too. Sometimes the girls ride."

The small rag rug she had written on her list for Matthew never appeared. Instead, there were several thick wool carpets. Anthony rolled each one out for her to see. One, large enough for the parlor floor, had a Middle Eastern design. Other smaller rugs had floral patterns, and the brothers patiently rolled them out for Mimi to see and consider where she wanted them. They placed them in several positions before she was able to decide. If the brothers had not been there, she would have danced on them. They felt so warm and soft under her feet.

As they passed, she stopped and ran her hands over each piece in disbelief, marveling at their grandeur. She put Matthew on the rug and watched as he kept pushing himself up on his hands and proudly turned his head this way and that. When he began fussing, Anthony picked him up off the rug, lifted him in the air, and made all sorts of expressive faces at him, and Matthew stopped crying.

"Tony, he loves the babies," explained Frank. "He and his wife have eight. One on the way." Then, looking up and holding his hands toward the ceiling, he said. "Maybe this time twins."

Anthony broke into a big proud grin, his eyes sparkling with joy as he shook his head up and down.

"And what about you? How many children do you have?"

"Ten. Me, my wife and kids, Tony and his family, we live in the same building on Mulberry Street. Downtown. You know where that is?"

"Of course, I do. I lived . . ." She quickly turned and picked up a chair and moved it to another spot in the room. "Of course, I know where Mulberry Street is."

There were side tables, an elegant dining room table, and eight ornately carved and upholstered matching chairs, which she had them place in the front parlor.

"This is good furniture," Frank said. "You sure are a lucky lady." Anthony's eyes opened wide and he gestured wildly in agreement.

"I know," she said without offering an explanation.

While the two brothers were there, Mimi behaved in a ladylike and professional manner, but as soon as the truck pulled away from the curb, she ran around the room and plopped herself on every piece of furniture. In her bare feet on the delicious thick parlor rug, she danced and sang "Come Josephine in My Flying Machine" just like Blanche Ring, and each time she sang "up she goes" she raised Matthew in the air like an airplane and laughed until he smiled. He was just beginning to giggle. Finally, exhausted, she lay down on the floor and smothered him with kisses. He moved his arms and legs in excitement.

They had never had electric lights on Eldridge Street, and she turned the lamps off and on. That evening in the lamplight she arranged and rearranged the furniture until every chair was exactly where she wanted it. Her mind never stopped spinning with ideas, and she wondered if she would ever sleep again. When she stopped her thoughts to listen to the surroundings, the quiet was like a peculiar buzz in her head. She couldn't even hear the wind blowing.

On Tuesday morning at eight, Frank and Anthony's knocking on the front door woke her. She had slept on the rug under blankets with Matthew close by her side.

"*Buongiorno,*" Frank said, and Anthony tipped his hat and smiled when she greeted them at the door. "Have you eaten, Mrs. Mimi?"

She was embarrassed to admit that she had no food.

As though he had read her thoughts, Anthony waved his finger at her like Mama would have, and from a bag hidden behind his back, like a magician he produced a loaf of Italian semolina bread and a package wrapped in brown paper. He opened the packages on the kitchen table and revealed a chunk of cheese and sausage. Pulling off a chunk of bread, he took a knife from his pocket, cut a chunk of the cheese and some sausage, and offered it to her. He reached out for Matthew and took him from her arms.

She hadn't realized how hungry she was, and the combination of the smooth texture of the cheese and spiciness of the Italian sausage was perfect with the crusty bread dusted with cornmeal. She looked up to see that the two brothers were laughing at her appetite.

"*Mangia, mangia*," Frank insisted. The way he said the Italian words, Mimi knew it meant "Eat, eat." (Just what Mama would have said: "*Esn, esn.*") "You like the provolone?"

"Thank you. You are so kind. I wish I could make you coffee. But I have no coffee and no pot. Or cups, either."

"You no worry, " Frank said.

First, they carried in the mattress for her bed. Then boxes. There were bed linens, duvets, quilts, towels, pots and pans, dishes, flatware, and glasses. There were boxes filled with kitchen staples: salt, sugar, flour, spices, canned goods, tea, and coffee. There were baking pans with such fancy designs, she delighted in their decorations.

"It will take me the rest of my life to put them away," she said. "Perhaps I should become a baker instead of a dressmaker."

Frank put a crown-like pan on her head, and then the two brothers kneeled in front of her as though she were royalty. They laughed and laughed. From behind his back, Frank produced a coffeepot.

"Ahh, a coffeepot," she said with excitement.

Anthony produced a bag of Hills Brothers coffee.

"Now I can make you coffee."

"Tomorrow," Frank said.

The brothers worked until midday, checking that the water ran, the windows opened and closed, that the stove worked; they even oiled the front and back door locks. At noon they bowed politely and set off to a job in Brooklyn.

"*Arrivederci!*" Frank said. "Bye, bye. See you tomorrow."

"*Arrivederci!*" she repeated, and waved Matthew's arm at them.

"*Buongiorno, amico mio,*" Frank said on Wednesday morning when they arrived promptly at eight. "Mr. Thomas *Wint'rop* sent this refrigerator for you," he sang like a song.

Frank and Anthony carried between them a brand-new General Electric refrigerator, which they plugged into the kitchen wall and explained would keep her food cold, so she wouldn't have to shop every day for fresh food or keep ice in a box. They accepted cups of coffee but explained they had a busy day ahead, and drank it while they worked.

"That's all for today," Frank said after making certain the refrigerator was working. "Oh, Mrs. Mimi, Mr. Thomas *Wint'rop* said you tell us what you want built in your shop. Me and Tony, we make it beautiful for you," Frank explained before they left.

"You must learn to say Mr. Winthrop's name properly, Frank," she bravely suggested, hoping she didn't offend. "Win-throp," she corrected.

He practiced several times until he was able to say it correctly.

"Is good?" he asked.

"It's perfect," she answered, standing at the door. She suddenly burst into tears and threw her arms around Frank.

"Oh, don't cry, Mrs. Mimi." Frank was very distressed and flustered. He patted her on the shoulder. "Not today. Okay? Mrs. Mimi. You think about. We make it for you. A beautiful new shop—any way you like."

Anthony poked Frank with his finger and then pointed upwards.

"Oh, yes," Frank said. "Tony wants me to tell you that he will make you a beautiful sign. With real gold. Special. Tell us what you want it to say. Think about it. Tomorrow, dear young lady. Tomorrow. Right, Tony?"

Anthony looked embarrassed and nodded in agreement with his usual grin and then began poking Frank in the ribs with his elbows, indicating that they had to leave.

"*Arrivederci!*" she said as she waved to the two brothers.

"*Ciao!*" Frank said. Anthony waved.

8

THE AGREEMENT

Lottie and Mr. Timothy Troy of Haber & Troy, Attorneys-at-Law, arrived at seven. They appeared an odd couple: Lottie being a solid, sturdy woman, and Mr. Troy a person who certainly and seriously controlled what he ate. He seemed all skin and bones.

It wasn't to be a social call. Mr. Troy represented the Winthrop family, whereas Lottie was there to be certain that Mimi understood the terms of the Winthrop agreement. Mimi noticed that when he removed the bowler, Mr. Troy's black hair, parted in the middle, seemed glued to his gaunt head, which made his appearance even more unattractive. The handlebar mustache did not hide the gloomy expression of his downturned mouth. In his impeccable pin-striped three-piece suit, starched and ironed shirt, and polished black boots, Mr. Troy was what Mimi imagined to be the perfect representation of a lawyer. He was clutching a black leather briefcase to his chest as though someone might take it at any moment. Mimi assumed he carried the agreement papers, which she was expected to sign. His briefcase was as polished as his boots.

When Mimi had first met him, introduced by the Winthrops after she was evicted from her place on Eldridge Street, he had seemed a kind man but one concerned more with papers, forms, laws, rules, and promises. This evening, any indication of kindness seemed absent from his eyes, even when he smiled, and despite his courteous manner he made her uncomfortable. He only pretended to like her, she thought. She was learning to recognize scorn beneath the surface of some people of gentility.

It made her stand straighter, hold her head higher, like Miss Spencer, the librarian. She pretended there was a book balanced on her head, and gazed more directly at Mr. Troy, as Lottie always told her to do. Even when he wasn't speaking.

She invited them into the upstairs parlor, where a fire warmed the room, offering Mr. Troy the velvet wing chair and Lottie a place on the sofa. She excused herself to get the tea. When she returned, she took her place next to Lottie.

Matthew was asleep in his cradle in the next room. The house was still. She could smell the remnants of her leftover dinner: the beef stew that had been too burned for her to eat. But then, she had no appetite, knowing the importance of this meeting. This was an important night. Mr. Troy, representing the Winthrop family, was here to have her sign an agreement—a generous one, Lottie had promised.

She listened intently and quietly as Lottie had instructed her, as he went over the terms that spelled out what the Winthrops would provide for her and Matthew in the years to come. It had been written simply, Mr. Troy explained. All quite generous, he assured her.

He took a sip of his tea, cleared his throat, and checked his pocket watch.

"Mrs. Milman, in order for there to be no misunderstandings, I am sure I need not tell you that the Winthrops are an important family both in New York and abroad. Families like the Winthrops must maintain their reputations in society. Any sort of"—he paused to find the right words—"*indignity*, particularly an egregious one of a child born out of wedlock—an illegitimate child . . ." he stuttered.

"I'm sorry, Mr. Troy. I don't understand."

His expression hardened as he leaned forward in his chair. "Don't understand?" Two vertical creases appeared at the bridge of his bony nose, and his scowl was fierce. "What precisely don't you understand, young lady? You were not married, *Mrs.* Milman. You lived in a squalid tenement on the Lower East Side. You were, quite simply, a dalliance. Nothing."

His tone and the word "nothing" brought back memories of Mr. Moskowitz's humiliation of Szymon. Through the thin walls of Eldridge Street, Mimi had shared Szymon's kicks, his bruises, his inability to fight back, and his rage. She was bursting with indignation.

"Mr. Troy!" Lottie cried out.

"Mr. Frederick Winthrop and the entire Winthrop family are pillars of New York society—men of position and affluence. *You*"—he pointed a finger at her—"*you* should have known better, *Mrs.* Milman." There was loathing in the way he said her name.

"She was a child, sir."

"Why, it's depraved and sin—" He stopped mid-word.

Stunned at his accusations, she reached toward Lottie, who sat beside her. It was as though her mother were again accusing her from her hospital bed. Once more forced to face the shame. Depraved and sinful—that was how the world of the Winthrops saw her.

"Mr. Troy," Lottie interrupted, putting an arm around her shoulder. "I must ask you to speak to Mrs. Milman with respect."

He paused to take a sip of his cold tea and then, taking a deep breath, wiped his mouth and sweaty brow with his napkin. When he next spoke, the scowl had vanished, there was the faintest indication of a smile, and his voice was again polite. "Let's be honest, shall we?"

"That would be for the best, sir." In the heat of the conversation's indelicate nature, Lottie's warm skin gave off her familiar scent of vanilla.

"It would be dreadful were any of the Winthrops' friends or business associates to learn about *your* . . . indiscretion."

"Excuse me, sir. *My* indiscretion? But, with all respect, sir, Frederick Winthrop was almost thirty and I was fourteen."

Lottie was shaking her head at Mimi, indicating wordlessly not to go on.

"Yes, there's that. But that said, Mrs. Milman, you might consider yourself . . . fortunate." His tone was oily. "The Winthrops feel for your sorry state but they certainly want no problems to arise in the future, which would embarrass you, the boy—"

Mimi interrupted. "Or their family?" She suddenly understood this game. Finally, it all made sense. *Sorry state?* She held more command than she realized. Timothy Troy had been sent to make her feel small and powerless when it was the almighty Winthrops who were worried. They had much to lose. Hadn't Lottie told her numerous times that the last thing wealthy people wanted was scandal?

"I believe we are ready for your signature." Taking his black fountain pen from inside his suit jacket, he offered it to her. Too eagerly, she observed. "Unless you have any questions?"

"Actually, I do have one question, sir." Her voice burst out like a Fourth of July firework, startling her as much as it did Lottie and the lawyer. She put her finger on the section of the agreement in which she agreed never to reveal the identity of Matthew's father.

Lottie gave her a questioning glance, her brows furrowed. "Mimi." *Know your place* was what Mimi heard in Lottie's tone.

She sat up taller, placed one hand on top of the other on her lap. "Clause sixteen, article three states that I must, under no circumstances, reveal the name of Matthew's father."

"That isn't something you want Matthew—or anyone, for that matter—to know, is it, Mimi?" Lottie whispered.

"Clearly, not as much as the Winthrops." Mimi grasped her palms in a tight grip, noticing how Mr. Troy kept his gaze on her. When he put the pen down on the table next to his teacup and then took his gaze off her to look at Lottie, Mimi was almost certain there was a conspiratorial connection between them. They had not expected her to question the agreement.

"How can I be certain that the Winthrops will not claim my son?"

"Hmm, good question."

"Just look at all they are providing you with," Lottie said, squeezed her hand as though to remind her that the family was buying her silence and assuring their own.

"I will discuss that with the Winthrops and get back to you in a day or two. I am certain adding that stipulation won't create a problem."

"I want to be quite certain of that." She considered Lottie's silent reminder of all they were offering her, and the reason. "They have been very generous."

"They are philanthropists."

"Is that a religion?" she asked.

"Philanthropists are people who have a great deal of money, Mrs. Milman, with more money than they know what to do with, so they give it to help others. Like you and the boy. To be remembered. People like the Winthrops, the Astors, and the Vanderbilts built this city. Its railroads and bridges. They fund libraries, museums, and schools. They also provide educational scholarships. Both Jonathan and Thomas want to be certain your boy has the finest education.

"And speaking of scholarships, Mrs. Milman, they have offered to pay your tuition at the Manhattan Trade School for Girls on Twenty-Second Street and provide you with a nursemaid to care for the baby while you attend classes."

"But, Mr. Troy, I must work to support myself."

"My personal advice is to allow yourself a certain amount of time to prepare. This shop will need to fit into the neighborhood and your new clientele. We have arranged for the Corsino brothers, whom I believe you've met, to help with any construction you may need."

"The Corsino brothers have been very helpful in getting me settled. They have already put everything in place."

"So I notice. Moving on." He checked the time. "You will soon learn that uptown is quite different than Eldridge Street."

"Yes, Mr. Troy. Lottie has already reminded me."

"Hmmm." He coughed. "In addition, I would add that the Winthrops would . . ." She was certain that he was considering his words carefully when he lowered his eyes, paused, and then took out his pocket watch before continuing to speak. "The Winthrops want to be . . . helpful in your and the boy's future, but they are a very private family . . . and have asked that, should you have any questions . . . questions related to our agreement . . . speak to me rather than with them. You understand?"

"Yes, sir, I do," Mimi said quietly.

"Excellent. I think you will find that this will work out extremely well for you and the boy. I will see that the changes we have discussed this evening are made, so you can sign the papers in the next few days, if you agree."

After showing Lottie and Mr. Troy out, she sat at the kitchen table, completely overwhelmed at the thought of all that lay ahead, the promise of all possible opportunities she could never have imagined. She was proud of the way she'd represented herself.

There was a sealed envelope on the table. Picking it up, she opened it and took out a check. Her breath caught in her chest. She couldn't believe the amount: one thousand dollars. It was more money than she had ever seen in her entire life. Twice what she and Mama had ever earned in the best of years. After an hour of sitting primly, acting grown-up, she was thankful that Mr. Troy was not there to observe her collapse into an eruption of childish emotion.

She knew how to keep a secret; would never breathe a word to any of her uptown customers or anyone, for that matter, about how she had lived downtown. That "squalid" room, as Mr. Troy called it. That she and Mama had worked in suffocating, dust-filled factories for pennies, and then come home after those long hours and sewed more—often until morning to finish orders. She would never tell anyone about poor Mama, who deserved better than to die in the public ward at Beth Israel Hospital. Hadn't she hidden her pregnancy?

Was this an agreement with the devil? No, she decided, it was an opportunity to put the past behind her and begin a new and better life.

9

HOME

On those days when the brothers arrived to work on her shop, she had coffee ready. They would bring food from their neighborhood to share: bread or wonderful flaky Italian pastries, some cheese, or meats.

One day she made Mama's hot borscht for them for lunch; another day *balandeliai*: cabbage filled with ground meat and rice and simmered in a light tomato sauce, then topped with sour cream.

She remembered all of Mama's recipes. The Corsino brothers loved her cooking, and she grew fond of Frank's gruff way and Anthony's quiet presence in her life.

"Our mom and pop came from a village in Sicily. They were fine woodworkers but when they came to New York they had to live in the city and find whatever work they could—with eight children—four sisters and four boys. Our pappa was a hard worker—and a saver—and no drinking." Frank waved his finger in the air and scowled. "He was good at building things and soon found work with furniture makers." His face lit up. "A craftsman. Everything he made was beautiful. Right, Tony?" Anthony grinned.

"You know? Tony makes beautiful picture frames—puts gold on them. It's called gilding," he explained. "Our grandfather taught him that. Right, Tony?" He nodded and looked sad. "Tony, he loved our grandfather. Now he makes frames for Mr. Jonathan Wint'rop—Win-throp," he said, pronouncing it carefully. "He paints and gilds ceilings in Mr. Thomas Winthrop's customers' houses. Big houses. Uptown. So grand. Life gets better and better. Right, Tony?

"Funny. When my brother was little, all he wanted was to learn to drive. He's stubborn. Right, Tony?" The two brothers laughed. "He had his mind set. He wanted a truck." Tony looked embarrassed and looked down at his hands, which were holding his coffee. "It's true, Tony. You're as stubborn as a mule." Anthony shrugged and laughed.

"Calling your brother a mule? That's not nice."

"This mule," Frank repeated, squinting his eyes and using his hand to emphasize that if he said his brother was a mule, then he was, "he worked day and night and saved. We all pitched in a little—until there was enough to buy the truck. Brand-new—an REO. Ransom Eli Olds. Right?" Anthony smiled with pride. "Our family, we lived in one room. Ten of us. Tony knew that if we could make furniture, and his frames, and if we had a truck, well, then we could deliver them. You gotta have a truck." He tapped his finger on his brother's forehead. "Brains! Now we own a whole building and a workroom!" Anthony beamed with pride as his brother pounded him on the back. "He may be quiet, but he's a hard worker." He paused before saying, "*Il cuore è grande*. His heart is big." He leaned over and kissed his brother noisily on the cheek.

"*Cuore è grande*," Mimi repeated, tapping her heart.

"Soon we'll have Mrs. Mimi talking Italian." Frank laughed and gestured with his hand.

Later that week, Mr. Troy came with the agreement, which now included the addition of a clause stating that *under no circumstances would the Winthrops reveal the identity of the child's father.* Agreeing that it satisfied her concerns, she signed. The lawyer picked up the agreement, squinted in order to look at her signature, rearranged the pages in some different order, and tidied their edges before placing them into his leather case. Her and Matthew's future was sealed with the snap of the brass closure. The Winthrop agreement had been made.

10

THE FUTURE

You're driving me crazy with all your ideas. Where do they come from?" Lottie complained one Sunday as they sat at Mimi's kitchen table.

"I can't help how my brain works. I think about how things look. Rooms. Gowns. Shoes and even hats. My brain just sees these things: fabric, color, shape, stitches, and designs. I imagine what accessories should go with every dress. When I see people walking on the street, I think about what they should be wearing." Mimi laughed. "Don't you?"

"No, I don't, child. I think about numbers in columns, addition and subtraction. I think about bills that need to be paid and money owed." Lottie was very serious when she spoke.

Mimi stood and began to clear the table. "There's enough room for you to live with us, you know. You could have an entire floor. You wouldn't have to pay rent."

"No, thank you, my dear." Lottie chuckled. "I'm perfectly happy where I am. But if you need me, I will come."

"Then I will make a room for you to sleep over when you visit. So you won't have to travel home late at night, or when it rains or snows."

"You *are* a dreamer, Mimi."

"Most of all, I want to create beautiful clothes. I see them in my head, swirling around and around." She spun around the room, dancing with Matthew in her arms, the child as gleeful as could be. "Like at a fancy Winthrop ball."

"Don't you spoil that boy, Mimi."

"But I want to. I want him to have everything."

"Let me hold my sweetheart," Lottie cooed.

"If anyone is to spoil him, it's you, Lottie." She handed Matthew into Lottie's open arms.

"Don't be ridiculous." Lottie began covering him with kisses. "I brought you a gift, Mimi. I think you will like it. It's in that bag by the door."

Mimi wasn't used to gifts. She unwrapped the package to find a sketchbook, pencils, a paintbrush, and a set of watercolors.

"Now you can put those dreams on paper," Lottie said. "Put Frederick Winthrop out of your mind. Don't allow him to get in your way. You and Matthew are safe. You've been given the opportunity of a lifetime. To make something of yourself."

With Matthew on her lap, and with her hands holding his wrists, Lottie moved his arms in the gestures of the song she sang in the loveliest voice:

> *Wind, wind, little baby,*
> *Wind, wind, little baby.*
> *Pull, pull.*
> *Hammer, hammer, hammer.*

Matthew laughed and waved his arms, eager for more.

"Where did you learn that?" Mimi asked. "You have the sweetest voice."

"Your mama sang it to you when you were a baby."

"Did she?" Mimi was bitter. "I don't remember her having a song in her to sing."

"Well, she did." Lottie looked cross. "Pay attention to your future—and Matthew's."

After Lottie had gone home, Mimi cleaned the kitchen and prepared Matthew for bed. She lay with him by her side in the four-poster bed, hoping to fall into sleep, but every creak, the moaning of the house, the wind in the garden, began to frighten her. She turned the lamp on. She hated the quiet of nighttime. Uneasiness crept into her thoughts. The house was too big. It had too many empty rooms to fill. She missed Eldridge Street, the sounds of people on the stairs. She wanted to smell food cooking and the fragrance of the Schenkeins' bread, to hear laughter—even the Moskowitz family's unrest. She knew she should feel grateful and listen to Lottie's advice, but instead she felt frightened.

At the same time, she knew Lottie was right: much waited ahead. The vision of her future. Possibilities. She concentrated on Matthew's breathing, held his hand while he slept, smelled his sweet breath close to her. All that this would provide for him as well.

When she was certain he was asleep, she went down to the kitchen to draw and paint those dreams that she had imagined in fleeting moments during the day, creating designs and watercolor sketches with descriptions written along their sides in pencil. She sang aloud to shut out the quiet. Hours passed uncounted. When she looked up at the clock on the kitchen wall, it was close to midnight.

She got ready for bed, tucked the covers around Matthew one more time, and slipped under the cool feather duvet, waiting for her cold toes and the bed space to warm—and to sleep.

When she thought about the new life ahead of her in this beautiful house, Matthew's education provided for and the promise of attending classes, she felt triumphant.

She was still angry at Mr. Troy's biting accusations and the reminders of Matthew's conception. The seduction—kissed and touched in the back of an automobile. Enticed by small gifts. Dazzled by the golden splendor of the Wolcott Hotel and the refrains of Viennese waltzes from distant rooms. Seduced by a gentleman twice her age. Childish ideas from the Grimm's tale of *Aschenputtel*, and her adolescent fantasies of being the wife of a Winthrop.

She could still envision every detail of that room, vivid as yesterday: the gilded mirrors, the Persian carpets, the naughty photographs, and the birds frozen under a glass dome. She remembered the feel of velvet pillows, the taste of his mouth, his hands awakening her senses, his fingers, whispers, and lips at her open bodice.

She was filled with shame because here in the dark, alone, without Mama beside her in that cramped, tired bed on Eldridge Street, with no one to see, hear, or judge her, the desire rose in her to feel those sensations again.

Raising her nightgown, Mimi ran her palms down her chest and across her breasts, imagining they were his hands, his lips, his breath, caressing the smooth skin of her belly and hips. Her fingers searched for that place of dark, wet mystery.

The inexplicable sensations she experienced, the commotion of longing unlike any other, the heat of mounting desire—the ravishing memory and hunger to have him inside of her—was unbearable and delicious. As he had opened each tiny button on the blouse she had worn that night like stars appearing in the night sky, she climbed and circled and soared wildly among the constellations in unearthly pleasure.

When the heat subsided and she lay in the cold stillness of the room, all that remained was disquiet and the pounding of her heart.

Unable to sleep, she slipped out of bed and bent over Matthew's crib to pick him up. Startled, he took hold of her fingers. She lifted him and carried him to the rocking chair, where she held him to her chest, breathed in the sweaty perfume of his neck, listened as his breathing and her own joined in syncopation and finally filled the house's overbearing silence. Holding his soft hand, she caressed each miraculous finger.

"We have just been given a future, my sweet baby boy," she whispered.

11

THE NANNY

You need a nanny," Lottie said as they walked to the Bethesda Terrace in Central Park. It was chilly for June. The sky, like a silver-gray watercolor, was filled with a variety of gray clouds. It had felt as though it might rain all day, but fortunately the weather held it back. Alice Winthrop had sent a new Heywood-Wakefield pram for Matthew, and they were showing it off.

Lottie stopped to tuck the blue blanket she had crocheted around Matthew. "Sound asleep," she whispered. "And she must live in. You can easily create a room for her on the third or fourth floor. She needs excellent skills and the willingness to work for a young mother like you."

"I can take care of Matthew myself."

"No, you cannot, young lady. Are you serious about your business? Are you planning to go to school?" She paused, clearly waiting for answers. "The Manhattan Trade School for Girls is a privilege that you must set your mind to. There will be classes and homework to do. You need to get that shop open as soon as possible. Someone needs to attend to Matthew. Not you and not me. You can count on me for Sunday adventures, but that's all."

She pushed Lottie out of the way and began pushing the pram. "I've scheduled interviews every morning from nine until noon for the past two weeks. I need to supervise the Corsinos' work and organize all of the things the Winthrops sent. I stopped counting at forty nannies. They were too old, too young, too stiff, too talkative, too stuck-up, too silly, too bossy, too uncertain, too know-it-all, and too know-nothing." She counted the ten things on her fingers. Lottie laughed.

"Don't give up. You'll find the right person." Lottie patted her hand and then took two apples out of her bag and handed one to Mimi. "Let's sit under the *Angel of the Waters* statue. It was designed by Emma Stebbins. Funny," Lottie said. "The *New York Times* said it resembles a servant girl dancing a polka. I read that her brother was a big shot and got her the commission. Pfff. It's always who you know, isn't it?"

They sat at the base of the statue and watched the people strolling on the plaza, many with infants and children. "Look around, Mimi. Tell me what you see. Nannies!"

Mimi was torn. She wanted to care for Matthew herself, but she wanted just as much to attend school and design clothes. When she saw all the nannies with their charges, she thought that it would absolutely bore her to tears—and then how would she accomplish her dreams?

On the following Friday, there was a knock on the side door just as the regulator clock struck nine.

"I'm Mrs. Edna Willikins." She looked Mimi up and down before holding out her hand. Mimi was taken aback by her heft and that she had to be less than five feet tall and wore a massive eight-button brown wool coat that made her look like a stuffed fowl. Her worn, dome-topped navy velvet cloche sat an inch above her brows and almost hid her beady eyes. She had pinned a corsage of wilted African violets at center front. But it was her face with its plump round pink cheeks, turned-up nose, and straight grim mouth that Mimi found unpleasant.

"Is Mrs. Milman at home?"

"I'm Mrs. Milman. Mrs. Willikins, please come in." Mimi led her to the chairs in the front of the shop. "May I take your coat?"

"No, thank you, my dear."

Mimi did not like being addressed in that condescending manner. As Edna Willikins entered, she kept sniffing distastefully. She sat stiffly in the chair with both hands holding her worn handbag upright on her lap. Mimi couldn't help but notice that her fingernails were dirty and that her boots were in need of repair and a good polish. The hem of her coat was edged with mud, the cuffs ragged.

She began speaking, before Mimi could begin asking her questions. "I like to make things very clear, Mrs. Milman. Right away. So there's no misunderstanding," she said. "First of all, I only take care of the infant. I don't live in. I leave exactly at five and I don't tidy up. I don't do dishes. I have bad knees, so lifting anything is out of the question."

Mimi interrupted. "Does that include my son?"

"How much does he weigh?"

She ignored the question. "What *else* don't you do, Mrs. Willikins?"

"What floor is the child's room? I don't climb stairs, and expect a full lunch and dinner. No stews or soups. Steaks, chops, and roasts only."

Mimi stood up. "Thank you for coming, Mrs. Willikins. I will be in touch with you."

"Don't you want to see my references?" She began opening her handbag.

"That won't be necessary."

"Well!" she huffed. "I came a long way."

When she left, Mimi watched from her front window: how her dome shape waddled down the street, her colossal coat swaying from side to side over two tiny feet, and that ridiculous hat perched atop like a teakettle cover.

Mrs. Willikins was the last straw, and Mimi was about to give up in despair, when Miss Ruth Meyers arrived at ten o'clock.

In her austere aubergine-colored dress with its white crocheted collar and her dark hair pulled back into a bun, she reminded Mimi of the heroine of Charlotte Brontë's *Jane Eyre*.

"Which agency are you with, Miss Meyers?" She knew the questions backward and forward.

"I wasn't sent by an agency. Lottie Aarons—she's a friend of my mother's—suggested I call you. She mentioned that you are a clothing designer."

"Yes, I am."

Miss Meyers had a thoughtful expression. Her eyes were hazel, with amber flecks. When she looked directly at Mimi as she spoke, Mimi realized that Lottie would have noticed that immediately.

"Lottie and my mother both worked at Hein and Fox."

"Is she still there?"

"Not anymore."

She had a gentle smile. "When my mother mentioned to Mrs. Aarons that the couple I work for will be leaving for California next week, and that I've been caring for their baby since birth, Mrs. Aarons suggested I call you."

"Where does your family live, Miss Meyers?"

"On Delancey Street. It's a very small apartment." She lowered her eyes. "A bit crowded. That's why I prefer live-in work."

"Near Iceland Brothers'?" Mimi asked.

"Why, yes." She looked surprised. "You know it?"

"A . . . a friend always talks about their blintzes, and their onion rolls," Mimi added quickly. "Please tell me about your family."

"Well, my father makes and repairs violins. He plays, too. We all do. I have two brothers and a sister. I'm the oldest. My father taught us all to play. My mother left factory work and went back to school and now she's a schoolteacher," she said with pride. "I graduated from high school with honors two years ago and then found a full-time live-in position on Lexington Avenue with a young family with a newborn. Here are my letters of reference." Taking the letters from her purse, unfolding them, smoothing them on her lap, she handed them to Mimi.

"Quite impressive, Miss Meyers. When might you begin?" she asked.

"May I meet Matthew? And would you mind showing me where I would be sleeping?"

"Of course. How forgetful of me."

This was all so new; it hadn't occurred to her. Perhaps Miss Meyers worried she'd be sleeping in a basement or under the stairs.

Miss Ruth Meyers held Matthew in her arms and Mimi was certain things would go well. She had a tender and kindhearted manner. Mimi could attend classes, see to the construction of the shop, and think about her business plan.

12

VISITING LAWRENCE LOFT

When she first visited Lawrence Loft's shop, he had showed her about. She tried to take in everything he said, to remember names and dates, but there were too many items: a pair, a place, a person, or a musical instrument. There were Chinese lacquered end tables, set among potted orchids and palms, that he said might trigger reminiscences of past occasions to his customers; a room visited, a place traveled, if their life was one of privilege—or if they wished to pretend it had been. There were sconces and candelabras, crystal candlesticks, bronze figures, and elegant chairs—Duncan Phyfe, he called them, and she wasn't sure if that was a person or a musical instrument. There were also sterling picture frames with velvet mats, items for the "proper" desk, and freshly ironed table linens "for those who entertained."

In his own travels, Lawrence explained, he had collected silver, platinum, and gold jewelry—vintage pieces inset with diamonds and emeralds; pale, clear amber with insect inclusions; turquoise, which he described as the color of an Arizona sky; seductive opals that intensified emotional states and released inhibitions; and lapis lazuli, once reserved for depicting the robes of angels in paintings. His explanations seemed made up of magical words that were a complete mystery to Mimi, but she simply appreciated their sounds.

Lawrence, as he preferred to be called, was long-limbed and angular. He lived above the shop and had a cottage on his grandfather's farm in Connecticut. At twenty-two, when not making the circle of seasonal social events in the city or traveling, he enjoyed reading and gardening. His suntanned skin attested to that. His longish sandy hair, pomaded in place, was so well managed it seemed never to be in need of a barber. He seemed the most sophisticated person she had ever met.

She admired his style: he tended toward tweeds, brown shoes, and an ascot or a bow tie. While his jackets and trousers were meticulously tailored and sedate, his custom-made shirts were always in colors that astonished Mimi's sense of color. Most men she knew wore white, cream, or blue shirts. Lawrence shocked with lavender, chartreuse, turquoise, or outlandish stripes, which he juxtaposed with disarming neckwear in contrasting oranges, purples, stripes, or checks. The cuff links he collected and wore were, he had explained, his signature, always unusual and made by an elderly artisan in Venice from objects Lawrence found while traveling. Each pair had its own exotic story. Sometimes Mimi wondered if he made them up.

"You will need a signature, Mimi. Be on the lookout. One of my customers only wears pale blue," Lawrence said. "Another always wore a choker at her neck. Oh, and Mrs. Fenwick-Morton always carries her Pekinese with a diamond collar—in a straw basket."

What one thing—an item of jewelry, a style of scarf or hat, a signature color, perhaps—would define who she was?

Mimi admired the study Lawrence made of his appearance, recognizing from her own experience the skill and attention to detail it took. She liked being with him. They were beautiful together. She didn't need to be told. And besides, beneath his polished surface, he was a gentle soul.

13

THE SHOP AT 1313 MADISON

Mimi was settling into the house and shop at 1313 Madison, close to Millionaire's Row. She was certain she would attract a decidedly more upscale clientele than downtown, and her classes at the Manhattan Trade School for Girls were helping her to prepare.

Frank and Anthony Corsino sanded the old floors, applied a black stain, and then polished and buffed them to a warm glow. They built doors, walls, counters, cabinets, and shelves in the warm cherrywood Mimi selected. She helped Frank and Anthony paper one wall in the entry with a quiet floral design of large pale burgundy cabbage roses with dark leaves on a silvery background. Some of her favorite laughter-filled hours were spent with the brothers. Her circle of friends was growing. Not yet with the sort she once dreamed, but with people with whom she worked.

Every Tuesday, Frank and Anthony's mother sent "her boys" with a pot of soup and a loaf of bread for lunch. On Wednesdays, when his shop was closed, Lawrence would arrive with elegant hors d'oeuvres for lunch, and on Thursdays the nanny, Ruth Meyers, served borscht—hot or cold, depending on the weather—which she prepared the night before. Lottie often came by to join them. Fridays they each brought their own lunch—with some Italian pastries from Mulberry Street, as they never quite knew who would stop by. They would sit around what would be her worktable for one hour exactly. They talked business, books, moving pictures, family, and news. Matthew always joined them at lunch in the high chair that Frank had made for him and named "His Majesty's Throne." One afternoon Ruth Meyers played the violin. Anthony never spoke but liked to sing; he could sing arias from Italian operas.

Frank and Anthony surprised Mimi with a gift of two yellow canaries in a standing polished-brass birdcage. Lawrence found a large ceramic pot in Chinatown and filled it with a fern. A young seamstress reupholstered in Hooker's green velvet the pair of chairs Mimi found on the top floor. Mimi arranged them so that the gentlemen or ladies who waited might look out onto Madison Avenue. Lottie sewed a pair of jacquard drapes to divide the front of the shop from work areas. A partial wall closed off the kitchen and stairways to the living areas.

One morning after a water pipe burst, everyone pitched in to help mop the floors.

Mimi admired Frank and Anthony, who were extraordinary craftsman. Just as she understood fabric, they understood how wood could be cut, carved, polished, and honed to perfection. She had asked for a large worktable in the center of the room, covered with canvas, and was astounded when they decided to put wheels on the large table so that the room could be rearranged when she had more work, hired seasonal help, or needed more space.

They built shelves to store sized muslin dress forms for individual clients, their mannequin stands below in a small rear room they built. In time, each dress form would be stenciled with its owner's name.

By watching her at work, they created the perfect container for the tools of her trade: the pins, needles, marking chalk, thread, scissors, tape measures, and folded wooden rulers, as well as a thread holder for sixty spools in a showy rainbow display of colors.

Probably the most beautiful thing in the shop was a cherrywood three-way mirror and alteration fitting platform the brothers made for Mimi's birthday. Anthony had hand carved the mirror's crown with cabbage roses and leafy vines that trailed across and down the sides of the frames, and he had gilded the roses and vines in real gold.

It sat on cabriole legs. The platform on which customers stood for alterations was decorated with a trim of gilded vines around the outer edge to match the mirror. It was truly a work of art.

On one wall Mimi pinned, with straight pins, idea sketches, images of dresses, gowns, and accessories torn from magazines. Scattered in between were inspirational references: birds, flowers, ballerinas, color combinations, moving picture actresses, and pictures of paintings and sculptures. There were silk flowers and bits and pieces of ribbons, trims, and fabrics she collected.

Most of the day the front of the shop was bright, filled with the singing of the birds. She had named them Tito and Enrico, after Tito Schipa and Enrico Caruso, both operatic tenors. There was the occasional jangle of the bell announcing the arrival of a potential customer curious to know what services she would provide when she opened for business.

Above the front door hung the elegant gilded sign Anthony had made, upon which was painted *Mimi Milman* in a florid Spenserian script to match the business cards that Lawrence designed and printed for her.

To the left of the front door was a lady's garment on a dress form. On Mondays, Mimi added silk flowers to the hat perched jauntily on the form's top knob. They were exquisitely made by one of her classmates: red roses, lilies of the valley, yellow daisies, or purple African violets. In the window on the right was a display of menswear on a mannequin. A silk boutonnière in the lapel was coordinated with the lady's.

Interest in her business began to grow as a result of both passersby and referrals, which began with Lottie telling the Winthrop wives, who told their friends, and then word traveled from one to the other along the social ladder.

Lawrence had spare tickets for concerts, opera, and theater, and frequently asked her to join him. His elegance inspired her to create a small wardrobe for herself. The budget that Lottie helped her put together included a special fund for her personal wardrobe. Mimi subscribed to the latest magazines and paid close attention to the women she saw in the neighborhood. They were her potential customers. She took notice of the detailing of Lawrence's fine clothes.

Lawrence took her to parties and salons. The wooden hangers in the armoire in her bedroom began to fill. He had the gentlest way of imparting to her the things she needed to know as her social life expanded and she learned from watching him.

14

GLORIA ARNOLD

It was a chilly Sunday, and Mimi and Lottie had come downtown to their old neighborhood to shop, Lottie for undergarments and Mimi for fabric.

"I feel as though I never left Eldridge Street."

"Well, you have. Madison Avenue and Ninety-Third Street is a long way away."

"There's still something comforting downtown, Lottie. The noise, the familiar smells, all the memories."

"Pfff! Uptown's better. Why do you wear such light colors? They show dirt."

"You must stop mothering me, Lottie. I wear pale colors because I *prefer* pale colors! You insist on that dreary brown wool—winter and summer. Why won't you let me make you something new and fresh?"

"Okay, okay. Don't be snippy." Lottie held her hands up in surrender. "I thought we'd agreed not to discuss my clothing choices."

They walked a block in silence. It irked her that Lottie refused to do anything she suggested to make herself look more youthful and attractive. But maybe she would simply surprise her. Would she refuse a new shirtwaist? A bit of a ruffle?

"Have you been reading about Gloria?"

"Gloria who?" Mimi asked.

"Your customer, Gloria Arnold. The socialite and heiress. The

Arnolds, who came over on the *Mayflower*," she said mockingly. "She's a friend of Jonathan and Alice Winthrop—and Frederick."

"I assumed she found another dressmaker. Someone cheaper. She cried poverty over my prices. She still hasn't paid me for some work. I don't miss *hondl*ing with her."

As they walked along crowded Orchard Street, men, women, and children, their heads down against the wind, jostled them. Vendors were packing up. Some propelled their wooden carts along the cobblestone streets, trying to avoid horses, carriages, and automobiles. The sound of wooden wheels on cobblestone was jarring.

"Well, she's missing. Since September! It was in *Town Topics*."

Mimi stopped still where she stood. "September? They wrote about Gloria Arnold in that scandal sheet with all the gossip?"

"I love *Town Topics*!" Lottie laughed. "Come. Let's go to Yonah Schimmel's. It's a bit of a walk. I'll tell you what I know about *Miss* Arnold." Lottie sighed. "She was on her way to look for a dress and simply disappeared. Button your top button and wrap your scarf around your neck," she ordered. "It's getting chilly."

"Yes, Mama."

"Don't be fresh, young lady."

"She owes me fifteen dollars."

"How many times have I told you, Mimi? Deposit and full payment on delivery."

"Maybe she's traveling."

"The paper said she disappeared wearing a tailor-made blue serge dress and coat and a small velvet hat decorated with two silk roses. No mention of suitcases!"

Mimi stood still. "I altered that dress and coat for her," she said angrily, "and then she begged me to make that velvet hat." Lottie was walking so fast, Mimi was getting out of breath. "It's getting windier and darker. Look at the clouds, Lottie. Snow. Anyway, I hope they find her so I can get paid."

"Send the bill to her home." Lottie shook her finger in her face. "Her family will pay. Believe me, they don't want any gossip that they don't pay their bills."

They waited at the corner to cross the street. "Next time, we'll go to Iceland Brothers' for latkes or blintzes." Lottie rolled her eyes with pleasure.

"How do you expect to fit into your new spring coat, Lottie?"

"What can I do? I love to eat!"

As they waited to cross Delancey, a passing horse and carriage barely missed them as they stepped off the curb.

"Slow down, you *meshuggener*!" Lottie shouted, and almost lost her footing on the cobblestones. "You coulda murdered us, you *momzer*!" she yelled even louder.

"Lottie, it isn't refined to shout at people on the street."

"Haven't *you* become the la-di-da lady!"

"Why, thank you." She ignored the sarcasm. "You need to slow down. I can't keep up with you. And I want to hear more about Miss Arnold."

Lottie walked more slowly. "One of her friends told the reporter that Gloria was off to buy this dress and planned to walk home through Central Park." Lottie paused—for drama, Mimi assumed. "And that was the last anyone saw of her. Awful. And to make things worse, the Arnolds didn't call the police for six weeks!"

"Why? I'd call the police if Matthew was missing for ten minutes."

"People like the Arnolds, the Vanderbilts, *and* the Winthrops *never* call the police. Never. It would be socially embarrassing." Lottie rolled her eyes. "God forbid the upper crust should be socially embarrassed. Well, here we are."

There was a crowd in front of the redbrick building on Houston and Orchard Street.

"What kind? My treat."

"Potato," Lottie said emphatically as they took their place on line.

"Oy! Mimi, look at that sky," Lottie said as they left the knishery. "Let's hurry. We'll eat while we walk. A storm's coming, I feel it in my old bones."

"It's impossible to eat a hot knish and walk fast." Mimi tried to catch up with Lottie, who was almost running to catch an approaching trolley.

They were relieved to get seats at the back of the trolley heading uptown; it was too long a ride to stand, and they shared sighs as they each bit into their freshly baked, golden knishes with the fragrant mashed potato mixture encased in delicate flaky pastry.

As the trolley passed through the Lower East Side, Mimi, who was sitting by the window, glanced out and watched the people on the streets, their hats and shoulders sprinkled with snow, moving briskly in the streetscape. The clean white dusting served to accentuate the pushcarts, sidewalks, awnings, cobblestones, the laundry and bedding still on clotheslines, which stretched between buildings, and on fire escapes. Women, their shoulders hunched up against the wind, leaned out open windows, pulling the laundry lines toward them, removing and shaking their laundry in the blustery wind.

"Aren't we lucky not to be working in the factories anymore?" Lottie sighed. "Those managers going through our purses at the door like we were *gonifs*." Her face contorted with those words. "I never stole nothing my entire life. I'd rather die than ever go back to that factory."

"Well, you work for the Winthrops now; you won't have to."

"And neither will you. With your *uptown* customers," Lottie said, holding her hand up and rubbing her thumb against her fingers, indicating money.

Mimi laughed. "Thanks to you."

Lottie patted her hand and smiled.

Yes, she might have wealthier, more stylish customers, but some of these people were too close to Frederick, especially Jonathan's wife, Alice Winthrop. Always asking personal questions. Mimi worried about Lottie's loyalty to the Winthrops and that, with a slip of the tongue, Lottie might reveal her secret, and then Frederick would find out about Matthew—and might take him from her. He had the money and those lawyers, Haber & Troy.

As if she had read her mind, Lottie patted her hand again and said, "Don't you worry, Mimi, your uptown clients will never find out about you and Mr. Frederick. Not from me."

"Or from me." Mimi felt heat rise to her cheeks, embarrassed that she had even thought Lottie would do anything like that. "Okay, so tell me more about Gloria Arnold," she whispered.

Easily distracted, Lottie opened her eyes wide, eager to discuss scandal. "So the Arnolds are so afraid of gossip, they didn't call the police for weeks," Lottie whispered. "Six weeks!"

The trolley stopped and started. It was a long, slow ride.

"And?"

"The police came to question the Winthrop brothers," Lottie said, and then, after a pause: "They heard that Mr. Frederick had been spending time with her on Long Island."

"Frederick and Miss Arnold?"

"Yes, *your* Frederick and Miss Arnold," Lottie's head shook up and down. "They attend all the same parties and balls. The la-di-da *Social Register*."

Mimi thought about the pictures in *Vogue* of their fancy balls and how she still secretly longed for their glamorous life. How different her existence would be if she were a Winthrop.

Glancing out the window, she noticed that the midtown streets were wider; automobiles and carriages replaced pushcarts. The people on the streets were more finely dressed, all the women with their corseted silhouettes. The European designers were showing looser, more comfortable clothing—shorter hemlines, too. She was struck by the change of class as the trolley moved toward midtown, and she realized that her world was also changing as she moved farther away from life on Eldridge Street and closer to Millionaire's Row.

Lottie put a hand on her arm, interrupting her thoughts. "You know, when I read about Miss Arnold's disappearance, I remembered Mr. Jonathan talking about a small dinner party he and Alice gave. Miss Arnold was there. So was Mr. Frederick. At the end of the evening, she couldn't find her purse and was quite distressed about it. Mr. Jonathan said she carried on something terrible. A ring that had belonged to her grandmother—gold with a small diamond—was in it. So the ring was missing."

Mimi felt for the ring under her glove.

"It was on my thirty-first birthday; that's how I remembered," Lottie said.

Mimi was struck by the date. A week after Lottie's birthday was the night she went to the Wolcott with Frederick. That was the night he had given her the gold ring with a diamond. The night he had taken her purse and never given it back to her. The night that had changed her life and her world. Mimi considered the timing. It was no coincidence.

"Everyone searched but they couldn't find the ring." Lottie paused for a moment. "Of course, they blamed the servants."

"Are you certain it was that exact date?" Mimi asked. "You know, he took *my* purse. The night he took me to the Wolcott Hotel. It was such a pretty one, too."

"Why would he take your purse?" Lottie frowned. "Anyway, I am absolutely sure of the date. It was *all* Mr. Jonathan and Mr. Thomas talked about at the office—that purse and that gold ring. They forgot all about taking me to lunch for my birthday for the very first time since I began working for them."

The driver clanged the bell at other vehicles, at horse-drawn carriages, and at every intersection.

Lottie smiled snidely. "They decided that Gloria must have *misplaced* her purse. Pfff! Misplaced! Then they agreed to ignore the entire incident." The wheels screeched every time they pulled to a stop. They both held on to the seats in front of them. Lottie nervously grabbed hold of Mimi's arm, as the trolley seemed to lose traction on slippery inclines. "Society has its own rules."

"Did they ever find her purse or the ring?"

"No, and this is just between us. Look me straight in the eye, Mimi. Did Mr. Frederick give that ring to you?"

She hesitated for a moment and then nodded with shame.

"Show it to me."

She removed her glove and held out her hand.

"That man is simply incorrigible. Stole it from one woman to give to another." Lottie took a deep breath. "So the police came to question the brothers." Her expression turned dark. "They asked Mr. Frederick where he was on the day Gloria disappeared. He told them, 'On Long Island. Hunting.' But that was a bald-faced lie!"

"He lied? To the police?"

"Said he barely knew Gloria. Believe me when I say, he knew her *a lot* better than 'barely.' Just his type. Petite and pretty. Quite the glamor girl. She wasn't interested in him. Made fun of him behind his back.

"Well," Lottie continued, "the police had no sooner left the office than the three brothers were arguing again, claiming that Frederick had lied, and him denying it. 'I was hunting,' he insisted. Then Mr. Thomas said—teasing, sort of—'*Bird hunting* in Central Park, you mean.' Then, Mr. Frederick struck Mr. Thomas. In the face! And then stormed out."

Mimi felt light-headed.

"Do you think they will find her?"

Lottie shrugged. "She's always in the headlines. Seen here, there, and nowhere!" She began putting on her gloves and hat. "We're almost at my stop."

"Do you believe Frederick had something to do with her disappearance?" Mimi asked.

"I do." Lottie leaned over and took a look out the window. "*Oy vey,* look at that snow! He's a wicked man with cunning ways. Women disappear. Be glad you are done with him. You take that ring off your finger and let's not discuss it again. Now, give me a hug goodbye and get home safe."

Lottie stood, pulled the stop cord, and carefully made her way to the front of the trolley. When it pulled to a stop, she climbed off. Standing in the snow, her shoulders hunched against the wind, she blew Mimi a kiss and waited for the trolley to move on.

Taking off her glove, Mimi looked at the little gold ring, took it off, and placed it in the change purse in her pocketbook.

1911

1

TRIANGLE FIRE

MARCH 26, 1911

Read all about it. Fire at the Triangle Factory! Read all about it," newsboys were shouting in the street.

When Mimi picked up the candlestick phone and held the receiver to her ear, she could hear Lottie sobbing. "Oy, my God. Did you hear?"

"The fire," Mimi said. "Yes, I heard."

"Did you read the papers? Terrible, terrible."

"Thank God, you convinced Mama to quit the Triangle," Mimi said. "All those young women—dead."

"I've read every newspaper article. The *Times*. The *Herald*. Such a fire! *Oy gevalt!!* Such terrible places, those factories! No one should work like that. *Es iz a farbrekhn.*" She sighed heavily.

"It *was* a crime," Mimi agreed.

"Downtown, it's like everyone knows someone who died," Lottie moaned. "I'm telling you. They shouldn't have ever locked those doors, Mimi. Worried we should steal things! They shouldn't have locked the doors," she repeated again. "I would have gone crazy, the way I feel about being locked in."

"Mama would complain that they kept the windows closed. Even in summer. No matter how hot it was. You worked nine hours, ten hours a day, she said."

"For seven dollars a week."

In her sorrow, it was good to hear Lottie's voice and acknowledge together that they had been part of and shared those experiences in the sweatshops. She thought she could keep it a secret, that it was behind her, but it was and always would be part of her.

"Most of those people were landsmen: friends of Blanck and Harris. They will have to live with that. A friend called to tell me that a woman we both knew, she had seven children—little ones." Lottie sighed. "She was *twenty-one*."

"Oh, no. Seven? May her memory be a blessing."

"Can you hear me, Mimi? I hope we shouldn't get cut off."

"I can hear you," Mimi shouted into the mouthpiece over the crackling sound. "My friend Rosie, I heard she jumped. From the ninth floor."

"I could never jump," Lottie said. "Listen, all this is making me too upset. I'm going to hang up."

"Wait, wait. When will I see you?"

"Soon, *meydeleh*. Those two, Harris and Blanck! The Shirtwaist Kings! They're in *such* trouble, those two," Lottie continued, having forgotten she had said she was hanging up. Mimi was certain Lottie didn't realize she was moaning in short bursts of pain. "Goddamned Russians! They swore . . . they swore that the doors weren't locked. Liars, the two of them!"

"One of my customers said, 'What do you expect? They were Jews.'"

"They said that? To your face? *Goyshe*, right?"

Before she could answer, Mimi heard a click and then a dial tone. She moved the speaker closer to her mouth and shouted into the receiver, "Lottie, are you there? Lottie? Hello?"

2

ESPRESSO AND NIGHT-BLOOMING JASMINE

APRIL

When she peeked through the windows into Lawrence's shop, Mimi saw that he had only one customer. She didn't want to disturb him and was about to move on when he looked up. His face lit up and, with a nod, he beckoned her in. He greeted her at the door with a kiss on each cheek, then stepped back to see what she was wearing and murmured, "Lovely!" It was her tailored cream-colored linen suit with a pencil-slim skirt and ruffles at the cuffs and neck.

"Come in, come in. I'll be just a few minutes. Finishing up with my customer."

Mimi watched from a distance as Lawrence pinned a brooch on the lapel of the young lady's forest-green jacket as if it were a medal of honor, then stepped back, one elbow resting on the other hand, his fingers gracefully placed on his cheek, his head cocked to one side, and admired his placement of the vintage platinum-and-diamond bar pin with its one large, dazzling square-cut emerald. It was precisely what she needed to complete her outfit. He led her to a mirror and said something that his customer seemed to appreciate, then stepped away so she might admire herself. Mimi knew the sale was made. He wrapped the brooch in a box tied with velvet, gallantly led his customer to the door, returned to Mimi, and then heaved a sigh of pleasure. "It was truly made for her!"

"Redheads are meant to wear emeralds."

"Absolutely." Taking out his watch from his vest pocket, he remarked, "It's half past two. Perfect timing."

"Oh, good."

"Come in the back and we'll sit—unless a customer comes," he added seriously. "Then I'll have to tend to business. Espresso?"

"Of course. Tell me, how is your grandfather?"

"I've told you he's slipping into 'humorous senility.' On Sunday night, it was almost dinnertime, and he was nowhere to be found." Lawrence shook his head. "I'd made a dinner for the two of us and called up to him in his study. I searched every room in the cottage for him—even the attic. Recently, he's taken to going up there to search through the trunks. He likes to put on his uniform and is proud that it still fits.

"I searched in the garden, the conservatoire, and all the surrounding woods, calling his name, and finally, just before sunset, I simply gave up and called the police. My poor dinner went uneaten!"

"Did they find him?"

"No. But then"—he raised his arms in wonderment—"the next morning he strolled into the house at ten, red-faced, disheveled, and quite out of breath, complaining that he was unable to find the dogs!" He laughed. "I said, 'Grandfather, you haven't had dogs in almost twenty years. You haven't hunted, much less ridden, for that long, either!' 'Is that right?' he asked. 'I guess I'll be off to bed.' And just like that he left the room and I didn't see him till the following morning. He had, of course, forgotten the entire thing and wanted a full breakfast!" Lawrence shook his head and laughed. "I haven't the slightest idea where he spent the night!"

When his laughter stopped, she saw the sorrow in his expression, which revealed the depth of his distress.

"Enough of my woes," he said. "I was thinking about you last night. Just consider: if you had been able to fit the key into the lock, I might have passed by. We might never have met. You have brought a ray of sunshine and friendship to Madison Avenue. How is school?"

He began his complicated method of making them both espressos while she placed spoons, napkins, and sugar on his little tea table. Then he pulled out the chair for her.

"I feel the same way about you," Mimi said. She had thought often what it would be like without him. He stopped by often just to say hello and chat for a minute or two. "I've received all As," she said with pride. "The Manhattan Trade School for Girls is one of only four vocational schools in the city and the only one that admits female students. Some days I spend four hours in classes," she moaned. "I miss Matthew."

Lawrence took down the porcelain cups and saucers. "It's only for a short time. You have an admirable work ethic."

"Do you think so?" She breathed in the fragrance of the coffee. "Most students spend five hours each day in trade practice: an hour and a half studying non-vocational subjects that could be applied to trade work, such as English, math, and textile design; and thirty minutes a day in hygiene and gymnastics. I've asked if I might skip those two, and Headmistress agreed, since I have some business and need time to spend with Matthew. Fortunately, Miss Meyers is perfect, but I don't want Matthew to forget that I'm his mother."

"I think you'll be fine without hygiene and gymnastics." He poured their coffee.

She stirred two sugars into the strong brew. "My teacher really liked my sketchbook of evening wear."

"I'm not surprised. What classes are you taking?" he asked.

"I take upper-level classes in dressmaking and lingerie. They excused me from making uniforms and aprons, lampshades and candle shades."

"Somehow, Mimi, I cannot imagine you making lampshades." When he smiled at her, something stirred in her chest: a longing. Could a man like Lawrence ever be interested in her?

"Lampshades are like millinery, and I like creating a hat to coordinate with a suit or dress that I design. They have classes in which we learn about different sewing machines. I don't enjoy that very much, but it's important." She sipped her coffee. "Headmistress wants me to study art history and literature."

"I agree. Which classes will you skip?"

"Perforating and stamping, photography, and slide retouching. I wanted to skip mathematics but Lottie insists that it's necessary."

"Couldn't run my business without math," Lawrence said. "Understanding business is essential to executive ability, male or female."

"You should join the suffragettes!"

"I believe in the cause." He stood and cleared the table.

She admired his long legs and athletic body.

"I'm so fortunate. Most of my classmates are looking for jobs."

"Immigrants eager to leave the tenements, I suppose. Perhaps one day you will hire them."

She searched his face for any expression of derision or judgment, certain he had recognized her, pleased that he looked sympathetic. "The school is helping the youngest and poorest of my classmates to be self-supporting," she said. "My dressmaking instructor told me today that I have the ability"—she paused and, as she felt color rising to her cheeks, felt concern about saying the rest—"and intelligence to become a fine designer, and if I continue as I'm doing, there are practically no limits! Isn't that something?"

"It doesn't surprise me in the least."

She saw affection in his eyes and wondered if he was shy.

"I'm quite determined to succeed—and I *could* hire the students to help me in my business, couldn't I?"

"Where does your drive come from?" His expression was quite serious.

She didn't want to tell him the truth. Those horrid sweatshops, their appalling conditions, the silent, endless days and nights of factory work, doing what they were told. Pennies for piecework. She couldn't explain how badly she wanted a different life from Mama, who had just wanted to get by, put food on the table, pay the rent.

She yearned to make beautiful garments, hungered to wear fine clothes—of her own making rather than someone else's discarded things. She never wanted to ever pick through barrels and

carts again for salvageable clothing—patch someone else's clothing from which no amount of washing could remove the sweat of
whoever wore it before. Rather, she imagined walking into a fabric
store and making her selection from a variation of fine fabrics in
every color.

"I'll take three yards of the raspberry taffeta and a yard of the
velvet—in the same color, please," she would say. "Oh, yes, and two
yards of that ecru lace." It had been her dream from the first time
she wrapped herself in cheap fabrics that Mama's customers carried up the flight of stairs on Eldridge Street. Packages wrapped in
butcher paper and tied with string. No one knew that she had made
imaginary gowns from Mama's woolen scarf with the blue flowers
and their bedsheet.

Mama, who refused to stand up straight, wore old slippers to
serve her customers, toadied and apologized, and would have sold her
soul for a dime. Mama, who let her customers take advantage of her,
haggle over her prices, and make her repeatedly ask for payment.

Tenement and factory work had beaten Mama down and stolen
her youth and dignity.

Lawrence, like everyone she met, believed that she had come to
the city from Watermill, a small farming town on Long Island. That
had been Lottie's idea.

"You haven't answered my question," he broke through her reverie.

"Sorry, I've had a dream of designing specifically for each customer. I want them to come to me because no one else in New York
City can make what I make for them."

"Tell me what else you're up to?"

"I have a lot of schoolwork, and Matthew needs me when I'm at
home. Fortunately, I have some income to carry me for this year. My
life needs to be in order for me to think creatively."

"I'm available to help, you know. Just ask."

"I do know that."

"There's a party Saturday evening. Clients of mine. Are you free?"

"Absolutely."

He gave her a sly look. "I'll bet you're up to some design mischief that you're not telling me about. Eh?"

"How did you guess?" She grinned mischievously. "My summer collection."

"And? Is that all you're going to say?"

"Well," she paused to consider. "It's airy and pale."

"Sounds ethereal."

"What's *ethereal*?"

"Delicate and fragile. It's how you look but not who you are." There was that delightful and distinctive sparkle in his grin. "You, Mimi Milman, are the best model for your own line. You must always be dressed in your designs."

"You think so? I've been taking your advice. Even when I go to the greengrocer, I wear my finest."

He closed his eyes. "I imagine you drifting down the grand staircase of a French cruise ship. Those dainty feet, your pale skin and hair captured by the light. Every eye is upon you; silk eddying around that willowy figure of yours. Of course, I'm by your side. Our photos would be in all the papers. The fabulous Miriam Milman . . . perhaps *Miriam* is more elegant than *Mimi*?"

"I think I'll stick with *Mee-mee*: it sounds French," she said. "And the effervescent Lawrence Loft." She continued his fantasy. "We do sound like film stars, don't we?"

Yes, she was falling in love with him, imagining, in her quiet moments, what it would be like if he took her in his arms and they kissed. Like something from the picture shows.

"We're seen aboard the SS *Whatever*, en route to Paris . . . " He paused. "On board is Victoria Mary Augusta Louise Olga Pauline Claudine Agnes."

"Oh, Lawrence." She laughed. "How do you remember all the queen's names? You should write for *Vanity Fair*," she teased. In awe of celebrities and persons of title, he always knew what King George V and Mary were doing! Not to impress but rather to enliven his stories, his conversation was always sprinkled with the names of luminaries and royalty.

The chimes on the front door rang musically.

"Alas, business calls. I'll tell you more about the party later. We'll coordinate what we wear."

"I love to browse. Don't mind me, and thanks for the coffee, Lawrence." She stepped through the curtain and meandered back into the front room, where she quickly turned herself into a customer.

Her spirits were lifted. She felt the same calm in the rhythmic orderliness of the shop as in Lawrence. Just as the soft lights were set at the perfect angle to make shiny objects sparkle, Lawrence had the ability to make everyone feel singular and special.

She ran her hand over the polished surface of a walnut tea caddy, its flowers created with inlays of varied woods. An exquisite lock and key suggested the box as the perfect place for keeping love letters or a small diary. Inside was a stack of note papers and envelopes tied with a velvet ribbon.

As she picked up the notes, the ribbon fell away, revealing a silver pen. It was the pen Frederick had given to her the first night they went to dinner. Mimi recognized the delineation of the delicate jasmine flowers and leaves on the silver, certain it was the very same one she had lost when she lost her purse at the Wolcott Hotel. It felt cool in her hand as she opened the cap and held it to her nose. And there it was, that familiar combination of floral and spice. Like the night-blooming jasmine in her garden with cinnamon and orange; Coty's L'Origan. She was that naïve, breathless child again. Words like bird's wings whispered on her neck, the prickle of air against her ears. The touch of lips on the palms of her hands. The rudeness of his tongue. An ember of fire stirred in her for the feeling of flesh against flesh—and then vanished, replaced by a shiver.

The wiser woman slipped the ribbon over her head, adjusted the pen on her chest, where it hung like a dainty pendent. She was surprised at her reflection in the mirror. The pen seemed insignificant for who she was now. How, she wondered, had it come to Lawrence's shop?

3

NEW CLIENTS

Jonathan Winthrop's wife, Alice, referred Gertrude Vanderbilt Whitney, great-granddaughter of Commodore Cornelius Vanderbilt, American shipping and railroad magnate. She was a renowned sculptor and one of the most stylish women in the city, and she immediately became one of Mimi's best customers. Tall and elegantly slender, she was often seen wearing beautifully cut English slacks with tailored silk shirts and long ropes of pearls. Mimi had never seen a woman wear trousers. It was bold and chic. Miss Gertrude paid her twenty dollars for one pair of wool trousers, more than Mimi had previously earned in a week. Pleased with Mimi's fabric ideas, inspired combinations she observed from Lawrence's elegant menswear, Miss Gertrude recognized her understanding of style and began sending her clients.

"I heard Gertrude Vanderbilt recommended you to Amanda Duchamp?" Alice Winthrop remarked as Mimi pinned the hem of one of her new party gowns. "Everyone watches what Amanda is wearing at parties and balls. She is quite avant-garde in her style."

"I've read in the magazines that everyone watches *you*." Alice Winthrop needed to be flattered, Mimi had learned. "Turn, please."

"She's well-read and refined—with the wittiest sense of humor. Educated in Florence and Paris. *Au courant*—and *always* shopping. She will be an excellent client for you, my dear."

"I appreciate every referral," Mimi said, thrilled to have a debutante as a customer.

"I introduced Amanda to Thomas, and he's *madly* in love with her! Don't tell anyone I said this, but he's just a bit old for her," she gossiped. "But you know, men love young women."

"He's a year younger than your husband, isn't he? Turn." Mimi asked as she measured the hem from the floor.

"Yes. Jon is sixty-one. As we all know, a man of fifty or eighty, for that matter, has his choice—if he has the money and power. The Winthrop men have that. I am so fortunate."

"Yes, you are, Mrs. Winthrop."

Alice Winthrop interrupted Mimi's thoughts. "Men of power enjoy seducing young women."

What was the edge she heard and felt in those words? An insinuation? Was she speaking of Amanda Duchamp or did Mimi just imagine that she was speaking of Frederick and her?

"Tom adores Amanda!" Mrs. Winthrop said.

Mimi experienced a twinge of jealousy. For a brief, childish moment, she had believed Frederick adored *her*. What must it be like to be adored? Had her father *adored* her mother? Why had he married her, only to abandon her after two weeks? Had he ever looked for her? *Hard-hearted*, Lottie always said about Mama. Was it any wonder? Mimi was determined that she would keep her heart open. Find joy in life.

"And, thank God, she's *quite* unlike Tom's first wife."

"He had another? What was she like?"

"Yes. *Poor* little Sarah Collingsworth-Winthrop," she said with great drama. "*So* sickly. That was years ago. Before you were even *born*, no doubt! She died within a year of their marriage."

Mrs. Winthrop had this way of emphasizing words like so many of Mimi's other uptown customers. When Mimi began speaking that way, Lottie said, "Stop that immediately. That does *not* suit you, Mimi. Know your place. You provide a service. Don't take on airs."

"How did she die?" Mimi asked. "Turn, please."

Mrs. Winthrop sighed and turned again. "She *always* complained about headaches and stomach problems. Peevish. I was against their marriage from the moment Tom introduced her," she said with condescension. "And poor Tom. She made him keep his darling Dora in the basement. And he *loved* Dora."

"He kept his wife in the basement?"

"No, no, silly! Sarah was his wife. Dora was his dog, and the sweetest fox terrier. He'd always kept wire fox terriers—since he was a boy. Then she died suddenly."

"Sarah died suddenly?" Mimi asked.

"No, Dora died quite suddenly. Sarah died quite slowly! Cook was certain that someone poisoned the poor thing."

"Poisoned the dog or Sarah?" She was quite confused.

"Both, probably! Anyway, the only person who was willing to keep poor Sarah company in her darkened boudoir was my brother-in-law Frederick. Made for each other, those two. Sarah and Frederick, I mean," she whispered. "Frederick was actually holding her hand when she passed. At home with her—alone. Women, dogs, cats, and birds are either dying or disappearing around that horrible young man. Oh, my dear Mrs. Milman. You've suddenly gone quite ashen. Are you all right? I don't suppose you've met Frederick? Such a dreadful person."

"I need some water. Excuse me for a moment." Shaken, she went into the kitchen and took several deep breaths. The stories about Frederick—particularly from his own family—were, to say the least, unsettling. Alice Winthrop seemed to insinuate that Frederick had poisoned Thomas Winthrop's wife, and what did she mean by *women . . . are either dying or disappearing*?

"Amanda has brought laughter back into my brother-in-law's life," she said, when Mimi returned to the workroom.

"How wonderful for him." She paused, leaned back to look at the gown's length. "It's quite lovely and modern. Coral becomes you. Brings out your lovely coloring. I think that should do it for today."

Alice Winthrop smiled, and turned this way and that, admiring her reflection. "Yes, I do like this color. You have a good eye. It's wonderful to wear a gown without a corset, in which I can actually breathe. Why did we ever wear them?"

She stepped off the dressmaker's stand and waited for Mimi to help her out of the gown. "Standing for fittings is absolutely exhausting. Jon and I are meeting Amanda and Tom for drinks at the Yale Club. I'll make certain she calls you. I want you to be very successful."

As Alice Winthrop kissed her on both cheeks, she was left wondering why she had asked if she had met Frederick.

4

AMANDA DUCHAMP

Mimi was thrilled when Amanda Duchamp called for an appointment. She quickly became one of Mimi's steadiest customers. Beginning with alterations, she soon depended on Mimi for new designs. Vivacious and enthusiastic, everything delighted her, and she entertained Mimi with constant chatter, describing parties and balls, people and places. Her desire for beautiful clothing knew no boundaries—or time limits—and Mimi realized she would need help in the shop. School exams would begin soon and it was important to her to do well. Besides, anyone could do alterations.

All the talk was about costumes for the Winthrops' masked ball. Mimi offered Amanda Duchamp suggestions and showed her samples of the latest fabrics, which so enchanted the young debutante that she asked that Mimi prepare drawings. Each night, kissing Matthew good night, Mimi went to her workroom to create sketches. For the first time there were no limitations to what she could envision. Headmistress encouraged Mimi, and created a special course schedule for her, recognized her work as part of her studies, and suggested Mimi hire several students.

One afternoon Amanda came to the shop for a fitting and gleefully held out her hand to show Mimi the Tiffany solitaire diamond *engagement* ring that Thomas Winthrop had surprised her with. They were the newest thing among society. The stone in Amanda's ring was enormous, a bold display of wealth and ostentation, Mimi thought, but couldn't help but compare it to the gold ring with its tiny diamond, which lay in the bottom drawer of her bureau, wrapped in an embroidered handkerchief.

"I've had the best idea! I'm going to surprise Tom with a pair of puppies. They will be my engagement gift to him. Wire fox terrier puppies! Two," Amanda confided. "They will make him so happy. He still misses his Dora."

Just as she was about to walk out the door, she stopped, turned to Mimi, and threw her arms around her. "You *are* a treasure, my dear Mimi. I think we will be great friends. Ta-ta."

5

MATTHEW

Mimi looked up to see Matthew peeking through the curtains. He must have heard the chimes as the front door opened, announcing Alice Winthrop's arrival. She had recently been bringing peaches from her Long Island orchard, and his merry dark eyes went straight to the basket on her arm.

"Come here, you beautiful boy." Mrs. Winthrop kneeled and held open her arms for him.

As Miss Meyers held his hand, he toddled precariously towards her. "And, yes, I've brought you a peach."

Matthew's eyes and mouth were open wide with anticipation, Mrs. Winthrop caught him with two hands just before he was about to fall, took his chin in her hand, and then ran fingers through his dark hair. She seemed to examine his face with pleasure.

"He's going to be quite handsome," she said, and then, holding him at arm's length, looked him up and down. "With those long legs, that mass of dark hair, he could easily pass for a Winthrop, couldn't he?"

Inquisitive, she was always prying into Mimi's background. She'd even had the nerve to ask about Matthew's father. Mimi had long ago learned to simply say, "I'd rather not discuss my personal life."

"Mama?" Matthew begged from Alice Winthrop's embrace.

"Be sure to say thank you to Mrs. Winthrop."

"Thank you, Mrs. Winthrop," he said with difficulty, as he took the peach.

"Matthew, I want you to call me *Auntie* Alice."

Mimi was startled.

"Thank you, Auntie Alice."

"No!" The word burst forth like a squall. "Mrs. Winthrop is *not* your aunt."

"I'm so sorry, Mimi." Alice looked genuinely alarmed.

Matthew fell and started crying. Mimi quickly picked him up. To protect him, she realized.

She recovered her composure, and found the breath to tone down her indignation. "I would really prefer he call you Mrs. Winthrop."

Alice Winthrop seemed frozen, her expression one of disquiet. "Excuse me, please." She stood, and quietly stepped into the small dressing room to change into her ball gown.

When she returned and stepped onto the alteration platform, she whispered, "Mimi, I meant no harm. Really. He's just the dearest boy!"

"Yes, he is, isn't he?" Mimi spoke with as much grace as she could muster. Matthew was still holding the peach in two hands, as she placed him atop a wooden stool with a dish towel tucked into the collar of his shirt. His little tongue licked all around his mouth as he bit into the fruit and juice ran down his chin. She kissed his forehead, and then quietly returned to measuring and marking the hem with white chalk. "Turn, please."

6

THE SALON

JUNE

Frederick arrived almost an hour late at Jonathan and Alice's home on Fifth Avenue, handed his coat and top hat to the servant, and then made his way across the mirrored grand hall, carpeted with a Persian carpet. Egyptian sarcophagi filled with tall ferns lined the marble floors, and white orchids on the turns of the double staircase reminded him of a line of Florodora Girls.

He could hear the sound of music and laughter emanating from the music room and would have been willing to wager that roast quail was on the menu.

At the stairway's turn, Louis Comfort Tiffany had designed and created six slender floor-to-ceiling stained glass window panels. Against a background of a starry sky, delicate lavender wisteria and pale green vines were depicted, a special gift from Jonathan to Alice. Frederick hated to admit, even to himself, that they contributed to the celestial atmosphere of the white marble staircase. Frederick had never forgiven Thomas for his refusal to help him design and build Raptor.

It had been years since he'd outsmarted his brothers on that piece of land off Fifth Avenue they had wanted for their school. They still held a grudge and avoided him as often as possible. Alice was always icy. It had come as a complete surprise to receive the invitation to this evening's dinner and salon, and he wondered what they wanted. Why had Alice sent him the invitation?

He stopped in front of an ornate rose mirror to adjust his vest and white tie, pulled his shoulders back, smoothed his pomaded hair, and then found the superior attitude he liked to show off in his expression. He couldn't believe the music emanating from the Bechstein in the music room. It was ragtime, the syncopated Negro music played at the Follies Bergère dinner theater. His brothers, both musicians, usually prided themselves on providing their guests with the finest of chamber music and musicians at their salons.

He opened the doors to the music room to find guests dancing a frenzied one-step, and it was none other than the composer himself, Irving Berlin, at the piano. He counted about a dozen visitors. It was all quite gay. He was immediately offered a glass of champagne and a caviar canapé. There were arrangements of irises and white, apricot, and lavender hyacinths on every available surface. The hyacinths, which were in full bloom, filled the room with their distinctively intoxicating scent.

"Look who's here," announced Jonathan, who was dancing with Alice. He made his way across the room to welcome him. Alice stayed where she was and nodded her greeting with her usual chilly smile. While he hated to admit it, she was beautifully dressed in a flattering silk, high-waist apricot gown, probably a Jeanne Paquin design, with the daring new hemline that revealed the ankles and allowed her to dance.

He recognized Thomas' supercilious fiancée, Amanda Duchamp's, laugh. Sarah, Tom's first wife, momentarily crossed his mind. He almost missed her. The rest of the guests were unfamiliar.

"We've been waiting for you." From his vest pocket, Jonathan took out their father's gold pocket watch, the one that Frederick had coveted. "You're late, and why the hell are you wearing a white tie? My darling wife has grown impatient waiting for you. Our guests are starved."

Tamping down his rage, he turned his gaze to an attractive woman standing by the piano, watching Berlin's hands on the keyboard. She seemed fragile, surrounded by light in her pale turquoise silk gown, which puddled at her tiny feet and over which she wore a sheer, luminescent chiffon duster. The sleeves of the coat, bordered with lace, draped like wings from her narrow shoulders, and Frederick caught glimpses of her delicate arms beneath. Her blond hair hung loose, with pale blue ribbons woven through in Botticelli style. She was framed by the floor-to-ceiling leaded glass windows at the end of the room, beyond which bloomed seasonal wisteria. She made him feel light-headed.

"And who is that little bluebird standing next to the piano?" he asked. She was smiling at something Irving Berlin was saying, and Frederick noticed, even at a distance, the way her expression spoke of her awe of celebrity.

"Louise Langford, a Florodora Girl," he said. "The Castles brought her from the theater. She'll be singing for us after dinner. Leave her alone," he warned. "She's underage. Where is that Dora Dunn you brought back from Paris?"

"Cora Dunn," he corrected. "I took her to Long Island," he said. "She was exhausting."

"*You're* exhausting." Jonathan snickered.

"Bugger off."

"Oh, please. You certainly can do better. Such a cheap, classless showgirl. How dare you bring her to our school?"

Frederick noticed, with some pleasure, how an angry flush rose to his brother's cheeks.

"Keep your lady friends where they belong, Freddy," he whispered. "You disgrace our company and family."

"Aha, Little Brother's arrived!" Thomas shouted in a jolly tone from across the room before he could respond.

He clenched his jaw as Thomas and Alice jauntily danced across the parquet floor to the beat of the ragtime. Alice, who usually scowled at him, was actually laughing, which only accentuated the creases that were beginning to appear on her face.

"Jon, I just love dancing with your wife!" Thomas had picked up a glass of champagne along their way. As always, he'd broken the rules and was wearing a colorful bow tie and matching cummerbund. This evening it was violet to match his boutonnière. He was quite flushed, and Frederick sensed he had already had a lot to drink.

"Once again you've held up dinner, Frederick," Alice chastised. "Our guests are famished."

"You certainly don't want to ruffle Alice's feathers, old man." Thomas poked him with his elbow to accentuate his remark. "Nothing could be worse than"—he paused for effect—"half-cooked quail." He then broke into laughter. Thomas seemed to think it was amusing to tease him with bird puns. When he refused to laugh, his brother said, "You remain absolutely humorless, Frederick."

When he patted his brother's stomach and said, "Santa won't need a pillow at Christmas," he was sure he heard Thomas growl.

"That's enough, boys," Alice said as her expression quickly changed from irritation to a forced smile "We have several honored guests this evening. Irving Berlin and Samuel Coleridge-Taylor."

"Coleridge-Taylor? The Creole from Sierra Leone?" Frederick said with scorn. "A mutt of European and African descent—a bastard—and married to a white woman?"

"Stop that. Behave yourself," Alice warned. She could be as haughty as a Sargent portrait, and he hated when she treated him like a schoolboy.

"Why would you invite me to listen to African music? Negro melodies," Frederick argued.

"Don't be a prig." Jonathan poked his shoulder.

"Irene Castle and her husband, Vernon, are here." Alice pointed. "Irene's sitting at the piano with Irving. You've heard of Vernon and Castle, the dancers? Just back from Paris."

"The Castles have promised to teach us some new steps: the Texas tommy, the foxtrot, and the grizzly bear. Are you up for that?" Jonathan teased.

"You know I don't dance. Since when have you become such liberals?" Frederick snapped, disappointed that one of the two most attractive women in the music room was married. "Entertaining Jews and Negroes."

"Well, my darling wife wants our guests to dance. You, too."

He was about to walk away, to make his way to the young girl across the room, when he felt the steely grip of Alice's hand on his arm.

"Would you excuse us?" she interrupted. Her expression was imperious and disapproving. "I want to speak to Frederick—privately—in the library. It won't take long."

"About what?" Frederick asked. His rage was at a boiling point. His brothers got under his skin, and Alice's unflinching disapproval emanated from her every fiber: her condescending expression, the tone of her rancorous voice, not to mention her sour breath. He wanted to find out what she wanted and then leave as quickly as possible—although the idea of delicate roast quail teased his appetite.

"Jonny, why don't you and Tom see to our guests? Frederick and I won't be long." Her ominous tone got under his skin. She stood on tiptoe to kiss Jonathan before pushing him away.

Taking his arm, smiling as though they were the dearest of relatives, Alice led him across the music room, through the dining room, down the long hall, and into the library, where she pulled the heavy oak double doors closed behind them.

A WARNING

"Sit down."

Alice pointed Frederick to an armchair by the fireplace, then sat across from him. "I want to make this quick. I can't keep our guests waiting. The police came around again this week asking about Gloria Arnold."

"Oh, that again?"

Primly, her hands placidly folded in her lap, she sat unmoving. Her mouth a grim line, her nostrils flared, her expression was hardened into a stern portrait. He imagined that under that exterior her heart was beating furiously.

His left hand was tightened into a tight fist through which blood coursed into every finger, pressing, throbbing as though it had a life of its own—an animal held in its grip. He imagined its breath being squeezed silent.

His right thumb and forefinger moved through the links of his watch chain, and one by one he counted each as Alice chastised and threatened. When he reached his vest pocket, he opened his fingers and held the gold watch—not his father's but one stolen from someone long forgotten. He felt the movement of the minute hand as it moved like the heartbeat of a falcon, and he was reminded of the divine arousal of his first adolescent kill.

"I've had a premonition about you," Alice said. "About you and Miss Arnold."

"One of your 'dreams'? Are you visiting that quack again? Professor What's-her-name? Isotta?" He laughed, but Alice was no fool. "Haven't they found her yet? Today the papers said Miss Arnold was seen in London. She's been seen everywhere, apparently," he said.

"You, young man, need to be very careful. As a matter of fact, Professor Isotta does speak of you, and I believe her. She describes you, describes Gloria. She even spoke of a missing gold ring. How would she know about Gloria's ring? It was just the family at that party."

"Hogwash!" he responded. But his heart raced. Anxiety rose in his chest. He couldn't remember to whom he'd given Gloria's ring. "I've never even met the woman."

Alice pointed her finger at him accusingly. "Women disappear around you, Frederick. I notice. Young girls. People are talking about you, and the police are showing a great deal of interest in our family. You are bringing dishonor to this family. And I won't have it."

He stood, walked toward her. "Stay out of my affairs."

"I will not be threatened."

He knew the power she wielded in the family.

"Your behavior is affecting your brothers' lives. We were at a fundraiser for the new public library and someone whom I will not name whispered that your brothers' names are being discussed for the board, but there's concern that Gloria's father has been telling everyone that the police have questioned you about her—more than once. This could affect your brothers' acceptance."

When he began to walk out of the room, she surprised him by taking hold of his arm.

"Sit down. I'm not finished with what I want to say."

Though she was a foot shorter than he, she stepped closer and pushed him back into the seat. "It's of the ultimate importance to the reputation of the Winthrop School and the corporation that your brothers be on that library board. Do you understand?"

"It's been almost a year."

"Well, the police are still looking for answers."

"As I told Tom and Jon and the police, I was nowhere near Central Park. I was at Raptor."

"Liar!" she said angrily. "I saw you. At the office. The day she disappeared. It was a Thursday. It's on my calendar. I met Jon for lunch. Do not expect me to lie for you. Your brothers may be willing. I'm not."

It amused him that he was not, in fact, lying. He had been in the city, then driven to Raptor!

A servant opened the library doors, announced that dinner would be served, and then quickly closed them.

"I want you to make sure that this Dora . . ."

"Cora."

"Whatever her name is. See to it that she goes back to France where she belongs. There are too many women vanishing in your life. Don't you believe for a moment that I haven't noticed," she cautioned, turned, and then walked out of the room.

"How dare you tell me what to do?" he shouted after her.

Had he been careless? he wondered. Alice was too smart for her own good. He would not be threatened. He poured himself a Scotch and sat at Jon's desk, swallowed the drink down in one mouthful, enjoying the burn as it slid down his throat, and then waited for it to quell his anger. He was torn between wanting to leave and being even more desirous of meeting the Florodora Girl.

Cora had bored him quickly. Though he would never have admitted it, Alice was right: she was vulgar. It was the chase. Watching the self-assured manner turn to distress and then to terror. He was glad to be through with her and certain that no one would ask about her.

He casually opened his brother's desk drawer, looked through the contents, and then, finding a Montblanc Rouge et Noir pen, slipped it into his pocket. Taking things that other people cared about gave him great satisfaction. Admittedly, once he possessed it, it had no meaning. It was the thrill of appropriation that mattered.

Emboldened by the liquor, as he walked through the dining room, he quickly searched the place cards on the table until he found that they had intentionally put him between Coleridge-Taylor and Vernon Castle and far from the ethereal blonde. He quickly changed the cards.

He hated Alice, but she always served a fine meal. Throughout dinner, observing Alice's expression, he could see that she was furious that he had changed the seating arrangement, but as Frederick knew, would never make a fuss. It just wasn't done. The dinner was delicious: oysters with mignonette sauce, smooth cream of mushroom and lobster broth, redolent of saffron, and generous with lobster. The roasted quail, surrounded by figs and potatoes, was divine.

He knew just how to charm showgirls like Louise Langford: he looked directly into her eyes, feigning that sincere interest in her ideas, tastes, and passions, listening intently to her inane answers to questions he asked, and always nodding his approval. She had little to engage him and yet he wanted her. He was enchanted by her dimples when she laughed, and told her so.

He was aware that Alice never took her eyes off of him throughout supper, and when Jon stood and lifted his champagne glass and made a toast to their honored guests, she looked at him with that steely expression, revealing just how much she despised him. He returned her gaze without blinking an eye while secretly worried that she would, as she had insinuated, reveal to the police that he was in the city that particular Thursday when Gloria disappeared.

He made certain that Louise Langford knew that he was an officer of the Winthrop Corporation and heavily invested in real estate both in New York and Europe.

At one point, he leaned toward her and mentioned the effect her seductive powdery L'Heure Bleue fragrance had upon his senses. When he suggested that she should always wear sapphires, which would enhance her ivory skin, he noticed the hungry sparkle in her blue eyes.

After chocolate meringues and coffee, he stood, helped her out of her chair, and then took her delicate hand in his. "I will say good night, Miss Langford. The last thing I want is to listen to Coleridge-Taylor's music after that fine quail and your company."

"Oh, too bad," she purred. "I'm gonna sing with Mr. Berlin."

"So sorry, my dear. Perhaps you'll sing for me privately some-time. May I say once again that I have been completely captivated by your dimples?"

She cocked her head and smiled as if for a camera. "I got them from my mother." She opened her mother-of-pearl case and handed him a card upon which her name was printed in a flourished Edward-ian script along with her telephone number. He held it to his nose. It was scented with her perfume. "Call me sometime."

"Very soon, Miss Langford."

The guests were moving into the Music Room. Brandy would be served, and Coleridge-Taylor would be performing, and Frederick was able to casually slip out the door unnoticed.

What, he asked himself, could he do about Alice?

1913

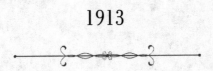

1

RECTOR'S

Frederick had arrived early at Rector's, on Times Square. They were celebrating the reopening of the new Grand Central Terminal. There had been a catastrophic train collision in 1902 that had killed seventeen and injured thirty-eight, and as a result, steam locomotives were banned. Within months the original Grand Central Depot, which had been built in 1871 by Cornelius Vanderbilt, had been demolished. A Beaux Arts building, the new terminal was elegant, majestic, and functional, and began service at one minute past midnight on the second of February with the promise to be the heart of the city.

Rector's was close enough to the station that fresh fish, oysters, and live lobster could be delivered daily. The restaurant quickly became known as a "lobster palace." Its spectacular interior was a mirrored paradise of green and gold, with tall potted palms everywhere. A thousand people flocked through the doors every day and night despite the pricey two-dollar dinner.

Charlie Rector employed a staff of 165, many lured from Delmonico's. They worked long hours starting at 10:00 a.m. with three hours off in the afternoon and then worked until 3:00 a.m., at salaries of twenty-five dollars a week. But despite the low pay, the staff wanted to be there.

Noisy and ostentatious, there was no grander place to make an entrance—to see and be seen. Actresses paused at the door, waiting for applause; showgirls arrived on the arms of older patrons, each hoping for a diamond trinket from the jewelry store next door, which stayed opened late into the night for just that purpose. Frederick loved Rector's—the later, the better.

Florenz Ziegfeld had invited him to a special after-theater party. How could he refuse? The showman, always in need of investors. liked introducing wealthy men like him to the young and willing dancers from Ziegfeld's Follies, the Florodora Girls, and Tiller Girls, who wanted to meet men of affluence.

"Here he comes!" someone shouted as the band played "If a Table at Rector's Could Talk," one of the best songs from the *Ziegfeld Follies of 1913*, playing at the New Amsterdam Theater. Glasses were raised in a toast. The room broke into raucous applause.

Every eye in Rector's turned toward the entrance to watch "Flo" Ziegfeld in evening clothes and with a startling young Follies girl on his arm, flamboyantly dressed in red ostrich feathers step through the city's first revolving door. They made their way across the crowded restaurant, waving and blowing kisses, while everyone clapped and stamped their feet. Glasses were raised in a toast.

"Enjoy the show, Frederick?" Flo asked, slapping him on the back. "May I introduce Miss Louise Langford!"

He immediately remembered her from the salon at Jonathan and Alice's.

"Miss Langford and I have met."

"Have we?" she asked, busily looking around the room.

Before they could sit down; more applause and foot stomping filled the room. Diamond Jim Brady and Lillian Russell had entered. Brady turned, went back out the revolving door, and then returned with two dark-haired beauties. The room exploded with applause. Brady's larger-than-life laughter could be heard above the din as he greeted everyone.

Frederick quietly asked Ziegfeld, "And who are those two gypsies?"

"The Dolly Sisters! This is going to be quite a party tonight! Don't be greedy, my friend," Florenz whispered. "I brought Louise for you."

"You and I met at the home of my brother, Jonathan Winthrop."

"Jonathan Winthrop, the portrait painter? He's your brother?" Her expression brightened.

"Yes," he hated admitting.

"I attend so many parties. Oh, yes, Irving Berlin was there. You left early."

"Did I?" He feigned surprise. The red ostrich feathers moved with every breath. "You know, Miss Langford—may I call you Louise?—you remind me of a cardinal in those feathers."

She lifted her eyebrow in amusement. "So I remind you of a bird?"

"Did you know that it's good luck to see one, and dreaming about one means that nothing can hold you back?"

"Is that right? Aren't you in real estate, Mr. Winthrop?"

"Frederick, please." Feathers on her sleeve brushed against his hand, reminding him of the intoxicating flutter of capture.

"Were you at the theater this evening, Freddy?"

"Was that you in the pink feathers?" he asked mischievously.

"We were *all* in pink feathers!" Her tone condescending, she batted her false eyelashes and her lips formed a red rosebud as she said his name.

"How could I miss *you*?" He took her chin in one hand, kissed her painted bow lips as he slipped his hand around her back, stirred by the velvet fabric and the satin of her bare skin.

Diamond Jim kept turning to look at Louise, much to Lillian Russell's annoyance.

"We seem to have a bevy of beauties with us tonight," Frederick said, with an indecorous wink and nod at the Dolly Sisters. He imagined the trip to Raptor, could almost hear the rustle of chiffon and silk, the feel of feathers, lace, and fur, as well as the scent of the varied fragrances of four women. He lifted his glass in the air. "To beautiful women! A toast."

They began with fresh oysters, lobster tails, and Newburg, shipped that morning from Montauk. There were boneless prime rib eye steaks, sweetbreads Toulouse, and grouse. Diamond Jim wanted it all. Charlie Rector saw to it that champagne and the finest wines flowed.

"Your appetite is pure theater, Jim," Frederick mentioned good-naturedly.

"I adore men with huge appetites," purred Louise. "They—"

"Well, that's *my* Jimmy!" Lillian Russell interrupted Louise, placing her arm through Diamond Jim's. "Jimmy and I once had a bet that if I could eat as much as he, match him course for course, he'd give me one hundred dollars. If either of us failed to clean our plate, that round was lost." Then, running her hands over her big breasts and down the sides of her voluptuous body, she said, "You better believe I collected that hundred dollars. You don't look like *you* have much of an appetite." Everyone at the table laughed.

Frederick understood that Lillian enjoyed behaving crudely in front of Louise. While still a beautiful woman at fifty-three, Brady's buxom companion, with her upswept Gibson Girl hair, its waves and puffs, braids and ringlets, looked old-fashioned next to Louise, but she was a fierce competitor.

"Still like to take you to Long Island for the weekend," he whispered to Louise. It was close to 3:00 a.m. Despite the hour, the room was filled with laughter, clinking glasses, and music.

"Long Island? Really?" Taking her compact from her purse, she primped her hair and with her pinkie finger placed rouge on her lips. "Sweetie pie, I have rehearsal in the morning and a matinee at two."

"I'd bet you don't need much rehearsing or sleep. Show me what you have in there." When he reached for her purse, she slapped his hand away. "Naughty boy."

"What would we do without Rector's?" Diamond Jim asked the owner, who was making certain their glasses were always full.

"You'd find another place!" Charlie Rector laughed. "You have to eat, don't you?" Everyone laughed. "In the meantime, how about Baked Alaska?"

"Bring *all* the desserts," Diamond Jim shouted. When the dessert tray arrived, there were cakes, charlotte russe, *baisers de dame*, éclairs, Nesselrode pudding, and brandied cherries.

"We could be there in time for a sunrise swim," Frederick whispered. Dessert never interested him.

"In February?" Louise pulled away from his embrace and yawned. "I must get my beauty sleep, sweetie pie. Rehearsal's at eight." She stood. "Perhaps next time."

"It's late. May I see you home? My car and driver are outside."

She allowed him to help her put on her coat. "I'm going to grab a cab. So nice seeing you again." She kissed him on both cheeks, turned her back in order to lean over and kiss Diamond Jim on the lips, blew a kiss to Lillian Russell, the Dolly Sisters, and Ziegfeld, and then was gone.

His humiliation quickly turned to fury.

2

THE WALLET

Mimi's dinner with Lawrence had been leisurely and they'd had a million things to talk about; the newly opened Grand Central Terminal, the election and what sort of president Wilson would be, their plan to attend the suffragette march for women's right to vote in Washington the following Monday. He surprised her and tucked the train tickets into an edition of Willa Cather's *Oh, Pioneers!*

"The paper says they're expecting thousands."

"Do you think I'll be the only man?"

"Not likely. The Corsino family is driving to Washington. My enlightened clients are coming with their husbands. Alice and Amanda insisted that Jonathan and Thomas attend."

"You'll need a constitutional amendment if women are going to be allowed to vote."

"Alice told me Inez Milholland will be riding a white horse," she said. "And there will be parade floats, bands, and mounted brigades. She'll be leading them up Pennsylvania Avenue."

"She's very beautiful," Lawrence said, folding his napkin and placing it on the table.

"She's more than beautiful," she replied. "Inez Milholland is a brilliant leader of the women's movement, graduated from Vassar, and earned a law degree at NYU. Wish I had the time to attend college. When we're with your friends, I'm somewhat ashamed."

"Well, don't be. You're perfect just the way you are: well-read, informed, articulate, and a creative genius. Perhaps one day you will decide to return to school. In the meantime, I find you open, enthusiastic, inquisitive, and . . . the best of company."

She smiled but thought, *Company? Is that all I am?*

He stood. "Well, my dear, I must go."

She was taken aback with disappointment. "So soon?" She pouted.

"I must." He bowed gallantly. "The bouillabaisse was exquisite, your company a delight. Is there anything you can't do?"

Make you fall in love with me, she thought as she stood and began clearing the table. This was to have been a special dinner. She'd searched for a bouillabaisse recipe in *Ladies' Home Journal.* The fishmonger, from Marseille, was impressed that she was making the dish: "He will fall in love with you, mademoiselle." Although she hadn't said so aloud, she wondered if Lawrence ever would. It had been almost three years.

He pushed his chair into the table as if saying, *That's that.*

She had wanted to sit close to him in the parlor after dinner. The day had been overcast and chilly, and she had prepared the fireplace in the parlor for a cozy fire after dinner.

"Tomorrow's a very busy day and I need to get an early start," he said. "Besides, I think I've had too much to drink." As he leaned toward her, she was certain he was about to kiss her but instead shook his finger. "Naughty girl."

He brushed her cheek with a kiss, and at the touch of his lips she breathed in his breath and the scent of the fruity Chablis the fishmonger had recommended. "Keep his glass full," he had laughed and winked. And she had.

His eyes had become heavy lidded, his expression dreamy and more relaxed with each glass.

"Were you trying to lead me astray?" he teased. He was close enough that if she'd had the brazen courage, she might almost have leaned closer and kissed him on the lips. Why shouldn't she let him know how she felt if he was too shy to take the initiative? She laughed as cheerfully as she could manage, hoping he hadn't realized what she had been about to do.

"Don't get up. Finish your coffee. I'll show myself out; I know the way. Our train leaves early tomorrow. We can see something of D.C. Then, on Sunday, I thought we might have a leisurely brunch and rest for the march on Monday. We have adjoining rooms. Thank you again for the bouillabaisse. I know what a lot of work it is. I'll cook for you next time." And he was gone, leaving her crestfallen.

She had fallen in love with him: his warmth, kindness, generosity, intellect, and because she could depend upon him. He made her laugh, kept her from doing impulsive things. He was soulful and understood her heart. She loved the depth of his gaze and the way he always took her arm on the street and was always ready with a handkerchief when she wept at the moving picture shows.

He had taught her so much over the past three years—about the city, art, literature, music, and social etiquette. They often spent quiet evenings reading poetry aloud. He invited her to parties, salons, and all the social events to which he was privy. Women would whisper to her, "He's smitten with you, head over heels, you lucky girl!"

She was overwhelmed with feelings that she was dreary and unattractive. He had every opportunity to kiss her—not on the cheeks but on the lips. She had waited for what seemed an eternity. Why, she wondered, was he so shy?

Seated in his chair, she finished what remained of his chocolate cake, running her finger around the edge of the plate, finding bits of frosting, when her bare foot rested on something under the table. He had dropped his wallet. It was too late to run after him. She would stop by and give it to him in the morning.

Rather than leave a mess for Ruth, she washed all the dishes, pots, and pans, put everything away, and then, exhausted, climbed the stairs to her bedroom, eager to get in bed and read for a while. Matthew was staying with Lottie, who had grumbled, "I'm too old to march for anything anymore! My ankles would swell up like a balloon and my old feet would hurt."

Mimi put the wallet on the nightstand, got ready for bed, snuggled under her duvet, and then took up a book Lawrence had recommended, George Bernard Shaw's play *Pygmalion*.

Professor Henry Higgins, a linguistic expert, wagers that he can transform an awkward cockney flower seller into a refined lady simply by polishing her manners and changing the way she speaks. Lawrence had written on the first page, *For my dear Mimi, Your story. Lawrence.* Was she dear? Was she his? She wondered as she began reading.

But by the end of the first act, she felt herself drifting toward sleep. She closed the book, turned off the light, and then waited to fall asleep but instead found herself tossing and turning. Sleep eluded her.

Finally, turning on the light, she opened the book to act two but the words faded in and out on the page and her eyes burned. She closed the book and picked up Lawrence's leather wallet, ran her fingers over the worn soft tanned skin, turned it over in her hands, struggling over whether to look inside. To trespass on his personal life.

It held twelve dollars, all facing the same direction, in order of numerical value. A driver's license, and a ticket for six shirts to be picked up the next day at the Chinese laundry. Lawrence would need them for their trip.

There was something folded inside one of the wallet's pockets: a photo, perhaps. Carefully, she pulled it from its hiding place, ashamed to be prying yet unable to stop her curiosity. It was in fragile condition, the halves barely holding together.

In the dim light of her room, she ever so carefully unfolded it, watchful that it didn't tear on the creases. Unable to see the faded photo, she held it up to the lamp.

A statuesque young man in white bathing trunks was standing with one leg on a rock with one hand on his hip. It had been taken near a still lake, with a horizon of fir trees in the distance. His blond hair disappeared against the brilliant sunshine of the day, while at the same time his expression, with its wistful and loving gaze as he looked directly into the camera, made Mimi's heart leap in her chest. He couldn't have been more than sixteen or seventeen.

On the back written in pencil, *Forever, Ben, 1909—Lake Mohonk, N.Y.*

3

LOUISE LANGFORD

For the next week, each evening after the show ended, Frederick, dressed in tie and tux in the back seat of his immaculate black Pierce-Arrow, and with two dozen red roses on the seat next to him, waited for Louise. His liveried driver stood at attention, ready to open the door.

The last one to appear, she stopped to sign autographs and chat with admirers at the stage door, while he impatiently drummed his fingers on the tufted leather seats. Finally, she would saunter toward the car, step inside, and, with a halfhearted hello, plop herself next to him like a bad-tempered adolescent.

Each night she demanded, "I want to go here" or "I want to go there." Always to a different club: Delmonico's, the Waldorf-Astoria, Reisenweber's on Columbus Circle, and finally Murray's Roman Gardens, which was her favorite because of its revolving dance floor, its indoor Pompeian Garden, and its vast open court with colonnades and pillars on each side, festooned with vines and floral décor like an open-air garden. She was in awe of the ceiling, which had been created to look like a starry sky with twinkling electric lights, moving clouds, and an artificial moon.

He grew increasingly irate at the way she turned her back to him and flirtatiously chatted with men at adjoining tables, inviting their attentions as though he weren't there—even going so far as to give them her calling card while she was his escort.

She firmly refused his invitations to Raptor and at the end of each evening insisted upon taking a taxi home—alone. He had his driver follow her to see if she was meeting other men.

She was no prettier, her waist no smaller, her breasts no larger, her hips no curvier, than any of the others. In actuality, she was less clever and amusing than most showgirls he had encountered.

She only brightened when others were about. Alone, she pouted and sulked. Nothing interested her other than to be beautiful and admired. Nothing she said interested him. Yet, no one had ever captured his imagination as Louise Langford, and her refusals increased his lust. He couldn't get enough of her. Wanted to possess her. This burning desire kept him awake at night. On those nights when sleep did come, she crowded his dreams.

BUSTANOBY'S

Jacques Bustanoby, whose prices were so high everyone called him "Bust Anybody," welcomed Frederick and Louise to his club one Saturday night in March. There was Latin music playing, and couples danced. Frederick jealously noticed how she edged closer to the café owner. Skin against skin, teasing, tempting—Circe, able by means of her charms and spells to transform men into wolves, lions, and swine. He desired her. He despised her.

He slipped a five-dollar bill into the proprietor's eager hand for a good table.

Bustanoby led Louise, Frederick in tow, to a spot where a potted palm hid them from the rest of the room. "Private enough?" he asked with a wink. "Yet, a view of the dance floor."

"Oooh, the band is playing tango music!" Louise became quite animated. "If only Frederick didn't have two left feet." She couldn't seem to keep her hands off the proprietor. Frederick took hold of her arm.

"You're hurting me."

"You're with me."

She pulled away, looked at her arm, and then said to Bustanoby, "Look what he's done to me."

"May I suggest a cocktail?" Bustanoby held the chair out for her. "Let me make the young lady our Coroner's Cocktail."

"What's a Coroner's Cocktail?" she mewed.

"Mix three chorus girls with as many men and soak in champagne until midnight. Squeeze into an automobile; add a dash of joy and a drunken chauffeur. Shake well and serve at seventy miles an hour. Chaser: coroner's inquest."

This, Frederick noted, was performed like some sort of vaudeville act.

"A cherry or an olive?" Bustanoby asked with swagger, and a wink at Frederick.

She took hold of Bustanoby's arm. "A cherry, of course!"

"I'll mix it for you myself." He gave Frederick a thumb's-up.

As he walked away, Frederick turned angrily and said, "Behave yourself."

"You don't own me, you know."

When their host returned with the drinks, Frederick took one sip and then pushed it across the table. "Strictly for the ladies."

"My apologies, monsieur. Allow me to bring you a bottle of our best French champagne. On the house. Oh, and with your permission, my friend, see that fellow at the bar? He asked if he might dance a tango with . . . Miss Langford?"

The young man at the bar nodded his head. Frederick couldn't help but notice the contrast of elegance and arrogance in the fellow's expression. His features—the chiseled nose, eyes that challenged in their boldness—were almost obscene.

"Absolutely," Louise said, clasping her hands together. Her expression had suddenly come alive: her eyes flashed, and she offered her most enchanting smile.

"While they dance, you and I will drink champagne. Yes?" Bustanoby put his hand on Frederick's shoulder. "And watch . . ."

Curious, Frederick agreed.

The young man sauntered across the checkerboard floor with the carriage of a matador, a primitive fire beneath his olive skin, and his nostrils flared as though he could smell her sex.

His bravado was intimidating. His chemistry stirred and infuriated Frederick. He was both attracted to and envious of the young man's sensuality.

"Unfortunately." Bustanoby patted the fellow on the back. "My young friend doesn't speak English yet. Rudi, meet Frederick and Louise."

Rudi bowed elegantly, held out his hand to Louise, and led her onto the dance floor. He dominated her, and as she leaned into his body and surrendered, Frederick watched while nausea rose in his throat.

"The lad is only eighteen. Just arrived. From Italy. Without a dime," he said, pulling one side of his thick mustache, and with a wink of his eye as the two began to dance. "I pay him ten dollars a week." Bustanoby laughed. "Even the name suits him, eh? Valentino. As you may notice, he has great appeal to women. Warms them up, so to speak. What do you think, my friend? Lewd and immoral, eh?" Bustanoby chuckled as he filled Frederick's glass. "He has this animal magnetism that women are attracted to. And Louise, she's a beauty."

Frederick couldn't take his eyes off the two, how they moved together as one. All eyes were upon them. He nodded his agreement, offered no resistance, when the youth requested, with a simple raising of his thick black eyebrow from the dance floor, permission to dance a second and then a third time with Louise.

His stomach churned, his bones felt brittle, his blood surged in rhythm with the music as they danced by him. Valentino's brutish animal bearing made Frederick feel meaningless and unmanly. He despised this stranger. Blinded by rage, he saw an accipiter, with its fierce concentration, diving with ease through tangled woodlands, eyes focused, and screeching as it approached its prey. The weeping of small animals rang in his ears: he felt the forceful flutter of birds' wings as they tried to escape, reminding him of the urges of his youth.

He had never wanted a woman more. Watching her surrender, he knew nothing would impede their journey to Raptor tonight.

"A Ziegfeld Girl, am I right?" Bustanoby asked, interrupting his preoccupation. "A ripe fruit, eh?"

"I'm getting tired of her."

"No, you're not. You are ravenous." Bustanoby laughed and refilled his glass before Frederick could respond.

When the music stopped, he leaned over and, patting Frederick on his back, whispered, "She is ready, my friend, for the picking."

"I'll take my check now, monsieur."

"On the house. Be sure to come again and bring your friends."

"*Grazie, signore, signorina.*" Valentino bowed courteously and, like a conqueror, flashed a wanton grin. Louise was breathless, flushed, defiance in her expression.

Surprisingly, she sat on Frederick's lap, took his hand, and then placed it on her chest, all the while looking up at Valentino. "I'm burning up," she said, sipped her cocktail too quickly, then offered Frederick the cherry with a provocative smile.

Her skin was damp from the exertion of the tango; her eyes with their vulgar black liner, lids painted in dark smoke gray up to the brow bone, were irresistible in their intensity. Her skin, which had earlier exuded the fragrance he had given her, Pleasure Gardenia—jasmine, vanilla, combined with gardenia petals—now smelled of Valentino's musky sweat.

She took a small round gold compact from her purse, and opened it, and he watched as she looked at herself as though he weren't close enough to hear her breaths. When she parted her lips to put on glossy red lip rouge, he saw the tip of her pink tongue. All pretense and guile.

"Let's go," he demanded, pushing her off his lap.

She pouted. "Wouldn't you like to watch me dance? Just one more?"

"You'd like that, wouldn't you?" Standing, he roughly led her toward the coat check.

"You've hurt my arm, Freddy," Louise whimpered dramatically. She turned her head once more toward the young Italian. Did she think he would rescue her? he wondered.

He helped her into her fox fur. "You're coming with *me* tonight."

She paused. "Buy me something sparkly first?" she purred.

As his car and driver followed, they walked to an all-night jeweler, where he allowed her to select a diamond-and-emerald bracelet. She held out her wrist.

"When we get to Raptor, the bracelet will be yours." He laughed.

When he pulled her roughly toward him by her wrists, then bruised her lips with a kiss, she pulled away, and he watched her tongue run across where he had bitten her lip. For the first time he saw a fierce light in her eyes, a challenging expression on her face.

"Promise?"

As the driver opened the car door, he momentarily caught Frederick's attention with a shadow of a smile. Pleased, he got in, slid over, and then held out his hand to Louise.

A feeling of anticipation rose in his chest. "Give me your purse so you don't lose it." For a moment she resisted, holding the small mesh evening bag, which hung from a gold chain, close to her chest. Then, with a sweet smile of submission, she handed it to him. He opened the clasp, dropped the bracelet in, and then put the purse in his coat's breast pocket.

The long drive to Long Island was always the best part: the dark enclosed space, the scent of gardenias mixed with the automobile's leather interior, the sheen of silk and the feel of fur, the coy way she would behave, and the fumbling amid the constant motion of the road. Touching and being touched while the handsome driver discreetly watched in the rearview mirror, envious of his employer. The heavy breathing and purring of desire. The excruciating struggle of holding back. Wanting—that was what drove him.

They would arrive at Raptor at about 5:00 a.m. Then the game began. He knew just how to lure them into the maze.

They tried to escape him, at first giggling like children, and then, growing more fearful, began calling his name, beseeching him to find them. He knew, by the sound of their voices, the mingling smell of fear and musk, exactly where they were in the maze. They were like frightened, exhausted rabbits.

Louise Langford missed rehearsals on Monday and the days that followed. Flo Ziegfeld received a telegram that she would not be returning. Like many of the chorus girls who went home with millionaires, she was never heard from again.

5

WINTHROP MASKED BALL

On the night of the Winthrop March masked ball, Mimi was certain she could hear the intake of breath from the mob of observers and press surrounding Thomas Winthrop's Beaux Arts mansion on Fifth Avenue when Miss Amanda Duchamp arrived in the open carriage that Mr. Thomas had hired. Mimi had taken the evening off to be sure she had an unobstructed view of the street outside the mansion as the carriages arrived and of the costume she had designed for Miss Duchamp. Fireworks exploded from Central Park, and the air was filled with the flatulent smell of rotten eggs and a pyrotechnic haze.

Mr. Thomas, in khaki and wearing a pith helmet, as President Theodore Roosevelt, the hunter on an African safari, was waiting to help Miss Duchamp from the carriage. He held out his hand for her. On the step, her dainty satin shoe, with a peek of pale blue ankle, preceded her bias-cut pale blue satin gown. Descending onto the pavement, her cape, which Mimi had made entirely of ostrich plumes, cascaded like a waterfall from the carriage onto the street.

Mimi had purchased hundreds of the costly feathers from Russian Jewish dealers on the Lower East Side who were involved in the fashionable and lucrative global feather trade in South Africa, where ostriches were reared and plucked, their feathers sorted, exported, auctioned, wholesaled, and finally sold. She had seen to it that each was dyed to match the French satin fabric of the gown. Miss Duchamp was a vision in robin's-egg blue, pearls, and diamonds.

Her three-foot-high headdress of cascading feathers perched atop her bobbed strawberry blond hair, a halo of wispy tendrils. Her skin was pale and powdered, her lips shocking red. Despite her diamond-and pearl-covered mask, the cheering crowd recognized her and began shouting, "Amanda! Amanda! Amanda!" as she walked toward the entrance to the Winthrop mansion, feathers fluttering in the breezy March evening air.

Miss Duchamp stopped and turned, allowing herself to be photographed. Mimi was thrilled when Amanda Duchamp noticed her waving from the crowd, smiled, and blew her a kiss.

Miss Duchamp and Mr. Thomas disappeared into the mansion, leaving Mimi overwhelmed with emotion she had never experienced before. She wondered what it was like inside. Through the windows she could see brightly lit crystal chandeliers and candelabras. She imagined its hallways and rooms filled with the fragrance of the gardenias Miss Duchamp told her Eleanor Winthrop had chosen as the floral motif.

But here she was, still outside, looking in, still feeling like the girl from Eldridge Street—and she always would be, she supposed.

As she tried to push through the mass of onlookers, guests continued to arrive.

"Who is that?" A woman pointed to an automobile from which stepped a tall guest in sixteenth-century costume that Mimi immediately recognized from Gustave Doré's illustrations for Perrault's fairy tales. His beard was a startling cobalt blue.

"It's Bluebeard!" Mimi exclaimed as the crowd shouted, "Frederick! Frederick! Frederick!"

6

AFTER THE BALL

Several weeks after the Winthrop ball, Mimi was summoned to the Duchamp Madison Avenue mansion, where a maid met her at the servants' entrance and led her through the kitchen, into the center hallway, and up the grand stairway to Amanda Duchamp's sitting room. The elegant staircase cascaded like a fountain of pleated silk. But rather than fabric, it was marble.

She was led through an open set of doors into Miss Duchamp's bedroom, its centerpiece a four-poster bed with a button-tufted velvet headboard, damask draperies at each corner, embroidered pillows, and a quilted satin bedspread. Mimi would have described the room as aglow in femininity with its combination of costly antique velvets.

Reclining languidly on one of two matching upholstered love seats by the fireplace, composed, and exquisitely graceful in a magenta, purple, and gold silk Japanese kimono that shimmered against the understated pale apricot and cream velvets in the room, Miss Duchamp reminded Mimi of a John Singer Sargent portrait she had seen at the Metropolitan Museum of Art.

"Mimi Milman is here, mademoiselle," the maid announced.

"Don't just stand there. Sit down," Miss Duchamp said, as though commanding a dog. She patted the cushion next to her.

Mimi sat upright, her ankles crossed and her hands clasped in her lap.

"My costume was a huge success. I admire your ideas. Sophisticated and modern. Finer than any of the Paris couture."

"Thank you, Miss Duchamp."

She opened a silver box and offered Mimi a cigarette. "I've been watching you. You have an extraordinary and, I believe, untapped imagination—more original than the French. Everyone talked about my costume."

Having refused the cigarette, Mimi admired the elegant way she placed one in a silver holder and then lit it with a crystal lighter. The fragrance was momentarily aromatic. She exhaled the ghostlike smoke that rose, intermingled with the room's dust light, and then vanished.

"Wherever there is a social event taking place in the city—at the opera house, Carnegie Hall, or the Fifth Avenue mansions—I wait outside in the rain and snow," Mimi said with pride. "I keep a sketchpad with me wherever I go." She could feel the heat of color rushing from her neck to her cheeks and was suddenly embarrassed that she had said too much, not known her place. Mama had always warned her of this. Yet she was unable to stop. "I love it. All of it: the colors of fabric, the sounds they make in motion, how they shimmer in the lamplight. I even try to name the perfumes in the air." She was breathless.

Miss Duchamp was laughing.

Mimi was suddenly self-conscious at the effusiveness she found difficult to keep in check when it came to fashion. "Excuse me, Miss Duchamp. I get carried away!"

"No, no, my dear. I'm not laughing at you. You are delightful. I get so tired of my dreary friends. They have so little real passion for life." She reached over and took Mimi's hands in her own, turned one over, and looked at the palm. "Have you ever had your fortune told?"

Mimi pulled her hand away.

Miss Duchamp stood and began pacing the room. "I asked you to come today because I want you to design my wedding gown." She paused, then raised her hands in a gesture of prayer. "Something absolutely splendid." Suddenly she was turning round and round, the fabric of the kimono floating about her. "Like nothing seen in New York—or Paris. I want something *outrageously* different from the traditional white lace bridal gown. And the last thing I want is a veil. I am not in need of a lampshade!"

Mimi wondered if she had heard her correctly. "*Your* wedding gown, Miss Duchamp?"

"You *must* call me Amanda." Her eyes sparkled. As suddenly as she had stood, she plopped on the edge of the love seat, picked up a small pillow, and held it to her chest. "I *had* considered Lucile."

"She made most of the gowns this year for the Vanderbilts and Morgans," Mimi said.

"Boring!" Miss Amanda stood and once again began pacing around the needlepoint rug.

"They're stunning gowns," Mimi said shyly, yet feeling dizzy with excitement.

"I know. You needn't try to convince me. But I think *you* will design something fresh and innovative. I want something *très américain*. Not French. Will you agree?"

"It would be an honor." While she wanted to throw her arms around Miss Amanda, she reminded herself that this was business.

"And your shop on Madison Avenue is practically in the neighborhood, so it will appear I'm visiting for alterations. You do understand everything about my gown must be confidential? Not even my staff can see it. Or the press."

"What about the press, mademoiselle?"

"I want it to be kept a complete secret. I want everyone asking, 'Who will design Amanda Duchamp's wedding gown?' I want everyone talking about it and then I want to shock and surprise everyone."

"Of course, mademoiselle." Mimi thought she would burst with joy even though she didn't understand the secrecy.

"Has anyone ever told you that you are quite pretty?"

"No, mademoiselle." Mimi looked down with embarrassment. Frederick had told her that she was beautiful. She had almost forgotten that Amanda was marrying into Frederick's family.

Just then, Thomas Winthrop burst into the room, strode across the carpet, and, with the proud and broad-chested bearing of a man who charged through life, took Miss Amanda into his arms and lifted her off the ground. He spun her round and round and then kissed her while she seemed to hang in the air like a ballerina. It somehow reminded Mimi of Thomas' brother Jonathan Winthrop when she and Matthew visited his painting studio on Union Square. He would lift Matthew up in the air, the boy shrieking with joy.

There was so much passion between them, it was obvious they were in love. Mimi felt invisible and was reminded once again that she was not much more than a servant. She took her eyes off the couple, gazed down at her hands, and allowed herself to consider that, despite how physically similar Thomas and Frederick were, they were completely different. Thomas Winthrop was filled with a lightness of being.

"Put me down! Put me down!" Miss Amanda screamed. "Thomas, darling, you must behave. This is Mrs. Milman. Mimi. She's my seamstress."

"How do you do, Mrs. Milman? A pleasure to meet you." He bowed slightly and held out his hand. "You must be the young lady I hear so much about."

Clearly, he did not wish to reveal that they were acquainted. Yet she was certain that she saw a flicker of a wink.

"Thank you, sir." She curtsied. "Congratulations on your engagement." She kept her eyes down and stood quietly, remembering her place. Miss Amanda's introduction was a reminder that she must not behave with any familiarity.

"We are discussing my wedding gown," Amanda said, turning to Mimi. "And Mimi has promised not to tell a soul. It must be a complete and total surprise—a magnificent one. *Vogue*, *Women's Wear*, and the *Times* will be hounding me. The European press, too, will want to know who is creating my gown. It must be an impressive surprise. Cross your heart, hope to die!"

Mimi made a cross over her heart.

"Mrs. Milman looks to me as though she is very good at keeping secrets," Thomas said.

"She does, doesn't she?" Miss Amanda said. "We will begin to-morrow at ten."

Mimi bristled. Without asking? Had it even occurred to Miss Amanda that she might have other appointments? "*My* seam-stress . . ." she had said.

"I'm very sorry, mademoiselle, but I have a fitting booked for to-morrow at ten."

"With whom?" she demanded in a tone Mimi had never heard before.

"Amanda!" Mr. Thomas interrupted.

"Would three o'clock be all right?" Mimi asked.

"All right. See you at three." It felt like a battle of wills.

Mimi stood, eager to leave. "I must be going. You will have my undivided attention, and we can discuss your ideas."

"*My* ideas?" Miss Amanda laughed. "It's *your* ideas I want. You convinced me that America must establish its own style without copying and refining French ideas. Well, then!"

She put one arm through Mr. Thomas' and the other through Mimi's; then they all walked through the hallway, down the marble staircase, into the elegant central hall with its black-and-cream marble floor, crystal chandelier, and floral fragrance. Like three friends.

Standing before a centerpiece of roses, peonies, and lilies on a round mahogany table, Mr. Thomas' arm around his bride-to-be, the couple appeared to Mimi to be ideally suited.

"See you tomorrow morning at ten."

"At three," Mimi corrected.

"That's what I said, dear. Three." Miss Amanda kissed her on both cheeks and then called for the butler to see Mimi through the kitchen to the servants' entrance.

SCHRAFFT'S

Mimi and Lottie waited for a table at the crowded Schrafft's restaurant on West Twenty-Third Street, advertised as "the daintiest luncheon spot in all the state." It was one of the new places for ladies to lunch and even hired female staff. From their table by the window, they could "people watch." The city was changing, modernizing: skyscrapers were creating a thrilling cityscape, and there were electric trolleys, making it easy for everyone to get around the city.

Spring was in the air and Mimi was wearing one of her newest creations: pale beige silk with a slightly raised nouveau empire waist, a draped neckline, and a layered skirt, and her straw hat was wide-brimmed and covered with flowers. Lottie was wearing her worsted wool suit with the six-gore skirt. She'd ordered it from the Sears catalogue for thirteen dollars and ninety-five cents plus 20 percent for its larger size—in brown, of course. She wore it in every season. Her hat was the same one she had been wearing for the past five years. She had newer ones but chose not to wear them.

They unbuttoned, gently removed, and folded their new kid gloves and placed them in their purses. Their hands remained in their laps.

"What a lovely day!" Mimi said, peering out the windows at the bustling street.

"We might share a dessert after," Lottie suggested with a sheepish grin as they waited for their overwrought waitress to bring them menus. "That is, if we're still hungry."

"I adore sewing for Amanda Duchamp," Mimi said. "Her figure is perfect. Alice Winthrop, too."

Without looking up, Lottie abruptly asked, "Does Alice Winthrop ask about Matthew?"

Mimi was taken aback by Lottie's question, having had concerns that Lottie might have confided in Jonathan's wife. "She asks a great many questions about my personal life. Why do you ask?"

"I don't know, but she questions me as well." Lottie straightened her place setting. "The one thing the Winthrop brothers don't want is a scandal. And you know how women love to gossip! Alice is too curious." She placed her napkin in her lap and smoothed it.

"Sometimes I think that she suspects something. She's always looking at Matthew as if she's noticing that he looks like a Winthrop. She's definitely suspicious."

"Well, don't give in to her suspicious nature." Lottie waved her finger at Mimi.

"Oh, my. No, Lottie. I agreed that I would never tell a soul."

"Your hair is lovely, Mimi." It was just like Lottie to speak her mind and then change the subject to something more pleasant.

Mimi patted her hair. "Do you like it? The minute I saw it in *La Mode*, I went to the hairdresser—with the magazine—and said, 'Off! Cut it off!' I know it is quite daring, but it's all the rage. I think it's time for you to have a new do. Have you ever cut your hair?"

"Women my age are used to wearing corsets, long dresses, and Edwardian-style hair. I must say that fringe of bangs is quite flirty!" Lottie smoothed her upsweep, gestured as if acknowledging the hopelessness of trying to be what she could not, and then turned her attention toward trying to get the waitress's attention.

"Oh, Lottie, let's cut your hair!"

Lottie paused and then her face lit up. "Should I dare?"

"Yes! I'll copy the photograph I have of Irene Castle. Don't you adore her style and her curly hair? Just like yours! And the bob makes clothes look so much more elegant. Speaking of the Castles, let's get tickets for *The Sunshine Girl*. Before it closes. Irene is wearing shorter skirts, too! Wait till you see."

"I'd consider the hair, but my ankles are too thick for shorter skirts," Lottie said.

Finally, the harried young waitress handed them their menus with an apology for how busy the tearoom was. "Beggin' your pardon, ladies. What'll you be havin'?" she asked with an Irish brogue, and then stood impatiently with her pad and pencil, waiting for them to order. Mimi would have liked longer to decide.

"I'll have the nut bread with cream cheese and pepper jam and a cup of tea with lemon," Lottie said.

"And you, milady?"

"I'll try the tomato rarebit on toast, And coffee, please."

The waitress moved on to the next table.

"'Milady'!" Lottie said, and then whispered, "Doesn't she remind you of little Irish Kathleen McGivern?"

"It's the red hair." Mimi paused to think about those terrible days working in the Triangle Shirtwaist Factory.

"The poor thing," Lottie said wistfully, and then quickly added, "To think it might have been us in that fire." She took a long sip of her tea.

"No sad thoughts today. We're here to enjoy ourselves."

Lottie looked up and nodded agreement.

Mimi paused before continuing. All she could think about lately was Amanda Duchamp. "You know, you were right. I quoted Amanda a higher price on her costume for the Winthrop March masked ball, like you told me, and she never batted an eyelash! She paid me for the changes she made from the approved design. Asking for more money terrifies me: I'm so afraid I'll lose business. You always give me the best advice, Lottie."

"When you're busy and your customers are desperate is just the time to ask for a bit more. Besides, the wealthy show off over who has spent the most," Lottie said. "Not like downtown people, like me, expecting a bargain." They both laughed.

"I have a wonderful secret to share with you. You must promise not to tell a soul."

"What's that?" Her eyes opened quite wide.

"Amanda has asked me to design her wedding gown!" she whispered.

"Her wedding gown!" Lottie clapped her hands in delight and then paused. "Once the news is out, word will spread quickly among your customers. Take my advice. It's time you only do the creative work. Hire the Galicians to do your sewing. They work hard and fast and have no ambition. And they won't steal your customers! But make certain they have a fine hand," she warned.

"What should I charge her? I've never done a wedding gown."

"I'll help you. It's a big ticket! Oy! You gotta ask for payments—a third, a third, a third! You'll have expenses. *Farshtaist?* Understand? Listen to me!"

She took pleasure in seeing Lottie's enjoyment of and expertise in pricing, bargaining, and business. "I'll do whatever you say. I have no head for numbers, like you. But she wants to keep it an absolute secret."

Lottie's expression changed. "Why a secret?" She shrugged. "Well, that's her business, isn't it? I'll go over what you should charge and what to pay the Galicians, so you make a good profit. They can afford it." She clapped her hands together with happiness. "In the fall, you should celebrate."

"I wish I could go to Paris. Take Matthew with me."

"Why not? Wedding gowns are costly, especially a Winthrop wedding gown. And you've put something away every week, right?"

"Thanks to you!"

The waitress arrived with their lunch.

"Oy! What a sandwich: cream cheese and pepper jam. Hoity-toity!" Lottie offered her sandwich to Mimi for a taste. "Give me a taste of your rabbit." Tasting it, she remarked, "This isn't rabbit; it's melted cheese and mustard. *Goyishe!*"

The two friends shared a laugh that the food was for Gentiles.

"*Vogue* had an article about Amanda. She went to Miss Ely's School, four years at Miss Spence's School, where she was said to be 'an especially brilliant pupil.' The article said that she's a competent horsewoman and enjoys yachting. Her maid told me that she's good with drawing-room conversation. Whatever that is!"

"Excellent qualities!" Lottie said with sarcasm as the waitress cleared their plates and gave them the dessert menu. "You must work on your yachting, Mimi! Shall we indulge in dessert?" she asked, then answered her own question: "Absolutely!"

"We'll have the ice cream cake, hot butterscotch sauce with almonds, and two forks, please," Mimi ordered, knowing Lottie's taste in desserts.

When the check came, Lottie insisted on paying, counting the change very carefully, and then, taking out her small notebook and pencil from her pocket, wrote down the amount.

"Let's go to Lord & Taylor's," Mimi said. "See what's new from Paris." They headed toward the Ladies' Mile.

8

FIRST FITTING

May

Amanda Duchamp spun around. "I am going to have the most beautiful wedding in the world!"

"Oh, do be careful. You'll prick yourself with the pins."

They were in Mimi's private workroom, hidden from view of the ten seamstresses she had hired from the Manhattan Trade School for Girls to sew Amanda's trousseau after interviewing her entire senior class. As a test, each had been asked to create a child's dress, which would be donated to the New York Foundling Home. Those chosen were of good disposition and character with fine patternmaking and sewing skills, and pledged to secrecy. They worked eight-hour shifts and Mimi paid them a fair wage.

Amanda stood on the platform in front of the three-way full-length mirror, shifting her weight from one hip to the other in the pinned muslin.

"You need to stand still or everything will be crooked."

"Yes, yes." Amanda was animated. "I read today that in Paris it's all about Paul Poiret and Diaghilev's Ballets Russes. Pantaloons and turbans. Have you seen Nijinsky dance? Oh, of course not!" She chattered like a magpie. She pinched her cheeks for color and then primped her hair.

"Miss Amanda, please, don't move about." Mimi sighed, pinning the side seams more accurately. "Turn."

"You simply *must* go to Paris, Mimi, dear." She tilted her head this way and that. "Do you think everyone will be . . . scandalized?"

"You said you wanted it to be *moderne*. Hems are rising . . . above the ankle . . . turn."

"It has no waistline, no ruffles or lace."

"Frills and flounces are yesterday. Like bustles and corsets."

"You *are* keeping it a secret, aren't you, darling?"

With a mouthful of pins, she nodded.

She came for fittings three times week, and her confidences were of such a personal nature, she led Mimi to believe she had a friend with whom she shared interests, especially fashion.

"You are amazing, my love!" She made a kissing sound. "Wait till you taste the wedding cake. I had a tasting yesterday . . . divine. Oh, dear, I'm so forgetful. I meant to bring a piece for you and Matthew."

Mimi wondered when her invitation would arrive. It would be rude to ask.

"Must have a ciggie!" Amanda jumped off the platform and took a cigarette from her platinum case. "Just wait until everyone finds out that you designed this gown. Everyone will want you." She lit her cigarette and took a deep drag. "I thought of keeping you a secret. All to myself!" Her exhaled smoke filled the space around her. "Oh, look at your sad face. I'm only joking."

The curtain parted and Matthew ran to Mimi's arms. She smoothed the dark curls off his face. "You must stay upstairs with Miss Meyers when I'm working, my sweet." Her heart was moved by his soulful expression. He was an easygoing child. "Run along, sweetheart," she said as Ruth Meyers appeared and led him from the room.

"You *must* be sure to read to him," Amanda declared. "You do read, don't you?"

"Of course I read," Mimi snapped. "Why *ever* would you think I don't? Turn."

"Oh. Now I've upset you. Sometimes I just say the *worst* things. Please say you forgive me? You are my dearest friend."

"Forgiven." What most annoyed her was Amanda's childish voice.

"Be sure to teach him his alphabet," she continued, as though she had never insulted Mimi. "Take him everywhere you go—museums, theater, and the opera—and when you travel," Amanda instructed. "It's important for a young man to be well-rounded, you know, if he is to make anything of himself. Just look at Thomas and Jonathan. Excellent students; spent summers sailing, hiking, riding, and, of course, learning to hunt. And traveling abroad. It's important that Matthew go to the best school. The friends he makes. His future depends on it. Where do you think you'll send him?"

"Hold still," Mimi demanded, unable to keep the annoyance out of her voice. She wanted to poke Amanda with the pin—right into her butt—and see blood.

"It's completely different for girls," Amanda continued her chatter. "My coming-out party was at Sherry's when I was sixteen. It was written up in the *Times*. All the handsomest boys from the best families! Be sure Matthew knows how to dance. Men who can dance are much sought-after. Thomas is an absolutely divine dancer. I have difficulty keeping him to myself at the balls."

Amanda's patter faded as Mimi lost herself in memories of what it had been like working in the factories and living on Eldridge Street—the hardships her mother had borne. None of her clients knew about her past, so why would she expect more from Amanda Duchamp?

"Thomas is brilliant—graduated summa cum laude." Amanda broke through her reverie.

"I don't speak French. Turn."

"That's Latin, silly. Everyone says Thomas is the finest architect in New York." She twisted to see the back of her gown. "I'm crazy about Jonathan, too. Frederick gives me the willies. Alice absolutely abhors him. And your friend Miss Aarons, the bookkeeper. She watches over him like a hawk. Why, I think, given half a chance, she would step on him—like a bug!"

"Why is that?"

"Because he's a thief and," she whispered as if they were not alone, "Thomas told me that if Miss Aarons didn't watch him, he'd steal their inheritance—without blinking an eye."

"Really? He told you that?"

"Thomas, Alice, and Jonathan think he's . . . *evil*."

"Evil?" Mimi was taken aback. Her heart was pounding, eager for information.

"Yes, evil. That's exactly what everyone calls him—at every opportunity, too. Are you all right? You look as though you've seen a ghost!"

"No, no. Just a long day."

"It seems showgirls find him charming. Alice says he makes women appear and disappear—like Harry Houdini." Lowering her voice to a whisper as though someone might overhear, she said, "And then there was Sarah Collingsworth-Winthrop. Thomas' first wife."

"What about her? Turn."

"She died." Then, with dramatic nonchalance, she added, "Arsenic. My maid told me Frederick fed it to her—when he was only sixteen. Sixteen! She heard it from Cook."

She felt woozy. "Did the Winthrops know?"

"Of course." Amanda's wide-eyed expression was reflected in the three mirrors.

"And they did nothing?"

"They probably pretended they didn't know. The family's good at keeping skeletons in the closet!" Amanda observed herself in the three mirrors, pleased with her likeness.

"What does that mean, 'keeping skeletons in the closet'?"

"Oh, Mimi!" She rolled her eyes. "I can't believe you've never heard the expression. 'Skeletons in the closet' are secrets. Now that I've told you a family secret, you're officially a Winthrop." She clapped her hands. "I've always wanted a sister."

"Perhaps I will change the sign above the door?" Mimi laughed. "'Mimi Winthrop's Shop'?"

"I'm exhausted." Amanda whined, and stepped off the platform. "Take this damn thing off of me," she demanded. "And don't prick me." Her superior tone startled Mimi.

9

THE INVITATION

Mimi waited for her wedding invitation, certain that Amanda would hand deliver it. But the Cartier engraved invitation Amanda had described with her name hand penned on the two envelopes never arrived.

She considered asking, "Amanda, dear, have all the wedding invitations been mailed?" She practiced in front of the mirror to make certain her expression was not overly eager. But each day, when Amanda stood on the fitting platform in front of the three panels of reflection, the moment never seemed right.

Amanda never asked if she had received it—if she was coming—or what she would be wearing, and Amanda always wanted to know what Mimi was wearing. People were noticing her clothes. The new *Vanity Fair* had photographed her at the opera with Lawrence and mentioned that she was "a designer to keep one's eye on."

Alice Winthrop never mentioned an invitation, either, when she came for fittings, but Amanda's friends spoke of nothing else while they were having garments fitted and altered.

In late June, Amanda began to complain at every fitting, "You can't imagine how many people have not RSVP'd. We need to order lobsters and Chateaubriands. The sommelier needs to know how many cases of champagne and wine. So rude! I asked Mother if we should follow up. She said one just doesn't do that."

"Oh, you poor dear," Mimi said, furrowing her brows in appropriate concern. "Why, of course. One should let one's hosts know immediately. Yours and Mr. Thomas Winthrop's wedding is the wedding of the year."

"And then the rudest thing happened," Amanda continued. "On Saturday morning I was playing singles with Tom in Southampton, and this woman on the next court—whom I barely know and was playing tennis with Frederick—shouted out, 'Amanda? I haven't received my invite.' Can you imagine? The nerve! I may have met her once or twice. Who does she think she is?" She scowled, shrugged her shoulders, and then, at Mimi's suggestion, turned.

10

THE GOWN

Mimi laid the pattern pieces onto the Chinese silk she had carefully dyed a creamy off-white and then minutely pleated them. Certain that each piece was correctly laid out on the bias before pinning, with a deep breath she picked up her scissors. Cut on the bias, the gown would have fluidity and a more interesting character, hug the small part of Amanda's waist, and skim over her slim hips. The front of the dress was shockingly shorter by three inches to reveal hand-embroidered mesh shoes with pearl-buttoned straps. Amanda's mother was having Cartier prepare six long strands of gold pearls, each with a diamond-and-platinum-clustered clasp.

She loosely sewed the pieces of the gown together with elongated baste stitches, and when she was satisfied that the pieces fit together properly—that each tiny pleat lay flat at its seam—she carefully ran the gown through the Singer and then placed it on Amanda's mannequin, which was set to Amanda's exact measurements and height. As she stood back to appraise its fit, she realized that she had been holding her breath. It was perfect.

Seated on the floor, she carefully weighted the pleats by sewing one of one hundred small gold South Sea pearls at intervals along the slightly ruffled hem. The layered top, cut at an angle, wrapped around the bodice and skirt in a graceful drape.

Mimi had searched for and found the sheerest cream-colored cut velvet for the kimono-style jacket and stained it with the palest washes of lavender, peach, and gold dyes so that it descended from the shoulders, front and back, like mist.

Amanda's hair was bobbed, with tendrils around her cheeks and neck. Mimi sewed a turban from twisted pleated silk and then embroidered it with gold seed pearls and diamonds, then added two snowy egret feathers.

11

FINAL FITTING

A week before the wedding, Amanda's car and driver arrived to bring Mimi to the Duchamp mansion in Southampton for the final fitting.

After greeting Mimi at the door, Amanda almost dragged her inside. "You're finally here. You must see our wedding gifts. Would you like a cold drink?"

"I would. It's been a long, hot drive."

"Bring my dressmaker a lemonade," Amanda told a servant. "Wait till you see all the gifts. There are seventeen candlesnuffers! It's all set up on tables in the music room. Mother's hosting a tea tomorrow to thank everyone who sent presents. They'll be like vultures hovering over our gifts, making all sorts of noises like barn animals." She laughed. "And I will be expected to be the gracious bride, oohing and aahing over all those candlesnuffers. Come, I'll sneak you in for a peek."

A servant opened the double doors. Mimi was speechless. The music room sparkled with white boxes, tissue paper, silk and velvet ribbons. In the garden she could see liveried servants carrying and setting up tables, chairs, umbrellas, and tents. All the roses bloomed.

Amanda gave her a push. "What are you waiting for? A band to play? I'll leave you to look. I've seen it already—as you can imagine." She kissed Mimi on the cheek. "Don't take any of the silver, my dear!" she teased. "It's been counted and listed."

Mimi felt a flash of indignation before smiling in amusement.

There were bowls, platters, embroidered linens, crystal, china, and silver pieces on display in their boxes in case they needed to be returned. A card that stated who had given the gift lay beside each item. She ran her hand along the crisp damask tablecloth as she walked the length of the room. A manservant followed several steps behind her, rearranging anything she picked up. She was nauseated by the overabundance. No one ever brought her the lemonade.

When the fitting was done, Amanda said, "The driver's here for you, my dear." She kissed her on both cheeks. "You may use the front door. See you on Sunday."

Mimi smiled. *Like family,* she thought, pleased. Of course, family didn't need an engraved invitation.

12

REFLECTION

It was a week before she was expected to deliver the gown and bridesmaids' dresses. The seamstresses had left for the night. The sounds of the Singers were silent. The shop was quiet except for the regulator clock on the wall, its soothing pendulum marking time. It was half past two. She had finished her third cup of coffee. Only one light over her worktable was lit. Matthew was upstairs, sleeping peacefully, as was Ruth Meyers.

Since she and Amanda were the same size and coloring, Mimi carefully slipped on the gown and jacket. Amanda's fragrance lingered on the fabric like a D. H. Lawrence poem. Was it L'Origan, she wondered, with its scent of night-blooming jasmine—sensual, rich, and sweet—that encircled her, intoxicating her with its floral intensity?

She walked on tiptoe the length of the workroom to feel the cool silk against her skin, the sway of the skirt, hear the almost indiscernible sound of the pearls at the hemline. She turned, serenely walked as she had seen brides do toward the gilded framed mirrors, then paused to look up and observe herself.

The color balanced and brought radiance to her pale skin, and the sheen and nuance of the pleated fabric created a quiet seductiveness appropriate to her age. She was no longer the fifteen-year-old naïve child who haunted her, kept her fearful and wanting. And in that private instant of seeing herself as if a stranger, she was aware of her own beauty and the marvelousness of this garment that she had created.

A second later, one passage of the clock's pendulum, the noise of a passing automobile broke through her reverie, and she paused to take one final look at herself in the mirror. It was in that one fleeting and unexpected glimpse outside of herself that she realized that she could leave who she had always been—where she had come from—and change how the world saw her. It was all in front of her: success, recognition, and a place in society for her and for Matthew. Not a marriage into a family built by old wealth. Rather, a life based upon her ideas and imagination. She took off the gown and jacket and hung them carefully.

She sat in one of the armchairs with her sketchbook and quickly began drawing a wardrobe of clothing that would allow her acceptance into a new world. There was no turning back. There was a rustle of wings under the velvet cover of the birdcage: Enrico and Tito settling themselves. When she next looked up, it was morning.

13

WEDDING DAY

Darling, I will send a car for you next week. Sunday at six a.m.," Amanda said. Her driver was waiting at the curb. "I want you there before ten. You must make sure I am dressed properly, that everything is perfect. Promise me you won't be late. Must run."

"Of course!"

"Oh, what would I do without you?" Amanda hugged her.

Mimi barely slept. She felt proud of all she had accomplished in terms of the designs, the work quality of the seamstresses, the fair wages she had paid, the planning and organization of the entire production—how smoothly it had all gone—all in a professional and timely fashion. And Amanda could not have been happier.

She arrived at King's Point the following Sunday wearing a costume of her own creation, designed to coordinate with Amanda's gown and those of her bridesmaids. It was a knee-length apricot-colored gauze surcoat, delicately embroidered along its cuffs and hem with cabbage roses and vines in mauve and pearl-gray thread through which one could see a long-sleeved silk sheath in a darker shade of apricot beneath. Her hat was a wide-brimmed pale straw, dyed to match the dress and banded with gauze and velvet cabbage roses. The seamstresses surprised her with a hand-painted coral-colored Japanese-style paper parasol to coordinate with the ensemble.

A manservant appeared when the car pulled up to the front of the mansion and escorted her to the servants' entrance, where he left her standing for quite some time.

"Excuse me. I'm Mimi Milman," she said when he reappeared.

"Follow me, miss," he said as he led her down the stairs to the servants' quarters.

"Pardon me, but I am supposed to help dress the bride and her bridesmaids. Didn't Miss Duchamp leave word?" Caught off guard, she was flustered and unsure of what she should do.

"No, miss. Her lady's maid will be assisting in her preparations."

Surprised at his condescending tone, she demanded, "And who are you?"

"I'm Mr. Franklin-Jones, house steward, miss."

"Well, Mr. Franklin-Jones, I'm certain *Miss* Duchamp wants me upstairs." Her breaths were rapid as indignation rose in her chest. "I'm the designer of her wedding gown, the bridesmaid's gowns—her entire trousseau." In the affront she felt at being treated like a domestic, she had forgotten the promise she had made to Amanda.

"Miss Duchamp left orders that she would like you to join the house staff," he said as two servants pushed by her in the small hallway carrying silver bowls filled with fresh fruits. They were dressed in their black uniforms and starched white aprons.

"The house staff?" she asked. How dare he suggest that she belonged downstairs! Mr. Franklin-Jones led her into the servants' hall and pulled out a chair at the empty long table.

"I think you misunderstood. She needs me with her this morning."

"You may sit here." He stood like a soldier, his voice scornful.

"I prefer to sit by the window." She allowed her voice to match his. A clock chimed eleven o'clock. "Please let her know I'm here. She asked me to arrive before ten."

"I will let *Miss Duchamp* know you are here, miss. Would you like a cup of tea while you wait?" He turned and walked away before she could answer.

She sat on a wooden straight-backed chair by a large window, her thoughts in a spin. It seemed a great deal of time passed before a red-haired girl of about ten, in a uniform intended for someone twelve or more, brought her a cup of watery tea and a dry biscuit, which she set on the side table. She reached out for the young girl's arm.

"Would you please tell Miss Duchamp that Mrs. Milman is waiting and that I've been here since before ten?" She took a few coins from her purse and put them in the girl's hand.

"Oh, no, miss. I'm not allowed upstairs. 'Specially today. I'm only allowed in the kitchen." She laid the coins on the table.

Through the multitude of windowpanes Mimi had a view of a somewhat bleak stone courtyard and the commotion of the day's preparations. Truck after truck pulled into the paved yard, and servants lined up to unload baskets of fresh fruits, flowers, and catered foods. The clock chimed noon. Several spotted terriers barked and got in everyone's way. There was a constant flurry of servants moving busily to and fro, carrying trays, bowls, flower arrangements, stacked linens—all in preparation for the wedding reception at one o'clock. Time passed slowly, and as the sun rose above the courtyard, its heat burned through the windows and merged with the steam and smells emanating from the kitchen.

Mimi felt sick to her stomach, lost and defeated. She gave in and ate the biscuit and washed it down with a swallow of cold tea.

Mr. Franklin-Jones called the staff to gather on the lawn. He waved to Mimi to come along. Mr. and Mrs. Thomas and Amanda Winthrop would be returning from church, he reported. Like soldiers, both upstairs and downstairs staff were led up the stairs and to the front of the mansion, where they formed a semicircle in order of position to wait for the bride and groom. Mimi was uncertain where she belonged, and the butler whispered to her to stand at the end of the line.

The midday sun was scorching, and Mimi stood for what seemed an eternity next to the Irish scullery maid. Drops of perspiration ran down her back. She felt like a common housemaid. When she started to open her parasol, the house steward, mouth agape and eyes wide, shook his finger at her in admonishment. Mimi closed the parasol.

A Rolls-Royce convertible came up the drive, and when it came to a stop, the footman helped Amanda step out of the automobile.

She was radiant. The gown fit perfectly, swaying like a dance with her every step. Photographers swarmed the car. She stopped to pose for the cameras, Thomas by her side, elegant and beaming. The bridesmaids fluttered around the pair like pale peach goddesses in their understated dresses and flouncy hats. Greeted at the front of the house, Amanda and Thomas moved slowly along the line of curtsying and bowing staff, stopping briefly to say thank you to each.

Amanda's gown, its creamy color perfectly suited to her skin, and her kimono jacket were breathtaking. She looked contemporary, unique, and startlingly glamorous—and yet bridal. Mimi was pleased to see that she was not wearing the lace veil she'd added at the last minute, and her eyes filled with tears as the couple finally approached her. Thomas recognized her and smiled.

Mimi did not curtsy but rather nodded her head.

"Mimi, dear," Amanda said. "So glad you could be here." Then, placing her finger on her lips, she whispered, "Remember. Not a word." Then the couple turned and went into the house.

While the wedding party celebrated upstairs, a special lunch was served to the staff in the kitchen.

At the dining table, Mimi listened to the staff discussing the guests.

"I didn't see Frederick Winthrop. Did you?" one of the servants asked.

"Let's not spoil the day mentioning his name," another responded.

"I heard he wasn't invited."

"Miss Amanda's maid said he didn't even send a gift!"

Amanda and Thomas took a few minutes away from their guests to greet and thank the staff. Thomas opened a bottle of French champagne and they toasted the couple. There was a cake—similar to the wedding cake, they were told—baked for staff.

When the coffee was served, Mimi asked Mr. Franklin-Jones to arrange for a car to return her to the city.

The ride was interminable, the driver silent. She sat in a corner of the car and put her tired legs up on the seat.

Know your place. Mama's insistent voice was loudest of all, shouting above all the rest.

But no one has ever created such a wedding dress, she argued silently in her head. She fretted over the creative energy she'd spent; the hours learning to pleat silk and dye velvet; the endless fittings; the putting up with Amanda's childish demands and petulance; the painstaking sewing by her staff; each of one hundred pearls sewn on by her own hands; and the weight of it all on her shoulders—and then barely a word of recognition.

All I got was a passing thank-you, she told Mama's ghost.

You expected more? Mama asked.

When she arrived home, all was quiet, and she fell into bed and a restless sleep.

> Mrs. Amanda Duchamp-Winthrop looked like a Greek goddess. The real thing!
>
> Who, everyone is asking, designed the gown? While we are left guessing, it will not be revealed until after the couple's round-the-world honeymoon.
>
> —*New York Times* on Monday morning

14

PRESS

Everyone wanted to see images of the beautiful couple on their honeymoon. Month after month, magazines featured illustrations by Joseph Christian Leyendecker, George Barbier. It seemed the world was smitten with the beautiful young bride and her handsome architect. The fashion journalists were rhapsodic in their descriptions of the bride's trousseau, her gowns and day dresses, their riding clothes and beachwear. Mimi remained silent. Like her agreement with the Winthrops, her word was her bond.

> The bride's lingerie is made of the finest linen, beautiful hand embroidery, real lace. Every stitch on the pretty garments has been taken by hand.
>
> Her trousseau is made of the most exquisite hand work in various materials; the linen is all of the best cambric, finer than a fine handkerchief. Six of the most beautiful sets are made entirely of linen, Valenciennes lace, and hand-embroidered.
>
> —*Vanity Fair*

And then, to Mimi's surprise, Amanda did keep her promise. Upon the couple's return in November, following their six-month honeymoon, she revealed that Mimi Milman was the designer of her gown and the clothing she had worn throughout her honeymoon. Suddenly, Mimi was being hounded for interviews.

SUCCESS

Mimi graduated first in her class and was no longer doing alterations, instead she was focusing only on designing gowns—and recognized everywhere she went.

With the help of the Corsino brothers, she redesigned 1313 Madison Avenue, creating a stunning design showroom on the second floor. She and Matthew were on the third floor with separate bedrooms and Miss Meyers resided on the top floor.

Lawrence had suggested to Anthony that he change the sign on the shop—that he remove *Alterations* and in its place add the words *Bespoke & Couture* to make it clear to her clientele and anyone passing that she custom made clothing for both men and women from hand-cut patterns and basted muslins, which were unique in terms of style and fit to their owner.

1915

1

AT THE OPERA

The sensual fragrance greeted Mimi as she entered the gardenia-filled lobby of the Metropolitan Opera House, which occupied an entire block between West Thirty-Ninth Street and West Fortieth Street in the Garment District. No matter how often she attended, no matter that she was twenty, successful in her field, and always clothed to perfection for every occasion, she was still reminded of evenings spent standing outside the grand mansions, waiting for the arrival of members of New York's society for parties and balls, her emotions stirred between awe, yearning, and envy. She observed every detail—then and now.

Miss Marjorie Curtis, a graduate of Miss Spence's school and a client who always arrived early, would most likely already be seated in the orchestra seat next to Mimi's. They frequently met at the opera and ballet, providing the companionship that society expected of single women attending events.

Pressed to move through the throng of attendees, Mimi brushed aside the old familiar feelings, reminded that her fashions were written about, photographed, and published internationally. With this realization, her breath swept through her, her chest filled with pride, and her carriage rose to meet her position. Mama had always warned her to remember her place, but that "place" had changed considerably in the past few years since she had moved uptown.

As she paused momentarily inside the concert hall, she noticed the students who were standing at the back of the opera house, librettos in hand. Long gone were the days when she had eagerly stood to see *Madama Butterfly*.

"Good evening, Mrs. Milman. Miss Curtis is already seated." The usher handed her a program and then led her toward her fifth-row orchestra seat on the aisle.

Mimi was aware that all eyes turned toward her. She wore a gown of her own creation, in signature cream silk—simple, slender, and perfectly draped—and outrageous in its originality. She walked down the aisle in considered slow motion, understanding how the fabric moved in waves that caressed her slender hips. She had learned how to enter a room.

When she reached her seat, Mimi's eye was caught momentarily by a dazzle of emerald-green taffeta. Turning toward the boxes, she was startled by the light reflecting off the satin and velvet and by the young woman's pale skin. It was the niece of one of the Morgans, recently introduced to society, a debutante of seventeen. Her gown was Mimi's creation.

When she had her last fitting, the young girl had flung herself into Mimi's arms, crying with theatrics like those of Sarah Bernhardt. "I want to throw myself into the river sometimes."

Ladies' Home Journal had turned down an article the debutante had written: "The Meaning of Roses." It seemed odd to Mimi that she would be expected to give comfort to a wealthy heiress. Not only was she rich but beautiful as well, with no end of suitors and a wardrobe of clothes as elegant as anything in the magazines. How could she want to die? Her life wouldn't end by one rejection. She was educated and received a generous allowance; her life consisted of parties and balls and a new dress or gown for each. She never seemed to take her writing seriously—until it was rejected.

She had even admitted that she knew little about roses and that her family had six gardeners to tend the garden. And there she was in a Diamond Horseshoe box with a tuxedoed gentleman who looked quite handsome. It was rumored that those lower boxes were named after Lady Astor's two-hundred-stone diamond necklace.

Then the young girl's companion turned his head from the shadows toward the light.

Mimi gasped. It was Frederick Winthrop.

Fortunately, preoccupied with each other, they had not seen her.

"Are you all right?" whispered Marjorie.

Mimi quickly covered her mouth. "Just a cough."

"Your gown is divine. I want one just like it."

Mimi smiled. She never made the gowns she wore for any of her clients. "But you look absolutely stunning in amethyst, Marjorie."

"Do I?" Pleased, she smoothed the bodice of her gown. "Isn't Maestro Toscanini attractive?" she whispered. "I heard that Geraldine Farrar told him at a rehearsal that he should follow her lead, since *she* was the star. And he said, 'The stars are all in the heavens, mademoiselle. You are but a plain artist, and you must obey *my* direction.'" She laughed. "Such vanity. They're always battling."

"Two giant egos."

"It's quite a torrid affair. But he's leaving the Met in May." Marjorie fanned herself briefly with her program. "There he is."

The maestro bowed slightly to the audience, then turned toward the orchestra and raised his hand. The lights began to fade. In the darkness, the orchestra began the Puccini overture. Mimi closed her eyes as she always did before performances, taking two deep breaths, waiting for the magic to begin, and relieved to be able to stop smiling.

When she opened her eyes, she was in a Japanese house with its terrace and garden. There were chrysanthemums everywhere onstage. In the background were the painted bay, harbor, and town of Nagasaki.

Geraldine Farrar was a force on stage and screen; her voice, like a child's, rose in such sweetness and naïveté that Mimi wept. Similar to her own experience at fifteen, Cio-Cio San would be betrayed by her first love and find herself with child. She would wait for B. F. Pinkerton as Mimi had waited for Frederick's return. But unlike Mimi she would commit hara-kiri.

It was her favorite opera; its poetic language in the love duets and the dramatic tragedy touched her deeply and personally. But this evening, having so unexpectedly seen Frederick, she could barely concentrate. She felt in a feverish tumult, torn between a desire to flee and curiosity.

At intermission, Mimi excused herself from her companion, who was eager to catch up with a tennis friend in the lobby. Mimi made her way out of the orchestra, through the hall, and up the carpeted staircase, searching for and finding with little difficulty the emerald gown and following, at a distance, the young debutante and her escort to the Founder's Room. Frederick's arm circled her tiny waist and he held her near. Each time he whispered in her ear, she twittered and fanned herself coquettishly. Mimi had found her to have the sense of entitlement rarely absent from the upper class.

She found it amusing how the pair paused in front of a mirror, each gazing at themselves. He reached up to brush an auburn ringlet from her cheek and then took a small box from his tuxedo pocket, which he opened to display its contents. Whatever it was caused the young woman to cry out with pleasure. Mimi watched as she donned each dazzling chandelier of emeralds, then searched his face for approval. Turning her head this way and that, moving in such a way that the jewels captured the light, she smiled up at Frederick with adoring gratitude. Mimi felt just the slightest twinge of jealousy. But then, emeralds diminished her. She preferred pearls.

"I wanted you to have these. They were my mother's," Mimi overheard.

Hadn't he said those same words to her when he gave her the silver pen, the perfume bottle, and Gloria Arnold's ring? He *was* a thief and a liar.

The pair meandered the private room and sipped champagne. Mimi was careful to keep out of their immediate view. She also had to avoid those who might recognize her. At one point, due to the crowded room, she was forced quite close to the pair and was certain Frederick looked directly at her. Did she imagine that he smiled? Nodded his head ever so slightly?

She turned quickly, suddenly fearful that she'd be confronted with this monster.

When the bell rang, Mimi made her way back downstairs toward the hall for the second act. As she walked through the doorway, she felt a gentle tap on her shoulder. "Excuse me, mademoiselle. I believe you dropped these."

Mimi turned to see Frederick offering her gloves. He smiled at her and bowed. His scent was overpowering.

"Have we met?" His expression struck her as lewd.

"I don't believe so," she said with disdain. She did not smile. Accepting her gloves, Mimi nodded her appreciation and then quickly turned and walked away before her eyes gave away her terror. Reaching her seat, unable to breathe, she paused to let others pass.

As Marjorie rambled on about whom she'd seen during the intermission, Mimi collected herself.

It was a relief when the lights went down. Once again she closed her eyes, folded her hands in her lap, breathed in the fusion of fragrances in the hall, and waited for the orchestra to play the melody that foretold the sorrow and tragedy that awaited Cio-Cio San. When she opened her eyes, all that mattered was the red velvet curtains opening on act two.

2

MATTHEW'S EDUCATION

Thomas and Jonathan had just finished their monthly meeting at the Winthrop School. It was close to seven o'clock. Lottie was eager to get home. It had been a long day.

She had her shorthand notes and dictation and would type the minutes and letters in the morning and get them to the post office. She was very proud of the speed at which she could take shorthand notes; 100 words per minute had won her first prize in school. On the steno machine she could type 150 words a minute by creating a series of dots and dashes similar to Morse code, but she preferred shorthand.

"What's Frederick up to, Miss Aarons?" Mr. Jonathan asked. "No good as usual?"

She paused, unsure if she should tell them. "Well, sir, a friend saw him at the opera Saturday night." She decided not to mention Mimi's name. "I'm sorry to tell you. He was with J.P.'s niece." As she closed her stenographer's notebook and placed it on the desk, she noticed the two brothers caught each other's gaze.

"Goddamn him!" Mr. Jonathan bellowed, slamming his palm on the desk. "She's seventeen!" He stood and began pacing the oak-paneled office he and his brother shared.

"Please excuse my brother's unseemly language, Miss Aarons."

"Of course, sir."

Mr. Jonathan was so different, so much more animated than his sober full-length self-portrait that hung on the wall behind his desk.

The painting captured his aristocratic expression, salt-and-pepper hair, and direct gaze as he stood proudly at his easel against a background of dark brown brushstrokes over a mustard base coat. There was the faintest shimmer of his Union Square studio behind him. What was missing, she thought, was his excitement for life.

Rather than holding a paintbrush, his favorite violin bow was in his hand. His beloved violin rested on the worktable among tubes of paint and brushes. He would never have put it there in real life. He had explained to her that it had been made in Cremona, Italy, in the year 1560 by a man named Amati and that it was a rare instrument. It was customary for him to play at the school's Christmas party. He was quite accomplished.

"If Morgan finds out, we're in trouble," Mr. Jonathan said, breaking through her musings. "He better not have taken her to Raptor. What a devil he is!"

Lottie was shocked to hear him say that about his brother, even if it was true. *Mind your business,* she told herself. She found talk of Mr. Frederick and his lady friends disturbing.

"You know, sirs, there's almost no one working at Raptor. This month I only made out checks to Cook and that Italian fella who takes care of the grounds and drives his automobile. Too good-looking for my taste—and a bit rough."

"Isn't there a housemaid?" Mr. Thomas asked. "An Irish girl. Pretty little thing."

"Mr. Frederick said he fired her, sir. But he didn't pay her wages." The brothers looked at each other.

"He doesn't like that I write the checks."

"All the more reason to keep an eye on him, my dear Miss Aarons."

"Well, I should be getting on home, if that's all right with you," she said, eager to get away from the discussion of Frederick.

"When you see Mrs. Milman, ask if she would bring Matthew to my studio next week. Jon and I would like to discuss where we will send that young lad to school."

"Wish it could be here at the Winthrop School," said Mr. Jonathan. "He's such a bright, curious little fellow."

"Can you imagine the gossip?" Mr. Thomas said. "He's only five and looks just like one of the family: those long legs, that mop of black hair. The Winthrop smile. No, no, impossible."

"Alice is always commenting on our resemblance."

"He may look like you, Jon, but he has my charismatic personality!"

Lottie looked across the room at the portrait Mr. Jonathan had painted of his brother in his library. Captured his likeness. He sat with assurance in an eggplant-colored velvet wing chair. His expression was as merry as the man, his features rounded, with the same blue eyes as Mr. Jonathan, their father Mr. Winston—and Matthew, even at five years old.

Mr. Thomas liked to be noticed and was dressed with his customary flair in his portrait in a burgundy velvet jacket, a ruby silk vest, and a ruby, burgundy, and yellow plaid bow tie. Mr. Jonathan had captured all the texture and luxury of the various fabrics and all of his brother's flamboyance. One long, elegant hand rested on his eighteenth-century terrestrial globe while the other patted the head of Dora, his beloved wire fox terrier, who sat by his side.

Mr. Jonathan looked quite uncomfortable. "First thing in the morning, Miss Aarons, find out—discreetly—if J.P.'s niece got home safely." The two brothers stood as she gathered her things and left the office.

"Use discretion, please," Mr. Thomas called out, repeating his brother's concern. "First thing."

3

VISITING JONATHAN WINTHROP

MAY

When Jonathan Winthrop opened the door to his painting studio on Union Square, he seemed to fill the doorway. He was a giant of a man.

"It's my favorite boy!" His face with its expansive waxed mustache broke into a wide and familiar grin. He swept Matthew up onto his broad shoulders and, galloping like a steed, carried the boy from the front hall into his studio and back. Matthew leaned over the top of his head and tugged gently on both ends of the mustache.

"Ouch!" Mr. Jonathan shouted, with dramatic anguish.

"Please, sir, put me down, put me down!" Matthew shouted gleefully.

Mimi loved seeing her boy so happy.

"Only if you agree to be the smartest five-year-old in New York City," Mr. Jonathan demanded. "Promise?"

"That's just not possible, sir."

"Hogwash! Who told you that?" Mr. Jonathan set Matthew onto a chair and patted his head. "Why, you can be whatever you choose, young man. Isn't that right, Mrs. Milman? But whatever you do, you better do it well." Turning to her, he remarked, "I must say, I look forward to his visits. He's such a charming boy. Makes an old man happy. You should be very proud. How have you been, my dear?"

"Very fine, sir."

At the time of the original signing of the Winthrop Agreement,

Mr. Troy had informed Mimi that the brothers would oversee Matthew's education. There would be arranged visits to Jonathan Winthrop's painting studio on Union Square but not to any of the family's Fifth Avenue mansions—ever. While Thomas might be there, their wives were not to know about Matthew or about the agreement. Lottie had repeatedly reminded Mimi not to allow anyone else in the Winthrop family to get close to the boy for fear that they or he might form attachments.

"Making quite a name for yourself, I hear," he said. "Everyone wants your designs. Especially my Alice. She shows me every article about you in the fashion magazines and press and points out your gowns at every event! She's quite fond of you—and Matthew."

"It's what I love to do. Matthew loves the peaches your wife brings from Long Island."

"A cup of tea?" he asked.

"That would be lovely. Would you mind if I sit by the window in your library today and read? It's so peaceful, the light is wonderful, and I enjoy looking out over Union Square. It's quite muggy outside. I think it's going to rain."

"Of course, please do, Mrs. Milman."

"I've had so much to do this month, running back and forth between New York and Philadelphia. Coming out parties!"

"Oh, my!" he said.

"Yes. At the Bellevue-Stratford Hotel in Philadelphia! Someone told me that the young ladies would sooner be arrested by the police than stumble on suitable husbands! They just want to party! And they *all* want gowns. This work keeps me on *my* toes."

"And what are you reading today?" Mr. Jonathan asked.

She lifted the book. "*The Song of the Lark* by Willa Cather."

"Excuse me," Matthew interrupted. "I'm reading *Treasure Island*, the book you gave me, Mr. Jonathan."

"It's important to read."

"I know, sir." His dark eyes were open wide and he shook his head in agreement. "Actually, Mother is reading it with me. But I know most of the words."

"Are you enjoying the story, Matthew?"

Matthew's expression broke into a proud smile. "Oh, yes, sir. I am."

Mimi threw her arms around her son and hugged him. She loved him so. "I'll leave you two." She handed them a basket. "I brought you a picnic lunch."

"Mama baked us gingersnaps, Mr. Jonathan. Two each!"

"Thank you!" Mr. Jonathan said, bowing gallantly.

She gave her boy a kiss on the top of his head. "Remember your good manners."

"Oh, yes, Mother. I *always* do."

"Mrs. Milman, my brother Frederick will be coming by for a sitting at three," he warned.

A chill ran through Mimi. "We will be gone before then, sir."

"Best if you were." He nodded.

KANNAUJ AND THE SCENT OF RAIN

MAY

Mr. Jonathan was looking out his studio window. "It's going to rain, I think. Did you bring a canoe? A gentleman must always carry one."

"But we don't have one, Mr. Jonathan. Besides, my mother could never carry a canoe."

"Why not?"

"Well, sir, it would be too heavy, and I couldn't help her. It wouldn't fit in your automobile or on a trolley, and besides, people would laugh at her."

"No one would ever laugh at your mother. And if they do, you be sure to punch them in the nose!" Mr. Jonathan put up his fists as if to box. Matthew believed that Mr. Jonathan and Mr. Thomas were the most exciting men he had ever known. Although they were brothers, they were different. Mr. Jonathan smelled of turpentine and paint, because he was a painter, while his brother Mr. Thomas smelled like his pipe tobacco and cologne and wore bright colors. He built grand houses.

Mr. Jonathan's studio on Union Square had tall windows, with light to paint by. It was a large space with a stage in the middle of the room where the people he painted stood or sat. His paintings were stacked everywhere—perfect for hide-and-seek.

He breathed in the distinctive smells of the studio, and, when Mr. Jonathan wasn't looking, stuck a finger into a puddle of dried paint on his palette, hoping it wasn't still wet.

Mr. Jonathan chose what was best for his models from all the chairs, tables, pillows, paisley blankets, and velvet throws. Plaster casts of classic sculptures, busts, hands, and feet rested on shelves, tables, and chairs in corners of the room. One of his favorite games was to put a hat from Mr. Jonathan's collection on each head. The one he liked the most was the collapsible top hat. There were picture books everywhere, even in piles on the floor.

"I need to work for a few minutes, Matthew. Can you be patient?"

"He has an angry face."

"That he does, my boy. You are a good judge of character. He's my brother Frederick."

"I thought you had only one brother, Mr. Thomas." He walked up to the painting and looked at the face. "He looks as though he's thinking bad things. Do you think he is, sir?" He stepped back to get a better look, the way he'd seen Mr. Jonathan do.

"What else do you see, Matthew?"

"He doesn't look very happy. Everything in the painting is very dark: the wall, the chair, Mr. Frederick's clothing. I don't think I would like your brother, sir."

"You're absolutely right!" He laughed and shook his head. "I admire your straightforwardness, Matthew. As a matter of fact, I'd much rather be painting you."

"Would you, sir? That would be a nice present for Mother."

"Let me do five more minutes on this damn portrait and then we'll play. How's that?"

"Will I ever get to meet Mr. Frederick?"

"I don't think so." Suddenly the smile just disappeared from Mr. Jonathan's face, and Matthew worried that he had said the wrong thing.

"Did I say something to make you unhappy, sir?" he asked.

"No, no. One day when you are grown, I will paint you." He turned back to his easel.

They sat on the floor, and Matthew made a puppet show with the wood models; people and horses with movable legs, arms, hands, and feet. Even the fingers moved. Perfect puppets for make-believe.

They ate the picnic lunch Mother had brought: cheese sandwiches, apples, and the ginger cookies. The rain beat against the windows.

"A deluge," Mr. Jonathan called it. "If it doesn't stop by five, you may have to paddle my canoe home."

"But, sir, that's too far to paddle?"

"My dear boy, paddling builds muscles and character."

After lunch, they sat on a deep windowsill. Opening the window, Mr. Jonathan closed his eyes and said, "Smell the rain?"

"What does rain smell like?"

"Close your eyes and take a deep breath, Matthew, and I will tell you a story about the fragrance of rain."

No one could tell a story like Mr. Jonathan—and without a book. Matthew closed his eyes, listening to the story and the sound of the rain.

"There is a village named Kannauj," he began. "In that village all the people make perfumes, and in Kannauj they found a way to capture the scent of rain. They steam flower petals over wood fires in giant copper pots to capture fragrances. Even mothers roll incense sticks in the shade while their babies nap."

"Where is Kannauj, sir?"

"Far away in India. It is four hours east of the Taj Mahal, a magnificent white marble palace built by the Mughal emperor Shah Jahan. He built it for his beloved wife, Empress Mumtaz Mahal. The shah and empress had shared a passion for fragrant oils and perfumes—jasmine oils, rose waters, the roots of grasses called vetiver. When she died in 1631 giving birth to their thirteenth child, Shah Jahan vowed he would never again wear perfume. I'll show you a picture of the palace." Mr. Jonathan knew just where to find the book in which there were pictures of the Taj Mahal.

"Mr. Thomas could build a palace like that, couldn't he? Mother says he's an architect."

"Someday you will fall in love, young man, and you can ask my brother to build a Taj for you and your princess."

"Oh, yes," he exclaimed with glee. "Mother will be my princess. I will ask Mr. Thomas to build her a palace. I will call it Taj Mimi!"

"Your mother is very special. She works very hard—for you, young fellow. You must always take good care of her. Be a serious student, a kind person. Make her proud of you, and see that no harm comes to her. That's what I did for mine."

"I shall, I promise. I want to be like you when I grow up, sir."

"Why, thank you. You are a kind person, which makes me happy." Mr. Jonathan patted his hand and put the book aside. "Here in New York City, rain smells of steaming asphalt; in the countryside, of grassy sweetness. Ocean rain smells briny, like clams. In the desert, storms fill the air with creosote and sage. The fragrance depends on the land and what grows there. But nowhere is rain's fragrance as powerful as it is in India. Some say that India's dry soil is the scent of life itself."

"I should really like to go to India someday," Matthew said.

"By ship or plane? Which would you prefer?"

"On a grand ship. So it will take a very long time to get there and back."

"We will see that you get the finest education and the curiosity to travel."

He wanted to tell great stories and know as much about the world as Mr. Jonathan and Mr. Thomas when he grew up.

Mr. Jonathan stood, walked to his desk, opened a drawer, and brought out a box of chocolates. "Oh, I forgot. You don't like chocolate," he teased, and put the box back in the drawer.

"But I do, Mr. Jonathan. I do!"

He laughed, opened the drawer again, and offered him the box to choose a candy. "Oh, that's not you. I get you mixed up with your brother!"

"But I don't have a brother, sir. You have two brothers, Mr. Thomas and Mr. Frederick, the man in the painting, who doesn't look very friendly."

"He isn't, my boy! As a matter of fact, Mr. Frederick is so unfriendly that he doesn't like children. Take a chocolate for each of my brothers." Then he whispered, even though no one was about to hear, "We try not to speak about Mr. Frederick. We keep that curmudgeon a secret."

"I like secrets! What is a curmudgeon, please?" he asked.

"One should always have a dictionary at hand." Mr. Jonathan stood and began searching for one. Finding it, he turned the pages and showed him the word. "There it is: 'curmudgeon: a miser; an ill-tempered person full of stubborn ideas or opinions.' Now, eat your chocolate and let's not speak of my brother again. Promise?" He took out his pocket watch to see the time. "He will be arriving in half an hour, so you and your mother need to be on your way. Come. Jump up on my shoulders. One more ride. To your dear mother."

They took a last gallop about the room and then made their way to the library and Mimi, who closed her book and welcomed him with open arms.

"You have a bright and darling young fellow, Mrs. Milman."

"Thank you."

"Always a delight to be with you, young man." Mr. Jonathan shook his hand with a firm grip. "Quickly, Mrs. Milman. Please take the back stairs. The car will be there. My driver will take you both home. I will see you again soon, my boy. Keep making your mother proud."

"Oh, yes, sir. Always."

"Hurry, Matthew," Mimi said, picked him up, and then carried him down the back stairs.

"I can walk," he protested.

"The car is waiting." She sounded angry.

5

THE LIE

It was just after six, one morning in August, and Mimi's bedroom was still dark when she awakened to sounds coming from Matthew's room. Or was it the cries of whippoorwills or doves?

Mama had told her when a young woman hears her first whippoorwill, if the bird does not call again, she will remain single for one year. If she makes a wish upon hearing the first call and keeps it a secret, she will marry. But if the birdsong continues, she is fated to remain single forever. Mimi quickly made a wish, then slid out of bed, grabbed her robe, and, still barefoot, crossed the hallway to Matthew's room. She had no time for silly superstitions.

"Whoo-whoo," she heard, and released her held breath.

Opening his door slightly, she peeked inside. He was kneeling, his small back toward her, lost in his imagined world. She watched while he moved his toy trains around and around the circular rag rug.

The rising sun was just breaking through the corner of the window, and the breeze fluttered the curtains as in her dreams. It almost blinded Mimi for a moment and then, as it rose higher, spread across the room, catching Matthew in its morning brilliance and filling the room with cheer. How she loved him.

She sat on the floor next to her dear boy and kissed him on the top of his head. He had set up a small world, a combination of railroad and battleship fleet, on the rug and was moving trains, ships, and toy soldiers with complete concentration on a destiny of his imagination, making sounds, giving orders, and telling a story.

"Where is my father?" he asked, out of nowhere Mimi could have imagined. He stopped and turned to look at her, waiting for an answer.

It felt like a lifetime. It was so unexpected. He was only five. Until that moment, he had seemed unaware that he didn't have a father. She was unprepared; she didn't know what to answer. What could she say? She reached out, brushed his dark hair from his forehead. It was inevitable that he would ask. But not this morning. Not today—not so soon.

"At school," he said, "Teacher asked us to tell something special about our father."

"What did you say?"

"I said . . ." He looked down into his hands and played with his fingers before answering. "I said . . . he was a painter. Like Mr. Jonathan. I told a lie, Mama. I didn't want to lie." He began to weep with shame. "But I had to."

He looked so distressed at that moment, she lifted his chin in order to look into his eyes, which searched hers for forgiveness.

"It's all right."

"Where is he?"

She didn't answer. Instead, she reached out and pulled him onto her lap, comforted his little body, rocked him, and kissed away his salty tears.

"I wish Mr. Jonathan was my father. Or Mr. Loft."

"I understand. But he isn't, Matthew. Mr. Jonathan and Lawrence are our friends."

The truth was too ugly, a crushing burden on her heart. Why must she share this sorrow with her innocent child? Not now. Maybe one day. Just not now. Her own shame surrounded her like death. Mama's death, which had accompanied the humiliation of her pregnancy, was forever connected in her being. She had broken Mama's heart as she lay dying. If she were to tell Matthew the truth one day, it would then be his burden. Jonathan Winthrop was larger-than-life and so kind and caring. Was it any wonder that the boy might fantasize that he was his father? And Lawrence, who planned outings—ice-skating, sledding, and snowball fights in winter; sailing, riding, and sports in spring and summer—was a role model. Was it any wonder Matthew saw him as a father figure?

"Is my father on a ship at sea?"

"Yes, he's at sea, Matthew," she lied.

"Maybe one day he will return, knock at the door. Just in time for dinner."

"Maybe he will," she said as he wriggled out of her embrace and went back to his world of make-believe. As if he had never asked.

In the kitchen, waiting for her coffee to percolate, Mimi realized that even if she had not signed the agreement with the Winthrops, she could never reveal the truth to Matthew.

1918

1

THE RIALTO

Mimi was waiting for Lottie at Grand Central Terminal's information kiosk, certain they would be late for the matinee of Cecil B. DeMille's *Old Wives for New* at the Rialto. Looking up at the station's painted ceiling with its starry sky, she was reminded of Szymon Moskowitz, the boy next door on Eldridge Street. She wondered if he'd seen this map of the constellations.

When Lottie finally arrived, Mimi noticed her shirtwaist was stained where she must have spilled her morning tea, and when they embraced, rather than the familiar fragrance of vanilla, which Lottie still considered suitable as perfume, she gave off a sour smell.

"Where's your hat?"

"Oy, I forgot it." Lottie's hair was unkempt.

"And I can see your brassiere!"

Lottie buttoned her shirtwaist as they rushed out of the station toward the Rialto.

There was no time to buy popcorn; they had to climb over people to get seats and then missed the newsreels and cartoons. Every time Lottie coughed, people turned to scowl at them. But all was soon forgotten in the drama on the silver screen.

After the picture show, heading back to the train station, an approaching storm grumbled. Lottie would stay overnight and spend Sunday with Matthew. Bumper-to-bumper traffic of stalled automobiles, buses, and trolleys running east and west jammed Forty-Second Street. A cacophony of impatient honking and clanging and the stench of gasoline exhaust lay heavy in the air like a mucky blanket.

Suddenly the sky turned charcoal gray; lightning split the atmosphere, followed by a thunderous clamor, and then came the downpour as everyone ran for cover. Lottie, equipped with safety pins, hankies, bandages, and breath mints, opened her umbrella.

"Let's make a dash for it," Mimi said.

"Let me catch my breath," Lottie begged.

In the station, heading to the uptown train, Lottie stopped every few steps. People rushed around them as a train arrived. "So we miss one train, we'll catch the next. You want I should drop dead?" Taking her arm, Mimi helped her down the steps, but the doors closed and the train left the station.

"There'll be another." Lottie was breathless. "I'm not sure I liked that moving picture. *Old Wives for New*. Old men lusting after young girls."

"I don't want to discuss the film."

"Why are you so cranky?"

"It's Alice Winthrop. She keeps mentioning that Matthew looks like a Winthrop."

"Well, he does."

"And she keeps saying terrible things about Frederick."

"Listen, Mimi, just do your business."

"But she brings it up. Are you afraid you'll lose your precious job?"

"You're twenty-four. You should know by now not to discuss personal things with customers. Definitely not Alice Winthrop."

"You're always defending them."

"Don't be ridiculous, Mimi. Remember, you have a career to consider. You made an agreement. *Farshtaist?*"

"Yes, I understand," she sulked. Lottie was infuriating.

The platform was crowded, the air muggy. They covered their ears each time a train passed in or out of the dark tunnel, shrill and jarring. Lottie kept coughing.

"That cough of yours is getting worse." There were patches of sweat at Lottie's underarms.

"It's nothing. So, what is Alice Winthrop saying?"

"Gossip. About Frederick. Things *you* keep secret."

"It's no secret. He's not a nice person. Now stop it. Where *is* that train?" Lottie mumbled as she leaned over the edge of the platform to look down the tracks.

Suddenly, Lottie seemed about to fall over. Mimi pulled her back.

"Oy! I got dizzy. All of a sudden. You upset me, Miriam."

"My name is Mimi," she insisted over the screeching brakes of an approaching train. "You're more loyal to the Winthrops than to Matthew and me. You and your damned job."

"*Shoyn genug* already! Stop!" Lottie's face was sweaty, her expression fierce.

The train inched forward on the platform before pulling to a noisy halt. The doors opened and throngs of passengers pushed to get out, and the next thing Mimi felt was Lottie pulling her onto the train with such force that she almost fell.

As the train entered the dark tunnel, Mimi saw her reflection in the window, pushed some straggled hairs into place, and rearranged the angle of her straw boater. Lottie's reflection looked forlorn and crushed.

They sat in silence. Fifty-Ninth Street, Seventy-Second. People got on and off.

Finally, Mimi said, "You work too hard. Why don't you take some days off? Go to Brighton Beach, stay at a nice hotel, walk on the boardwalk, get sun."

"I don't need days off, and I don't like being by myself," Lottie insisted petulantly. "Besides, everywhere you go, there's Spanish flu."

"What's that?"

"Don't you read the newspapers?"

2

THE STORM

When they got off the subway, Mimi sensed the storm that had caught them earlier was brewing again: the damp, earthy smell that preceded a spring rain. There was an ominous silence, not even a bird sound, although she noticed a tribe of low-flying starlings headed toward Central Park. The streets had already dried, but the air was thick and the night felt like more was on its mind as they walked to the house.

Ruth Meyers had prepared a rich mushroom barley soup and baked a seeded rye bread for their dinner, and Matthew greeted them at the door, hungry and eager for their attention.

"Lottie, I know just what route we will take in Central Park tomorrow." He chattered away throughout the dinner, mostly sharing with them his school studies about India, stopping only for Lottie's fits of coughing. Ever since Jonathan Winthrop had told him the story about Kannauj, Matthew had put up a map of India in his room and attached flags showing the route from New York City to the city where they made the perfume that smelled like rain. He filled the awkward space of silence between Lottie and Mimi with an eight-year-old's exuberance about his classwork, unaware of the argument that had begun on their ride home from the moving picture show.

Mimi responded enthusiastically, but her anger at Lottie's resistance to sharing news of Frederick, like a dog with a bone, had settled into a constriction of her jaw.

After dinner, they played the Landlord's Game, the object of the game being to accumulate as much wealth as possible. The player with the most in cash, cards, and houses at the end of the game was the winner or "millionaire." Every card and every house counted for one hundred points to the holder or landlord at the end of the game. Lottie was banker, Mimi held the cards, and Matthew counted the spaces with their markers. After enthusiastically winning with five million dollars, he excused himself and went up to his room to get ready for bed, eager for his trip the next day to the park with Lottie.

They cleared the table, with Lottie's persistent and phlegmy cough breaking the silence. There was a rolling sound of distant thunder.

"Leave the dishes," Mimi finally spoke. "Go to bed. And please take some cough syrup."

"You're still angry, aren't you?"

The lights flickered and then the rain began—not gently but a deluge that bounced off the pavement and beat against the windows. Lightning pierced the darkness.

"You were inexcusably rude to me." The words fed her cough.

"I don't trust you," Mimi responded. "I want to know who are you loyal to: the Winthrops, who pay your salary and invite you to their Long Island cottage, or to me?"

"That's unfair, Mimi, and you know it." Lottie tried to strike a match to light two candles on the kitchen table. Tried again and again.

"Give those to me." Mimi grabbed them from her hand, striking the match and lighting the candles. "It's not unfair at all. I think you tell them about Matthew. About me. I think you report on us. Like a spy."

When the candles were lit, she observed Lottie's expression—her eyes, raw, red-rimmed, and pinched, her mouth a grim line, her chin trembling with rage, one hand pulling at her collar. "How dare you accuse me of being disloyal? You would have none of this without me."

The electricity suddenly went out and the only light in the kitchen came from the candles.

"Move on with your life," Lottie said.

"You should talk." Her rage matched the storm. "You have no life of your own beyond bookkeeping. Your little book filled with numbers—nickels and dimes. Living your life vicariously through those articles you carry in your purse." She was unable to stop herself from lashing out at Lottie. As if part of an operatic scene, thunder, rapidly followed by lightning, filled the silence between them. Mimi put her hand to her mouth to stop the torrent of her vile temper. All she had said—words she could never take back.

"Why are you and Lottie shouting?" It was Matthew, standing in the shadow of the kitchen doorway in his nightshirt and barefoot. His voice caught her by surprise. "Tell them what about me, Mama?"

"Matthew, it's nothing. Go back upstairs, dear." Had he heard? He was eight, surely old enough to understand.

Instead, he ran into her arms. "Why are you angry at Lottie?"

When a lightning strike reverberated through the kitchen window, he tightened his grip on her. "I'm scared, Mama."

"Count, Matthew. See how long before the thunder comes." She held him close as he counted the moments, wishing she could protect him—from his fears, from the inevitable truth. Wishing she had never said what she had to Lottie. "It's nothing—just an argument between friends."

"Sometimes good friends don't agree, Matthew," Lottie said.

"But you're arguing about me," he said.

Mimi looked at Lottie, waiting for her to explain.

Lottie kissed him on his cheek, placed a hand on Mimi's shoulder. "We could never be angry at you. We love you, Matthew. Come, I'll put you to bed."

She could hear Lottie's coughs and sighs, the steps creaking under her feet as she and Matthew climbed the stairs. At the kitchen window, looking out into the darkness—the storm beating down on the peach tree in the garden—she was afraid the awaited fruit might be lost.

3

MORNING

"Wake up, wake up, Mama. Something's wrong with Aunt Lottie. I knocked on her door over and over and she doesn't answer." He was tugging on her arm. She was annoyed to be roused this way and momentarily unwilling to give up the warmth of her duvet for whatever awaited her on this chilly March morning. The crows that had settled on the roof of the building next door were making a terrible commotion.

She sat up and put her arms around him. "Okay, I'm almost awake. Give me a good morning kiss."

"I knocked four times." He kissed her quickly on the cheek while pulling at her arm. She stretched, sat up, and felt around for her slippers by the side of the bed. "Come, let's go see what's keeping that sleepyhead Lottie from waking up."

She slipped out of bed, put on her robe and slippers, then climbed the stairs to the third floor and knocked on the guest room door. Matthew waited at the bottom of the stairs. An early riser, Lottie was usually the first one up, putting up the water for her tea, setting the table for the three of them, and pouring cornflakes in her favorite cranberry-and-white transferware bowl with the English country garden scene and border of leaves and roses.

"Lottie? Would you like me to bring you your breakfast on a tray?" There was no response.

"Lottie?" She knocked a little more assertively and called again.

"Are you all right, Lottie?" When there was no reply, she was suddenly worried.

She opened the door and in the morning light took in the freshly painted room, canary yellow with lilac trim on the windows and doors, and on the night table the bouquet of fresh pale blue, purple, and green hydrangeas she had bought specifically for Lottie's visit. Lottie refused to treat herself to anything she considered excessive, like fresh flowers.

The room was filled with sorrow, as if all the deaths in the city—in the world—had been held captive, waiting for her. Lottie. Friend. Auntie. Confidante. Mother. She lay gracelessly sprawled on that bed, its silk duvet thrown aside, her left leg and arm hanging over the side.

The *Saturday Evening Post* lay open on the floor where it had fallen from her hand.

Mimi closed her eyes to the ugly indignities of death. The enormity of the moment was incomprehensible. She stepped across the threshold with the intention of taking Lottie into her arms when she heard Matthew's footsteps on the stairs and then, remembering the looming danger of disease, quickly closed the door behind her.

"Mama. Is Lottie sick?"

"You didn't open the door, did you?"

"No, Mama. I only knocked and called her name." He looked frightened.

It would have terrified him, she thought, to see Lottie, her eyes and mouth agape, having undoubtedly gasped for her last breaths.

"We need to call an ambulance," she said. "We mustn't go in the room."

"But Lottie's all alone."

"I know."

"Is she dead?" His eyes filled with tears.

She slid to the floor, took him in her arms, and, holding him close to her, rocked back and forth as they wept. Sounds emanated from her chest, laments she didn't recognize as her own.

She was filled with regret for all the ugly things she had said. She could never take those words back, wanted to beat her chest

with her arms, but they were filled with Matthew, who needed her
more. She felt hollow and full of shame.

"What do we do, Mama?"

His voice, his questions, gave her purpose—brought her back to
the moment and what needed to be done. Lottie's death, its proximity,
was frightening him.

"Come, sweetheart." She stood and, still holding Matthew's hand,
went downstairs. He stayed by her side. "Why don't you wake up Tito
and Enrico and feed them, change their water while I call the hospital? And get your book and your mask from school. After you've taken
care of the birds, you can read while we wait. Mt. Sinai Hospital is
on One Hundredth Street, so it shouldn't take them long to get here.
We'll sit together in the front of the shop so we will know when the
ambulance arrives."

She went to the kitchen to make the call.

As she waited, she watched and listened as Matthew ran here
and there to care for the two birds. She was calmed by the familiar
sounds of the canaries awakening as he removed the velvet cover, the
cage door opening, and then the commotion of the two excited yellow
birds hopping back and forth to avoid his hand, yet eager to be fed.
The sounds of seeds and then water being poured into the appropriate trays were comforting, and soon the canaries settled onto their
perch and began their warbling duet as the morning traffic—delivery
trucks, taxis, and automobiles—began to pass by the shop. She took a
deep breath.

Rather than sit in a chair by himself, Matthew squeezed in beside
her, nestled under her arm, and opened *The Swiss Family Robinson*,
and before long he was deeply immersed in the story.

He paused after some time had passed. "You won't die, will you? You
were with Lottie all day yesterday. At the moving pictures."

"I'm feeling fine, really I am. I have no cough, no fever." She put her
lips on his forehead. "Let's check your temperature, why don't we? And
we must wear our masks, even when it's just you and me. All right?"

He nodded and read several more pages.

"What will we do without Lottie?" he asked, as though he could read her mind.

"We'll learn to manage. We will talk about her. Her memory will be a part of us."

When the ambulance arrived, Mimi showed the nurses the way to the guest room, opened the door, and stood in the hallway.

She wanted to remember Lottie always: how it felt to be in her soft encompassing embrace—the comfort that Mama could never find a way to give. Her ability to reassure Mama, Matthew, and her that everything would be good. Supporting their dreams. She remembered how, when she was a child, Lottie had allowed her to brush her waist-length auburn hair, which she chose to hide in an untidy upsweep. Lottie had been a part of all of Mimi's accomplishments, making them joyous moments. She had never stopped loving for a moment. It was Lottie who had believed in her, encouraged her—shown her the way. And she realized that it was Lottie who had determined the provisions of the Winthrop agreement.

If only she had paid closer attention. Lottie had loved and cared more about her than her own mother.

Matthew stayed by her side as the Red Cross nurses, starched and prim and carefully masked, brought Lottie, discreetly covered by a white sheet, down the two flights of stairs on a stretcher.

"May I hold her hand? Kiss her forehead?"

"Oh, no, ma'am," one nurse said, then held her hand up and cautioned, "Stay back, please."

She felt Matthew's hand slip into hers. "Mama," he whispered. "You mustn't. We need to care for each other."

"And keep the boy away," the second nurse said brusquely. "Be sure to keep wearing those masks, the two of you. You know, ma'am, there's to be no funerals, no religious ceremonies."

They gathered all the information they needed, carried Lottie's body to the ambulance, slid her body inside, closed the doors, and then drove off. Out of the corner of her eye, Mimi could see the motion of curtains in the windows of the buildings across Madison Avenue.

It wasn't even nine o'clock and Lottie was gone. It had taken less than ten minutes. There would be no sitting shiva, no celebration of her generous life.

It seemed almost impossible to get out of bed on the days that followed. Miss Meyers was a great help, getting Matthew to school every day. There were still customers to serve, orders to fill, garments to be finished. Mama had taught her that work was a priority. There was no time for self-pity or indulgence. Lottie had taught her that she could do that well. Lottie had been her strength, her support—her friend.

Unaware that Jews do not give flowers at a funeral, Alice Winthrop sent an enormous arrangement of white lilies, suitable to fill a mansion.

"Where will you put them?" Matthew asked. "They are bigger than our house!"

"It was very thoughtful of the Winthrops to remember Lottie," she told him.

In the evening, she went to Lottie's apartment in order to empty her belongings. Left to sort through her possessions and papers, Mimi felt uncomfortable about the intrusion. The drawers of Lottie's dresser were lined with paper, and while they were decorated with sprays of bell-shaped lilies of the valley, the fragrance was vanilla.

In the closet she found stacks of round boxes filled with Lottie's cherished collection of hats. Hats for spring: they had bought silk flowers and grosgrain ribbon at B. Altman & Company and laughed at the fussy old women making demands of the salesgirls, whose patience was tried. Her fall hats were dark straw with birds and feathers. Lottie had only one winter hat, a luxurious gift from Alice Winthrop, made from Hudson Bay seal. It had been a particularly cold winter, and Lottie loved that large beret. She would pull it down over her ears and sigh with pleasure. When Mimi took the hat out, she found a letter, yellowed and fragile with age. The handwriting was old-fashioned and schoolgirl tidy. Here and there, words had been crossed out and rewritten.

She sat on Lottie's upholstered bedroom chair, and as she looked at the handwriting, recognized it as Mama's. The stamp was missing, and she remembered Lottie had given Matthew the stamps from Marijampolė for his collection. Curiosity got the better of her and she opened the envelope.

It was written in pen and ink in Yiddish. She knew just enough words to read it and was surprised to learn Lottie's full name.

July, 1893

> *Dear Charlotte,*
> *Today I picked flowers for my wedding. I wished you were here.*
> *Jacob met me, even though Mama said I was not to see him alone. He went through the woods so no one would see him. He is so handsome, he makes my heart beat faster. I can hardly wait to be his bride.*
> *I hope you and Yitzak are happy. Do you have a house with a garden?*
>
> > *Your friend,*
> > *Rivkah*

Mimi couldn't believe her Mama had written the letter—had never known her to have hopes and dreams, even passion. The young girl who wrote that letter had no idea what lay ahead in the harsh, joyless world of New York City—or what her life would become.

4

DEATH EVERYWHERE

It was difficult to empty Lottie's apartment of her belongings and watch what remained loaded on the peddler's wooden wagon: bed, sofa, table and chairs, dresser—all covered with sheets and tied up with rope. Mimi watched from the sidewalk as it noisily clattered over the cobblestones until it disappeared. Frank and Anthony took Lottie's clothes, her beloved hats and buttoned kid gloves, downtown to Henry Street Settlement to be distributed to the poor.

What remained was the photo of Lottie taken by Jessie Tarbox Beals on the same day the photographer had photographed the Winthrop family. Lottie sat at the Winthrop's grand desk in a wing chair, her accounting book held in two hands on her lap. She looked directly into the camera, her expression unfamiliarly fixed and without animation. Jonathan Winthrop's self-portrait hung behind her. The photographer had captured a moment when a beam of sunlight broke through the window and created an aura around her head and the wisps of her persistently unruly hair. She wore the tortoiseshell combs Mama had brought with her from the old country and given to her in gratitude for taking her in. Mimi found them in a drawer and put them into her own hair. The photograph in its pale velvet frame now rested on a table by the side of Mimi's bed along with Lottie's hatpin collection in the pincushion Mama had made. The prettiest was a faceted amethyst in a brass setting. Most were "working-girl" pins, or simple black-and-white beads.

What had begun mildly in the spring became more infectious by September. In November the influenza was even more virulent. Highly contagious, it raged like a beast as it spread throughout the city—and the world. There was the constant sound of ambulances on the streets. Mimi joined her neighbors in peering out from behind the drapes to see where they stopped. To count the dead. Everyone spoke in horror about how within hours or days of symptoms appearing, the skin would turn blue, the lungs fill with fluid. Suffocation and death often followed.

Once their dinner was eaten each evening, the dishes washed and put away, and Matthew kissed good night, dread seeped through the cracks and crevices, slipping noiselessly through open windows—unwelcome—whispering that death was everywhere.

5

THE PANDEMIC

I miss my family," the nanny told Mimi. "But the buses and subways are crowded and everyone is coughing. They've ventilated the cars, but I still think it's too dangerous."

"I can understand your concern, but it wouldn't be safe for you, Ruth. Speaking to your family on the telephone will have to suffice until the Spanish flu is over."

"Three cousins moved in with them recently and my father isn't well."

"That must be worrisome. This can't last forever. I cannot tell you how much your being here matters to me, to Matthew, and to the business. I will ask the Corsino brothers to deliver food to your family, if that would help."

Frank and Anthony delivered and picked up work from her staff of seamstresses so that they might work at home. Every day and night she took Matthew's temperature and her own. Everyone was living in terror. If she had not paid attention before, she now read newspapers and listened to whatever news was available about this horrific squall of disease sweeping the world and, like the Great War, leaving millions of dead in its wake.

She spoke with Lawrence every day, to be sure that he was well; they took turns leaving food for each other. She missed him and their time together, longed to sit across from him with espresso and cookies. Waving through windows would have to suffice.

Frank and Anthony Corsino came by regularly with food their wives prepared: giant meatballs and layered dishes with pasta, sauce, and cheeses and Italian pastries from Veniero's—enough to feed a family of eight. They wouldn't come inside.

6

"THAT MRS. EPSTEIN, SHE'S THE DEVIL"

It became necessary for Mimi to go downtown to Orchard Street in June for fabric, buttons, trims, ribbons, and lace. It felt strange, almost painful, to be in her old neighborhood without Lottie, whom she missed even more than Mama. They would have caught up about their lives and gossiped a little, then might have decided on the spur of the moment to go to Iceland Brothers' for blintzes. Lottie would have slipped the leftover onion rolls into her napkin and put them in her handbag. They have tried to stifle their laughter—behave properly—as they left the noisy restaurant.

She avoided the main thoroughfares, those streets where swarms of dirty people, many unmasked and looking sickly, pushed and shoved one another to shop from the pushcarts. She had grown unused to the disorder, filth, and chaos of the Lower East Side. The thought of the influenza that was sweeping the city only made her repulsion worse. She didn't want anyone or anything to touch her and kept her arms and purse close to her body.

"Well, if it ain't Miriam Milman."

The familiar voice startled Mimi, and she turned to see who was speaking, surprised to be recognized in her mask.

"All high and mighty, ain't ya?"

It was Mrs. Epstein from the third floor, who, despite not wearing the required protective covering, was barely recognizable without an infant on her hip. She squatted on the bottom step of a tenement hugging a bag of potatoes. Her brown hair, which always flew in every direction, hung limp and filthy around her shoulders. Gaunt and sickly, she had the appearance of someone who had outwitted death and lived to regret it. Mimi remembered how Mrs. Epstein dragged her children about, thrown things at her peaceful husband, and spat on poor Szymon Moskowitz.

"How are you, Mrs. Epstein, and how is Mr. Epstein?" she asked. "And the family?"

Alongside bags that seemed to hold all of her belongings, Hannah Epstein sat with legs splayed, soiled stockings carelessly mended in too many places, with swollen ankles and feet seemingly forced into a pair of scuffed, broken-down slippers. The sleeves of her shirtwaist were rolled up to reveal scabby arms, and when she wasn't coughing, she sucked on the stub of a cigarette, which she held between thumb and index fingers like a man. Mimi could hardly believe how filthy her hands were. There was a bruise that began on her right eye and traveled along the bridge of her nose and across her cheek in the mottled shades of a sunset—from mulberry to brown, then ochre.

"Heard about ya," she growled. "Ya think you can forget where ya came from, don't ya?"

"Do you still live on Eldridge Street?" Mimi asked, forgetting the building had been demolished. "And how are the children?" She ignored the woman's insults and condescension.

Mrs. Epstein suddenly broke out with a deep hacking cough. Gasping for air, she gathered the snot in the back of her throat and spat onto the sidewalk. Mimi was horrified. That was considered illegal and a finable act.

"Dead. They're all dead, miss." She barely got the words out. "Or do you call yourself 'missus'? How's that bastard kid of yours?"

No one had ever called Matthew that. Not in her presence. Her heart felt too small for her chest, like shoes that no longer fit.

"I guess you didn't get the illness. Probably didn't even touch ya, did it?" Mrs. Epstein wheezed. "All safe and tidy—*uptown*." She said the word as though it were the plague itself, then dragged on her cigarette one more time before throwing it into the street.

So surprised by the unexpected confrontation, Mimi couldn't move. Could not walk away. Mrs. Epstein was mistaken. This cruel infection knew no boundaries. Yet, Mimi was unable to find the courage to shout their names: Lottie; Thomas' wife, Amanda; their little daughter, Emily; and one of their newborn twins—so young, they hadn't yet been named. Jonathan and Alice's children: Philip, Frances, Margaret, Henry, and Jonathan Junior. Poor Alice Winthrop, sick with fever herself, had insisted upon caring for those five children and almost went mad with grief when they died—all on the same day. And would Hannah Epstein care that Anthony Corsino's wife, Isabella, and their three-year old daughter, Gabriella, died, as did Frank and Giana Corsino's baby boy, Luca? But what purpose would it serve to argue with this poor soul?

Instead, she stood there, dressed in her bright coral linen suit with matching B. Altman & Co. kid gloves, the perky straw hat with the bright gingham bow and her red-and-brown leather boots, silently accepting the wrath of the woman Mama recognized as "the devil."

1920

1

PROFESSOR ISMERELDA ISOTTA

C ome with me, Mimi. She's extraordinary," Lawrence pleaded. "Her place is downtown. I've always visited her once a year. Now that the pandemic is over, she's available once again. I didn't believe in what she does. She's not a magician. No ghosts or visions. She doesn't contact the dead. She just *knows*—in some strange inexplicable way.

"I don't need anyone to tell me my future, Lawrence. I know exactly where I'm going. Hard work will tell me my future," she insisted. "They're quacks who prey on the poor, especially poor women."

Her mother had worked with a Russian immigrant, Esther, and whenever Mama had fifteen cents to spare, they would visit her on Houston Street. Mama would insist Mimi go with her, no matter how much she begged. The apartment smelled just like Esther, who smoked one cigarette after another. "You're throwing your money away," Mimi told Mama. Esther believed if you put a penny inside a coffee maker, the penny would turn to gold. Every time Mama tried, it broke her coffeepot!

"Lawrence, I simply don't believe in clairvoyants."

It wasn't so much that she didn't believe in them as she didn't want to go with him to Houston Street. He had no idea she had lived on Eldridge Street. She couldn't endure it if he made snide or disdainful comments on how squalid her old neighborhood was.

"I promise, you will enjoy the experience," Lawrence said. "It will be my treat!"

"They're just stage performers. I read about them in *Ladies' Home Journal*."

"So, enjoy the theater."

During holiday dinners, Esther would grab Lottie's hands and try to predict her future. Lottie wouldn't stand for it and hated that Mama wasted fifteen cents. Esther told Mama she saw her on a "fancy vacation" in the country, which Mama loved hearing. She had come from a farm and longed to be back. For days Mama would go on and on about Esther's vision of her country vacation—the country roads, trees, ponds, and fields of flowers.

Mama confided in Mimi that Lottie didn't want anyone to know that she had paid a certain Professor Abraham Hochman to find her husband. Every single day women would wait on the mind reader's stoop on Rivington Street—with all their children—hoping the professor would locate their missing spouses. They would pay him a dollar. Not fifteen cents.

Professor Hochman had told Lottie that her husband probably changed his name, making him impossible to be found. A lot of husbands did that. Had her father changed his name? Mimi wondered.

"Oh, try it," Lawrence said, interrupting her thoughts. "I'll pay for you. Maybe you'll learn about your future."

"All right. But she better not tell me I'm going to take a trip to the country."

"I promise you, there will be no spirits or ghosts, the table won't rise off the floor, and no long-lost howling relatives will appear."

She had fully expected they would be heading somewhere dark and dirty. But the professor lived in a three-story residential building near Mulberry Street.

There was a discreet sign: *Professor Ismerelda Isotta*. She and Lawrence climbed one flight after another of marble stairs until they reached the top floor. The floors on each turn were tiled in a black-and-white checkerboard pattern, and the odor of sautéing garlic and onion wafted throughout. Professor Isotta's front door was painted a shocking turquoise, and there was a gold-winged bust of a cherub above the brass door knocker.

Mimi could hear the shuffling of slippers before the door opened, revealing a woman's silhouette, which she was unable to see clearly, as she was backlit by the lamps in the railroad apartment's long hallway.

"Professor," Lawrence said, bowing.

"Mr. Loft, good to see you." Professor Isotta beckoned them to enter.

"My dear friend, Mrs. Milman."

Professor Isotta took both of Mimi's hands in hers, closed her eyes, and remained that way for so long that Mimi became uncomfortable, finally pulling her hands away, embarrassed.

"Forgive me, *Miss* Milman." She nodded her head slightly and opened her eyes. "Your hands tell me things about you."

Lawrence always introduced her as Mrs. Milman. Why, she wondered, had Professor Isotta so distinctly called her "Miss"?

As Mimi's eyes adjusted to the light, she was able to see that Professor Isotta was a petite woman of a certain age, perhaps sixty, yet carried herself with the confidence and grace of a ballerina. As she turned toward the light, Mimi first noticed her pale skin, which seemed never to have seen the light of day, and then how her lips were penciled with a bold line, darker than her lip rouge. Her piercing eyes were circled with Moroccan kohl, and she wore thick black false eyelashes. Her dark, piercing stare made Mimi feel uneasy. Professor Isotta offered no welcoming smile. What Mimi had believed to be a lace mantilla was actually profuse, black, undulating hair.

"Mr. Loft, please have a seat in the waiting room." She pointed the way through a doorway. "We shall be about thirty minutes. Manuel will bring you an espresso."

"You are in good hands, Mimi. I'll be waiting for you."

"Come with me to the parlor, my dear."

As she followed Professor Isotta down the hallway in the dim light, Mimi was able to discern that she wore a garnet velvet caftan that swayed around her body. The scent of stale cigarettes and her overpowering perfume, with its heavy rose and violet scent, followed her like a thick shadow.

At the entrance to what appeared to be the parlor, Professor Isotta held the draperies slightly apart and beckoned Mimi into the chilly room. The four walls were draped with dark burgundy velvet, and centered under a chandelier was a small table covered with the same material. There were two chairs. Like a mysterious moon, a glass orb seemed to be floating above the table.

"Please take a seat," the professor said, indicating the chair opposite hers, then sat down herself.

Mimi sat for several moments, looked around, hoping to get her bearings and locate a door or a window, but without success.

When she looked across at Professor Isotta, her elbows were at her sides, her fingertips resting on the edge of the table. There was an ornate silver ring on every finger as well as her thumbs. The clairvoyant radiated stillness. She looked down for several moments, slowly lifted her heavily lashed lids, and then, while looking into Mimi's eyes, seemed to be listening to something internal and distant.

The light from the chandelier began to dim.

"Place your tongue on the roof of your mouth and take a slow deep breath."

Mimi was aware of the sound of her own noisy breath as the oppressive scent of roses filled her nose and lungs. She counted the seconds.

"Release the air through your lips. Continue to do this until you are comfortable, then close your eyes, my dear, and do it without opening them," she said. "Now give me your hands, Miriam."

Mimi was taken aback at hearing the name only Mama had ever called her.

"Please, Miriam," she repeated.

Mimi cautiously extended both hands.

"Take another deep breath. Release."

At first, she felt her own pulse, the difference between her cool hands and the warmth from the psychic's palms. But after several slow breaths—in and out—her heartbeat and the temperature of her blood matched those of her host, and there was an inexplicable oneness. She felt connected and calm. After what seemed like an eternity, Professor Isotta spoke slowly. "Miriam"—her name sounded like a song—"something is holding you. Holding you back from life. From a success that wants to be yours. That achievement is close to you." There were long pauses between each sentence. "But so, too, is danger. You will never get what you want as long as it has a hold on you." She was quiet again, and in the dark, Mimi heard her struggle to breathe. Time passed—how long, she couldn't tell.

Ismerelda Isotta let out a long and pained groan before crying out in anguish. "Take care . . . there is a hawk . . . water . . . he knows his way." She paused, barely able to finish the sentence. "He is a madman, Miriam."

Mimi opened her eyes, pulled her hands free of the psychic's grip, and stood up, knocking the chair over. She could barely breathe. Terrified, she rushed around the room, searching for the opening in the drapes. Finding it, she ran down the hall toward the door, and almost fell on the stairs leading to the street. She stopped and leaned against a building, shaking with fear. It was her dream.

Lawrence caught up with her, took her in his arms, and held her until the trembling stopped. "I'm so sorry," he repeated again and again.

"I don't want to talk about it. Please. Take me home."

As they rode uptown in the taxi, which took them through the downtown streets—so familiar, so much more real than Madison Avenue—she felt raw. How had Professor Isotta known her dream?

Lawrence in his genteel way never asked what had happened, or apologized again. It was as though the experience had never occurred. But Mimi was haunted, and understood that she would never be safe from Frederick Winthrop.

2

LAWRENCE

Banging echoed through the house, which startled Mimi, and her book fell to the floor. She realized she had fallen asleep while reading a debut novel by a young writer, F. Scott Fitzgerald. *This Side of Paradise* was about the privileged, their narcissism, greed, and peculiar love.

Tiptoeing to the window, opening a portion of the deep green velvet drapes wide enough to peer down at the side door, she was shocked to see Lawrence—without a hat, jacket, or vest, and his shirt torn off at the shoulder. He was shivering in the warm spring night. She ran downstairs to open the door and found that he had fallen to the ground. In the moonlight, he looked like a fallen soldier. When he lifted his head, there were cuts and bruises on his face, his left eye was swollen shut, and a large gash on his forehead was bleeding. His hair was caked with dried blood. She sat down beside him on the ground and took him in her arms and rocked him as she would have comforted Matthew if he were wounded, murmuring over and over, "It's all right. It's all right."

"I'm so sorry." He could barely speak. Tears were running down his cheek. "Help me."

"Let me take you to Mount Sinai." She was surprised that he hadn't gone to a hospital immediately. "Were you in an automobile accident?"

"No, no. No hospital. They will ask questions."

What questions didn't he want to answer?

"I'm so ashamed." Sorrow racked his face; his body trembled.

"Then let me see what I can do. Let me help you inside. We'll need to be very quiet so we don't wake Miss Meyers or Matthew."

When he could stand, she helped him up and led him into the kitchen. Once he was seated, she gave him water and began tending to his injuries. She bathed his face and hands. His pale green shirt was stained with watercolor patches of blood. His pants were irreparably torn at both knees.

He looked away. "Please don't look at me. I'm so ashamed."

"Ashamed of what?" She lifted his head, wiped the tears away with a wet cloth. It was then that she saw the depth of sadness in his eyes—eyes that usually shined clear and azure.

"They beat us," he whispered.

"Who beat you?"

"The police. I was at a party." He looked away. "With friends."

"But why would the police beat you at a party?" She was trying to put a cold compress on his swollen eye. He took hold of the cloth and pulled it out of her hand.

"We were in a club in Harlem."

"In Harlem? What were you doing in Harlem?"

"It's the only safe place for people like me."

"What do you mean, 'like you'?"

"I'm a pansy, Mimi." He looked away. "A gay boy."

"What does that mean—a pansy?"

"It means"—he paused, taking hold of her hand—"I prefer men."

"I don't understand." She pulled her hand away. She didn't want to hear more. She wanted everything to be the same as it had been. Lawrence, self-assured and dependable.

"Mimi, I don't make love to women." His voice sounded gentle. "I make love with men. I'm queer. Homosexual."

She could hear the clock ticking in the silence between them. Then, she stood, collected the cloths, the bowls filled with water, and carried them to the sink. She filled the coffeepot, took down two cups, searched for spoons . . . anything rather than look at him. She kept her back to him so he wouldn't see the tears filling her eyes. When she turned around, which seemed to take forever, she went to him and held his head close to her chest.

"Oh, my dear, dear Lawrence. No wonder you didn't make love to me after my bouillabaisse dinner." Suddenly she burst into laughter and Lawrence joined her.

"You didn't know? Silly goose."

"I've led a sheltered life, I'm afraid." When she leaned down and kissed his forehead, he gasped from the pain.

She poured the coffee, added milk to her own, and put the cups on the table.

"There was a drag ball in Harlem. I went with a friend." His face lit up as if he momentarily forgot his pain. "You would love it, Mimi. Black men and white—they dress up as women in sensational ball gowns, and then there's this outrageously decadent fashion show with music and prizes. There are straight men and women as well in the audience. It's quite gay. The partying is fabulous." He stirred two spoons of sugar into his coffee and sipped it, recoiling from its heat on his cut lip.

"My friend Edward and I were having such a good time. You know how I love to dance."

Mimi tried to imagine him dancing with another man. How shocked society would be.

"Suddenly the police broke down the doors. They were hitting us with their nightsticks, in the head, our legs, pushing us to the floor, and then kicking us with their boots. Arresting everyone they could get hold of. Edward was arrested. I . . . I managed to get away." His breaths faltered. "I ran. I didn't help anyone." He rested his head in his hands.

"You did what you had to. They might have killed you."

It was difficult to listen to his animated description of this secret life he led—of loving men—and she realized that her own secret might not astound Lawrence after all.

1922

1

DAVID GERSONOV

Mimi had made her way, stylishly late, to the Grand Stairway and slowly descended into the Captain's Suite. It was the last night's celebration aboard ship. The RMS *Baltic* had sailed across the ocean and would arrive in New York in the morning. Her Paris event had been a huge success and, as a result, on board ship, were many potential American customers.

She was wearing the gown she had designed especially for this occasion in off-white silk charmeuse. British archaeologist Howard Carter and his workmen had just entered the tomb of King Tutankhamen in the Valley of the Kings in Egypt and found it intact. She had been unable to think about anything else.

She had cut the fabric on the bias and draped it across her breasts, where it appeared to hang from a flat-collared beaded neckline similar to an Egyptian necklace woven with gold threads, crystals, and pearls. The back was daringly low-cut. She wore hammered gold cuff bracelets on both wrists, and the Egyptian-inspired earrings were intended to catch the light from the chandelier. She felt every eye upon her.

He was standing at the bottom of the staircase, holding his chin with one finger on his lips, when she caught his eye. He took his hand away from his face, his eyes lit up, and then quite suddenly his entire face broke into a remarkable grin. She lost her composure and began to laugh, and as she reached the bottom step, he reached out his hand for her.

"I've been waiting for you," he said, which made her burst into laughter.

Despite the music, chatter, laughter, and decorous waiters carrying champagne and caviar canapés through the crowded Captain's Suite reception room, he had gotten her attention.

"Oh, have you, now?"

"I'm David Gersonov."

"Mimi Milman," she responded.

"The designer," he said, still holding her hand, which he tucked under his arm—perhaps to make certain she didn't get away. Surprisingly, she didn't mind.

"Why, yes."

"A pleasure. Care to dance?"

She nodded, and they made their way to the dance floor. She was aware of the touch of his palm on her bare back. The orchestra was playing "Mi Noche Triste," a tango. David danced with musicality and a confident lead.

Between songs she noticed that, while he wasn't handsome, he had a rather amiable face—one that lit up every now and then. He seemed without pretense and comfortable in his own skin.

All she had time to learn before the band announced they would take a short break and she was swallowed up by an admiring crush of devotees was that David lived in the city and that he was a photographer. As the women pushed him aside, she laughed and shrugged her shoulders to suggest that she was unable to resist. He blew her a kiss and disappeared in the throng of guests.

He stayed on her mind, along with the disappointment that they had not met earlier on this particular voyage. It was rare that she traveled without Matthew. She played out in her imagination how they might have had a shipboard romance, or at the very least, she might have offered her business card, asked for his, and let him know she was interested in seeing him again. She found him extremely appealing.

The next morning, when the ship reached the port of New York, she searched for him, but it was too large a crowd, between those disembarking and those greeting the arrivals—with everyone waving, shouting, throwing confetti, and presenting balloons and flowers.

Lawrence had cabled to say he would be waiting with fresh tulips and a taxi, and he was. He quickly whisked her away. Her trunks would be delivered later in the day.

She looked David up in the phone book and a week later called him to invite herself to his studio to see his work. He was pleased. She was taken aback to recognize the Union Square address.

"Your studio is in the same building as Jonathan Winthrop's."

"Yes, it is. Do you know Jon?" David asked.

"Why, yes, he's like a—" She paused, searching for the right word. "He's like a grandfather to my son. We occasionally visit his studio. What a grand place it is! I believe losing five of his children to the epidemic took its toll on him."

"Yes, he's lost some of his vitality. My place is not so grand, but it has great light from the north. You didn't mention you have a son," David said with surprise, although not with displeasure.

"I barely had time to get your name!" She laughed.

"I was thinking you had to do some work to find my phone number," he teased.

"My luck, you are the only David Gersonov in the directory."

"Damn, my client is at the door. Give me your number. Let me call you back."

When he telephoned, he asked, "Can you come by next Tuesday? I'll show you my photos and expect you to tell me about your son, and also how you know the legendary Jonathan Winthrop."

He called her again at eight the next day to say good morning, and they spoke again that night, and every night for longer and longer periods of time. She wasn't used to this sort of attention, and yet he put her at ease. David wanted to know who she was other than what he'd read about her in magazines and papers. She was relieved when he forgot to ask her how she knew the Winthrops.

Each day she awoke eager to hear his voice and looked forward to his calls when her workday ended, and then something began to stir in her that she hadn't felt before. But she was hesitant.

David told her about his parents' journey from Russia to Canada, then to New York, where he'd attended the Ethical Culture School and studied photography with Lewis Hine, who inspired in him the belief that a picture should tell a powerful story.

He described the friendship he formed with photographer Paul Strand, who introduced him to Alfred Stieglitz and Edward Steichen, who were photographing city life, ordinary people on the street, unaware that they were being photographed: the poor, immigrants, workers, the blind and disabled. While the second industrial revolution was transforming the city, they captured its underbelly. He spoke of this period of his youth with fervor, and she was moved by his passion.

Her seamstresses, Miss Meyers, Frank and Anthony Corsino, even Lawrence, commented that something was going on that she wasn't telling them. She admitted to Lawrence that she thought she was falling in love with "the fellow I met on the ship."

"That's supposed to be me," he complained. Mimi assured him that he would always be her most special friend.

"You can come with us wherever we go," she joked.

2

PHONE CALLS

Tell me about your daughter."

"Yes, my darling daughter, Lenny. She's four and the light of my life: feisty, articulate, and curious."

"That's a great combination."

"'Brave lion.' That's what her name means," he said. "Although she's not very brave—yet. She lives with her mother in Brooklyn. Monique and I met in France during the war. I was working as a photographer—until I was injured and sent home. Monique was pregnant and we returned to the States together and fortunately Lenny was born here, so she's an American citizen. She's a redhead like her mother, and I believe she has my heart."

"So you have a brave heart?"

"I do."

"Why didn't you stay in France?"

"It was having Lenny that pulled me in a more commercial direction. I had responsibilities: rent to pay, food to put on the table." He paused. "I've been very fortunate." He sounded wistful. "So tell me about Matthew," he said, clearly wanting to change the subject, Mimi was certain, and she was not one to pry or prod.

She was in her robe and slippers, seated on a wooden kitchen chair, which she'd moved near the rotary telephone, the handset cradled between her ear and shoulder. The wood-paneled kitchen was dark, the light from an oil lamp on the kitchen table reflected in the surrounding windows. Matthew and Miss Meyers were long asleep, so she rudely put her feet on the kitchen table.

"What would you like to know?"

"Whatever you want to tell me."

"Matthew's twelve, attends Riverdale Country Day. He's bright and curious."

"You sound *very* formal."

"Do I?"

"Is there a problem with Matthew?"

"No, of course not."

"Your voice changed. You sounded guarded. Would you rather not talk about him?"

"I suppose I'm protective."

"May I meet him?"

"Someday," she said, surprised by her resistance.

"You see?" He laughed.

"You know, till I met you, I kept my personal life private."

"I'm not prying. I want to know who you are, Mimi. Get to know you. Be a friend."

Be a friend? No one had ever said that to her. Everyone and everything in her life was business—except Matthew: he was personal. She kept everyone at a distance. Pretended to be more grown-up than she felt. Only Lottie had known who she was. Lottie alone had known Mama, Matthew, and Frederick Winthrop—understood the silence she had agreed upon with society. She sat up in the chair. A moth was fluttering madly around the oil lamp, "searching for the moon," Szymon Moskowitz had once told her.

David interrupted her thoughts. "You're very quiet. You haven't responded to my telling you that I want to get to know you."

She hadn't realized how long she had been silent, watching the moth, lost in her consideration of the distance she created with people she met—and that perhaps this was the reason she often felt alone in the world. She was so cautious about revealing the truth about herself.

"To be honest, I've never had a friend, David. Only my 'aunt' Lottie. She wasn't my real relative. She was a friend of my mother who looked after me when my mother died." She paused. That had been easier to say than she would have imagined. Her memories seemed strung together like pearls. "I grew up on Eldridge Street. My mother, Lottie, and I, we all worked in the factories. When my mother died, I was lost. Lottie was like a mother to me," she admitted, and then grew quiet. She closed her eyes, remembered Lottie's face.

"How old were you when your mother died?"

"Fifteen."

"Is that when Matthew was born?"

He asked so gently, it seemed as if the brass birdcage door had suddenly been opened and she had flown out. "Yes," she answered, and wondered if he had heard her sigh, heard the sound of her wings.

"Do you miss it?" she asked. "The work you loved."

"Sometimes. But I set aside time every year and work on a personal project, something that matters, you know?

"Last year I took a series of photos of immigrant families," he continued. "People affected by the Emergency Quota Act. After the war, there was such high unemployment and intense anti-immigrant feeling—a great deal of anti-Jewish sentiment. That damned quota system. We allowed so few immigrants from eastern and southern Europe. I was reminded of my own parents coming here from Russia and what it must have been like for them. Where are you from?"

"I was born here. My mother came from Marijampolė in 1893. She expected to find my father waiting for her. They had been married for about a week when he left. He gave her a ticket to use in a month. She realized she was pregnant on board the ship."

"I think I know what happened," David said. "He wasn't there."

"How did you know?" she asked. The story had just poured out of her, the secrets of her childhood, which she had held tightly bundled in her chest.

"It's a story one hears again and again: the husbands that simply disappeared because there were too many children, too much responsibility. So many marriages were arranged. It's part of the immigrant experience, Mimi."

"David, I've never told anyone about that part of my life."

"Why? Are you ashamed of who you were before you were *the* Mimi Milman?"

She had no answer.

"You know, when I worked on my project, I got away from the portraits of society ladies, the *Social Register*. My new work felt"—he struggled to come up with the right term—"*real*. It reminded me of the decency of my old buddies." He paused again. "It mattered."

She didn't know what to say, she was so moved by his openness.

"I've been offered an exhibition at the Salmagundi gallery."

"Oh, David, how exciting!"

He paused. "Mimi, I see Lenny every Sunday and we usually go to the zoo. At present, she is madly in love with a brown baby goat. Is Matthew too old for the zoo? We could all go together sometime."

"I'd like that." She tried to sound at ease.

"What about your ex? I assume there is one."

"David, I'd rather not discuss that right now."

"Of course."

The awkward silence between them was the first. It felt enormous. She wondered if it was possible to tell him. Was the agreement she made at fifteen with the Winthrops binding forever? She could never have a meaningful relationship and keep that secret. She could never have a loving relationship with a man who wouldn't understand.

David filled the awkward space with easier questions and humor before they said good night.

THE STUDIO ON UNION SQUARE

David was waiting for her on Fourteenth Street in a three-piece off-white linen summer suit and a sporty tie, and on seeing that broad, open smile, Mimi was relieved to still find him appealing. Tuxedos made the man, they said. So did three-piece white linen suits and a suntan. He looked her up and down with admiration, opened his arms to greet her, and whispered, "Exquisite. And you smell good, too."

She wore her silk chiffon dress, cut on the bias, with splashes of peach flowers against a creamy background with a ruffled uneven hemline. Her straw trooper's hat was circled with a band of flowers she'd made from the dress fabric. Beige silk stockings matched her patent leather, cut-out shoes.

"I think it's the Veniero's pastries you smell."

"Those, too. Come. We'll have to take the back stairs. The elevator's down . . . again. It's in sore need of repair." He took hold of her hand and led her toward the back entrance of the building. "It's also more romantic. If you get tired, let me know, and I'll sling you over my shoulder and carry you the rest of the way," he joked.

"I think I'd rather perish on a landing," Mimi said. "I'll sing a death scene aria."

"I could call out your name from the fourth floor." He sang out beseechingly Rodolfo's plaintive calls upon Mimi's death in the last act of *La Bohème* with a great deal of drama and wringing of his hands.

"You know your Puccini! But don't give up your day job!" she said, as she started climbing.

She remembered earlier times: racing down these same stairs, carrying Matthew, rushed and breathless, and desperate to avoid meeting Frederick. Worrying that if he should recognize her, he might ask Jonathan why she was there—ask who was that child. While it was years ago, it seemed like yesterday.

She thought of Frederick less and less. Her life was so full. On the occasion that his name was mentioned, or she thought she saw him on the street, or at a social gathering, it was like peering through a window at the person she had once been: somewhat familiar but mostly a stranger she no longer recognized. Just history.

David stopped on the landing of the third floor. "Are you all right? You look pale. Perhaps we should have taken our chances on the lift?"

"A bit out of breath."

"My offer stands." He held out his arms. "Over my shoulder. I'm in quite good shape."

"I've noticed." She laughed.

"Oh, good!" He reached for her hand and pulled her up, and they continued up the stairway side by side. "Onward," he said.

He looked directly into her eyes when he spoke to her, as though trying to read her reactions. Somehow she was unable to look away. Then he would break into that smile she remembered from the ship. It had made her laugh even before she knew him.

Watching him ahead of her on the stairs, she couldn't help but notice the way his pants revealed the muscles of his buttocks, thighs, and calves, and she imagined him as a lover.

He stopped to wait for her on the fourth-floor turn. "You're flushed. Is it my good shape or the stairs?" He struck a comical strongman pose.

Taking a deep breath, she smelled the familiar odors of oil paint and turpentine.

"It even smells the same," she said.

"One more flight," David said, "and I'll give you a glass of my best Chianti!" He held out his hand.

After giving Mimi a glass of wine, David opened the leather portfolio on his worktable.

"Please," he said, indicating that she should look at his work.

She carefully picked up each of the twenty-by-thirty black-and-white prints, which were primarily portraits of women of all ages. Some were of actresses, some were of society women, and several were of his daughter, Lenny, caught in motion. She took her time looking at all of them.

"You're too quiet," he finally said as he collected and stacked the photos he had shown her, and then put them aside. "Don't keep me in suspense," he pleaded. "This is who I am, you know."

"Oh, I'm sorry, David. They're stunning."

He breathed a sigh and released his breath. "I wanted you to like them." He leaned forward. "What is it you like?"

She closed her eyes, gathering her thoughts in order to turn her emotional response into words.

"Well, you capture the fabrics—the way light and shadow play on the textures. That's the designer speaking," she explained. "I am astounded with how you've taken the picture at just the perfect moment."

"I try!" He laughed, held his hands up like a camera to his eye, and then, just when she felt that awkward moment of being photographed, he made the clicking sound of the shutter.

"So that's how it's done." She laughed.

She picked up a photo. "Ah, this is my favorite." She held it for a few minutes to gather her thoughts. "She's a very exotic woman. It's as though she's sitting in a veil of sunlight. You're choice of lighting accentuates the lace—its sheerness here and there—and her skin." She pointed to the particulars.

"The darkroom is my friend." He seemed pleased that she had noticed.

"She's quite seductive—the way her head is tilted down and she stares up and directly at the camera. Were you in love with her?"

Her question went unanswered. David suddenly leaned forward and kissed her, and she was startled and pleased.

"Thank you," he said.

"For the kiss?" she asked.

"I rarely thank women for kisses." He laughed. He took the photograph from her hand and put it and the rest back into the portfolio. "For seeing what I see."

"Would you consider photographing my collection?" Mimi noticed that he paused, somewhat uncomfortably. "What if I said that you could do whatever you wanted?"

"If I could do whatever I wanted, I just might kiss you again."

She felt the color rise to her cheeks.

"Seriously? You would be putting a great deal of trust in me," he said.

"What if I am willing to do that?"

"We would need to spend a great deal of time together," he teased, brushing a wisp of hair behind her ear, which stirred feelings of arousal.

"That sounds like a good idea. Would you?" she asked.

"Kiss you?"

"David, be serious!"

"Only if you will let me photograph you—frequently. And if you and Matthew will come with Lenny and me to the zoo this weekend."

"I want to see your project photos."

"In time."

1924

1

THE SALMAGUNDI CLUB

It was always the same laughter, murmurs of gossip, sideward glances, fleeting fragrances, and pretentious banter, familiar and tiresome. Now that she had acquired international recognition, Mimi preferred her workroom—the quiet contemplation, the discussions of process, and the curiosity and ideas of her young seamstresses, all amid the whirring of Singers—and her time with David.

A year earlier, when fourteen-year-old Clarissa Nowak, a student at the Manhattan Trade School for Girls, presented her initial samples, her work stood out among her classmates'. Mimi immediately saw that her design work, even at fourteen, was sophisticated, original, and imaginative. The headmistress whispered to Mimi that Clarissa was their most promising student but at the same time in need of some attention as to her somewhat willful behavior. She was living on Hester Street with her father and nine siblings. Her mother had died in childbirth during the pandemic. Her father had been a professor at the Academy of Fine Arts in Warsaw, teaching drawing and painting, and now, in America, worked as a sign painter, determined that his children would have every opportunity for an education. Clarissa said that he held on to the belief that if he could only learn to speak and write in English, he might teach at a university.

Mimi met with Clarissa's father and offered to provide her with a scholarship and paid opportunities to work on special projects.

Professor Nowak was pleased, proud of his oldest daughter, and accepted Mimi's offer with humility. The child was as dependable as she was gifted. The school allowed her to use work time as credit toward her degree and in place of some classes, as Mimi herself had done when she began.

Every now and then, when working with Clarissa, Mimi quite forgot that she was still a child. They collaborated, bounced ideas off each other like colleagues. Clarissa was confident in her opinions and willing to argue. Often, Mimi thought to herself that Clarissa was an old soul. She had wisdom and a grounded sense of being in the world—often far more than one would expect in someone her age. Mimi loved Clarissa like a daughter but had to be prepared for those moments when her obstinate adolescence showed itself.

The shop had been quite busy preparing for the summer social events, and Mimi had hired six additional seamstresses as well as bead workers. Everyone wanted glitter! Professor Nowak had agreed to allow Clarissa to spend particularly busy weeks with Mimi during school breaks so that she wouldn't have to make the long daily round trip to and from Hester Street.

Mimi was determined to introduce her young charge to the city's cultural world, to prepare her for success, and invited her to join them at David's gallery exhibition on lower Fifth Avenue.

Mimi took a taxi to Hester Street where Clarissa lived. Looking at the shabby tenement, Mimi considered how difficult it must be for Clarissa, her father, and eight siblings enduring in their two-room apartment.

When Clarissa stepped out of the darkened doorway, she seemed to personify the sun, wearing a garment she had designed specifically for the occasion, a simple afternoon dress made from lemon-yellow linen with a crisp bow at the shoulder. Both the bow and the buttery felt cloche hat she had made to accompany the chemise celebrated her delicate profile and radiant skin.

"You look like a ray of sunshine, Clarissa!" Mimi swelled with pride at the way her fifteen-year-old protégée presented herself. "Did you make the hat as well?"

"Yes, I did. I actually just finished sewing the hem a few minutes before you arrived. Do you think it's proper for the party?"

"Absolutely proper."

"That's what Papa said." She suddenly seemed childlike as she self-consciously smoothed the skirt over her knees and pulled up her white gloves. "Matthew's not coming?"

"He has exams and needs to prepare. He sends his apologies." Clarissa's disappointed expression did not go unnoticed.

As David had warned her, the gallery on Fifth Avenue between Eleventh and Twelfth Streets hosted a group of people unfamiliar to Mimi. There were none of the usual faces that she saw at the opera, ballet, concerts, and parties. Instead it was a Greenwich Village crowd, many of them David's friends and associates, men indifferently dressed in black, grays, and browns, without ties, many in need of a haircut and a good shave. They offered the women strolling the gallery rooms the means to show off their Dada- and Surrealist-influenced outfits, intended to shock and amuse—a costume party of sorts. Hats that were works of art, with fabrics, colors, and patterns that were mismatched, and even a young woman dressed like a Russian peasant without shoes. Mimi, used to celebrity, found herself feeling conventional and overdressed, even in her Japanese-influenced cream-colored kimono-style suit with black trim.

David welcomed them. He was very pleased with the way the gallery had hung his photos. The building with its separate gallery spaces was crowded. Clarissa, interested in drawings and engravings, wandered off, and Mimi meandered slowly about the different rooms, more interested in listening to the conversations, intrigued by the things people said at these events.

The painting gallery was of no interest to her; it displayed representational landscapes of country scenes and bucolic meadows. She preferred the brilliant, aggressive colors of the Fauves. "Wild Beasts" correctly described their works, particularly Henri Matisse, whose energy she admired and whose palette inspired her recent designs.

David, like a homing pigeon, returned to Mimi's side, slipping his arm through hers. "They've sold six of my photos," he whispered.

"Oh, how wonderful."

"Your Clarissa seems to be handling herself with poise," he said.

They made their way through the gathering, searching for Clarissa, and finally found her.

"She's graceful and self-assured, isn't she?" Mimi remarked.

"You have a wonderful way with your staff."

"Clarissa is more than staff!" She laughed, leaning into him. "She's my right hand."

"I thought I was."

"You are my heart," she whispered.

They stood together like two proud parents, watching Clarissa. But Mimi felt uneasy. There was something too bright, too eager, in the schoolgirl's expression. It was the teenager. Her pale cheeks were bright with flush, her smile too radiant. Her animated blue eyes coyly darted this way and that but returned to the face of the person to whom she was listening. She kept her graceful, slender fingers near her mouth as she leaned toward him. Though only a schoolgirl, her manner was, Mimi observed, overtly flirtatious. In her yellow dress and hat, amid this murky bohemian set, she seemed the center of attention.

It was a man to whom she was adoringly listening, his voice as smooth as silk, velvety, with bass tones like the resonant sound of a cello rising above the gathering in the room.

Even if he hadn't turned, Mimi knew in her skin, bones, and blood that it was Frederick Winthrop—despite the years that had passed—who was talking with Clarissa.

Impotently, she watched as the child accepted his card, smiled with appreciation, and then placed it in her purse.

Time stopped, the murmur of the crowd vanished, everything Mimi felt was internal, her heartbeat a whirring sound like the rush of water or air.

She had no memory of dropping her wine glass, never felt her hand let go. Staring light-headed and lost at the pale floor, she noticed the glint of splintered crystal and then felt the comfort of David's arm as he pulled her toward him.

"Are you all right?" David's voice brought her back into the room.

Frederick turned his head toward her, a lewd smile for Clarissa frozen on his face.

"Mrs. Milman," Clarissa called out. "Are you alright?"

Propelled forward, out of David's embrace, Mimi took hold of Clarissa's arm, speaking firmly. "We must be going."

Frederick was staring at her with an inquisitive expression, his memory of her, she was certain, just out of grasp, like a forgotten word on the tip of his tongue.

Clarissa sulked. "We just got here."

"It's time to go, Clarissa," Mimi said in an assertive tone.

David stepped in, gathered her and Clarissa, and guided them quickly toward the door.

But Frederick followed them. "I'm Frederick Winthrop," he said, reaching out for Mimi. "I'm certain we've met. What is your name?"

She pulled away, fearful that he would take her chin in his hand, tip her head back, look into her eyes, and recall. She didn't want him to remember her. Lost for words, she was unable to say her name. She must protect Clarissa—and Matthew.

"You found my gloves at the opera once," she said.

"Ah, yes," he said, nodding courteously.

"Excuse us, Mr. Winthrop," David said, opening the gallery door. Taking hold of her arm and Clarissa's, he walked them outside into the cool evening air.

She turned and looked back over her shoulder to see Frederick standing at the door, watching them. She hailed a passing taxi and, taking hold of Clarissa's arm, got in.

"We'll be fine, David. You need to stay here. I will see Clarissa home."

The two were silent in the taxi as they headed to Hester Street. Clarissa scowled while Mimi was filled with a rush of memories, unexpected and overwhelming. Downtown's shadowy landscape filled her nostrils with the remembered stench of the sweatshops—her lost childhood. The narrow streets and buildings brought back Mama's death. When they passed Seward Park, she recognized with a chill the bench on which she had met Frederick Winthrop. The violation, stolen touches, and favors from an unsuspecting child. Her own lusting after foolish things. Stolen things—a perfume bottle, a pen, a ring. Rage filled her mouth, chest, and belly. Now he hoped to do the same with Clarissa. She would never allow that.

2

CLARISSA'S LIE

Life was changing—especially for women. The 1920s began with passage of the Nineteenth Amendment, giving women—if they were white—the right to vote.

Mimi noticed the change in conversations with her clients. Of course, they still gossiped but also wanted to discuss the world, politics, educational opportunities, the status of their marriages—and even career possibilities. It was very clear to Mimi that for these women of privilege, the 1920s were a time of expanding choices.

The discussions among her clients and those of her seamstresses were paradoxical. The lives of the young women in the workroom still offered fewer choices and opportunities.

Having started her own path to independence earlier than most, Mimi was finding the success she had dreamed about. And yet, she felt caught between the women who lunched and the women who sewed. Except for Clarissa Nowak, who seemed to be caught between both, mostly because she showed so much potential and because Mimi took interest in her future.

Mimi's clientele could drive and spend their own money. They could go out at night, unchaperoned—smoke, drink, and party. Yet, when they stepped out dancing and partying, they needed their hemlines raised to show off their legs, and wanted their clothes to sparkle.

Mimi remained passionate about her work, challenged by the

latest simplified columnar silhouette of garments that accentuated athleticism and youth over mature proportions. Her patrons needed little coaxing to shorten their hemlines to reveal more leg. Without corsets, evening wear was no longer restrictive but rather designed to facilitate the rebellious motion of the Charleston, the foxtrot, the shimmy, and Mimi and David's favorite: the tango.

The surfaces of the garments she designed became her canvas. Colors that surprised were the *Mimi Milman* palette. Her youthful clientele liked to be noticed, and beaded garments made a glittery statement, particularly on the dance floor. It *was* the Jazz Age.

Clarissa had called to ask if she might take Saturday afternoon off to meet a friend from school at the Liberty Theater. There was a matinee of the new film *The Thief of Bagdad* with Douglas Fairbanks. Mimi had read the reviews and understood it to be a wholesome swashbuckling adventure, and so she agreed. She was eager to see it herself.

Later that afternoon, Clarissa called. "Hello, Mrs. Milman? It's Clarissa Nowak. I'm calling from a pay phone! On the street!" Her voice was so formal, Mimi had to stifle her laughter.

"How was the picture show?"

"Very exciting! Especially Douglas Fairbanks. He's *so* handsome! You and Matthew would enjoy it." After a brief pause, she continued. "May I get something to eat with my friend's family?"

Mimi looked at the clock. It was a little before three. "How will you get home? I wouldn't want you taking the subway or trolley by yourself."

"They will bring me home."

"Enjoy yourself, dear, but remember your good manners." The child deserved some fun. "Be sure to thank them."

"Of course, Mrs. Milman, I will."

3

UNCHAPERONED

It was six, and Clarissa had not arrived, nor had Matthew and Miss Meyers returned from the park. Where was everyone? Mimi fretted. She paced the workroom and constantly checked the time. She made herself a cup of coffee and sat at the kitchen table.

Suddenly she thought about Clarissa meeting Frederick at the Salmagundi Club the week before and the expression on the impressionable child's face. Flattered, undoubtedly. Adoring of a wealthy gentleman's attention. Would Clarissa lie to her?

After Mimi and Clarissa had hastily fled the gallery opening the previous Sunday, she had spoken sharply to Clarissa in the car. "You must stay away from Mr. Winthrop." She had turned to her in the back seat of the taxi and recognized that adolescent flash of defiance in Clarissa's expression. It occasionally showed itself at the shop.

"He seems a gentleman, Mrs. Milman, and said he might have business for my father."

"What sort of business? He is *not* proper company for you,"

"Why not?" Clarissa demanded, then realized her insolence. "I'm sorry, Mrs. Milman."

She was terrified for the safety of the child. While extraordinarily talented, she had an unruly streak that occasionally showed its angry face and with which Mimi struggled.

"You're my charge, Clarissa. Your father and Headmistress have given me responsibility for your well-being. You need to pay attention to your work."

"Yes, Mrs. Milman."

"You can't just go to a gentleman's home because he asks you," she added. "Certainly not without a chaperone, and Mr. Winthrop knows better."

"A chaperone?" She had turned, a forlorn expression on her face, to stare out the window.

"Yes, a chaperone." Mimi had forgotten that Clarissa lived almost as she had as a child, knew nothing of propriety nor the perils of men like Frederick Winthrop. Her father wouldn't understand the danger, either, the Winthrops being of such impressive power and wealth.

"I'm sorry. I wouldn't want you to have concerns about me." Clarissa turned back toward her and smiled apologetically.

Now Mimi had reason to be concerned. Clarissa was a willful adolescent. If she was with Frederick, they could well be on their way to Long Island. To Raptor.

The idea terrified her. When she imagined the child in the back seat of Frederick's car, she could barely discern the difference between Clarissa and herself. It was as though it were 1910 and she were once again in the back seat of his Pierce-Arrow. And where were Matthew and Miss Meyers?

Though she had been driven to the North Shore's Gold Coast by her clients' drivers over the years, Mimi would be hard put to know the routes to the Vanderbilt, Astor, Whitney, Morgan, or Winthrop estate. She considered calling the Corsino brothers but realized that it was the Winthrops she should be calling. Let them take care of their errant brother, and besides, any one of their cars would be faster than Tony's truck—and they would know the way.

She rang up Jonathan Winthrop, relieved when he answered the phone himself.

"Jonathan Winthrop speaking."

"Jonathan, it's Mimi Milman."

"Good afternoon, Mrs. Milman. To what do I owe the pleasure of your call?"

"Your brother." She paused, breathless. "Your brother Frederick, I believe, has taken my apprentice Clarissa to his place on Long Island. She's fifteen."

It took a moment of complete silence before he responded. "When?"

"Late this afternoon, and if she's with him, she's in danger. We need to stop him."

"Fifteen, you say? How the hell did he meet your apprentice? Damn him. We must get there quickly before it's too late. It's almost five. Thomas is visiting. We were going to our club for dinner."

"Well, I think you should cancel your dinner plans. We need to get to Raptor."

"Does anyone else know?" he asked.

Just like a Winthrop, she thought. *Concerned about scandal.*

"No one," she assured him. "I didn't want to upset her family."

"Good thinking. Let's keep it that way. Just the three of us."

"We'll have to hurry. I can tell you both the details on the way."

"Can you be ready in ten minutes?"

"Of course."

Just before she hung up the receiver, she heard him bellow, "Thomas!"

That family would do anything to avoid ignominy, and she would do anything to rescue Clarissa, whom she loved like a daughter— albeit a rebellious one.

After hanging up, Mimi ran upstairs and changed into comfortable tweed trousers, a tailored shirt, and a pair of sturdy oxford shoes, then tied a pullover sweater around her shoulders. She left a note for Matthew and Miss Meyers explaining that she was going to Long Island with the Winthrops. On her way out the front door she grabbed gloves and a scarf. She worried about leaving without knowing where

Matthew and Miss Meyers were, but was certain the nanny could handle things. Clarissa could not. The clean-shaven Winthrop brothers were already waiting at the curb, the motor running.

Despite her concern about Clarissa and her annoyance with Matthew, who had gone to the park with Miss Meyers to meet a school friend, Mimi had done all she could do to keep from laughing at Thomas' attire when he jumped out of the car, insisting she sit in the front seat. He looked ready to play golf in his pale beige tweed knickerbocker pants, short baggy trousers gathered just below the knee; knee-high laced boots; a red-and-yellow argyle knit sweater; and a red bow tie. But even with his rather outlandish attire, which would make any other man look foolish, he was able to carry it off with aplomb. Somehow, Mimi found that it suited his jaunty personality.

Just then, Matthew ran across Madison Avenue and immediately went over to the car. Miss Meyers was still half a block away.

"Matthew! How are you, young man?" Thomas said, pounding him on the back. "Look how tall you've grown. Fourteen, eh?"

"How's Riverdale Country Day treating you?" Jonathan asked.

"Fine, sir." He turned to Mimi, said, "Sorry, Mother," and gave her a peck on the cheek. "Teddy and I were starved and we convinced Miss Meyers to stop for a hot dog."

"Oh, thank heavens. I must help the Winthrops. There's a note on the table."

"Are you going in this swell car?" he asked eagerly. "May I come?"

"You may not. It's business," she lied.

"Oh, please," he begged.

"Sorry, Matthew, not this time." Thomas patted him on the back. They were almost the same height, and the family resemblance was startling, Mimi noticed.

"We've got to go." She pushed him toward the building. "I shouldn't be too late."

As Jonathan pulled away, she waved at Matthew and Miss Meyers, who were waving back. She was pleased to be sitting in the front seat of the pristine white convertible, its top down. The speedy 1920 Rolls-Royce Silver Ghost Tourer had been a good choice, with room for four—once they rescued Clarissa. Mimi had occasionally seen Jonathan driving around the city in one of his six automobiles, but this was the fanciest! And leave it to Jonathan to be elegantly dressed in an off-white pullover shawl-collared sweater and dark gray corduroy pants.

"Let's go," she said, reminding herself of their mission. If she was wrong, it would at least be an adventure.

"What the hell is holding up traffic?" Frederick asked.

"There's some sort of accident up ahead," his driver, Carlos said.

"Well, then get off the goddamned road. Take a side road."

"Traffic is at a standstill, sir."

An hour passed. Carlos insisted there was nothing he could do.

He was not only impatient but furious. Clarissa had resisted his advances along the way, instead engaging him with a string of maddening questions, curious to know all about him, and then had quite abruptly fallen asleep while he was telling her about the years he had lived in Paris.

Not even the starts and stops of traffic along the way had woken her.

At long last, they arrived at Raptor's front gates, and he rolled down the back window. The scent of leather and Clarissa's powdery fragrance were quickly overwhelmed by the briny ocean smell. He gazed out upon the moon, a pale sphere rising. The sky was a crazy quilt of blue cloud formations on a pale magenta background. As it made its slow journey toward the sea, the brilliance of the orange sun revealed that Sunday would be a scorcher. They drove past the leaf-covered tennis courts, their nets sagging forlornly; rolling unkempt lawns; the English garden, once manicured, now grown wild.

The chauffeur drove unhurriedly along the winding gravel driveway lined with Italian cypresses toward Raptor, his arm rested nonchalantly on the open front window, and Frederick noticed how he almost affectionately caressed the car's exterior with its twenty layers of black paint. The driver's gaze shifted to the rearview mirror, and as he surveyed the inactivity in the dark leathery interior of the plush back seat, his expression was one of . . . disappointment, Frederick assumed.

"We need a plan," Mimi said.

"I've brought three flashlights," Thomas said when they were out of the city.

"Perhaps we should check the cottage first?" Jonathan said. He was speeding and the trees seemed a blur.

"If he's having a dinner party, there will be other guests," she said.

"Frederick? Have a dinner party?" Thomas laughed. "That'll be the day! He only has his old crotchety cook, who can barely make toast if I remember correctly, and that strange chauffeur. Have you visited lately, Jon?"

"Not for years. He is not fond of Alice. You?"

"I did stop by—unannounced—last year. He had a housemaid at that time, and she said there was no one home. He's never forgiven me for refusing to design the place." Thomas chuckled. "As I expected, Raptor looks like something from a Gothic horror story. It's not the sort of place you ever forget, is it?" The two brothers laughed.

"I'll say," Jonathan said.

"His Duesenberg was sitting in front of the entrance. That chauffeur of his was polishing it," Thomas continued. "He was home, I was sure of it. The hood of the car was still warm."

"Getting back to our plan," Mimi said. "We must be quick and thorough—and find Clarissa."

In an attempt to pass two slow cars, Jonathan just missed an oncoming car in the other lane. Mimi closed her eyes, certain they would smash.

"Whatever you do, don't go into his damn maze," Jonathan said as though nothing had happened. "I doubt you'd ever be seen again."

She was shaken when Jonathan said that, remembering how Frederick had described the maze to her—with affection and pride. This whole experience with Clarissa was reawakening forgotten memories. Would she have been in peril if she had agreed to go there with him? What would he have done to her that Jonathan and Thomas were so worried about? All the gossip about young girls disappearing and Lottie's cautions over the years suddenly came to mind. Perhaps it was not just rumor after all.

As Carlos drove past the maze, a flock of small laughing gulls flew into the sky, surprised by the automobile. The air was filled with their raucous cackling. When the car reached the mansion's entrance, Frederick breathed in the feline aroma of the surrounding yaupon holly hedges. The mansion stood like a dark bastion against the glistening calm steel-gray Atlantic, the turrets breaking the seemingly endless horizon.

Clarissa's youth had made Frederick forget that he was almost forty-four. While his hair had thinned slightly, turning salt-and-pepper around the temples, he was certain that his reflection remained aristocratic. Women still found him attractive.

The girl had piqued his interest the moment he saw her, all aflutter at his every word. A determined little thing, ambitious and inquisitive, with no embarrassment about her Lower East Side upbringing; her father, once a professor, now a common sign painter. She had worn, at his request, the same sunny yellow chemise. Without the cloche, he noted that her flaxen hair was long and rolled up at the nape of her neck. Strands had come loose along the ride and fell across her shoulders in a most seductive manner.

The interruption by her rude employer and David Gersonov at the gallery had been unexpected. Initially, he'd felt thwarted but then gratified when he considered that he had just enough time to give her his card, get her phone number, and invite her to his supposed dinner party. Such an eager expression. It had been some time since he had felt such erotic yearning.

His sister-in-law Alice's warnings had concerned him, the repeated questioning by the police about Gloria Arnold had shaken him, and then all the time and emotional distress with Louise Langford had put a serious dent in his appetite. He had decided after Louise that self-involved showgirls were tiresome.

In recent years, he had satisfied his urges by returning to smaller, simpler prey, which he called "red crossbills"—the finch-like, red-haired Irish girls who arrived on American shores eager to find work on the Gold Coast. He loved observing how, when disquieted or demeaned, beginning with a pale rosy blush at their shoulders or collarbones, the color would appear on their pale skin, tiptoe up their necks and then, as their anxiety grew, bloom on their freckled cheeks like stargazer lilies.

Cook would say, "Peggy ran away," "Maggie, the new girl, took off with the young fellow from town," "Clodagh, the one from Belfast? Gone." Irish girls, always wanting to please, disappeared all the time, barely noticed, easily replaced, and then life moved on.

"Cook hired a new girl, Mr. Winthrop." Like a mind reader, Carlos interrupted his thoughts. "A pretty little thing. Looks like she's left a light on in your study, sir."

Was that an impertinent smirk he noticed?

When the car came to a stop, Clarissa awoke, sat up, blinked at the sunset, and yawned. "Are we here? I am really sorry, Mr. Winthrop. I must have fallen asleep," she said, patting the skirt of her dress into place. "We've been busy at school preparing for exams." She attempted to roll up the hair that had fallen. "And my position with Mrs. Milman," she chattered. She rubbed her eyes with the backs of her fingers, ran her hands along her cheeks, and spread her arms wide. "Is this your house?" Clarissa looked about. "All of it? It's like . . . like something out of a fairy tale. When will the other guests be arriving?"

Carlos helped her out of the car. "Will that be all, Mr. Winthrop?"

"Bring us tea in the garden, Carlos, and then you and Cook can have the weekend. I'll drive the young lady back to the city. See you Monday morning."

"Thank you, sir." He bowed, got back in the automobile, and drove toward the garage.

"Mr. Winthrop, I thought there was to be a party."

He was stirred by her boldness. Ignoring her question, he took out his watch.

"I wanted you to see my home at sunset. Come, we'll sit right over there by the fountain, where you have a view of the ocean, and have tea, and then I'll show you Raptor. These are the moments when it is at its most beautiful." Taking hold of her slender hand, he brought it to his lips. "The ocean, the moon and stars."

"But you said there'd be a party."

"My dear"—he put his arm around her—"please call me Frederick. 'Mr. Winthrop' makes me sound a hundred years old. Please accept my sincerest apology. There will be no dinner party tonight. Perhaps another time."

He noticed how her brow furrowed and the wide-eyed girlish expression vanished, replaced by petulance. She tried to pull her hand out of his. He patted hers but did not let go.

The chauffeur brought a tray. "Cook wasn't expecting you and the young lady, and she and the new girl have already gone." He served the tea. "This is Mr. Winthrop's favorite, miss. I prepared it just as you like it, sir."

"Have a good weekend, Carlos. I'll be in touch to let you know my plans. I may be traveling in Europe for a while. Maybe I will convince the young lady to accompany me."

Clarissa laughed nervously. "I'm only fifteen, sir, and I need to finish my studies."

"You can always study. How often do you have an opportunity—an invitation—to see the world? Do finish your tea before it gets cold."

"Good evening, sir, miss." Carlos bowed and walked back toward the house.

They sat looking out to sea, and Frederick waited for her to empty the cup.

"Good, that should warm you. It gets chilly by the water. Come."

"Why doesn't anyone tend your garden?"

He shrugged. "I'm not very interested in plants and flowers."

He had long ago ceased caring. "The place is overgrown with fox-tails and this damned Chinese wisteria has spread its runners, seed, and suckers everywhere. The vines have smothered, strangled, and crushed everything around them."

He pointed with pride at the wooded area. "It's my bird sanctuary and reserve that I care about. It has trees, a salt marsh, a lagoon, and numerous ponds. Ten, actually. There are all sorts of wildlife: small chipmunks, field mice, rabbits, frogs, songbirds. They, in turn, attract the hawks. Look!" He pointed at a pair of hawks soaring and circling together on a draft. "See those two? Cooper's hawks. You can recognize them by their long, banded tails. They have a twenty-eight-inch wingspan. Aren't they breathtaking?" He was exhilarated. "Even in the dark they can see their prey from up there. Once they spot what they want—a small bird or a rabbit—then it's only a matter of seconds. They swoop down, take it in their talons, carry it to the water, and drown it. Oh, that is something to see." He checked his pocket watch again.

"Oh, how awful." Clarissa shuddered. "What time is it, please? I must get back to Mrs. Milman's. She will be worried about me."

"My dear child, stop worrying." He laughed, pulling her toward him, feeling her body resist. The sedative in her tea should have been working by now. "Come, let's walk a bit before it gets dark."

When she delighted in seeing fireflies, he asked, "Have you ever been out of the city?"

"No, sir."

"How charming. Please call me Frederick."

"Frederick." She was gazing up at him, smiling as she had at the gallery.

"Come. I want to show you my pride and joy. My maze."

She stumbled and he took hold of her arm. "Be careful you don't fall."

The maze was some distance from the cottage, and he quickly led her along the path toward its entrance. It was an eighteenth-century lay-out with a confusing and intricate network of passages, choices, and dead ends. He had chosen yaupon holly for the hedges, which, now at more than seven feet high, dwarfed his six-foot, two-inch stature. In the center was a tower with a spiral-shaped external staircase, its only purpose to confuse. He stopped at the maze's entrance.

"I had this copied from one at Villa Pisani in Stra, Italy, along the river Brenta between Venice and Padua," he boasted. "I was twelve when my brothers and I visited. They said that even Napoleon was unable to find his way out of it."

"No way out?"

"Extremely difficult! The Greeks believed that a Minotaur . . . "

"What is a Miniter?" she interrupted.

"Min-o-taur," he corrected. "A mythical creature with the head and tail of a bull and body of a man. It waits in the center of the maze."

"Is there one in yours?" She looked alarmed.

"I doubt it, my dear." He laughed as he led her inside its walls.

"It's awfully quiet in here."

What was it, he wondered, that excited him about the sound of uneasy girlish laughter?

"You won't leave me?"

He ran his hand along the yaupon hedge, amused that its botanical name was *Ilex vomitoria*: the bright red autumn berries were considered highly toxic to humans; as few as six caused vomiting, and twenty promised death. He felt giddy, like a young lad again, capturing cedar waxwings in the park, made all the easier when they were drunk on berries.

He put his arm around Clarissa, and this time she offered no resistance. The narcotic was finally taking effect. He paused, holding her face up to see that her lids had turned heavy, her gaze distant and dreamy. Her cherubic mouth was slack. He took her hand, brought her fingers to his mouth, kissed her palm.

She giggled and weakly attempted to pull her hand away. "I'm—I'm feeling—very—strange—tingly. I should sit." Her speech was slurred.

He kissed her, felt the soft cushion of her lips, how relaxed she was—like the small birds of his youth, warm in his pocket. He felt the visceral surge of exhilaration, the insistent pulse in his hand, knowing that she was growing weaker. *Mustn't rush things,* he reminded himself, taking a deep breath. He wanted to feel her anguish, his hands around that slender throat, carry her to the water. Her resistance, her struggle, his own power—and then the drowning. In control at every step, he told himself. In the moment. *Nothing must go wrong to spoil my pleasure.*

Letting go of her hand, he allowed her to stumble forward. Watched in the rising moonlight as she staggered from side to side in the confusing passageway.

"Can you hear me?" he murmured. "Clarissa?"

She turned toward the direction of his voice. Reached out for him. He stepped back into the shadows. Unable to hold on to anything, she stumbled. "Where are we? It's dark. I—I want to go home. I don't see you. Please, Mr. Winthrop. Are you there? Take me home."

She turned this way and that. He stepped closer. Put his hand on her shoulder—ever so gently. Startled, she reached for his hand as he moved away from her.

Mimi felt Thomas' hand on her shoulder. "Jon's an excellent driver, Mrs. Milman. We are making excellent time."

There was a sudden kettledrum of sounds, followed by a flash of lightning across the horizon.

"Quick, pull over. We'll get soaked," Thomas shouted from the back seat.

They pulled to the side of the road and Thomas jumped out of the car to help Jonathan pull up the cover. Within moments, it began to pour, suddenly and ferociously. The wipers could barely keep up.

"I'm afraid I didn't listen to the weather report before we left," Jonathan laughed.

The windows fogged. There was no visibility, and Jonathan could only follow the taillights of the car ahead. The automobile filled with the dank smell of wet clothes. Mimi wanted to open a window.

"Fortunately, Frederick prefers his chauffeur to drive slowly," Jonathan said. "We just might pass them!"

She remembered, as if it were yesterday, those three clandestine

drives through the city with Frederick—her first automobile rides—
and his furtive touches and her first kisses. When a quick turn in the
road threw her to the side of the automobile, her thoughts snapped
back to the present, her fear that they might not save Clarissa.

"If it stops raining, there may still be a moon tonight. That will
definitely help us find her." Tom leaned forward. "Remember, Jon,
that night at the Breakers, when you were searching for—"

"Please, Tom, no amusing stories. We need to stay focused," said
Jonathan. "Don't forget that Raptor's enormous."

"Then we must stay close together," Mimi said. The slap of the
window wipers, the rushing sound of the torrent against the convertible cover, and the sour stink of male sweat were dizzying. "Jonathan,
how will you let us know if they are in the house?" she asked in an
attempt to keep them focused.

"Ah, yes, good question."

"If they're there, why don't you ring the bell on the veranda,"
Thomas suggested.

Jonathan swerved in and out of the lane, passing cars, splashing
up water on both sides, and just seeming to miss other cars by a hair.
She felt nauseous and worried that they would not get to Clarissa in
time. Thomas handed her a blanket from the back seat.

"Thanks. We must get there before anything happens to her," she
said.

"Don't you worry, my dear," Thomas reassured her.

"I believe there is plenty to worry about," she said.

They rode on in silence. She could barely see what lay ahead.

The sound of Clarissa's breathing was shallow.

"I'm here." Frederick whispered, and then as she turned, he
stepped away from her again. His heart was racing. He relished toying
with her like a cat with a mouse.

"Where?" she pleaded. "Where are you? Please. I'm feeling dizzy.
I might fall."

No light made its way through the smooth, contorted whitish-
gray branches or the small, shiny dark green leaves, all of which had

thickened over the years. Each path in Raptor's maze had branches, which presented more and more choices and ever-greater potential for getting lost. The sounds of trapped animals were muffled. Her voice had grown feeble, her calls plaintive. The ponds were close. He could easily carry her the distance. Touch that moment when her being ended, her heart stopped. When he finally heard the sound of her body falling to the ground, he found her, picked her up, breathed in her scent, and then carried her out of the maze toward the reserve.

With little traffic and driving at top speed, they made up for lost time.

"Not a light on in the place," Jonathan said as they pulled up to the mansion. The rain had stopped.

"We need to stay together," Mimi insisted. "Where might he take her?"

"The maze," said Thomas. "It's quite slippery from the rain. Would you like me to take your arm, Mrs. Milman?"

"That won't be necessary. I'm wearing sturdy shoes."

They made their way to the high walls of vertical shrubbery. She shone her light into the entrance and with her usual sense of adventure stepped forward but was overcome with a sudden breathlessness. Jonathan reached out, took hold of her arm, and forcefully pulled her back. Admittedly, she was relieved that he had stopped her.

"There's no way out," Thomas said. "My brother designed it that way."

"Shh," she said. "Do you hear anything?" They stopped to listen for the sound of voices. There was only the cawing of a pair of Cooper's hawks circling above them.

"Let's search the reserve." Thomas pointed the way. "The moon is bright enough to see where we are going. He may be taking her there. It's quite secluded. Follow me, Mrs. Milman. It will undoubtedly be muddy."

The temperature was dropping, and she slipped the sweater over her head, put on gloves, and wrapped the scarf around her neck. A brackish scent blew off the ocean. What a damp and chilly place this had to be in winter.

Clarissa was easy to carry, as she offered no resistance, and Frederick made his way through the reserve toward the ponds. The moonlight guided him. His thoughts wandered over which pond to choose—Peregrine, Night Hawk, Goshawk, or Cooper's Hawk—and decided on the last, and deepest. His heart raced with excitement.

Frogs were beginning to croak, while storm clouds attempted to hide the moon's light, leaving a fiery magenta-and-purple sky above the ocean. The air was filled with the chorus of cicadas and the sparks of fireflies. Mosquitoes, attracted to the damp, surrounded Mimi as they entered the reserve. She swatted away a flurry of gnats, some of which flew into her nose and open mouth. Branches and dry weeds scratched her arms and legs and poked through her clothes as she pushed through the dense growth. All she could think of was rescuing Clarissa. Like a daughter to her, a headstrong one. Part of what made her so creative was her stubborn insistence on her ideas. In their design discussions, Clarissa often held out for her concepts with a fierce tenacity. At times she reminded Mimi of herself, while at other moments she showed herself to be more of a revolutionary. It would serve her well in the future. Mimi was certain that one day she would be an avant-garde designer. But her decision to lie and defy Mimi was not about fashion; it was adolescent and dangerous.

She looked around for Jonathan and Thomas and realized that she had been separated from them, but it was too dangerous to call out. The reserve was deep and, without knowing her direction, seemed endless. Fortunately, she heard the sound of the ocean on her left side. That would be her compass. The night sky was now clearer. The beam from one of the flashlights broke through the branches of the trees, blinding her momentarily, and she quickly made her way toward the brothers.

"They're just ahead," Thomas whispered, and pointed. She heard the flapping of wings as wild birds and waterfowl, disturbed by their surprise entry into their peaceful domain, flew into the air.

Jonathan held out his arms to stop them from moving farther, indicating that they should turn off their flashlights and, with one finger to his lips, be quiet. From behind a cluster of scrub oak and pitch pine trees, she could see the clearing and Frederick carrying Clarissa like an offering, her head and limbs dangling lifelessly. Were they too late? He was at the edge of a pond. It was all she could do to keep herself from shouting Clarissa's name. He was going to drown her!

Suddenly, Thomas rushed into the clearing, forced his brother to the ground just as he was about to enter the water, and then pulled Clarissa out of his arms

"Get away from me!" shouted Frederick, caught completely off guard.

Jonathan yelled, "Is she breathing?"

"Yes, but she's unconscious," Tom answered. "I wonder if he's drugged her."

"Get her to the car and keep her warm!" Mimi wanted to go with Clarissa but she was frozen where she stood.

Stunned at seeing his brothers, Frederick slipped off the grassy incline, and his foot slid on algae-covered stones on the edge of the pond. "Damn. Help me, for God's sake, man," he called out to Jonathan.

His brother remained motionless.

"Give me your hand, Jon," he ordered as he attempted to stand, but the pond was the largest of the ten and deeper than he had thought. He grabbed for rocks along the lip, but one after another they came loose, with nothing for his hands to grasp, and as much as he tried to find his balance and foothold, the slimy floor of the pond pulled him deeper. The water was cold and he was soon up to his knees, water seeping into his boots, mud sticking between his toes. Soon he was ankle-deep in the sludge and his legs grew heavy. Again and again, he strained against the muck in an attempt to pull out a foot, but it was a hopeless struggle. He lost one shoe and then the other in the mire.

"Tom!" he shouted. "Don't leave me here!" He searched the shore for his brother and caught a fleeting glimpse of him as he disappeared from the clearing, carrying the girl. He continued to struggle but was losing his ability to stand, sliding farther away from the edge of the pond. If only he could get hold of the rocks, he might be able to pull himself out. But he couldn't do it alone. "Jon, for Christ's sake, help me!" he begged.

But Jon just stood there, a woman at his side, her mouth covered by her hands in apparent horror. Jon spoke to her, and when she took her hands away, he was certain he recognized her: the woman from the gallery, Clarissa's employer.

"Help me." He reached for something to grab hold of. There was nothing but hydrilla. The aquatic weeds broke off in his hands. Every effort to find his footing failed. He shouted, "Find a tree branch! Hurry!" He tasted the muddy water. "Thomas, help me," he called upon seeing his brother return. "I'll drown." He stumbled deeper, pulled backward toward the pond's center. His clothing was sodden and made heavier by the stones he had put in his pockets in order to weigh down Clarissa's body. There was no solid bottom for his feet to stand on. Beneath the slick surface, the water was thick with vines, which entangled his feet, legs, and thighs.

He grappled and grabbed at the rootless coontail, with its stiff forked leaves and thorns, as he was sucked deeper and deeper, his strength dissipating. He tried to paddle with his arms, but the suck and the weeds hindered his efforts. He gasped for air—or did he call out for his mother? Then his mouth filled with grit and he gave up, surrendering to the blackness.

Mimi was surprised by her own calm as she watched Frederick struggle and sink to his death. Jonathan might have chosen to rescue his brother but did nothing. Thomas had arrived back at the clearing. They stood wordlessly unmoved at the theater of Frederick's fitting demise. How many young girls had he brought here to Raptor? Had the rumors—whispered and suppressed—been true? Were there others at the bottom of these ponds? she wondered. If so, justice had been served.

"How is Clarissa?" she finally asked.

"She's in the car, still unconscious. I covered her with blankets. He drugged her. I just wanted to make certain you're both all right."

"We need to get her home," Mimi said.

"What should we do about Frederick?" Thomas asked.

Jonathan sighed. "I should probably call the police."

"His cook and chauffeur are gone. The house is empty," Thomas said. "I helped myself to towels and dry blankets."

"If you call the police, Clarissa's life will be ruined, which I would not like to see happen." She spoke with assurance in her tone and was pleased that Jonathan and Thomas both looked at her with respect. Neither had a response. "And . . . if you call the police, there will be a terrible scandal, you know. Who knows what the police will discover." When she saw them make eye contact, she knew that they understood what she meant.

Thomas finally spoke. "We'd all be ruined. It would be a terrible disgrace."

Could they agree to conceal his death?

"No one ever comes to Raptor," Jonathan said.

"We can give Cook and the driver their wages, tell them Frederick's gone to Europe, and close up the house," Thomas added.

"We would have to agree to keep it a secret," Jonathan said. "Besides, there is nothing to connect us to his drowning. I didn't push him; he slipped."

No one spoke for several minutes. They looked at one another in turn.

"You both need to decide," Mimi said. "Quickly. We must all agree before Clarissa awakes. I'm willing to keep silent, but the three of us must agree."

Jonathan and Thomas looked at each other again, and then turned to her.

"So, do we have an agreement?" she asked.

They nodded their heads.

All that remained was a shimmer of moonlight across Cooper's Hawk Pond's black surface. All else was still. As they walked back to the automobile, Mimi was relieved that they had saved Clarissa and that the child's reputation would be untarnished. The fresh earthy scent of rain filled the air, a momentary reminder of Matthew's favorite story and the realization that she would never again have to worry about Frederick finding out about Matthew and taking him from her.

Despite the now clear and starry night, Jonathan drove more carefully back to the city, and they made excellent time. Thomas carried Clarissa up the stairs to Mimi's guest room and the brothers said their good nights and then left. Miss Meyers helped Mimi get Clarissa out of her damp clothes and into a nightgown, then tucked her into bed. Mimi waited by her side until she regained consciousness. She seemed confused and tried to speak.

"You went to Mr. Winthrop's home against my warning," Mimi reproved her. "You acted quite foolishly. But even worse, Clarissa, you lied to me. That disappointed me."

"I am so sorry for any trouble I may have caused, Mrs. Milman," she said with sincerity. "All I remember is walking in the garden and feeling frightened."

"Shush, shush," Mimi soothed her. "Mr. Winthrop was quite worried and called his brothers. Since you are my charge, they thought it best that I come along."

"Mr. Winthrop is such a kind gentleman, Mrs. Milman. He gave me a lovely gift. It's in my purse." She looked about. "Oh, I left it behind. It was the loveliest peach, carved from very old ivory. It belonged to Mr. Winthrop's mother. The peach opens and inside is a small baby boy who grew up to be a great hero named Momotarō. It was so precious."

"I didn't see your purse, Clarissa. You must have left it behind."

"I hope I haven't lost it. It was so dear."

"I'm sure it was. Get some rest. Tomorrow's a new day and we have a great deal of work to attend to. I don't wish to speak further of this incident."

The ticktock of the regulator clock's brass pendulum swinging back and forth was the only sound in the silent workroom. When the Winthrop brothers had brought her home, it had dependably marked 11:47 p.m. Mimi sat on the edge of the alteration fitting platform, eyes closed, listening to the comforting meter of its strokes. Time passed unnoticed.

She'd been aware of speed in the race to Long Island, aware of the tempo of the Atlantic's waves pounding the shores, but lost track of time, actual minutes and hours, in the search for Clarissa and in those last moments of Frederick's slow-motion death in the moonlight. Watching, with Jonathan and Thomas Winthrop by her side, there at the edge of the pond—near enough to do something, with time enough to reach out. Shocked that they did nothing, yet relieved as well. Her life had never been about such things as life and death—or choosing death. But she had known clearly that she must protect Clarissa and Matthew.

Opening her eyes, staring into the three mirrors, the one frosted globe overhead reflecting three midnight moons and casting dark circles under her eyes, she barely recognized herself: expressionless, the crease between her brows like a gash, and shadows beneath her cheeks. Who was this stranger in the mirrors? Who had she become? What had she consented to, and could she keep yet another agreement with the Winthrops?

There were leaves and pine needles in her tangled hair, a small cut on her cheek. She picked the pieces from her hair, held them in her palm, counted them, listened to the air filling her nostrils; tasted muck, briny sand, and dead leaves; felt a measured throb in her knees and tried to piece together the events of the evening. Had she fallen?

What she did remember was how quickly Frederick had disappeared underwater except for that last moment—an eternity—when his mouth and nostrils were already beneath the surface. Would she ever unsee that one instant when all that remained was his wide-eyed and inescapable terror?

Would she ever forget the return to the city, Clarissa's head on her lap, counting the child's breaths, the measures of her pulse, as if nothing else mattered?

She was bone-tired. Turning her eyes from her reflection, she leaned forward and with both palms rubbed her knees in a clockwise movement as she swayed back and forth in time with the brass pendulum and, like Mama in her red rocking chair, allowed herself one loud moan of exhaustion.

1926

1

MATTHEW AND
THE SCENT OF RAIN

Mimi intended to drop in on Lawrence and stepped out into the garden to gather some flowers to bring. She was kneeling on the ground, about to cut the daffodils, when she took a deep breath and recognized the distinctive fragrance of impending rain.

Whenever it rained now, she thought of Matthew and their recent trip to India.

She closed her eyes and breathed in slowly and considered her travels. It was unlike the moist soil and decaying plants of the rain forest of South America. None of the fragrances of fresh-ground spices at the Marrakesh souks, where she'd bought tins of cinnamon, coriander, and cumin. It was not the smell of wet sage that combined with the thunder and lightning and driving rain in the Sonoran Desert in Arizona. And it was most definitely not the essences from that trip she had taken with Matthew to Kannauj. No, New York's summer rain was distinct: the sweet, earthy scent of the drops hitting the city's hot, dry pavement.

When Matthew was about five, they were on their way home in a downpour from one of his visits with Jonathan Winthrop. Talking a mile a minute, he told her the story Jonathan had told him that afternoon about an Indian village named Kannauj where they made a perfume that had the scent of rain. It was as though he'd memorized every word. From that day on he never ceased asking if one day they might visit the village. She made a small flag attached to a pin to mark the spot on the world map Matthew had on the wall of his bedroom. When he was seven, he gave a talk to his class about the trip he wanted to take one day to India, to Kannauj, and to the Taj Mahal. The following year he took red embroidery thread and plotted their journey by ship using information he gathered from his set of encyclopedias, *The Book of Knowledge*, a gift from Lawrence. When Matthew's teacher took Mimi aside one day to tell her of her son's remarkable enthusiasm for geography and the relationships between people and their environments, Mimi decided to make the trip a celebration of his sixteenth birthday in December

"I'll make all the plans," Matthew said with glee, and immediately set to work. Like Lottie, he carried a notebook with him and every now and then would give an enthusiastic shout and write something on the pages, which he had organized into categories: "Travel," "Cities," "Things to See," "Things to Eat," etc.

Knowing that Matthew would want to take several books, Mimi made him a version of the haversack used in the Great War.

It had been an arduous eight-thousand-mile trip to India by ship and then by train to rural north-central Uttar Pradesh until they reached the ancient city. It seemed that Matthew was born to travel; his good spirits, curiosity, and engagement with fellow travelers were a delight. He carried Upton Sinclair, L. Frank Baum, and Jack London, none of which he ever tired of reading again and again, and was determined to finish the new book, *A Passage to India* by E. M. Forster, before they arrived at their destination. He had a knack of asking questions of people they met, drawing them out. At the ends of certain conversations, with some secret criteria, he would ask if he might have an address and immediately add each into a school notebook. When Mimi asked him why he asked a certain person, he would simply lift his hands, raise his eyebrows, and shrug.

Aboard the ship, a kindly college professor they met at dinner suggested that Matthew keep a diary of the trip and the next morning at breakfast presented him with a leather-bound journal.

It was a dusty four-hour drive east of the Taj Mahal to the shop on the banks of river Ganges. Such a strange way to spend Matthew's sixteenth birthday, Mimi thought. They made their way along the streets to the perfumery owned by a shopkeeper, Munna Lal, who had three thumbs. He carried on the traditions of his father and grandfather. In the shop, metal shelves were crammed with glass bottles and tins of all sizes filled, according to the labels, with oils and extracts of jasmine, rose, three kinds of lotus, ginger lily, gardenia, frangipani, lavender, rosemary, wintergreen, geranium, and many more that Mimi had never heard of. Matthew was enthralled. Despite the summer heat, they toured the facilities with his guide, and Matthew listened patiently to everything the gentleman, dressed all in white, explained to him about their history and production.

There was no electricity, no industrial machinery, not a suggestion of modernity. Daylight streamed into open rooms where craftsmen, practicing the skills they inherited from their fathers and grandfathers, tended fires under copper cauldrons. The fires had to be closely monitored so that the heat beneath stayed warm enough to evaporate the water inside to steam—but never so hot that it might destroy the aroma. Mr. Lal had made the rain fragrance since opening for business.

"Sir," Matthew finally asked politely, "may I smell your perfume that smells like rain?"

"Of course, young man." Mr. Lal beamed with pleasure that Matthew knew about his attar. "Did you and your mother visit the Taj Mahal?"

"We did, sir. At sunset. My mother and I agree that it is the most beautiful building we have ever seen."

She was tempted to tell Mr. Lal about how Matthew, at the age of six, had promised to build her such palace, but thought better of embarrassing him, and luxuriated in her sweet memory. He was growing up. She had noticed him eyeing the exotic Indian girls.

"Here in India, we call fragrant oils attars. The Mughal emperor Shah Jahan built the palace in memory of his beloved wife, the empress Mumtaz Mahal. She died in 1631 giving birth to their thirteenth child. These oils—these attars—were their passion, but after the empress died, the shah never wore perfume again. However, today we still capture fragrances the same way they did then."

"But, sir," Matthew asked, "I understand how you can make perfume from flowers or spices, but how can you capture the smell of rain? It's elusive."

"Excellent question, young man. Please close your eyes and listen to what I say." He waited until their eyes were closed and then continued. "City rain smells of steaming asphalt." He paused, giving them time to imagine the fragrance he described. "In the countryside, rain smells like its sweet grasses." He paused again. "Ocean rain smells briny, of fish and sea life." He paused once more. With her eyes closed, Mimi had become aware of his English accent and the melodic cadence of his dialect. "But nothing, nothing, smells like the rain here in India, where great dry swaths of desert are inundated with the most dramatic seasonal storms on earth. Do you know about our monsoons, young man? "

Mimi loved listening to his voice and knew that Matthew was enthralled.

"Yes, we studied India in school, and I did extra research for this trip."

"Good! Indian monsoons shape everything, you know—from childhood to culture to commerce. People who visit here say that the smell of long-awaited rains soaking India's dry soil is the scent of life itself." He said this with great pride. Despite his paunchy face and huge protruding belly, he was a man of perfumes and poetry. "Without opening your eyes, put your hands out in front of you, please. Palms up."

He placed a bottle in Matthew's hands. "Now you may open your eyes," he instructed.

Mimi saw that Matthew was flushed with pleasure. The light of joy was in his expression and eyes. His dream was coming true. She watched as Matthew twisted off the gold bottle cap, closed his eyes, and breathed in the scent he had traveled so far to smell. "Mother! Mr. Jonathan was correct." Placing it under her nose to smell, he cried, "It does, doesn't it? It smells just like the earth."

"It is the fragrance of dry clay steeped with water from a pond," said Mr. Lal. "Do you smell rain?"

"I do," Matthew said. "Not the same as rain in New York City."

"Mr. Lal," Mimi said, "I grew up on a street in New York City named Eldridge. We were very poor. When it rained, the stench of horse dung, cabbage, and sweat filled the air. I doubt that anyone ever made perfume from that stink."

"Probably like Mumbai, where there is much poverty. But here in Kannauj, the soil is warm and rich from the minerals, and that allows us to create rare perfumes."

"You know, sir? My mother is like a rare perfume."

Mimi was unable to believe he had said that. He was that age at which boys are often embarrassed by their mothers.

It was a trip that Matthew would speak of often, and each time Mimi heard him tell the exquisite story, her heart was filled with the gladness she had felt that day.

1927

1

THE LETTER

"Mail's here, Mimi." David dropped it on the kitchen table next to her. "How was your walk? There's coffee."

He poured himself a cup and gently kissed the top of her head as he sat down. "Wish you'd come with me," he said. "Spotted a red-tail."

"Tomorrow, I promise." She looked up to see the smile she knew was waiting. It was one of the many things she loved about him.

"I think I'll make some eggs. How about you?"

"Yes, one," she said.

As he fussed at the stove, she picked up the pile of mail and quickly sorted it—bills, bills, and numerous invitations: she could tell them from the envelopes, her name in florid calligraphy on the cream linen paper. At the bottom was a beige square envelope with a two-cent red George Washington stamp.

"A letter from California," she said. "Pasadena."

The handwriting on the folded sheet was formal and Spenserian.

> *Dear Miriam Milman,*
> *You might not remember me, but we were neighbors on Eldridge Street when we were children. You were very kind to me at a time when such emotions were out of my realm.*
> *My brother Igor recently sent me this photo of the building we lived in on Eldridge Street, and there you are in the first-floor window with your son.*

Last week I read a New York Times *article about you and was pleased to read about your successes. It reminded me of how our lives began, that you were the only person who saw the good in me, who listened when I spoke about the stars, planets, and galaxies, and that you taught me to read and write— providing a passage to the future.*

After leaving home, I found a way to attend school, and was accepted at the University of Chicago. I've been able to look through some of the most powerful telescopes in the world and see the universe.

My wife, two children, and I live in Pasadena, California, a city of roses and oranges, where I work with Edwin Hubble at the Mount Wilson Observatory.

You and I have both come a long way from 245 Eldridge Street and I simply wanted to let you know of my gratitude for all you saw in me. I have never forgotten.

Respectfully,
Dr. Szymon Moskowitz, PhD

Mimi took a deep breath, smelled the butter, heard the sizzle of eggs frying, and sipped her coffee. She looked closely at the photo— Schenkein's Bakery on one side of the front stoop and the linoleum store on the other, the gossiping wives in the doorway, henpecked Mr. Epstein on the top step. At the parlor-floor window, beside Matthew, little Mimi looked out onto the street, her wistful expression unforgettable—so distant from everything that awaited.

1928

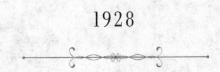

1

RAPTOR

There remained one piece of unresolved business for Mimi. Was she driven by curiosity or the residue of the longing that had consumed her youth? Or was it her need to live out the childish fairy tale of Aschenputtel, the German Cinderella, by the Brothers Grimm? She wanted to return to Long Island in the daylight—to see Raptor. David asked if she wanted him to come along and understood when she said it was something she needed to do alone.

In early October she reserved a ticket for a narrated tour along Long Island's Gold Coast but also hired a private guide, who met her at the end of the formal tour.

Rita Langer, wearing a long white sweater over a pleated red wool skirt, and sturdy walking shoes, had the air of someone used to life in that affluent part of Long Island but from slightly outside the right circles. The dark roots of her Jean Harlow platinum-blond hair indicated that the color came from a bottle and was in need of a touch-up.

"Raptor was built around 1905 by multimillionaire Frederick Winthrop, the youngest of three brothers. He would have been about twenty-five at the time," Rita explained as they approached the mansion's front steps. "He was a protégé of Frick. Not one of the more elegant cottages! As you can see, it has suffered from neglect."

Mimi would have described Raptor as eclectic and severe—all bricks and sinister turrets. It looked different from what she remembered the night they rescued Clarissa. With its small windows, she expected the interior to be dark and joyless. However, she was not there for the architecture but to find answers.

Rita chuckled. "No one would ever have suspected that Frederick was a Winthrop." She took Mimi's arm, led her toward the front door. "His father and two brothers were philanthropists. Freddy was . . ." She paused before opening the front door. "Well, we'll get to that later. Come, let me show you the cottage. Take your last breath of fresh air, dear!"

"I've done some reading about Jonathan and Thomas Winthrop," Mimi said as they stepped through the door. "But there's almost no information about Frederick."

"Freddy was the family's black sheep!"

Mimi found it somewhat unprofessional that Rita, a local guide, would call Frederick Winthrop by such a familiar nickname.

"He was in real estate in Manhattan and amassed land holdings—stole from his own family, they say. Nobody liked him except, surprisingly, the ladies. Especially showgirls. He liked 'em young! Must have had an unrealistic view of women: a grown man lusting after adolescent girls," Rita continued. "Girls in costumes. Don't you think?"

"I suppose."

"Raptor was decorated inside and out with classical-style heraldry. A lot of second-rate stained glass and dreadful gargoyles." Rita continued with her tedious rote tour, guiding Mimi through the hallways, and pointing out all the details, none of which interested her.

Mimi observed, "Not the cheeriest place, is it?" There was a musty smell in every airless room, and she found it difficult to breathe despite the closeness to the water. The velvet drapes were moth-eaten; the wallpaper, stained from water damage, was peeling; and the few remaining pieces of what once might have been colorful silk-upholstered furniture had faded to a murky gray. It was like a set for a bleak stage play.

"To say the least." Rita led the way upstairs. "This was the master bedroom. Not much left to see." She opened double doors, crossed the room, and beckoned Mimi to see the view from the windows. "He had a nice view of the ponds. There's ten of them—all named after hawks, as a matter of fact." She laughed. "And that's the bird reserve over on the right. You wouldn't want to be in there on a dark night! He had a thing for birds."

"What sort of 'thing'?" she asked.

"He was a birder."

"Really?" Mimi responded cheerfully. "My son and I help count hawks in Central Park every year. You seem to know so much about him. Why Frederick Winthrop?"

"Quite a few of the guides have taken a special interest in old Freddy Winthrop. He came from such a fine family. Philanthropists. His family didn't think much of him. One of his older brothers, Thomas, the architect, refused to design *or* build this house, and they say there wasn't one of his brother Jonathan's paintings to be seen. I mean, Jonathan Winthrop painted anyone who was anybody, particularly the Fricks. He painted a portrait of everyone in his family but Freddy—at least, as far as we know! Odd, don't you think?"

"Rather," Mimi concurred.

"He kept to himself. Didn't socialize."

"Did he ever marry?"

"There were rumors he had several wives but no one ever saw them." Rita rolled her eyes and then, pointing to the view from the window, stepped aside so Mimi could see the ponds and in the distance, the ocean. In which pond, she wondered, had he drowned? It looked so pristine from this bird's-eye view. "Nice view," Rita noted, then looked at her watch. "Why don't we go downstairs?" She led Mimi along the marble hall, past mirrors in gilded frames, and started down the center staircase.

"No parties? Balls?" Mimi asked. "Music salons? He loved music."

Rita stopped suddenly and looked at Mimi with a strange expression.

Realizing what she had said, Mimi quickly added, "So many people who lived in these mansions were supporters of the arts and of music. I'm certain I read somewhere that the Winthrops were music enthusiasts."

"A strange man. I doubt even the Fitzgeralds knew he existed!" Rita laughed. "His cook, quite the gossip, apparently told strange stories about his comings and goings in the early hours of the morning. And after they dug up the . . ." She stopped in mid-sentence.

Stunned by those words, Mimi felt for the stair rail for balance. "Dug up the what?" she asked, suddenly feeling light-headed.

"Oh, I'll save that for later." Rita winked and smiled. "Anyway, he gave the place up, walked away." She opened the doors to several empty rooms. "Around 1924, 1925," she said with a shrug. "No one ever saw him again."

"I need to sit for a moment," Mimi said. "The air."

"Yes, it does get to you, doesn't it? Come, I can open the doors onto the loggia. You look tired. Wish I could offer you a cold drink. Well, at least there's a breeze off ocean." Rita led her through the living room and opened the French doors, which allowed a breeze to enter the musty old room. "This would have been the ballroom."

All that remained of any grandeur it may have ever held was the maple parquet floor, which needed a good polishing. Mimi walked out onto the loggia, a covered space running along the length of the mansion, similar to a porch but with columns on the open side.

Rita stood next to her and pointed. "Over there are the ten ponds and the bird reserve, as I said. Freddy hunted and killed birds there." She pointed to the left. "Those hedges? That's all that's left of his maze. The town came and cut most of it down. Too dangerous. No way out! And with all the town kids nosying around, just too dangerous."

"Why were they 'nosying around'?" Mimi could hardly contain her curiosity.

Rita walked over to a mirror, opened her purse, and put on bright red lipstick.

"Town kids, everyone, was nosying around once the news got out. Some kids snuck onto the property last year, partying and swimming in Peregrine Pond, and they found ladies' garments in the bottom of the pond."

"What?" Mimi was astonished.

"So the sheriff came to investigate," Rita continued with great animation. "And it turned out there were remains of two females. Then"—the pitch of her voice rose higher and higher—"they found *more*. Four in Goshawk. Four in Night Hawk. They were pretty certain they were young women. So they dredged all ten ponds. Eighteen women. Eighteen! All young, they said, from the looks of the remains. Can you believe it?" Her face was flushed.

"Who were they?" Mimi asked.

"No one will ever know. There's no way to recognize those poor girls. Everyone says they were most likely the Irish maids. No one would have missed *them*."

When she asked, "And no men?" Rita shook her head. Mimi could barely breathe. "How did you hear all of this?" she asked.

"I just love the history of this town. There are dirty secrets in every corner."

"'Skeletons in the closets'?"

"Exactly! That's the Gold Coast for you! Hey, you okay? You went as white as a sheet."

"I think the temperature's going down. It's so interesting, but I should get going soon."

"It turns out there were searches for missing girls in Connecticut, Rhode Island, Massachusetts, and New York City where the Winthrop family lived. Going back to when he built the place. Can you imagine?"

"What an incredible story!" Mimi barely knew what to say. "Eighteen?"

"Yeah. Maybe there are even more they didn't find. If they ever find him, Freddy would be convicted of eighteen murders. Sentenced to death."

Mimi took a deep breath to slow the racing of her heart.

"His fortune was estimated at over five million dollars. Everyone wonders if he had any kids. The police weren't able to find any. His brothers, they ran a fancy private school in the city, the Winthrop School."

"Yes, it's still a very fine school."

"All the tour guides joke about being old Freddy Winthrop's kid!

Can you imagine? If you had someone come to your door and tell you . . ." She paused. "Do you have any children?

"Yes, I have a son. He's eighteen."

"Imagine if someone came to your door and told you your son inherited five million dollars!"

"From someone who killed eighteen women?" Mimi shuddered.

Rita shrugged. "Who knows what any of those Winthrops did to earn their fortunes?" She lowered her voice to a whisper. "Ready to see the study?"

"You know, it's getting late and I'll need to get to the train station soon."

"It's the pièce de résistance, I promise you! Follow me." Rita grabbed Mimi's arm and practically dragged her down the hallway until they stood outside the doors to the study. "You won't believe this." With a dramatic flourish, Rita opened the doors. "Ta-da!"

As the doors slid apart, Mimi put her hand to her mouth to stifle the gasp of air that rushed down her throat.

2

THE STUDY

It took several minutes for Mimi's eyes to adjust to the dark room. Inside the study, the wood-paneled maple walls were hung with large-format hand-colored Audubon prints of birds of prey; condors, eagles, hawks, ospreys, and black vultures devouring their victims.

"Twenty-four. Almost life-size—valuable, too," Rita said with pride, as though they were her own. "First editions published by Havell. I wouldn't mind having just one!"

Throughout the room, every surface was covered with murky displays of stuffed predators under grimy glass domes and in dusty glass cases set one on top of another. Each consisted of a carefully constructed nature scene, brown and sooty with age. There were glass bottles filled with murky liquids and unidentifiable bird and animal specimens. She turned away from stuffed hawks, their claws holding field mice, rabbits, or other hapless creatures, labeled: *Barn Owl Clutching a Rat*; *Sparrow Hawk Grasping a Fish*; and *Ferruginous Hawk Clutching a Rabbit*. There was death everywhere. She was barely able to look at any more. "I prefer my birds alive." She laughed out of nervousness. "Or on a plate."

"First, he cleaned the skins." Rita's description was well-practiced. "Then scraped away fat and tissue with a sharpened spoon or dulled knife. They were washed in soapy water, and then plaster of Paris was used to dry the skin."

Mimi felt woozy. "Could you perhaps open a window, Rita?"

"Afraid not. There are none." She smiled politely and then continued her lecture in detail, taking what seemed almost perverse pleasure in the telling. Mimi needed to sit, but there wasn't a chair in sight. "Everyone who comes to Raptor wants to see this room." Rita took a fan from her pocket. "A bit warm, isn't it?" she said, fanning herself.

"Rita, I'm not feeling well. I've seen enough."

"Anyway, where would you see a room like this? Crazy as a coot." She spoke in a whisper, as though they might disturb someone as she closed and locked the study doors behind them. "Our tour is only of the mansion. You're welcome to stay and walk about outside."

"I want to see a little of the gardens." Mimi handed Rita a gratuity. "Breathe the sea air,"

"You are too generous. Thank you. The trolley should meet you at the front gate in twenty minutes. Did I mention that the police found a drawer full of ladies' evening purses in his bedroom?"

"Something to remember them by?" Mimi guessed.

Following a path toward the ocean, she found a bench and sat to gather her thoughts, when suddenly a male Cooper's hawk appeared: steely bluish gray above, warm reddish bars on its underside, and thick, dark bands on the tail.

Slowly turning circles on its broad rounded wings and screaming one note, "Kak-kak-kak," the bird landed in a tree, its stern red eyes fixed on the ground, waiting, then dove into the shrubbery. There was a flurry of struggle. When the hawk emerged, a helpless rabbit was gripped in its claws. Squeezing the prey, it dove into a pond, holding the rabbit's head underwater until its squirming ceased.

When the echoes of Mimi's cry ended, the garden was still and silent once more, except for the sound of the ocean waves. She stood and quickly headed along the path toward the gate and waiting trolley, which would take her away from this terrible place.

ACKNOWLEDGMENTS

First and foremost, here's to Jonathan Burnham for believing in my ability to create characters. To Regina McBride, writer, teacher, and a gentle mentor for more than thirty years, who guided me to the inner lives of the people who inhabit my stories. To Nancy Parent for her boundless knowledge, insights, and unwavering encouragement. To Katherine Schwarzenbach for clarity and the ability to keep me balanced on this bumpy trolley ride.

Every writer should have a writers' group as smart and candid as Michael G. Farquhar, Ned Racine, Melina Price, Paul Pattingale—and Fran Yariv, always there in my mind's eye.

What would I know without Carnegie Hall historian Gino Francesconi, Erica Clark at the Carnegie Observatories; Helen Golay, owner of The Corner Bookstore at 1313 Madison Avenue; and Daniel Lewis, Senior Curator at the Huntington Library? Thanks to Dr. Eddy Portnoy at YIVO, for teaching me how to find a missing husband; to John A. Harris' *New York City: Vintage History* for photos that inspired Mimi's story—and the librarians who found the books.

A toast to my savvy editor, Sara Nelson, whose vision and wisdom made my story shine, and the Harper team: Edie Astley, Heather N. Drucker, Katie Teas, and copyeditor David Chesanow. Thanks to the Marly Rusoff Literary Agency.

ABOUT THE AUTHOR

ALICE SHERMAN SIMPSON, an accomplished graphic designer and visual artist, has taught drawing and design at the Fashion Institute of Technology (FIT), the School of Visual Arts, the New School, and the Otis College of Arts and Design.

Her unique handmade, hand-painted books about dance are in more than forty international special and rare book collections, including Harvard, Yale, Stanford, New York Public Library, Lincoln Center Library for Performing Arts, and the Victoria & Albert Library.

Her stories have appeared in *Persimmon Tree* magazine (New York) and *Jerry Jazz Musician* magazine, and she was nominated by the *Writer's Voice* (New York) for Best New American Voices. Chapters from her debut novel, *Ballroom* (Harper), have appeared in *Writer's Voice* magazine (New York), *Words & Images Journal* (University of Maine), *TangoDanza* magazine (Berlin), and a limited edition *Tango Bar*. She lives in South Pasadena, California . . . and still dances the tango.